*There must be places for human beings to satisfy their souls.
Food and drink is not all.*

—John Muir

When they reached the cliff, they saw a valley so magnificent that even time stopped in hushed awe.

"Por Dios!" the woman whispered, her breath catching in her throat as she gazed across miles of empty sky into a valley which seemed far too beautiful for this world. Her immediate impression was of an incredibly deep gash in the earth filled with a thousand contrasting shades of green meadow and forest. Here and there, she could see the sparkle of river fed by glistening waterfalls tumbling out of heaven.

She closed her eyes for a moment and then opened them again. Yes, it was all true. Before her lifted sheer granite cliffs whose size mocked anything she had ever seen. The cliffs soared higher than eagles. They stood aloof, carved and stained by the ages. Stamped on their stone faces were eyes that bled rivers. One monolith leaned over the valley and another was halved like an inverted bowl topped by a snowy mantle. The cloud shadows played with the sunlight, constantly altering the stern stone faces.

Her throat tightened and tears came to her eyes . . . she was looking at heaven on earth. . . .

*Leave it as it is. You cannot improve on it, and man can only
mar it.*

—President Theodore Roosevelt

YOSEMITE

GARY
McCARTHY

PINNACLE BOOKS
KENSINGTON PUBLISHING CORP.

PINNACLE BOOKS are published by

Kensington Publishing Corp.
850 Third Avenue
New York, NY 10022

First Printing: July, 1995

Printed in the United States of America

For my sunshine girl,
my bonny Monica Marie

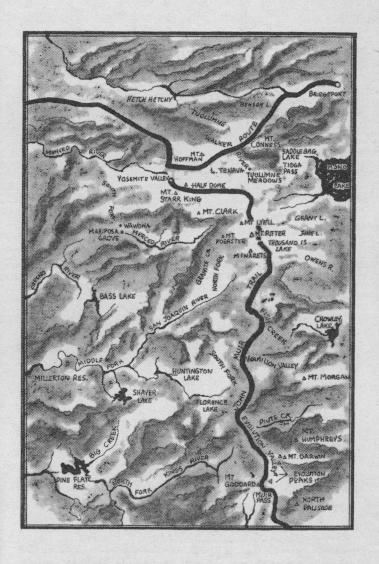

Prologue

Western Sierra Nevada Foothills, circa 1800

Jacinta could no longer endure being tossed violently about in the rough Spanish carreta where she lay gasping in pain, cradling her unborn child.

"Rafael, por favor!" she cried, trying to raise herself off what remained of their bags of corn and flour.

But her husband did not hear Jacinta over the screeching protest of the cart's wooden axle. Tears filled her almond-colored eyes. Jacinta was sure that the cart's incessant pounding was going to kill the child she carried, if it did not take her life first. How many days had this torture lasted? Six . . . or was it seven? Jacinta had lost track of time since she and her husband had robbed the great house of Don Luis Montoya, taking gold and many precious things before fleeing his vast hacienda.

"Rafael!" she cried again, throwing herself up to gaze wildeyed over the side of the cart. "Por favor!"

At last, Rafael turned and noticed her pain-stricken expression. He drummed his bare heels against the washboard flanks of his pony and it trotted toward Jacinta.

The sight of her thin and dirty husband brought comfort but also heartache to Jacinta. How well she remembered the first moment their eyes had met that day when Captain Rafael Lopez had led his cavalry past the Mission of the Holy Cross founded by Father Lasuen only a few years earlier at Santa Cruz. What a magnificent sight Rafael had been, dressed in full uniform with colorful helmet plumes waving! In a single heartbeat, Jacinta had fallen in love with Rafael's grace and mastery over his soldiers and his dancing white Andalusian stallion. That very day he had won her heart.

Now, floating in a sea of pain, Jacinta gazed up at the dark storm clouds. When the cart stopped, its sudden cessation of motion caused her head to spin and her stomach to lurch with nausea. Jacinta gripped the sides of the cart, panting and waiting to hear Rafael's calm assurances that she and their unborn child were not going to die. That very soon they would enter a sanctuary of beautiful mountains where friendly Indian people would hide and protect them from the pursuit of Don Luis's avenging Spanish soldiers.

An immense condor floated out of the clouds overhead. Jacinta stifled a cry of distress as it began to circle directly above, obviously a harbinger of the black death that already had claimed most of her coastal Yokut people.

"Jacinta!" Rafael exclaimed, reaching over the cart to clasp and squeeze her hands. "Jacinta, everything is all right. Please, be still!"

His voice dissolved her fears. And when Jacinta opened her eyes, Rafael's fine, shaggy head blocked out the sight of the condor. He smiled, cracked lips framed by a thick black beard.

"Rafael," she asked more urgently than ever before. "How much farther to the mountains?"

"Not far."

He leaned over the side of the cart, then slipped an arm under her back and raised her just a little so that she could gaze eastward. "See," he said happily, "the great Sierra Nevadas."

"But . . . but we have seen them for days now and they do not appear to get any closer!"

"We will be in the pines by tomorrow," he promised. "We have crossed the San Joaquin River and now we follow the Merced to a beautiful place. Jacinta, surely you remember how your own people told of a hidden valley filled with waterfalls and huge cliffs? One whose people call it Ahwahnee."

Jacinta knew that this legendary place, whose name some Miwok said meant "grassy valley" while others said meant "place of the gaping mouth," was shrouded in mystery, said to be so beautiful that it was part earth, part spirit world. Jacinta had heard of it, but she was not sure that she believed such a paradise could actually exist. "Yes, Rafael, I remember, but . . . but what if it does *not* even exist?"

"It *must* exist!" Rafael said passionately.

Jacinta managed to nod but then blurted, "But what if the people who live in Ahwahnee kill all invaders? Especially those who bring the black death."

"They will not have heard of that death," he answered, looking aside for a moment before continuing. "Jacinta, we bring them gold and much treasure. Trust me, they will welcome us. The Ahwahneeche will help you bring our baby into this world and we will live long and well among them."

"But what of the black sickness!"

He gulped. "It . . . Jacinta, it will have no power in such a place."

She desperately wanted to believe this. Rafael was wise and educated while she was not, but . . . "Rafael, what if . . ."

"Shhh," he hushed, growing impatient with all her questions as he eased her back down to rest in the cart. "You must not talk or worry so much, querida."

"Rafael," she breathed, gripping the wooden sides of the carreta. "I cannot bear the hard shaking much longer. Could we not . . ."

"No," he said gently, but with firmness. "Jacinta, you *must* hold on just one day longer. You are much too weak to walk and you could not ride my pony or the donkey. There is no other way."

"But if we could just *rest,* even for a few hours."

"Soon," he promised, dredging up a smile. "But first we require an Indian medicine woman to help you give birth to our first child."

Jacinta rolled her head back and forth, wanting to agree but afraid that both she and the child would die if she could not soon lie still and rest. "Yes, I know Rafael, but . . ."

He gently placed his fingers over her lips to still her protest. Rafael reeked of horse and sweat. Jacinta saw the pain and red suffering in his eyes and it suddenly made her ashamed for she realized again that his suffering, though different from her own, was just as terrible. She knew her proud husband felt nearly overwhelmed by guilt. So overwhelmed that he could not even sleep. Rafael had gambled everything to save her and their unborn child from the black death, hoping against hope that the merciless soldiers of Don Luis would not overtake and torture them to death.

"Jacinta, instead of worrying, pray to God that we soon reach the mountains and find Ahwahnee," he told her once again.

"Should I pray to your god or the gods of my Indian people?" she asked, forcing a smile because this had always been a joke between them.

His face softened, but he could not muster laughter and said, "My darling, pray to both. What can it possibly hurt?"

"Nothing," she replied in a voice that she did not recognize as her own.

"We will travel just a little farther today, querida," he promised. "Then we will go to the trees and make camp."

"Would your soldiers really follow us this far? Across the rivers and for so many days?"

Before Rafael could reply, they both heard the distant and ominous rumble of thunder. Rafael's head jerked sideways and Jacinta grabbed his beard, pulling his head around so that she could look directly up into his eyes. "Rafael?"

"No," he said, eyes skittering back and forth across the land they had passed like wild, caged things. "Jacinta, they would *never* follow us this far."

Jacinta saw through his well-intentioned but clumsy lie. The soldiers *were* coming. With a deep sickness welling up where their unborn child lay still and waiting, Jacinta realized that her husband had probably known the soldiers would never stop coming. They were, after all, the proud and now shamed hunters of a captain who had betrayed his allegiance to Spain for the love of nothing more than a common Indian woman. Don Luis would not even have to offer a reward for the head of a thief and a deserter.

Yes, Jacinta thought, finding it impossible to beat down her rising terror, the soldiers of Spain *were* coming.

One

The Ahwahneeche hunter wore a deer mask and hide as he paused beside the churning torrent of the lower Merced River. Mamota, son of Chief Utal, gazed south, studying the vast expanse of California's rolling foothills carpeted with a brilliant profusion of golden poppies interspersed with showy scarlet clusters of fuchsia, bugler, and the tall, stately red columbine. Canyon and blue oak trees dotted the landscape, their massive boughs tickling the bellies of dark thunderclouds that marched in from the Pacific Ocean. Already, the leaden storm clouds were stacking against the peaks of the Sierra Nevadas, clashing and growling. Mamota anticipated that rain would soon drive the elk back into the shelter of these cottonwood trees.

"Where are they?" Oati asked in a voice that barely carried over the gusting wind.

"They will come," Mamota promised with more confidence than he felt. "This storm will drive them to us."

"I hope so," Chala said, looking back toward Ahwahnee.

"Maybe," Hosu, said anxiously, "we should return to the mountains now."

Mamota chose to ignore the suggestion for they had yet to overtake the herd of elk they had been following for the past few days. And they also were hoping to come upon a band of wild Spanish horses.

But today there were neither horses nor elk in sight, only the approaching storm. Like his companions, Mamota felt extremely vulnerable whenever he ventured beyond the hidden valley of Ahwahnee. In that place, which his branch of the Miwok people had claimed for so many generations, there were always good spirits in the waters, the land, and even the winds, all ready to protect The People. If Mamota were there now, he would be lying with Tuani in their u'-ma-cha, a sturdy conical-shaped winter house made of cedar poles covered with bark. Tuani would have acorns roasting in their fire and they would be warm and dry and enjoying each other under a pile of soft animal skins. They both wanted children and making them was the pleasure they would have on such a cold day as this while the rain played upon the grass, the rocks, and forest.

Like his companions, Mamota wore only a breechclout under his disguise of a deer's head and hide. The doe's vacant eyes had been replaced with a mallard's green-feathered plumage while twisted branches of manzanita appeared as the forked horns of a young buck. Weighing less than ten pounds, Mamota's disguise fit so perfectly that it would not slip off even when he was forced to chase a wounded animal through heavy forest.

A jagged bolt of lightning stabbed the crown of a nearby foothill. A moment later, Mamota felt the earth shiver and he could not help but wonder if this was a warning given them by the Great Spirit not to leave the Merced River and expose themselves to the storm and their enemies.

"Mamota?" Oati asked. "We must find the elk now—before the storm."

To delay any longer would indicate weakness. "Yes," Mamota said, rising from a crouch and stepping away from the trees.

"But what if we are seen?" Hosu asked.

Mamota knew that Hosu was very worried about the Po-to-en-cies, a warlike tribe, also of the Miwok family, whose ancestral hunting grounds the Ahwahneeche were now violating.

"On such a day as this, they will not be hunting," Mamota answered, "and so . . ."

Mamota's voice trailed away and he shrank back into the trees, catching a flicker of movement to the southwest. The movement vanished in less than a blink of the hunter's eye.

Mamota turned to his companions. "Did you see that!"

"No," Oati replied, frowning with concentration. "What was it?"

Mamota shrugged, for he did not know—yet.

"Po-to-en-cies?"

"No."

"Then an uzamati?" Chala asked, already fearing the thought of facing the mighty grizzly bear.

Mamota did not think he had caught a glimpse of the great bear, although it was not uncommon to see the massive creatures brazenly loping across the Sierra foothills.

"A horse, I think."

The young Ahwahneeche brightened. Wild Spanish horses which had escaped from the missions and ranchos to multiply in the great warm valley below were highly prized for their flesh.

The mystery was solved just a few minutes later when a thin, bearded man astride a red pony crested a hilltop less than a mile to the southwest. Mamota could see that he was not an Indian because of his height and the fairness of his skin. He had the look of a Spaniard although it was a mystery what he was doing out here so far from the coastal missions. The man wore no shirt or hat, which was unusual for a Spaniard and gave Mamota the impression that the rider was very upset and in a great hurry.

The elk herd that the Ahwahneeche had been stalking suddenly bolted out of a ravine and fled toward the northern foothills. A moment later, Mamota realized they had been startled by the screeching protest of a two-wheeled Spanish cart being pulled by a donkey. The cart had pole sides and was filled with sacks, probably food and clothing.

Mamota squinted but still could see no driver in the cart. He decided that the donkey was simply following the pony, oblivious to its very agitated and impatient rider. Waving his hands excitedly, the man dismounted, attached a rope to the donkey's head, then remounted and began to yank. But the donkey was stubborn and refused to go faster than a walk.

"I think he is a thief," Chala said with contempt, "a thief among his own people."

"What are we to do about him?" Oati asked, looking to Mamota for an answer.

"Nothing."

"But he has robbed us of elk!"

"They were not ours."

Oati frowned and pressed his argument. "In repayment, we could take his pony, donkey, and treasure."

"No good would come of that."

"They would be of great value to our people."

"Oati is right," Chala seconded. "The cart probably has food and blankets. These gifts would be cause for celebration among The People."

Mamota could see that Oati had won Chala to his way of thinking, which was not surprising because the man on the red pony appeared to be armed with only a long sword, no match against Miwok hunters. Even so, Mamota shook his head.

"But why not?" Oati asked.

"Ouma has prophesied many times that white men would bring death to the Ahwahneeche."

"But how could Ouma, even with all her powers, know that this is just *one* Spaniard with much treasure? We could kill him without even being seen for he comes straight to us. Perhaps he was sent by our spirits to bring us treasure. Ouma could not know this."

Mamota saw the logic of Oati's thinking and knew he would be considered weak if he were too timid to attack even a single runaway thief. And it was true that they were looking at a rare opportunity for bounty, one almost without risk. He was about to relent when a body of fast-moving horsemen appeared on the western horizon.

"Look!" he whispered, pressing close to the ground.

"Spanish soldiers," Oati said, shrinking back a little into the protection of the trees. "They are chasing the man and his noisy cart. I was wrong about the spirits. We must go!"

Mamota, however, shook his head.

"But they have muskets!" Hosu whispered, voice rising with anxiety.

Mamota edged deeper into the cover of the trees. "We have been told that the Spaniards always have muskets."

"We should go now," Chala urged. "Ouma is right. The whites are very evil and we have no medicine to fight them."

But Mamota had no intention of leaving just yet for he was

caught up in the drama that was about to unfold. He had seen Spaniards before, but always at great distances and moving away. Now here was a chance to view them closely, to see if they really had great medicine that no Ahwahneeche could hope to defeat. As for the chase that was now about to end, there was little doubt of the outcome because it was obvious that the four Spaniards would quickly overtake the cart.

When the man on the red pony glanced back and saw the Spanish horsemen angling to cut him off from any chance of reaching the river, he cried out with alarm, then surprised Mamota by leaping from his pony. Taking up a stick, the man beat the donkey into a shambling, braying trot before remounting and hurrying on.

"If he left the donkey behind," Mamota reasoned out loud, "he might still escape into the river."

"Yes," Oati said, "he is blind with greed."

As the cart gathered speed, it began to shriek as if it, too, were in mortal fear of being recaptured by the Spanish soldiers.

"The fool!" Oati hissed, gripping his bow and leaning anxiously forward. "Why can't he leave the cart!"

"Because," Mamota explained as a head lifted above the sides of the cart, "it carries his woman."

The Ahwahneeche saw at once that this was true. They watched for several minutes and then Oati broke their silence when he declared with resignation, "They will both die."

Mamota nodded as the Spaniards raised their muskets.

"And they will kill *us* if we are caught here," Hosu said nervously.

Mamota did not fear detection. After all, if the Ahwahneeche could deceive elk, they could easily hide from the Spaniards whose attention was focused on their quarry.

Thunder rumbled and a few cold splashes of rain pelted Mamota but he did not feel them because he was mesmerized by the skill of the Spanish horsemen. Like all the Ahwahneeche, Mamota had heard of their mastery as horsemen from other Indian peoples, but he had not really believed that a man could actually cling to a beast moving at great speed. He had been wrong. Mamota could now see that the Spanish horses sailed over the land like the fish-hunting eagle whose talons skimmed the rippling waters. Nothing could long escape their grasp.

"Maybe we could do something," Oati ventured, his voice eager and excited.

"Against Spanish muskets?" Mamota asked, clenching his bow.

Oati said no more as Mamota watched the Spaniards swoop down on the fleeing couple. The lead rider fired. Mamota was shocked by all the smoke and the sharp crack of thunder. He saw the red pony stagger while its rider slumped forward. It appeared certain that pony and rider must both fall, but neither did. The pony resumed its choppy stride while the man pushed himself erect. It was clear that the Spaniards were not the only men who could ride.

"Now he turns to fight!" Hosu exclaimed, clapping his hands with delight.

They watched as the thief sawed his pony around to face the onrushing Spaniards. The wounded man drew a dagger from his belt and raised it defiantly. He shouted with a ringing challenge a moment before he charged the Spanish horses.

"He *is* brave," Oati whispered.

The wounded man's unexpected charge threw the Spaniards into a state of complete disarray. Two of them fired but missed. The third, however, was more accurate, and the red pony took the full force of the musket blast in its face, neck and shoulders. The animal somersaulted through the onrushing Spaniards, bowling one of them over and pinning its rider. The three remaining Spaniards finally managed to turn their charging horses back but the animals were nearly crazed by the pony's blood now drenching the colorful wildflowers. It was all their masters could do to get them under control. The thief, despite his many back wounds, dismounted and ran to the cart, where he began to beat the donkey toward the trees. A moment later, he pivoted away from the cart and ran south.

"Now the man deserts his woman," Chala said, admiration turning to disgust.

"Yes," Mamota replied, "but only to draw the enemy away from her."

The Spaniard whose horse had fallen was frantically attempting to push his mount off his pinned leg and then get to his feet. His companions separated, two going after the badly wounded thief, the other after the woman, who had crawled to her knees and was screaming at her husband and the soldiers about to take his life.

The donkey began to bray piteously and Mamota saw the woman trying to escape the cart, but then falling again. As the cart neared the trees, Mamota jumped to his feet and stared, knuckles stretched white against his bow as the cart lurched violently and overturned. The woman spilled against the forest. Behind her, the onrushing Spaniard was unable to pull up his horse in time to avoid plunging headlong into the trees.

"The woman *must* get up!" Mamota breathed, himself rising to his feet.

Being so heavy with child, she tried but failed.

Oati nocked an arrow to his bowstring and cried, "Mamota, we must help her!"

Casting all reason aside, Mamota also nocked an arrow and jumped forward, racing toward the unsuspecting Spaniard and the helpless woman. She was struggling to crawl into the forest but the Spaniard wheeled his horse directly into her path. He dismounted and calmly drew his short, heavy-bladed sword before advancing. When the woman clumsily threw herself forward to rise and strike him, the Spaniard danced away with mocking laughter. He raised his sword with both hands and began to circle the woman. At last, Mamota found a clear line of fire through the trees. He drew his bowstring, took aim, and an instant later his arrow murmured softly through a narrow corridor of forest until its obsidian point disappeared into the Spaniard's back.

The man staggered, then reeled about to gape at Mamota and his onrushing hunters. He was large, with a thick black beard and a hooked nose. Though mortally wounded and outnumbered, he took a few jolting steps forward, eyes blazing with hatred. Oati shot him again, bowstring chirring like quail taking wing. The Spaniard collapsed, blade hacking spasmodically at the decay of autumn leaves.

Mamota rushed to the woman's side. She was barely conscious. Her skin was on fire and her breathing was labored. When he tried to lift her to her feet so that they could all escape to the river, she found a Spanish dagger in her dress and tried to bury it in Mamota's heart but instead sliced it across his ribs.

Mamota tore the dagger from the woman's grasp. She struggled to fight him while he indicated to the others that they must drag her back deeper into the trees. The heavens growled and cold raindrops began to pierce the overheard canopy of trees.

"Mamota, we must leave this place," Oati urged, "or the other soldiers will find this dead man and come after us."

"Yes, and to hide our tracks," Mamota said, "we must keep to the rocks!"

Mamota knew they could not afford to leave tracks that the other pair of Spaniards would find and follow. But when they tried to lift and carry the woman to the river, she beat them away, sobbing uncontrollably. Now that Mamota could see her closely, he realized that she was too weak to walk more than a few steps and that created a dilemma that he did not want nor had expected to face.

"We *must* leave her!" Chala urged. "Leave her before the other two come and find us."

"Leave her?" Mamota mumbled, turning away with a shake of his head. "No, Chala. I can't leave her."

"But . . ."

"We must finish this fight," Mamota heard himself say as he turned back to face his hunters. "It is too late to run now that we have killed this soldier and made enemies."

"Then what will we do!" Chala demanded.

Mamota closed his eyes and called upon the spirits of Ah-wahnee to come to his aid with wise council. To act foolishly now and lose his hunters was a far worse possibility than death. After a moment, the answer came and Mamota opened his eyes. His voice was calm when he said, "We will carry the woman to the river and lay her on a flat rock, where she will draw in the Spaniards. But they will not see us until it is too late."

The young hunters looked at him for a moment, then Oati nodded, saying, "Mamota is right. We cannot run away now. We must kill the other Spaniards. Kill *all* of them."

The rain began to fall heavily, slanting through the tall trees. The Ahwahneeche overwhelmed the woman and carried her to an open resting place beside the river. They removed their hunter's disguises and used them to cover and shield the shivering woman. Then, without further discussion, they melted into the rocks and the trees, each seeking a place of ambush.

Mamota chose a high rock that afforded an excellent line of fire. As the minutes passed, his attention was drawn to this same great river born of the highest mountains to cascade into his Ahwahnee, giving all things life. Surely this river would now watch over the Ahwahneeche and protect them from the power of the Spaniards and their terrible muskets. As time passed, Mamota allowed the familiar and comforting sound of his beloved river to wash away the bloody image of the red pony mutilated by a single, shattering blast of smoke and fire.

When he felt soothed and confident that he would prove victorious, Mamota removed his quiver and carefully selected his finest arrow, the one with the feathers of the hawk and the black obsidian head traded from his Mono brothers on the far, dry side of the mountains. Mamota reminded himself that such an arrow already had slain one Spaniard and there was no reason to believe it would not do the same again.

A bolt of lightning struck a treetop, which erupted in a shower of smoke and hissing flames. Mamota eagerly embraced this as yet another sign that the Ahwahneeche would destroy their enemies. He eased forward to peer over the edge of his high rock. He could see the prostrated Indian woman, enticing as a morsel of meat.

But the two Spaniards were not fools. When they finally appeared and saw the woman, instead of rushing forward as Mamota had hoped, they dismounted and tied their horses. They advanced cautiously, muskets waving back and forth like fingers of death. When they grew near the woman, they ducked under a rock and huddled together, voices indistinguishable over the rumble of the river.

They wore black, flat-rimmed hats and heavy leather vests. Like the man they'd hunted and shot, they were bearded, sharp-featured with high cheekbones and prominent noses. As they peered into the rain, Mamota realized that they were as wary as wolves.

At last the soldiers seemed to reach some agreement, some plan of attack. When they stepped back into the falling rain, the pregnant woman finally saw them. She shrieked with defiance and began to drag herself toward them. To Mamota's surprise, the soldiers retreated a few steps before raising their muskets. At that instant, Mamota knew that he could wait no longer. He fired but missed. Obsidian scored against granite. His shattered arrow ricocheted into the river.

The Spaniard's chin snapped up as Mamota's hand reached to retrieve a second arrow. An instant later, Oati's arrow pierced both the Spaniard's cheeks. Blood spilled across the man's lower teeth and he tried to scream as his musket clattered to the rocks. He sagged to his knees, a swarm of arrows finding his body. The remaining soldier turned to run but died before he had taken more than a few choppy strides toward his horse.

Mamota and his companions emerged from hiding and hurried to gather around the pregnant woman. Mamota asked her name, but she did not understand and began to cry. They gently carried her out of the storm to rest under the same rock where the Spaniards had taken shelter moments before they died. The woman had regained her senses and now indicated with sign language that she wanted her husband.

"He is dead," Mamota explained, using signs which the woman still could not comprehend.

When the woman grew even more insistent, Mamota took his companions out to find the thief's body. First, however, they cut the braying donkey from its leather harness and began to open the sacks of bounty spilled from the cart.

"Mamota!" Oati exclaimed. "These are great prizes!"

Mamota was not so certain. Most of the sacks contained jewelry, which he considered to be of little value. There were rings, necklaces, plates, and cups. They would delight the women, but the only thing of real value to him was a very sharp Spanish dagger whose handle was encrusted with bright red and green stones. Mamota decided he could probably trade the dagger to the Yokut or the Mono. There were also several bags of corn and flour. And three leather pouches heavy with the yellow flakes that were found in the rivers. In a fit of disgust, Mamota poured out the yellow dust, but he knew enough to keep the fine leather pouches.

They were admiring their newfound wealth, which included the sad-eyed, noisy donkey, when they heard a faint call of distress. Jumping for cover, the Ahwahneeche hid behind the overturned carreta, sure that they would soon be attacked either by more Spaniards or the feared Po-to-en-cies.

But the call belonged to the lone Spaniard who had been knocked down by the thief's last, desperate charge. The man kept hacking his sword at the body of his dead mount in a feeble but desperate attempt to extract himself. But the soldier could get no power into his blows and was mostly striking the saddle. When the Spaniard saw the Ahwahneeche approaching, he began to curse and slash even more frantically at his dead mount. Mamota halted well beyond the Spaniard's reach. He squatted on his heels as he considered the consequences of taking this man's life. He had slain men before, but always in the heat of battle.

Killing a helpless man was completely against Mamota's nature but he also knew that he could not afford to allow this man life, for to do so might bring swift revenge. There being little choice, Mamota rose to his feet and lifted a sword he had taken from one of the other dead Spaniards.

The soldier slashed a final time at his horse and tried to free his leg. But when that failed, he pulled a silver cross from beneath his tunic and began to chant what Mamota supposed was his death song.

Not wishing to interrupt the Spaniard's prayers, Mamota and Oati went out to retrieve the thief's body for his wife. The thief was lying facedown in wildflowers. Mamota inspected his mutilated back because he wanted no doubts to remain in his mind about the power of muskets. Satisfied, he rolled the dead thief over and studied his face. Mamota decided such bravery demanded a moment of respect and he wanted to remember this man in death.

Several minutes later, Mamota and Oati carried the man back to his woman. But as they passed, the Spaniard raised his head and began to howl with mockery. His laughter was so evil that Mamota involuntarily shivered. Oati nocked an arrow and the Spaniard gagged on his laughter.

"Kill him," Mamota ordered as the Spaniard squeezed his eyes shut tightly and again began to pray.

This unnerved Oati.

"All right, let him finish speaking to his god," Mamota allowed.

The Spaniard prayed a long, long time, words clashing against the thunder of the sky. Finally, he was done and he opened his eyes and stared through Oati, nodding.

"Maybe," Oati said, a tremor in his voice, "we could just leave him?"

"Ouma warned us of their powerful medicine," Mamota said. "This man would lead others against us out of revenge. They might even follow us into Ahwahnee."

Oati must have agreed because he drew his bowstring and killed the Spaniard.

Two

Jacinta felt it would have been a blessing if the Spanish soldiers had killed her along with her brave husband. Now, because these Indians had saved her life, she was expected to go away with them and have her baby. If they had not interfered, her ordeal and suffering would be over because she, like most of the other Indians who had lived and worked on the ranchos near Santa Cruz, would be dead.

Life's only remaining sweetness were her memories and the best among those were of Rafael. Of how he had so ardently courted Jacinta and then, despite the ridicule of his fellow soldiers, defiantly married her in the mission church. But when the black sickness came and Indians began to die in the terrible plague, Rafael had been afraid that Jacinta and the child she carried also would die. So they had fled, but not before her Rafael had plundered. *That* had been their great sin, not the fleeing. Don Luis Montoya had sent his soldiers after them and they had not been able to reach the mountains soon enough to escape.

And so now, as Jacinta lay within the hated cart amid the worthless spoils that Rafael had insisted would buy them new friends and freedom, she felt a terrible dread. No good would come of this, especially when the Ahwahneeche realized she was the carrier of a black death. And so, if it had not been for her unborn child, Jacinta would have used a dagger to cut her own throat.

As the hours dragged into days, Jacinta wondered how far the Indians would take her into these rugged mountains. The Ahwahneeche had hitched the donkey back to the cart and left the rolling, open foothills following the big river into the deep forest, a forest cool and heady with the sweet incense of cedar and pine. There were birds and animals unlike any Jacinta had seen before and even a grizzly, which had reared upon its hind legs and challenged them for several moments. The donkey and horses had gone insane with terror, but the Indians had rushed at the great bear and sent it ambling away, woofing like a great cowering dog.

Later that afternoon, Jacinta had opened her eyes to watch a clumsy-looking porcupine sway atop the highest reaches of a lightning-charred pine. All around her were leafy giants that tried but never quite succeeded in blocking out the sun and the sky. Jacinta found pleasure in watching beams of silvery sunlight pierce the overhead canopy of leaves to dance like sprites upon the soft, moldy forest floor.

As their party climbed ever higher, the trees had gradually changed from oak and cottonwood to pine, spruce and maple. The air cooled and the river ran faster, often boiling with froth. The Ahwahneeche changed too, becoming almost playful. It came as a shock to Jacinta to realize that these hunters were little older than boys, a fact incompatible with the efficiency of their attacking and killing Spanish soldiers, men trained in the science of war and accustomed to victory and conquest.

Jacinta realized that the Ahwahneeche had been uncomfortable exposing themselves in California's great open valleys.

Along with their growing excitement, she felt their reverence for
the forest. Sometimes, when coming upon a particularly immense specimen of the red-barked giants, their voices dropped
to whispers, like padres passing before the altar. But above all,
Jacinta noted the extreme care they took to ensure that they could
never be followed. They used limbs to wipe out every trace of
their passing. Beds of pine needles were smoothed, rocks and
even pebbles crushed under the wheels of the carreta were collected and thrown into the river.

The storm that had plagued them in the valley with cold, in-
termittent rain had fled eastward, leaving soft white puffy clouds,
reminding Jacinta of Spanish galleons sailing into the harbor at
Santa Cruz.

On the third day after Rafael's death, the Ahwahneeche nearly
killed the poor donkey, forcing it to drag the heavy cart up an
impossibly steep and crooked trail they made by furiously hacking away brush until their new swords grew dull and stained with
pitch and the oil of heavy brush. Jacinta felt certain that the cart
would overturn and crush her to death as it rolled down the mountainside. But the Indians used vines to somehow keep everything
moving and upright until they finally slithered over a high ridge.
The donkey was so exhausted it could only wheeze. The Indians
beat its flanks until it staggered to the very edge of a cliff, where
they halted before a valley so magnificent that even time stopped
in hushed awe.

"Por Dios!" Jacinta whispered, her breath catching in her
throat as she gazed across miles of empty sky into a valley which
seemed far too beautiful for this world. Her immediate impression was of an incredibly deep gash in the earth filled with a
thousand contrasting shades of green meadow and forest. Here
and there, she could see the sparkle of river fed by glistening
waterfalls tumbling out of heaven.

Jacinta closed her eyes for a moment and then opened them
again. Yes, it was all true. Before her lifted sheer granite cliffs
whose size mocked anything she had seen plunging into the California coast. These cliffs soared higher than eagles. They stood
aloof, carved and stained by the ages. Jacinta saw stamped upon
their stone faces eyes that bled rivers. She marveled at granite

layered upon more granite, one monolith leaned over the valley
and another was halved like an inverted bowl topped by a snowy
mantle. Despite her pain and exhaustion, she delighted at the
cloud shadows which played with sunlight, constantly altering
the stern stone faces, moment to moment.

The home of these Ahwahneeche people was indeed worthy
of the Miwok legends. This *was* a spirit place so beautiful that
Jacinta's throat tightened like a fist. She scrubbed tears away
with the back of her arm, realizing that the Indians were watching
her closely to gauge her initial reaction to their secret paradise.
Oh dear God, she thought, if only her Rafael could have seen
this heaven on earth! He would have wanted to stay forever. There
would have been no need to steal the wealth of Don Luis because
all that was required to be happy in Ahwahnee was love and life.

The effect of seeing their home again had no less powerful an
effect upon the Ahwahneeche. In preparation for making a grand
and triumphant entrance down into their valley and, amid much
laughter and teasing, they stripped away their deer masks and
breechclouts to don articles of salvaged Spanish clothing. Jacinta
had to look away when Hosu chose to wear Rafael's pants, which
she had often mended. The new outfits were far too large and
the Ahwahneeche appeared ridiculous wearing hats that rested
on their ears and pants that could have been raised to their armpits. But they were having fun as they began their triumphant
parade down into their valley.

"Por Dios," Jacinta whispered again, making the sign of the
cross as the cart lurched over the rim of the world. The Indians
beat the donkey, which began to bray piteously as they edged
down a game trail that even a goat would have refused.

Jacinta hugged her womb and prayed for a quick end to her
misery. She lost all track of time, but hours must have passed
because the shadows were long by the time the cart finally
bumped into a meadow. With shouts of greeting, the villagers
crowded around to examine her along with the gold and silver
jewelry, flour and clothing. Apparently, their excitement unrav-
eled the last of the donkey's mind because it began to bray louder
than ever, causing everyone to laugh.

Jacinta's eyes fixed on a child, a small girl about five years old who was gazing at her with wonder. She was beautiful, and Jacinta, despite her sorrow, smiled. The child advanced, one hand held behind her back, until she presented a handful of wildflowers. Something inside snapped and fresh tears filled Jacinta's eyes. Confused by the tears, the child turned and fled. But the other people of Ahwahnee continued to press forward with curiosity, flowing around the carreta like their beautiful Merced River flowed around its many sparkling sandbars. They also engulfed the hunters, some hugging, others just dashing here and there in a frenzy to examine the strange and beautiful Spanish treasures.

The weary horses and braying donkey were also greatly admired and fussed over although Jacinta could not help but feel sorry for them. She suspected that they would last no longer than the time it took for them to be butchered and devoured. Next to the horses and the weapons, Jacinta herself was the cause of the greatest interest and excitement, particularly among the women and especially one slightly taller than average dressed in a very beautiful buckskin outfit decorated with red beads and fringes. She wore a matching necklace and earrings made from shells and the scarlet head feathers of a woodpecker. Her hair was long and bound by a garland of white feathers. In one hand she carried a gourd that she rattled and, in the other, a pouch that she shook toward Jacinta as if to ward away evil spirits.

Jacinta could not keep her eyes off the handsome woman, who stared at her with more than a passing interest. Unable to hide her curiosity, Jacinta looked at Chala, then pointed to the woman.

"Ouma," he said, bowing slightly to what Jacinta was sure was the Ahwahneeche's shaman, or medicine woman.

Hearing her name spoken as if in introduction, Ouma stepped forward, gourd rattling like a snake. When Jacinta shrank back, Ouma stopped the rattling and gently placed the buckskin bag on Jacinta's distended womb. Words without meaning flowed from her lips and Jacinta found them comforting. She smiled, but the shaman's eyes dropped to her womb as she began to chant.

The other villagers fell silent and watched until Ouma finally stopped her chanting as a short, stocky man also wearing buckskins and jewelry marched forward. In addition, he wore a feathered belt sewn on buckskin and fringed with pieces of abalone shell. A black tattoo ran from his lower lip straight down over his chin, neck, and body until it disappeared into his breechclout. He was at least sixty and missing most of his teeth, yet he appeared to Jacinta to be well fed. He was the only man wearing a feathered headpiece, made of black crow or raven feathers standing straight around a bunch of smaller, multicolored feathers.

He bowed very formally to Jacinta and intoned, "Utal."

Jacinta eased her legs out of the cart and attempted to stand but would have collapsed if Chala and his brother, Hosu, had not grabbed and held her erect.

When Chief Utal turned to Ouma with concern, she said, "This woman has a sickness."

"Then you must heal her with your medicine," Utal ordered.

Ouma bent to her knees and reached around Jacinta's big waist, then pressed her ear to her belly. For several minutes, while all the Ahwahneeche stood in silence, Ouma listened for the heartbeat of life. It was difficult to hear anything, for the mother was wheezing. Finally, though, Ouma was sure of a faint heartbeat.

"The baby lives," she pronounced to Utal. "But the woman is possessed by an evil spirit."

"What is the matter with her?" Mamota asked, for he had been secretly worried about the woman's fevers and delirium.

"Bad spirits," Ouma said vaguely.

"Her husband was brave, but a thief," Mamota told the chief. "The Spaniards followed and killed him."

"How do you know this?"

Mamota gestured toward the cart with its sacks of food and treasure.

The Ahwahneeche were very impressed. Their women pushed even closer to see the gold and silver plates and cups, a candelabrum and other riches that were pleasing to the eyes but whose function was a mystery.

"If her husband was a thief, maybe this woman also is evil," the chief said, looking sharply at Jacinta as if he might catch her in an unguarded moment and divine the truth.

"She is *not* evil," Ouma said. "But bad spirits have possessed her. I will drive them from her body."

"And from the body of the child she carries?"

"Yes," Ouma said. She looked around at The People, adding, "It will take much power to do this, but my powers are strong."

"This is true," Chief Utal agreed. "Take her to rest."

Ouma tried to hide her excitement. This was a great day and, when she purged the woman's fever and delivered her child, Ouma knew that her already-lofty standing as the Ahwahneeche medicine woman would soar.

"Beware of her," Kimia, the oldest woman in the village dared to warn Ouma. "I think she is evil."

"She is past her time to give birth," Ouma argued strongly, "and has suffered both from the death of her husband and her hard travels."

"Maybe, but I still think her evil," Kimia persisted.

This annoyed Ouma because it was just like old Kimia to stand apart in the face of triumph and celebration in a feeble attempt to gain importance and attention.

"Keep away from her," Kimia advised, "for all people of the outside world are evil."

Overhearing this, Mamota hurried over to Kimia to defend the visitor he had helped to rescue. "Kimia, this woman is very brave," he announced, speaking in a loud voice so that all could hear. "She tried to kill the Spaniard who raised his sword to cut her head off. She even tried to kill me."

To prove this, Mamota lifted his cloth shirt and displayed the long, ugly scab across his ribs.

"She did that?" Chief Utal asked.

"She did not know that I was a friend," Mamota explained. "She was protecting not only herself, but her child."

"This is true," Ouma agreed. "She is very brave."

Kimia, however, remained suspicious of the outsider. "If her husband was a thief, so she is a thief and should be stoned."

Ouma turned and lifted both rattle and buckskin bag as if to strike Kimia. The old woman turned and quickly shuffled out of sight.

Ouma spit at the ground to indicate her disdain. Then, addressing Hosu and Chala, she said, "Bring her to my u'-ma-cha. Hurry!"

Ouma led the grand procession through the village while it was all that Jacinta could do not to faint. She did notice that this village was quite large. These people lived in conical huts about a dozen feet in diameter constructed of thick, overlapping slabs of cedar bark laid upon a framework of tall poles. Inside many of them, Jacinta could see cooking fires set in rock rings, the smoke exiting the top where the poles were joined.

There were a few dogs in the camp, but no horses or other animals save a large, pet raccoon that humped its back a little then spit and hissed when Jacinta passed. Besides the bark huts, she noted several huge earth-and-bark-covered lodges that were obviously half-subterranean and would hold more than a hundred people. Jacinta also recognized the familiar sweat house once used by the men of her Yokut villages when she had been a child. But the Spaniards had long since destroyed them as pagan—like so many other tribal things now only dimly remembered.

"Koom-i-ne," Ouma pronounced grandly, as they moved through the hastily emptied village.

Behind them, Jacinta heard the donkey begin to bray until its voice suddenly died. She twisted around, struggling to see the little animal which had become like a friend in suffering. At the sight of the poor beast, which had tried so valiantly to carry her to safety and was now being repaid with death, Jacinta's eyes filled with fresh tears. Shrugging off the hands of Chala and Hosu, she covered her face.

"What is wrong with her?" Hosu asked, wary of the knife that this woman still carried.

"She is just tired," Ouma explained, looking back toward the slaughter of the donkey and one of the horses. "And maybe the donkey's good spirits also protected her."

"It was a stupid and slow animal," Chala said. "I doubt that it will even taste good."

"Never mind then," Ouma said, gently taking Jacinta's arm and leading her toward her hut. "Woman, you will not have to eat the flesh of your noisy friend."

Ouma placed Jacinta on her own bed of rabbit skins. She was proud of her hut because it was considerably larger than the others of her village, except for that of Chief Utal. Because she was

shaman and medicine woman, Ouma used two fire rings, one
within the other. The center fire ring was smoldering and the one
circling it had a foundation of rocks. Ouma would shift rocks
from the fire to the outer ring, then use a collection of beautiful
reed baskets to cook and prepare her food and medicines.

Now, with Jacinta watching, Ouma stirred a basket of steaming
acorn mush and used a big river mussel shell to sample the food.
She smacked her lips and grinned, pleased because all the bitterness was gone and she was sure that the woman named Jacinta
would find it tasty. But when she offered a shell of the food to
Jacinta, it was firmly declined.

Ouma frowned because, if this woman died, she would lose
face among The People. "You must eat to keep your strength for
the baby," she warned Jacinta, even though she knew the stranger
would not understand.

Ouma took another mouthful of acorn mush, tracing the food
down to her belly. She smacked her lips and rubbed her stomach.
Ouma did not think she could have made things any clearer.

But the stubborn woman shook her head again and then she
closed her eyes. Angry and insulted, but very determined that
this woman would have to obey her instructions, Ouma ate all
the food because she would also need strength in the days to
come if she hoped to save Jacinta.

Late that afternoon, Ouma prepared a strong tea of spearmint,
whose boiled leaves were very effective for stomach troubles,
fevers, and diarrhea. For good measure, she added the leaves of
incense cedar because of their great power to heal. And finally,
Ouma added a sprinkle of the finest young blossoms of the low-
land sage, guaranteed to break even the most raging fever.

It was almost evening when she was finally ready to cure her
patient. Touching her sleeping patient's forehead, Ouma decided
that she had never encountered a higher fever.

"Wake up," she ordered, slipping one arm under Jacinta's neck
and using the other to reach for her medicine.

When Jacinta awoke with a start and tried to pull away, Ouma's
patience slipped. She set down the bowl of medicine down and
yelled into the woman's face, telling her that she was ungrateful
and stupid.

"Drink!" she ordered.

Jacinta, eyes wide and feverish, tried to drink, but the medicine was too hot and she choked, then spit it out. Coughing and with tears filling her eyes, Jacinta pushed Ouma away and dragged herself back against the wall of the hut, reaching for her dagger.

"You are a fool!" Ouma scolded.

Jacinta only glared at her until she lapsed into a feverish sleep. Ouma quickly disarmed the woman and tied her hands and her feet. She was furious at Jacinta and could not understand why the woman was being so difficult.

"Now you'll drink," Ouma vowed, as she grabbed Jacinta's lower jaw and yanked it downward, then poured her medicine into Jacinta's mouth and throat. Jacinta tried to spit the medicine back up but Ouma was ready for that, too. She pressed her weight down on Jacinta's forehead and kept her mouth clamped shut. Some of the medicine escaped, but Ouma could see the woman's throat work and knew that most of it had gone down.

Jacinta screamed. Ouma folded her arms across her breasts and gloated. This was a battle of strong wills, one that Ouma had no intention of losing.

Jacinta hadn't the strength to fight very long. The next day she meekly submitted to the awful-tasting medicines although her fever did not abate and she felt, if anything, even weaker. When Ouma wasn't preparing medicines, she chanted and once even tried to place her lips on Jacinta's forehead in order to suck out the fever. Jacinta made it clear that she would take medicines, but nothing more.

Despite the great variety of awful-tasting medicines she was forced to consume, Jacinta could feel herself growing weaker by the day. Her fever would not break and it continued to bleed away even her dwindling reserves. Jacinta knew that she was dying. She had seen enough of her friends die to know the signs: a persistent and raging fever, nausea, diarrhea and cold sweats, pounding headaches and nightly hallucinations. Over and over, Jacinta tried to make Ouma give her something that would induce labor so that she could deliver her baby. Once that was accomplished, Jacinta would have no regrets if only her child would live to be healthy and the black death would end with her. The belief that her child would be loved and nurtured in such a beautiful place was a great solace as her body wasted away.

On warm afternoons, Chala and Hosu carried Jacinta outside where she could enjoy the sight of a waterfall gaily tumbling off the high cliffs to spill onto the valley floor. She could feel its power, hear music in its whispering thunder. The Ahwahneeche called it Cho'-lok and its playful mist reminded her of spun silk, the kind that the rich Spanish ladies favored. After taking her medicine, Jacinta would watch the waterfall and listen to the birds and the breeze sighing through the tall pines. If there was an afterlife other than the heaven promised by the padres, she thought it must be in Ahwahnee.

It also pleased her to watch the children play. Jacinta convinced herself that the half-Spanish child in her womb would become special among these children and perhaps even repay the kindnesses that they had shown her dying mother. But, in addition to these hopeful thoughts, Jacinta also struggled against a dark vision that filled her with despair and brought tears as bitter and scalding as the potion that Ouma brewed. This vision was that she would carry her child straight to the grave before it could be born.

"You must give me something different!" she demanded of Ouma one day, knocking her medicine aside and pointing to her unborn child. "You must help me bring my child into this world!"

Her voice was weak but so insistent that Ouma finally placed both hands on Jacinta's belly, closed her eyes, and began to chant.

Jacinta grew even more upset. "No, no!" she cried. "No more prayers!"

Ouma gently pulled up Jacinta's soiled dress, then leaned over to place her ear to the womb. She listened so long that Jacinta grew impatient.

"Ouma, my child *is* alive!"

Ouma listened and finally nodded. Looking determined, she went away for several hours, returning with berries and leaves whose appearance was foreign to Jacinta. Ouma crushed the berries and leaves, adding powders that she kept hidden in a leather pack, and boiled water to make a tea.

Jacinta, weak and exhausted, placed both hands on her womb and pushed downward, looking at Ouma with feverish eyes.

"Sí," Ouma said.

Jacinta's eyebrows shot up. "You speak Spanish!"

"Sí." Ouma smiled.

"My Lord, but why didn't you say so before now!"

Jacinta was ecstatic. Now she could tell Ouma everything about Rafael and her past. About her mother and her family, all dead, taken by the disease. And about the missions and the padre's Christ and all the beautiful . . ."

"Sí," Ouma began a singsong chant as she prepared the tea. "Sí, sí, sí!"

Over and over the medicine woman chanted this single word and Jacinta lapsed into a crushed silence, knowing that "sí" was all the Spanish Ouma knew and there would be no last, precious sharing between them before she died.

That night, Ouma's new medicine was the worst-tasting yet, but it caused Jacinta finally to begin her labor. She felt the first strong contractions and cried with happiness, praying that she would have the strength to live long enough to deliver her child. All through that afternoon the contractions came, always quicker and stronger. Ouma was joined by several of the other village women, who alternately fussed and worked to help her deliver the baby. The pain Jacinta felt was sweet and she reveled in it, knowing that she was giving away life to create new life.

By early evening, however, Jacinta thought that she could not possibly summon up any more effort to push. But Ouma had one last concoction, a sweetish red liquid that dulled Jacinta's pain and gave her a fresh burst of strength.

"It finally comes," Ouma said, gently pulling the slick newborn from Jacinta's womb. She wiped the child's face clean and slapped it on the back. The baby started, then opened its eyes and began to wail.

"You have a girl," Ouma said, as one of her helpers used her teeth to nip the umbilical cord free, then tied it with a strip of rawhide.

Jacinta lay panting, feeling as if every bone in her body had been crushed to powder. She barely had the strength to open her eyes and stare as she lifted the child up before her face.

"Una niña!" Jacinta cried, using the Spanish word for girl. "Una niña!"

Ouma nodded, thinking this was the name that Jacinta had chosen for her daughter. The infant's hair was thick and black, like an Indian's, but her skin was more golden than brown, no doubt the legacy of her Spanish father. Ouma was especially pleased that the child's skin was cool, meaning that she had not inherited her mother's wasting fever.

"Anina!" Ouma exclaimed as she proudly raised the squalling infant up before the other women.

The Ahwahneeche women beamed and giggled. The child cried even louder, a good sign that it had a strong spirit and body and the will to survive. Everyone was very happy. But when they looked down at Jacinta, their smiles died because Jacinta had slipped quietly into the spirit world.

Three

Almost a month later, in the village's hang-e or ceremonial roundhouse, Chief Utal and the surviving elders of the Ahwahneeche gathered in grim silence. Ordinarily, such a meeting would be a celebration, as it had most recently been when Mamota and his hunters had returned to Ahwahnee safe, victorious, and with much treasure. But now things were very different. Most of the elders were visibly ill, feverish and shaking with ague. Utal himself was running a persistent fever but, when his son Mamota, the brothers Hosu and Chala as well as their medicine woman, Ouma, were ushered inside, he drew himself erect.

"Mamota," Chief Utal said, speaking forcefully to his only son, "did the Spanish soldiers bring the black sickness upon The People?"

Such directness was rude and unlike an Ahwahneeche in matters of importance, but Mamota understood his father's desperation. "No," he said. "They were strong."

"Then it was the woman," old Hoo-a-mi proclaimed.

"Yes," Mamota said quietly.

"Then her child also carries the sickness."

Mamota did not know if this was true. He turned to Ouma, who had taken the child and cared for it as if it were her own.

Ouma took a deep breath. She had anticipated this charge and had tried to prepare her defense, but in the face of so much misery and death, she knew that her chances of saving Anina were slight. "The child has no sickness."

"She must die!" Hoo-a-mi shouted, head swiveling back and forth to his surviving friends on the council. "If we kill the child, then we kill the sickness."

Ouma thought of the baby now resting in its cradleboard, a child conceived in a world of sickness and death, fear and thievery, and yet one that glowed with good health and exhibited a calm serenity and whose eyes were filled with trust. In truth, Ouma had lost her heart to Anina and had mortgaged her fading reputation among the Ahwahneeche to save the child.

"Is it not true that we might save The People by killing the evil woman's child?" another elder demanded to know.

Ouma saw the others nodding their heads in firm agreement. Her heart sank and she could do no more than stammer, "The child is strong medicine for The People."

" 'Strong medicine'!" one of the elders exclaimed bitterly. "We are *dying!*"

Ouma's rattle lifted and shook. "The black death is very strong, but not all are dying."

"I am dying," Chief Utal said quietly.

Ouma loved her chief and fought off tears. How many of The People had already died? Two out of every three and more every day despite everything Ouma could do. There were those in the village to whom her name was a curse. Others who begged and pleaded with her to save their children, their wives or husbands, and their parents. Usually, her medicine had failed and so she had failed as well.

"Ouma, can you make new medicine?" the chief asked with little hope.

Ouma closed her eyes and began to chant, calling up the oldest and most venerated spirits, spirits who had ignored her almost-constant supplications because they had always been as free and fickle as canyon winds. But maybe, Ouma prayed, they would be listening now, seeing the sadness of the elders, coming to guide her hand and her heart to the right way and bringing life where there was now only death.

"I will make new medicine," she promised, opening her eyes and speaking only to Chief Utal. "Strong new medicine."

"The *child* is the evil among us," Eti-am said, voice shaking with anger. "She is the cause of our death. Her black medicine is stronger than Ouma's medicine. I say that we kill her now."

Ouma took a step backward and her heart raced with fear. "This is not true!"

Chief Utal turned to gaze into the council fire as if its flames might give him wisdom. Ouma felt the doubts of the tribal council surrounding her. Mamota had lost his wife, Tuani, and now seemed to walk in darkness. Chala and Hosu were glassy-eyed with fever and death was closing upon them. Oati had lost both his parents and confessed that he, too, expected to die.

Utal started and raised his head to speak. Ouma's breath caught in her throat because she could see the verdict in Utal's sad old eyes. A verdict of death for the child.

"My people, listen," Ouma said quickly. "I can prove that the child is good medicine. I can show you this."

"She cannot be allowed here!" Eti-am hissed. "If so, we will be cursed forever in the spirit world."

But Ouma was already dashing outside, where she snatched Anina from the arms of old Ei-y-ee and hurried back to face the elders.

At the sight of the child which so many thought evil, the old men began to shout in anger. Hoo-a-mi climbed unsteadily to his feet and shouted, "Kill her!"

"Anina has great medicine!" Ouma proclaimed. "She alone can bring back the spirits of those that have died of this sickness. She will become a great shaman for our people."

Even at these words Hoo-a-mi might have drawn his knife and attacked if Ouma had not raised her medicine rattle, the very same rattle that she had used to save Hoo-a-mi's own child two years before. The old man froze, then sank down on his meatless haunches, face fierce and accusing.

"How do you know this?" Utal asked quietly.

Ouma swallowed and looked down at the infant cradled in her arms. She prayed for strong words. If her words were not strong, Anina would die and so would all the Ahwahneeche.

"I had a vision," she began slowly, trusting for a power greater than herself to speak through her tongue. "I had a great vision that we would leave Ahwahnee . . . but someday return."

"We *are* leaving," Hoo-a-mi spit. "In death!"

Ouma's head and rattle began to shake. "Many yet live! Enough to remain a people, if we listen to the vision."

Utal leaned forward, his expression intent. "Where does your vision tell us to go?"

Great words swirled like spirits through Ouma's mind. She swayed before the council, speaking now without conscious thought. "Chief Utal, we must go far away from this sickness and death. Far away."

"But we cannot go to the valley of our enemies," Utal said, brushing a hand shakily across his eyes. "We are too few now to fight the Po-to-en-cies."

Ouma began to chant softly and the spirits raised her mind to a higher place, higher even than mighty Cho'-lok, whose nearby upper and lower waterfalls fed the grass of this valley. Higher even than the mighty half face of Tis-se'-yak, the Woman Turned to Stone.

"Tell us," Hoo-a-mi pleaded.

Ouma's vision brought to mind the ancient Ahwahneeche legend of the evil witches of Cho'-lok. And although she had not told this legend for many years, it was so strong that Ouma knew it must be the one true explanation for all the terrible things that were happening now.

"As you all know," she began, "just below the waters of Cho'-lok live the evil spirit women called Po'-loti."

"But that legend tells of snakes!" Eti-am wailed, raising his thin arms. "Snakes, Ouma, not sickness!"

Ouma ignored Eti-am. "Long, long ago, when a maiden from this ancient Ahwahnee went to the river below Cho'-lok, she dipped her water basket and discovered that it was filled with snakes. Frightened, she poured them all back into the river. Because she needed water, she tried again and again as she moved up the river toward mighty Cho'-lok, but always it was the same."

"We have already heard this story."

"Shhh!" Utal hissed.

Ouma's eyelids quivered and everyone watching feared that the interruption might have erased her vision, but finally, she began to speak again, and with greater power. "When the maiden reached the great pool of water fed by Cho'-lok, she bent over to try once more, but a mighty wind caused by the evil spirit women knocked her into the pool. She sank to the bottom and saw the spirit world, but just as she was about to enter it, the Po'-loti took pity and gave her a child."

Ouma turned dramatically toward the opening of the hang-e. "When the maiden returned to her village, she was very cold and wet and her people warmed and covered her with warm skin blankets. But when the woman's mother lifted the blanket to see the Cho'-lok child, this angered the evil Po'-loti, who used a great wind to sweep everyone from the village back into their pool."

Ouma passed a hand shakily across her eyes. She could feel the tension and it gave her a sense of power. She lowered her hand and said, "And none of those people were ever seen again."

The spell over Ouma was broken. Ouma's mind cleared and the child in her arms cooed softly. Ouma smiled at Anina but did not see her because she was still gripped by the vision and entirely at a loss as to its real meaning and the subtle changes that the spirits had made in its telling, particularly in the birth of an underwater child. What *could* this mean?

The elders, too, wondered at the child which had never been spoken of before. However, they knew that a shaman was allowed to see many new things in the old stories.

Finally Chief Utal said, "But what have the water spirits of

Cho'-lok and the birth of that child to do with the black sickness?"

Ouma surprised even herself by announcing, "The Po'-loti have given us back Anina. *This* is the child born under Cho'-lok."

This statement brought a gasp from many of the elders. Old Ati-lo jumped to his feet and began to dance and sing praise to the spirits. His voice, singsong and shrill, caused Mamota to exclaim, "But I don't understand, Ouma. And . . . and our People are still dying!"

"But not all," Ouma snapped. "Mamota, someday you will be chief. *Listen* to the spirits! They will save many of us if we follow the river over the mountains! The Po'-loti saved Anina for a reason and that was to tell us to follow the river before we *all* die!"

"I think you have no strong medicine to keep away the black death," Hoo-a-mi declared bitterly. "And you see no vision!"

Ouma fell to her knees and Anina rolled from her arms. Snatching up her rattle, Ouma pointed it at Hoo-a-mi and made it clear that she was about to put a curse on him. The old man jumped to his feet and scrambled out of the hang-e. Extending the rattle out before her, Ouma waved it over the others, causing even Chief Utal to shrink back with dread.

"When should we go?" Utal asked in a thin whisper.

Ouma closed her eyes and listened for the spirits for several heart-pounding moments, and then she said, "Tomorrow."

"And what of the child? Do we throw her back into the pool to appease the Po'-loti?"

Ouma pretended to give the matter some very careful deliberation. She closed her eyes and rocked back and forth on her knees. At last sure that she had the council's complete confidence again, she picked up her baby and shook her head. "No, this one was born of the river and, like the river, someday she will return."

Not all the elders were completely convinced, but when Utal, sick and desperate, nodded his head in agreement, Mamota and everyone else did the same. After all, the chief thought, eyes pulled to the infant at Ouma's feet. If the Po'-loti really had created this half-breed child with Spanish blood to save the last of the Ahwahneeche, then Anina would become great among The People. Much greater even than Ouma.

Preparations were made hastily and, although Ouma's vision was seized upon by all the surviving Ahwahneeche, the mood was not of joy and salvation, but of sorrow. The dead were burned in their huts, acorns were emptied from the chuck-ah granaries and then these buildings were burned, too. Only the great hang-e ceremonial houses were left untouched, for it had been decided that the good spirits, if any were left in this valley of death, would need a sanctuary until one day Anina led The People home. Never before had Ahwahnee heard so much wailing of women or seen such misery and death.

Mamota constructed a simple travois for his father but, when told of this, the chief refused to leave. "I am going to die," Utal said. "And so I stay to sing thanks to Po'-loti and ask that Anina, born of Cho'-lok, one day bring The People home again."

"How long would this be?" Mamota asked, trying to hide his tears.

"Long time," Utal finally said. He actually smiled a little and added, "One day Anina will tell you."

"Then you really believe in Ouma's spirit vision?" Mamota regretted the question even before it was fully spoken. Of course his father believed the vision.

But Utal gazed down at his hands and considered the question so long that Mamota began to have his doubts. And just when he was about to express them to his father, the chief raised his chin and said, "What is there *but* to believe?"

There was no answer to this question. Until this black sickness, Ouma's powers had always been great. Maybe, with Anina's presence, they would be again. There was nothing else to think, so Mamota touched his father, then went to help those too weak or sad to help themselves.

Ouma prayed, chanted and made her strongest medicine all that night. In the morning, she felt stronger than she had since the sickness had begun to spread among her people. She packed all her small baskets and leather pouches containing medicines but only a fraction of her belongings in a single cone-shaped basket. Ouma would carry Anina in a Miwok cradleboard which she had already bartered for with healing medicines that had, unfortunately, failed to protect a woman and her children from the sickness.

The People were waiting. Ouma could hear them outside her hut. The sun was rising and, as the one with the vision, she was expected to lead, but Ouma was not sure exactly where they were to go. Last night she had even taken a strong dose of the monayu root in order to summon up new visions, but the medicine had failed and left her groggy and depressed until dawn. Ouma felt a growing conviction that the spirit woman of Cho'-lok would get her feet to wherever it was that The People were supposed to live. It grieved her to leave behind so many medicines, a few almost impossible to collect. Would she be able to find tama, whose pulverized leaves had saved many of the people? Ouma doubted it, so she took as much of it and other similar medicines as she could carry.

Lifting her burden basket and the cradleboard, Ouma took one last look at her dozens of baskets of flowers, leaves, bark, and the powder of healing roots. It was a collection passed down from her grandmother, to her mother, and then to Ouma. In a final moment of weakness, Ouma decided that she would not burn her hut like the others. Her hut, along with the ceremonial roundhouses, was too alive with good spirits.

"Ouma," Mamota said when she emerged, "The People are ready."

She looked at faces streaked with smoke and tears. Their beautiful valley of the Ahwahnee was cloaked in a deathly silence, as if even the birds had died. Ouma squared her shoulders and, with Anina cradled in her arms and the huge cone basket filled with acorns, a rabbit-skin blanket, and her most important medicines, headed straight for Cho'-lok.

Mamota caught up with her after saying a last farewell to Chief Utal and a few others too weak or old to make this desperate pilgrimage. "Ouma, why are we going this way?"

"To say good-bye to the Po'-loti and ask for their blessings."

"But look what their evil has done to The People!"

Ouma did not have to look. She had seen death more intimately than anyone in the village. In just a month, she had failed hundreds of times and had very, very few successes. She did not need to turn and study their burning and smoldering homes, u'-ma-chas, sweat and ceremonial houses. No, she could smell death riding on the hot, smoky wind.

The People who followed her were very reluctant to approach mighty Cho'-lok, with its great upper and lower waterfalls. They averted their eyes from the great pool below while Ouma alone stood near the base of the lower waterfall and asked the Po'-loti to change their hearts and give her the strength and the vision to lead the surviving Ahwahneeche to a new land. But there could be no place so beautiful as Ahwahnee.

That morning seventeen more of The People died trying to climb out of Ahwahnee. Six were children whose deaths cut the hearts out of the Ahwahneeche, who had thought they had no hearts left. In the late afternoon, they crossed the final mountain ridge that afforded them a view of their valley. It was poisoned with the smoke of destruction. They could not see the valley meadows, shimmering waterfalls, or even the great river which fed and formed all.

"It is just as well," Mamota said, eyes distant.

"We'll return," Ouma vowed.

"Perhaps," Mamota said bitterly, "if I had not decided to save that woman . . ."

"Then we would not have Anina and the Po'-loti would have brought the sickness anyway."

Mamota almost choked with relief. "I want to believe that. I want to believe that I brought *life,* not death to our people."

"I saw the vision," Ouma said quietly. "You brought life."

Mamota staggered into the trees, to cry where he could not be seen.

"Come," Ouma said, leading up toward a lake where the water was cold and pure and the evil spirits would not follow, where huge granite cliffs and domes flowed upward to the east and the mountain canyons cradled deep, white pillows of snow.

* * *

That night, the wind blew hard in the mountains and more of The People died. Forcing herself to ignore the piteous cries of those too weak to go on, Ouma pushed higher at first light, still afraid of the evil spirits and the sickness. At the end of the second day, they came to the high alpine Tuolumne Meadows, where the Ahwahneeche had hunted and traded with their Eastern Sierra neighbors, the Mono Paiute, for as long as Ouma could remember. This country was rugged and beautiful, with vast open spaces and soaring rock escarpments. A thin blanket of snow still ringed its highest ridges and peaks.

"We will stay here," Ouma announced, knowing that the mountains to the east led down to a huge white lake crusted with salt and alkali beside which the Monos fished and hunted in a harsh and pitiless land.

"We can't stay here in the season of cold moons," Mamota said.

"I know."

"Then . . ."

Ouma turned her face into the west wind. Fields of wildflowers graced the Tuolumne but Ouma knew they would not last long, no longer than would the remainder of her People if they did not push on to the eastern deserts, to their unhappy fate with the Mono Indians.

"Can we go back before the snows?" Mamota asked.

"No. We must live in the desert."

Mamota turned with dejection and walked away. He could not yet accept the cruel future of the Ahwahneeche, but he would by winter.

The next day Mamota, Oati, and the other Ahwahneeche strong enough to hunt went after deer, which were plentiful. The women began to forage and make rabbit snares, as well as to prepare for fishing in the alpine lakes. There would be plenty of food for The People until winter, food enough even to make gifts for the Mono.

The real question in everyone's mind was whether the Mono

would accept The People and allow them to stay until Anina became a woman who would someday announce that it was finally time to return to their beloved Ahwahnee.

Four

Mono Lake, California

Ouma's eyes had grown very dim over the many years since she had led The People to safety across the Sierras. But in springtime, when the warm chinook winds blew off the high mountains, the scent of Sierra pines carried her back to Ahwahnee.

She and Anina sat on a crusty white rock beside Mono Lake basking in the sun and listening to the Indian women sing as they harvested pupa larva from the salty lake waters. But there was no happiness in Ouma, for she knew that her days were down to a precious few. She could not possibly survive another cold winter in this hostile desert. And had it not been for Anina's great medicine and power, she would already be dead. And so a deep sadness was upon Ouma, a sadness coupled with a fierce urgency to return once more to Ahwahnee so that her bones would not join the dust of this hated desert.

"What are you thinking?" Anina asked quietly, although she was sure that she could guess Ouma's troubled thoughts.

"I can smell the pines of Ahwahnee today," Ouma said, closing her eyes. "And I can hear her song in the wind telling me to come home."

Anina had guessed correctly. Each spring when the snow began to melt on the mountains and tumble down to this barren lake, Ouma always became homesick and melancholy. She would mope around the foothills for weeks, shunning the Mono village while she prayed to be delivered back to Ahwahnee.

The old woman sighed mournfully. "Anina."

"Yes?"

"I am going home."

Ouma announced this every spring so that Anina was not surprised or concerned. "Of course, Mother."

"I am!"

Anina smoothed her buckskin dress. She would have to make very strong medicine to calm Ouma's troubled spirits. But the pilgrimage that Ouma had in mind was out of the question. Because of her fragile health, Ouma would not last a week in the mountains. Anina began to run a mental inventory of her medicines that would calm Ouma. Like all The People, Anina delighted in spring and the end to the bitterly cold winters, but it was distressing for Ouma.

"You *must* speak again with Mamota," the old medicine woman was saying. "You must tell him that, just because he married a Mono woman and has been accepted as a chief among these people, he is still Ahwahneeche."

"I will tell him," Anina said, nodding her head dutifully. "But I have told him every spring and it does not matter."

"Then speak to his son, Tenaya."

"Tenaya also has a Mono wife and sons."

Ouma wasn't listening to her daughter. "The black sickness is gone from Ahwahnee. I believe that the spirits call us to go home again."

"I know, Mother."

Anina took Ouma's hand. It was impossible to try to explain to Ouma that, as beautiful as Ahwahnee sounded, *this* was now their home. This was the place where Anina had lived since earliest memory. This was the place where Ouma had brought her when she was less than one month old and had taught her to speak, to think, to make medicine. And although her real mother might indeed be buried in Ahwahnee, *this* was her home.

Anina was content with her lot and reasonably happy. Over the years she had earned not only the respect of her people, but also that of the Mono who considered her medicine stronger than that of their own shaman. Anina had taken great pains to use the best of both Ahwahneeche and Mono prayers and medicines so that no one could dispute her powers.

Ouma's voice shook with frustration. "Anina, I will *not* die in this hated place!"

"Yes, Mother."

Ouma scowled at the dead lake. "Anina, you should not like it either. The wind blows too hard and carries stinging sand. The summer is too hot, the winters too cold. And all we eat here are pine nuts, ka-cha-vee, and pe-aggi!"

Anina could not argue those points, although she thought the pine nuts were every bit as tasty as mountain acorns and that the Mono's fly pupa, ka-cha-vee, were a delicacy. Pe-aggi were cat-erpillars, which the Mono trapped by the thousands when they left the pines to burrow into the ground. When properly dried and seasoned, they also were delicious.

"We eat rabbit, fish, and birds, too," Anina reminded the old medicine woman.

"Only the ones that you catch for me," Ouma groused. "The Mono are too lazy to catch or trap. And anyway, they are not as good as the game in Ahwahnee."

"Nothing has ever been as good as Ahwahnee," Anina said with amusement.

"Anina!" Ouma said, her voice growing desperate. "If Mamota will not take The People back to Ahwahnee, you must talk to his son, Tenaya. Tenaya is young and unafraid." Ouma allowed herself a small smile. "And he *always* listens to you."

"That is not so!" Anina protested.

"He would have married you if you had not been a medicine woman."

"Shhh!"

"Well," Ouma said smugly as she rested her chin on the back of her wrist and stared out at the lake. "It is true."

Anina studied the old woman's leathery face and her cloudy eyes. She thought about how Ouma had saved her life and the lives of her people so many years ago. And now . . . now all she asked was to return to Ahwahnee so that she could die.

Aware that Ouma was waiting for some promise, Anina said, "Tenaya does listen to me and he is brave. But Mother, we all fear the black sickness and the spirits of the evil Po'-loti who live in the water under Cho'-lok."

"I will make strong medicine," Ouma promised, then quickly added, "we will *both* make strong medicine, so that the Po'-loti will be happy to see us again. So happy that they would protect The People from any more sickness or death."

Anina hoped this was true, but serious doubts assailed her, for she had heard many times how most of The People had died of the terrible sickness some twenty summers ago. "But if we took the last of The People and our medicine failed . . . the Ahwahneeche would be no more!"

"We are becoming Mono," Ouma said bitterly. "By the time that you are an old woman like me, they will be no more. We are the last of the true Ahwahneeche."

Ouma had not heard this talk before and it troubled her very much. Yes, she was Ahwahneeche, but she was also Mono by having always lived among these people. And although she did not want to think about it, Anina supposed that she was also part Spanish. Spanish was a name and a blood that meant nothing to her but whose influence was evidenced by her unusual appearance. Anina was uncomfortable being much taller than other Indian women, taller even than most of the men and lighter-skinned. Her features were sharper, too, especially the nose and the shape of her chin.

Anina took no pride in her odd appearance. Had she not been the adopted daughter of Ouma, the most powerful woman among the Ahwahneeche, her physical appearance would have been a cause of severe childhood torment. Even now, Indian men thought her ugly. Her only childhood friend had been Tenaya, whom Ouma called the last chief of the Ahwahneeche.

"Talk to Mamota," Ouma pressed with desperate urgency. "And if he will not listen this time, then speak to Tenaya. Tell him that he would be our chief in Ahwahnee, but he will never be a leader among these stupid and lazy Mono."

"I will talk to Tenaya," Anina promised.

"Now, *please.*"

Ouma's voice carried such desperation that Anina rose to her feet. She scanned the choppy lake with its crusted white pinnacles and two large islands, where thousands of seagulls and other birds came to lay their eggs and which was the source of life for the Mono, even though the lake was salty, impossible to drink. There was no black sickness here, but neither was there a trace of beauty or any chance to do more than grub out a hard day-to-day existence.

Have faith in Ouma, Anina told herself. *Have faith in the one who saved The People before and will do so again. Have faith!*

Taking heart with those thoughts, Anina went to see Mamota and Tenaya, as she had every spring during the last few years, to plead that The People return to Ahwahnee. And although she made up her mind that she would be much more insistent today, in her heart, Anina did not think that the outcome would be any different.

As always, Mamota and his son Tenaya listened very respectfully to Ouma's arguments for returning to Ahwahnee. Anina closed by using her most convincing threat, saying, "My mother says that, if we do not return to Ahwahnee this spring, she will die next winter and The People will cease to exist."

Mamota, old and in failing health, scoffed. "Your mother has great power, but her day is past. Our people are happy here."

Anina's hands clenched, for she knew this was simply not true. There was not, nor would there ever be, any happiness in this place for a true mountain people.

"But Mamota," she managed to say, "how can you—among all our people—not smell the pines and remember the great waterfalls and grassy meadows of Ahwahnee?"

Mamota bristled. "You speak out of place!"

Anina's eyes flashed. "I speak for my mother."

"She is not even your *true* mother."

Anina glanced at Tenaya, openly seeking his support. Tenaya was strong and handsome, like a brother. He was the only one who had ever looked and spoken to Anina as if she were attractive and a friend. The others wanted the power of her medicine when they were ill or dying, yet had never let Anina forget that it had been her mother who had introduced the black sickness to The People. Only Tenaya had never held the black sickness against Anina and had treated her with great respect, perhaps because his father had always held old Ouma in such high regard.

"Tenaya," she said, "I promise both you and your father that the evil spirits of the Po'-loti have been appeased and that they will not make a sickness for The People again."

"Ouma cannot know this for certain," Mamota said, after long reflection. "Even her medicine could save only a few of The People."

Anina could see how this was going to end. As in the past, Mamota would sympathize and then even promise to give the matter some serious consideration. But, in the end, the answer would be the same—the last of the Ahwahneeche would stay, intermarry, and exist until they could not be distinguished from Mono.

Anina suddenly realized that this was no longer acceptable because it really was Ouma's last springtime. Squaring her shoulders and ignoring Tenaya, Anina looked right into Mamota's eyes and told the worrisome old chief, "My mother is unwilling to die in this place. If you will not lead the people to Ahwahnee, then I will take her myself."

Mamota's gaze dropped to his lap. Several moments passed before he said, "Ouma would die in the high mountains before she could reach the valley of the long grass."

"Then at least she would die happy."

Anina came to her feet. She realized she had crossed the line and there could be no more talk. "Chief Mamota, we will leave very soon."

"Father," Tenaya said, breaking his troubled silence, "Ouma once saved The People. We cannot allow her to die in sorrow. I must help Anina return to Ahwahnee."

Mamota blinked with surprise and shook his head as he prepared his words. "But my son, you are needed by your family."

Tenaya rose to his feet and lifted his chin. Never before had he opposed his father, and now he did so with a tremble in his voice. "Father, I must be allowed to see Ahwahnee."

Anina's heart filled to near bursting with gratitude. She and Tenaya had often talked of returning to Ahwahnee, but it had always been just talk. And, when Tenaya had married a Mono woman and sons were born . . . well, Anina had herself given up on their dream. But now, in just these few moments, her whole life was changing. And who could say what awaited them in Ahwahnee? Maybe a new and happy life, but maybe, too, a terrible sickness and the black death.

Anina tried to hide her fear even as she wondered if her medicine would be strong enough in the place her people had always called home but which, for her, was just a storied world that existed only in her mind.

"Father?" Tenaya asked, clearly seeking Mamota's support and approval.

Mamota looked deeply into his son's eyes and Tenaya met his steady, probing gaze without flinching. At last, Mamota's chin dipped, giving his reluctant but vitally important consent.

Anina did not remember what was said next by Mamota. She found herself running as hard as she could through the Mono camp and out to their hut at the edge of the forest, where the old Ahwahneeche shaman sat rocking and singing her ancient prayers.

"Ouma! We are going back to Ahwahnee!"

Tears began to channel down the deepest wrinkles of Ouma's brown cheeks. Anina sat cross-legged beside her mother and hugged her tightly because she was suddenly very afraid. Afraid of the black sickness that might yet await and the dreaded women spirits who lived in the pool of the waterfalls of Cho'-lok. Afraid even of finally seeing Ahwahnee, whose spiritual and physical beauty could not possibly live up to the fabled stories. At least, not in this world.

When the Ahwahnee who had survived the black sickness learned of the expedition, not one of them volunteered to go over the mountains. Some even pleaded with Ouma and Tenaya, claiming that the evil spirits would follow them back to this place and find the last of The People and destroy them. When the Mono Indians heard this, they too became alarmed. And so, Tenaya quietly joined Ouma and Anina to steal away in darkness that very night.

The trail up to Tuolumne was long and arduous, so they took three horses. The Mono did not eat horses but used them to pack venison or trade goods. Ouma was unfamiliar with the animals but rode anyway because of her weakened condition. Anina, however, chose to lead her horse, which was loaded with supplies.

All that first day, there was an air of danger and even, Anina thought, of possible doom. They camped at Tuolumne and rested for two days before they pushed on, Ouma always chanting and singing after making prayers and medicine through most of the starry night. This was high country, still ringed with snow. Ouma alone had been beyond the Tuolumne with its deep, blue lakes alive with trout, where eagles floated on rising currents and bighorn sheep watched them atop soaring pinnacles of stone. Anina delighted to see fields of wind-washed grass and flowers. There were weatherworn and twisted whitebark and bristlecone pines that hugged the earth as if afraid of the sky. Everywhere, immense monuments of granite punched holes in the belly of cloudless sky.

Instead of growing weak, Ouma found new strength and seemed to grow younger with each passing hour, especially when they began to follow a river fed by immense snowfields and ribbons of silvery streams flowing across vast escarpments of rock. Almost always, the water channeled into deep, shadowy canyons or vanished under snow, only to reemerge far below, boiling out of the hard belly of the mountain.

"Can you yet feel the evil spirits of the Po'-loti?" Tenaya asked anxiously one afternoon when the sky opened up and the temperature dropped very suddenly.

"No," Ouma said, shaking her head. "I think it is too cold for them up here."

"But they will see us if we follow this river to Cho'-lok, won't they?" Anina asked.

"We will leave this river and enter the valley a different way. I have thought much about this and it is best."

Neither Tenaya nor Anina was willing to dispute the old woman's strategy in this new and ruggedly beautiful land. Later that day, giant hailstones sent the horses into a frenzy. Thunder cannonaded between the highest peaks and lightning bolts etched across the darkening canvas of sky to strike the tallest mountaintops. The Ahwahneeche scrambled for cover under the overhanging rocks while being scolded by a fat, yellow-bellied marmot who objected to their hasty intrusion.

The Sierra squall passed in less than an hour and when the sun burst resplendently across the bald, snow-glistening peaks, they hurried onward, rivers now churning downslope with fresh vigor, the air still frosty enough to send steamy plumes from the nostrils of their skittish desert horses.

The next afternoon, they entered heavy forest and, at sunset, discovered the great sequoia trees that Ouma had often described to Anina. No words, however, could have prepared her or Tenaya for these passive giants. The trees stood in a grove all by themselves, as if too arrogant to associate with the lesser trees of the mountain forests.

"Their limbs are larger even than the trunks of most trees," Tenaya said with astonishment.

It was true and, late that night, Anina awoke to see Ouma, arms and legs outstretched, hugging one of the sequoias and speaking to it as if it were a much-loved friend. The sight moved Anina to tears and, as she watched the stars wheel around in the galaxies and overheard the old woman's hushed whispers, she was reminded that they *were* going home, to Ahwahnee.

Early in the morning, while Ouma slept at the base of the tree, Anina and Tenaya walked softly among the giants. The forest was alive with the sounds of birds and the deer were plentiful. Moss clung thickly from the sides of the trees and, in the shadowy places, snow melted, forming a thousand little rivulets that ran under a thick carpet of pine needles.

"I never imagined anything could be so beautiful," Tenaya said, climbing up onto one of the fallen sequoias and placing his hands on his hips to gaze upward through the leaves so incredibly high above.

"Neither did I," Anina replied, feeling almost heady with the bouquet of cedar and pine.

"Anina?"

"Yes?"

"Do you feel evil spirits here?"

"No."

"Or sickness?"

"No. I feel . . ."

Anina's brows knit as she tried to find the words to describe how wondrous this forest made her feel. She had never seen anything that even remotely compared to the aura of its quiet majesty. "I feel beautiful," she said finally.

"You *are* beautiful," Tenaya said, looking away with sudden embarrassment. "I have always thought you especially beautiful."

Anina struggled with confusion. "Then why did you not ask me to marry you?"

It was a bold question, but one that Anina had asked herself so very, very many times.

"You are a medicine woman," Tenaya replied. "The People would suffer without your power once Ouma is gone. My father said that if you married, your power would not be so great."

"Your father said that!" Anina was suddenly angry. "Did he also say that your power, as chief, would also be diminished because of a family?"

"I have no power," Tenaya said without rancor, refusing to be drawn into a fight. "Even my father has no power anymore."

Anina considered that for a moment and supposed that it was true. And yet . . . yet she could hardly believe that Mamota had dissuaded his oldest son from marrying her. What had the old chief been thinking? He who had left his first wife's spirit in Ahwahnee and then had taken a second wife at Mono?

"Are you angry with me?"

Anina *was* angry. And despairing. She loved children just as much as Ouma had loved her. And the thought of becoming old like Ouma without a companion was depressing.

"I would have married you and given up my power as a medicine woman," she admitted without shame.

"That is nice to know," Tenaya said quietly. "But if The People are to return to Ahwahnee, they need all of your power. Otherwise, the Po'-loti would kill us even if the black sickness did not."

Anina wasn't afraid of the Po'-loti and when she said so, Tenaya sounded quite worried. "I hope that they did not hear you say that and you should not say it again," he cautioned. "To do so would make them even angrier."

The forest magic was gone. Turning her back on Tenaya, she started to march away but he grabbed her arm.

"Anina," he whispered, "will you stay angry with me?"

Still furious, Anina's chin dipped.

"But why?"

"Because you did not listen to your heart but instead listened to your father."

"He is wise."

"He is old and too afraid to lead his people back over these mountains."

Tenaya considered her words for a moment and then he released her and they both walked in silence back to Ouma.

Two days later, they came to the edge of a great cliff and stared into the valley of Ahwahnee. Ouma smiled with such joy that Anina forgot all about Tenaya's stupidity and lost herself in the view from high above their beloved Ahwahnee. It was a sight such as Anina had never seen before. Soaring mountains, cliffs, and peaks all cradling a great valley through which a river ran, fed by dancing, sun-dappled waterfalls.

For long moments, they gazed at the paradise before them and then Tenaya broke the murmur of the wind when he forgot about Ouma's near-blindness and asked, "Which is mighty Cho'-lok?"

"It is there," Ouma said, pointing without actually seeing.

Tenaya asked, "How do we get down there?"

"There is a way," Ouma said, her voice serene. "And I will show you."

Anina felt as if she had been waiting forever to join with the valley below. She could see that, along the north walls, the sun shone brightly while, along the south, there was shadow. There were beaver in the streams that fed the great river and deer were everywhere. Once, Tenaya pulled up short and motioned for them to ride their horses back into hiding.

Anina quickly saw the reason why. An uzamati, one almost as large as a horse, was ripping apart a tree, though for what purpose Anina could not imagine. Anina was in awe of its massive body corded with muscle and its long, fearsome claws. She could feel her mount quivering with terror, but the bear was so preoccupied with its work that it did not notice them. Tenaya led them in a great circle around the animal, whose energetic grunts and growls had silenced all other life in the forest.

"I have never seen anything so terrible," he confessed after they had traveled a safe distance and could no longer hear the grizzly. "My arrow would only tickle such a beast and bring us death."

"This is true," Ouma said. "In the old days, it took many hunters and arrows to kill an uzamati. And even then, we used dogs to keep the animal at bay while the arrows did their work."

She smiled, now almost toothless. "But Anina, the fur and the skin are rich and warm!"

"I hope not to find that out," Tenaya said, constantly looking back over his shoulder.

Ouma cackled with mirth and led them on down a steep game trail, although it was a mystery both to Anina and Tenaya how she remembered such trails from so long ago. When they finally asked about this, Ouma replied. "Long ago I collected the seeds and medicines up this path. Anina?"

"Yes, Mother?"

"We will come up here often and I will help you gather medicines. But there is no time for this now."

"Will that uzamati still be close about?"

"Yes," Ouma said without hesitation.

"Then perhaps we should look elsewhere, Mother."

The remark brought more cackles from Ouma, so loud that both Tenaya and Anina worried that the grizzly might stop its attack on the tree and come to investigate the sound of their voices.

"The uzamati," Ouma warned, "are everywhere in Ahwahnee."

This was not very comforting news. At Mono, the great bears rarely came down from the mountains. When they did come, the Monos would swarm from their huts and either chase them away with loud noises or try to kill them. Failing both, they fled to the lake and allowed the bears to plunder their precious stores of winter food.

By late that afternoon, they were riding across a deep, grassy valley where deer gazed at them with curiosity rather than fear. There were many golden eagles, too, but not one noisy seagull. Anina found it amusing to watch a pair of coyotes as they leaped and bounced through the tall grass hunting rabbits and ground squirrels.

"Where was . . ." Anina's voice faded into silence as a bear and its cub lumbered out of the forest, then stopped and stared at them. Rearing up on its hind legs and sniffing the air, the mother bear began to grunt and their horses to dance with fear.

"Uzamati!" Tenaya exclaimed, hand reaching to pull an arrow from its quiver.

"No!" Ouma snapped. "It is a *different* kind of bear. It is black without a hump on its back and much smaller. Is this not true?"

"That is true," Tenaya said, relaxing.

"Be still and it will pass," Ouma cautioned, even though she could not even see the mother bear.

Trembling a little from within, Anina stood frozen and, after several minutes of posturing and showing its displeasure at their appearance, the bear drove its cub back into the forest.

"Where is the old village of Koom-i-ne?" Anina asked.

"This way," Ouma replied, leading them across the meadow.

They were moving toward what Anina was certain was Cho'-lok, and she was filled with apprehension when she thought about the evil spirits that swam in its cold, deep pool. Were the evil spirit women called Po'-loti still waiting to destroy the last of the Ahwahneeche? Anina was hoping that, without people to torment for so long, they had left this place. If not, did she and Ouma really have strong enough medicine to stop them from bringing back the sickness?

"There," Ouma said, pointing but not really seeing, "is what's left of Koom-i-ne."

Anina saw the remains of the once huge and prosperous Ah-wahneeche village. There wasn't much left to see. Many long winters had passed and even the great ceremonial house, as well as all the sweat houses, had collapsed.

Ouma dismounted and went straight to her old hut, one of the very few that had not been burned during the time of the black death. The poles supporting her u'-ma-cha had withstood the winters and the bark skin of incense cedar that encircled them was still intact.

"Anina!" she cried, hands pulling the bark away. "Come inside and see what I have for you!"

She sounded as young and excited as a girl. Anina helped her open the u'-ma-cha and then slip inside, where Ouma began to grope around in the dim interior for the old medicine pouches and small baskets filled with precious Ahwahnee herbs.

"Aiiyee!" Ouma cried with alarm. "The Po'-loti, they came here and took all my medicines! Everything, gone!"

As her eyes adjusted to the poor light, Anina could see that this was true. There were just moldy remnants of leather, hulls of seeds and withered grasses, shriveled tops of black roots and shafts of what had once been branches with precious leaves gained by a young Ahwahneeche medicine woman unafraid to venture high into the mountains without fear of the terrible uzamati.

All this Ouma felt with her thick, twisted old fingers before she buried her face in her hands and began to weep.

"It is all right," Anina said, embracing her mother. "We will soon gather them together. They will come back to you, just as our people will come back."

"She's right," Tenaya said, squatting before the hut and wanting also to be a comfort. "The *mice* ate your medicine, not the evil spirits of Cho'-lok."

"They only made it *look* like mice," Ouma said, face streaked with tears. "They could see that I was returning and this is a warning."

"Mother," Anina said gently, "it *was* mice."

But Ouma did not believe them. She kept raking the ground with her fingers, blindly searching for evidence of the Po'-loti but finding nothing but mouse droppings until her fears were finally put to rest.

That night Ouma began to make medicine, but Anina wanted nothing more than to lie beside the pines and gaze upward at the stars while the waterfalls tumbled like glowing thunder in the silvery moonlight. The meadow where she and Tenaya slept was lush with grass and wildflowers. Nothing, not even Ouma's fixation on the wicked Po'-loti, could spoil the magic of this valley that they had heard about since childhood.

"Is Ahwahnee everything that you expected?" Tenaya asked, rolling over onto his side to gaze at Anina.

"And more," she replied. "I never will leave again."

"But you *must* return for The People."

"You return for them as their chief," Anina replied. "Tenaya, I have decided to remain here. Ouma will never go back. Anyway, she would not have the strength."

"But it is foretold by Ouma herself that you will lead The People back here someday. Not me, not my father. *You*, Anina!"

"Tenaya, even Ouma can be wrong."

"But not this time," he insisted. "Don't you see that The People would never follow anyone else back to Ahwahnee? They will come only if you promise them that the black sickness is gone and that you are now ready to lead them home."

Anina started to argue, but Tenaya's worried expression caused her to reconsider. And, after a few moments, she could see that he was right.

"But what of Ouma?" Anina asked. "She is not strong enough to ride back over the mountains again."

"She could stay," Tenaya suggested. "We could leave her much food. She would be happy waiting for us. She could make her medicine and we would return in only a few weeks."

Anina was unwilling to part from Ouma, who had been with her since birth and had never left her side. To be without Ouma, even for a few weeks, was unthinkable. What would she do if anything happened to her mother? And what would happen if the black sickness still lingered in Ahwahnee to steal away that beloved old woman's life?

These thoughts were so terrible that Anina refused to consider them until morning.

"I am going to sleep now," she told Tenaya. "Do not speak to me anymore. If you wanted to tell me what to do, you should have taken me to wife."

"I have already explained why I could not do that."

"Then you had better leave me alone and go to sleep!"

Tenaya jumped up and stomped off to sleep somewhere else in the grass. That was fine with Anina. She wanted to think only of Ouma tonight, not of a handsome but foolish young man.

Anina and Tenaya remained six days in Ahwahnee, collecting food and medicines for Ouma. They left on the seventh after an uzamati slaughtered one of their horses and drove the other two into the forest.

"I fear for you," Anina said, as she prepared to follow Tenaya back over the mountains to bring The People home.

"I am not afraid of anything but the Po'-loti," Ouma told her. "Anyway, I have strong medicine now."

Anina hoped so. Together, they had made much medicine since arriving. And since it was not autumn and the time of the acorn harvest, Anina helped her mother fill her u'-ma-cha with precious herbs whose powers Ouma said were very strong.

Just before parting, Anina was almost overcome with fear. She clung to Ouma and cried, "I am afraid that I might never see you again, Mother!"

"I promise you that we will meet again."

"In this, or the spirit world?"

"I cannot say," Ouma replied, looking very serene. "I can only promise that there will be no more black sickness or death and that the Ahwahneeche will be together again. I see this clearly in visions."

Anina nodded and wiped the tears from her eyes. Ouma looked so happy that it was impossible to feel bad now. And besides, Ouma's visions were always true.

"There is something else," Ouma said, looking now at Tenaya as her expression grew stern. "In my visions, I also see white people gathering outside Ahwahnee like vultures around fallen prey. They must *never* be allowed to enter this place."

The old shaman's voice turned shrill and her failing eyes rolled about wildly. She lifted her hands in supplication and cried, "Hear me well, Tenaya, I say *never!*"

"I understand," Tenaya said, looking shaken. "When the black sickness came before, it . . ."

Tenaya caught himself in time, but Anina understood what he had been about to say and there was no point in making Tenaya feel even worse by correcting him that no white had ever been in Ahwahnee, only a half-white, that being herself.

"I am sorry," Tenaya whispered. "Anina, you have always been one of The People. As much as myself or anyone. And you will be our next medicine woman because your powers are great, like those of Ouma."

"And you will be a wise chief."

Anina turned from Tenaya, kissed her mother's cheeks, and then shouldered her own pack. Ouma had insisted that she take some of the new medicines with her in case they were needed to help The People return.

Then, not wanting to make this farewell any more painful, Anina struck out across the meadows toward the high eastern cliffs. She left so suddenly that Tenaya was caught by surprise and had to run to catch her.

"Why did you not say a better goodbye to your mother?" he asked after they had reached the steep trail that would carry them out of Ahwahnee to the high Tuolumne.

"Because," Anina said, attacking the trail and saying no more.

"Because why!" Tenaya called after her.

Anina did not look back. All she wanted to do was to climb over these mountains, gather The People, and return to her mother as quickly as possible. She would drive herself and Tenaya relentlessly. And if The People were too fearful to come back to Ahwahnee, then she would leave them behind and Ouma's prophecies would have no more meaning than smoke rising into the sky.

"Anina!"

She whirled to glare down at him. "Tenaya, sometimes you just talk too much!"

"As a chief, I am *supposed* to talk more than others."

"Hummphh!" Anina snorted before she turned around and attacked the slope.

* * *

All that night, Ouma prayed and made medicine, bargaining with the evil spirit women of Cho'-lok. In the early morning, she heard their singing and watched them floating in the mist of that great waterfall. The Po'-loti danced for her, weaving a spell and casting a rainbow that fed into the center of their deep whirlpool.

Ouma understood now. She prepared herself for a great ceremony in acceptance of their invitation. Wearing her abalone shell comb in her silver hair and dressed in her finest buckskins, she marched proudly to the edge of their pool.

"I accept your invitation to become your medicine woman for all time."

The rainbow shimmered, the falling water danced with the wind, all telling Ouma that the Po'-loti were very pleased. Smiling, she entered their water and allowed the whirlpool to spin her gently down to live with them forever.

Five

Sierra Nevada Summit, November 1833

The young Kentuckian named Ezekial Grant sat perched on an icy rock, gazing into the slanting snow and thinking about food. He was six feet tall, slender, and athletic with wet, shoulder-length brown hair plastered around a long, narrow face dominated by an aquiline nose. His friends teasingly said that Ezekial's prominent nose cut the wind, which allowed him to be the fastest foot-racer in Joseph Walker's exploration party.

Ezekial, however, knew that a man's nose had nothing to do with anything but his smelling of such things as fried chicken and his mother's apple pies. He could not stop thinking about his mother's chicken floating in thick gravy. Also of succulent buffalo steaks, juice sizzling over hot coals. Of pork roasts, mutton, and venison smothered in wild mushrooms, onions, and garlic.

Ezekial shook his head. Dear God, there should at least be venison up in these freezing mountains!

But dammit, there just wasn't.

Ezekial tried to ignore his growling belly and the shivering cold that penetrated through buckskins and a buffalo robe to turn the very marrow of his bones to ice. He had begun to doubt that Joseph Reddeford Walker's stranded party was ever going to escape these terrible Sierra Nevada Mountains. And he wondered how many more of their starving horses would have to be slaughtered in order to keep them alive because, dear Lord, they were getting down to a precious few.

"Zeke!"

Ezekial twisted around to see Hugh Barrett tromping through the driving snow. "Yeah?"

"They're butcherin' another horse. Better get over there else you'll not get your share."

Ezekial thought about climbing to his feet and marching through the snow to the campfire to chew some of the tough, stringy horse meat. He even rocked forward a little, as if to stand, but his heart wasn't in the effort and so he just gave it up and kept staring into the falling snow.

Hugh came to stand beside him. "Zeke, if you don't eat, you'll die."

"I been eating, but just now I'm not quite hungry enough to eat horse again."

"It's all we've got."

"I'll eat later." Ezekial looked up. "Hugh, I been thinking about this fix we're in and it seems to me that there ought to be *some* damned way that we could get down off'a these cliffs that are keepin' us outa California."

"We been lookin' both north and south. You been lookin' as hard as any of us, Zeke." Hugh slapped snow from his beard. He was a short man, but powerful, and the best shot in the outfit.

"Yeah," Ezekial said, "I've been lookin'. But we've seen a few game trails goin' down the sides. Might be they're even Indian trails. Might be that we could get down 'em."

"But not a one was wide nor flat enough for our horses."

Ezekial had a ready reply. "Ain't goin' to be no horses left to save if we don't get down ourselves. We'll have et 'em all."

Hugh squatted on his heels and pulled his own buffalo robe up tight around his whiskery cheeks. "I thought I seen some hard winters in Missouri but this one sure does take the prize. Mr. Walker, he's got to drive our horses over these cliffs. After we get down, we can eat their carcasses."

The idea of their horses plunging to their deaths at the base of the cliffs sat poorly with Ezekial. And, if the game trails petered out and the Walker party couldn't descend to the dead horses, then where would they be? Up here, stuck on the mountaintops as they'd been for the last two weeks without even stringy horse meat to keep them alive.

"Drivin' the horses off the cliffs could be a big mistake," Ezekial allowed. "Hugh, it could get us starved to death since there's so little game up this high in bad weather."

"Sure, but we keep searchin' for a way to get down from the mountains but we're comin' up empty. None of us ever seen such cruel country."

"It ain't the country," Ezekial explained, "it's just the weather."

"We shouldn't ever have come." Hugh rubbed his hands briskly together. "This whole thing has been ill-fated from the very beginnin'."

Ezekial couldn't argue the point. Under the overall command of Captain Benjamin Luis Eulalie de Bonneville, a graduate of West Point, Walker had been dispatched from Utah Territory to scout the Sierras and to trap beaver all the way into Spanish California. The party's mission had seemed especially promising since most of the land that they were crossing was unmapped and its beaver sure to be a virgin harvest. So they had followed the Humboldt River across the Great Basin of Nevada to its terminus and then forged ahead until they had bumped smack into the eastern slopes of the Sierra Nevadas.

Finding the mountains ablaze with autumn colors, none among Joe Walker's party had even remotely considered that they might become trapped by an early winter storm. But it had happened and now, at an elevation of over nine thousand feet, things were desperate indeed for Walker's rugged party of fifty-eight veteran Indian fighters and fur trappers.

For what seemed forever, they had been struggling to extract themselves from this labyrinth of dizzying cliffs, towering peaks, and endless box canyons. Oh sure, they'd come upon some Indian trails, but they were so directly up and down the mountains as to be impassable for a horse. And without horses, how would they ever hope to return across the Great Basin in order to rendezvous with Bonneville in Utah's Bear River Valley?

"I was thinking," Hugh said, darting his tongue in and out to melt snowflakes, "that we could go back."

"To Utah?"

"Yep."

Ezekial considered the searing desert they had crossed and its bad water and their skirmish with the hostile Paiute Indians. "I don't think so."

"Well, why not? I'd rather die fighting Paiute than freeze to death up here."

"We'll find a way down," Ezekial said hollowly. "Mr. Walker, he ain't going to allow us to die."

Hugh wiped his running nose with the back of his sleeve, then said, "Walker is a good man, I'll grant that. He's brave and smart. But, Zeke, he ain't God nor Jesus—he's human and all humans make mistakes. Even my dear mother, rest her soul. And this time, Joe Walker has made a big, big mistake."

Ezekial considered the words, but he was so tired and hungry that he had difficulty fixing on any one thing for more than a few moments. Ezekial knew that he should climb to his feet and go back to camp, but a melancholy was upon him and he needed to be alone.

"Hugh, cut me a piece of horse meat and roast it along with your own. You do that and I'll do the same for you next time."

Hugh sniffled, wiped his nose again, then held his gloved hands up before his face and made sure that he could still wiggle his fingers. The wind stiffened and plucked loose snow from the ground, hard little ice pellets that mixed with the softer flakes that never stopped falling.

Hugh climbed heavily to his feet and stared at his friend. "You could freeze out here by yourself, Zeke. You ain't more than twenty yards from camp, but you could just as easy freeze. Come on and sit by the fire and chew."

"I'll be along directly. I promise."

"Is it the notion of forcing the last of our horses over a cliff that's stuck in your craw?"

"Yep," Ezekial admitted. "I remember what they looked like back when we outfitted the party in Missouri."

"They was once all fine animals," Hugh agreed. "Ain't much to look at now, though. Never saw horses so thin. Never saw men like us so thin neither."

"We'll survive this," Ezekial said. "But I don't think any of our poor horses will ever again be sound, even if they do survive."

"We've got to worry about *ourselves,* Zeke. Not the horses."

"I know. And this storm has to blow over sooner or later."

"Yeah, but it might not stop snowin' 'til summer."

Ezekial had also considered that possibility. These weren't like any mountains he'd ever fought with before. "Say, do you recollect that last big canyon we saw? The one with the Indian trail leadin' down to it?"

"Everyone but you agreed it warn't nothin' but a deer track," Hugh grunted.

"I still think it was an *Indian* trail. But no matter. I was sitting here remembering how pretty that great big canyon it led down into appeared when the storm broke for a couple of hours. Hugh, can you remember how the sun burned that river to pure gold and that big rainbow nailed the clouds to the rocks just below our feet?"

Hugh cracked a smile. "I remember seeing a half-dome rock that looked like a fist punchin' out of the earth. And them frozen waterfalls hanging over the canyon. Hell, it was more the size of a valley than a canyon."

"Hugh, I am dead sure that there are Indians livin' down there."

"Nobody saw no Indians."

"The Indians were there," Ezekial persisted. "I could *feel* them."

Hugh scowled. "All I could feel was the cold. But even if there were Indians, they mighta been even feistier than the Paiutes. Might be they would have wanted to kill us. And with us havin' ate most of our horses and bein' so weak, we'd have put up a damn poor fight."

"But if they were friendly, they would have helped."

Hugh cocked his shaggy head and then he shook it back and forth. "I think maybe you're so hungry that your belly is nibblin' away at your mind."

Ezekial cracked a smile that caused his badly chapped lips to split and bleed.

"I better get back or that horse will already be eaten," Hugh said, glancing over his shoulder.

"I'll be along."

"Best you do directly," Hugh cautioned, "before we start the usual fightin' and clawin' over the bones. Walker's Louisiana Creoles and them half-breed scouts are hungrier than winter-starved wolves."

"I'll be along," Ezekial repeated.

When Hugh was gone again, Ezekial rose to walk over to the edge of a high cliff whose base he could not see and whose width he could only imagine. This was yet another lost and unmapped canyon softly filling with snow. How could they ever get out of these high mountains? And what if his hunch was right about that one beautiful canyon filled with meadows and rainbows?

"I'm going back," Ezekial said to the wind, which spun his words into the blowing whiteness. "I'm going back tomorrow."

The next morning Ezekial went to speak to their leader. At thirty-four, Joseph Walker was ten years older than Ezekial but they were good friends. Walker had personally selected Ezekial for his California party, but now, when Ezekial asked permission to reexplore that one great valley, Walker shook his head.

"Sorry, Zeke, but there wasn't any way down that mountain-side."

"There was that one trail."

"Too narrow and steep for horses. Besides, we couldn't trace it very far down. Probably another dangerous dead end."

Ezekial was not a man to argue, but lives were at stake and it was time to gamble. "But . . . but maybe it widened just after it disappeared from our sight, Mr. Walker. You remember how it cut off to the right after it ducked under that one big overhanging boulder."

"What I remember is how that trail was sheathed with ice where a stream froze across it," Walker said. "And how that clear ice dropped sharply away so that a man or even a damned goat would fall to his death. That's what I remember."

"But what if I circled above that patch of clear ice?" Ezekial asked. "It seems to me that . . ."

Joe Walker shook his head. "We'll keep moving north until we find a safe way down, Zeke. The trail you're talking about was just no good."

"But there were *Indians* down there," Ezekial persisted. "And, if we could even have gotten halfway down, maybe they'd have helped us."

"Forget the canyons. We'll keep moving north," Walker ordered, his voice edged with dismissal. "And I'll expect you, being one of the men I most count on, to follow my wishes."

Ezekial tried to hide his disappointment and even rebellion. After all, if he tumbled to his death, at least he was trying to find a way down. "Yes sir."

Walker placed his gloved hand on Ezekial's shoulder. He had piercing black eyes that could sometimes read a contrary mind. "Ezekial, the way out of this wilderness is *north,* not south. Now, I'd like you to gather more firewood and then branches for the horses to feed upon. Bark is the only thing that seems to be keeping them alive."

"Yes sir."

After Ezekial gathered wood and branches, he made a decision to duck out of camp and go back to explore that trail leading down into the Indian valley. If all went well, he might even save the last of their horses.

"What the hell are you up to?" Hugh asked, catching him as he started to slip away.

"Hugh, I'm going to lower myself down across that ice," he confided. "That's why I'm taking all this rope."

"Damnation," Hugh growled. "That's disobeying Mr. Walker's orders!"

"I'll be forgiven after I figure a way off these mountains."

Hugh glanced over his shoulder at the rest of the party huddled around their smoky fires. Through the blowing snow and wind, only their silhouettes could be seen as they tried to roast meat and keep halfway warm. He turned back to Ezekial. "You're going to need some help."

"Maybe not."

"Zeke, do you reckon we could do this and be back in time to eat tonight's horse?"

"Yep."

Hugh dipped his chin and stared at the ground, considered things for a moment, then said, "And there'd really be no good reason for Mr. Walker to even know we crossed his orders?"

"No reason at all."

"Let's go," Hugh said. "I sure as hell don't want to get caught stumbling around out here after dark."

Ezekial slapped his friend on the shoulder. "We're going to be heroes," he pledged. "We're going to find a way down to an Indian village where they'll feed us all the venison and beavertail we can eat."

"You always was a dreamer," Hugh said, pulling a big coil of rope off Ezekial's shoulder so that he could better handle his flintlock rifle. "You always see a pot of gold under every rainbow."

"And you always see fresh cow plop," Ezekial replied.

It took them four hard hours of tracking through the falling snow to reach the steep, dogleg trail that snaked over the face of the mountain. The wind had picked up even harder and snow was swooping up the mountainside, cutting hard into their numb and ice-crusted faces. "You're a crazy man to go down there," Hugh shouted.

"Won't take but fifteen minutes to get past that clear ice and see what's on the other side of that boulder," Ezekial said, tying one end of the rope around his waist and the other around the base of a stout pine tree that was about twenty feet back from the cliff. "I promise that this won't take any time at all."

"What am I supposed to do up here at my end?"

"Pray."

Hugh wiped his running nose. "What am I *really* supposed to do, dammit?"

"Take hold of the rope and ease me down across that ice. Once I get a good look around that corner, I'll be able to decide what happens next."

"Just don't go beyond the rope," Hugh warned.

"All right," Ezekial promised. "I've no more wish to die than anyone else, even if I can't stand the thought of eating more horse meat."

The mountainside ran for about fifty yards before being obliterated by the storm and Ezekial remembered that a long chute of snow interspersed by boulders ran for several thousand feet down to a talus of rocks. The trail crisscrossed back and forth across the chute all the way to the bottom. The worst section of trail was at the top because it was narrow and the footing looked extremely treacherous. Fortunately, there were some thick manzanita bushes that a man could grab hold of as a last resort. Ezekial knew that the tricky part was going to be that patch of clear ice.

"Hugh, are you ready?" Ezekial asked.

"Hell yes! Just go easy. I recollect that it was a long, long way down."

"I could maybe sled to the bottom."

"You'd be torn apart by the trees and rocks if you weren't buried in an avalanche," Hugh said grimly. "Mark my words, if you get across that ice and around that boulder, you'll be at the end of the line and the trail had better be a whole lot easier than this first part."

"It will be," Ezekial said, trying to sound confident. "I remember, when the sun broke through the clouds, that the bottom half looked easy."

"For a mountain goat . . . maybe."

Ezekial wasted no more time with small talk. It was already midafternoon and the storm was intensifying. So he flashed Hugh a grin and stepped over the edge, cutting hard into the snow with the upper edges of his boots. He could feel Hugh playing the rope out and was damned glad that he hadn't tried to do this alone.

"Keep it comin'," Ezekial shouted as the wind tore his words away and the flying snow made him half-blind.

Ezekial was scared, but determined. He was in a hurry, but did not hurry. Instead, he just kept his head down and his feet close to the ground. The footing was treacherous, with a solid base underneath a thin crust of snow. When he finally reached the patch of ice, Ezekial pressed his upper body to the mountainside and, using his knife like an ice pick, he inched along until he managed to traverse the spot.

"Keep the rope coming!" he shouted, feeling resistance. "Keep playing it out!"

The immense boulder that blocked the next section of trail from view looked to be precariously balanced and ready to crush anyone crazy enough to cross under its shadow. Ezekial ducked his head and plunged forward, breath catching in his throat until he passed back out into the storm.

He had to raise his head to shield his eyes from the blowing snow. Through frozen eyelashes, he could see another ice patch just ahead, and then the mountain seemed to flatten a little and the trail grow wider. Maybe, he thought, if Walker's men could chop the ice away and widen the trail to this point, a way could be found to get past the overhanging boulder and then over this next small patch of ice. After that, it looked like a very promising route down into the valley. At least, what he could see appeared to be a passably safe trail.

Ezekial took another step forward but came to the end of his rope. He gave the rope several sharp tugs but when that didn't bring a response, he cupped his hands to his mouth and shouted, "More line!"

But the rope did not slacken. "Hugh, more line!"

Still no response and a sudden gust of wind almost spun Ezekial off the trail into the long, shadowy snow chute.

Ezekial took several deep breaths and stared hard into the storm. He was quite sure that he had found an escape from the mountains. Of course, it would have to be improved in order to have any chance of saving the horses, but once this storm passed and visibility was restored, it wouldn't be all that difficult. There were men and ropes enough to navigate this escape route. But something compelled him to go a little farther and so he gave another couple of sharp yanks on the rope.

"Ahhh!"

The terrified scream was a spike driving into Ezekial's heart. He had just time enough to turn before he saw his friend hurtling downward, arms windmilling, face an icy mask of horror. Ezekial started to yell for Hugh to grab the rope but saw that it was already in his friend's hand. An instant later, he realized that Hugh must have untied the rope up above in order to give him a little more line.

Ezekial dug in his heels, leaned back and tried to break his friend's fall. He might as well have tried to stop a train on its tracks. When Hugh flew past and then began to somersault through the snow, his falling weight jerked Ezekial skyward and he began to tumble downslope faster and faster.

A roar filled his ears and darkness dropped over Ezekial like the heavy black lid of a Dutch oven. An instant before losing consciousness, Ezekial felt a bone in his right leg snap. The next thing Ezekial knew, he was fighting to throw off a great weight that crushed his lungs, filled his mouth, and brought him to the brink of insanity. Somehow, he burst through the heavy snow and began to gulp huge drafts of air. Tears froze on his cheeks, and the fire died in his lungs as he wiped vision into his eyes with the back of his sleeve.

"Oh, God," he choked, "thank you!"

He was buried in snow up to his chin and his right leg refused to work properly. It took a longer time still for Ezekial to dig himself out of the avalanche and roll onto his back, face turned up to the blowing snow.

"Hugh?" he called, sitting up. "Hugh!"

His voice was batted around by the wind. The trees sighed, branches bent, aching under snow.

The rope was buried, but he found it just under the surface and tore it free. Crawling and shouting, Ezekial followed, pulling himself hand over hand until the rope vanished into the depths of the snow. He began to dig.

"Hugh!"

Hugh was buried in the fetal position, curled up tight, with the rope wrapped around and around his neck and his thick, muscular body. His face was blue, his ice-crusted eyes open and staring.

"Jesus, Hugh, I'm sorry!"

Ezekial collapsed beside the deep grave of his friend and sobbed until the canyon shadows crept over them both, causing the temperature to plummet.

There was such an awful silence coming upon him that Ezekial could scarcely bear to think about survival. In a feeble and vain effort, he cupped his hands to his mouth and called up toward the mountain men whom he would never again see or hear. All the while, flakes of wet snow silently covered the rough ridges of the avalanche, the bits of rock, torn trees, uprooted manzanita, all obliterated from view.

It was then, while staring up at the high, frozen cliffs that Ezekial realized that he would never be found. He buried his face in his hands but discovered he could not weep. So he slapped the snow off his clothes and began to think about living.

Six

Ezekial knew that he had to leave the exposed avalanche field and find shelter or he would soon be just as dead as poor Hugh Barrett, whose bloodless face now stared up at him from a shallow snow bowl. Ezekial took a small measure of comfort because there wasn't a hint of accusation in Hugh's expression. He even looked content, with his face powdered by the falling snow.

Hugh seemed to have suffocated upright and could not be pulled free. Ezekial could do no more than cover his friend's head, dragging a few small rocks over to protect it from scavengers. Wanting to do more, Ezekial cut a strip of buckskin from his shirt and used it to fasten two sticks into a cross.

"Hugh, if I make it back to the boys, we'll see you get a proper burial," Ezekial pledged, jamming the cross into the fresh snow.

During Ezekial's long tumble, the force of the avalanche had torn his buffalo robe away and buried it somewhere. Wearing only wet buckskins, Ezekial began to shiver violently, and he knew that finding shelter was his first order of survival. So he eased down the field of snow until he found a slanting crevasse that dropped about eight feet into a talus of huge rocks. There was enough light filtering into the crevasse to reveal large underground caverns, many of which were cluttered with broken trees and branches, probably the victims of earlier avalanches.

Ezekial took a deep breath and decided he had no choice but to slide down among the rocks. Entering headfirst so as not to risk further injury to his broken leg, he eased downward until he was out of the storm and the killing wind. To his great relief, Ezekial had not lost his powder horn, flint, steel, and tinder. He was grateful to find dozens of mouse, rat, and ground squirrel nests packed in under the rocks. He sprinkled black powder on a pile of dry sticks and leaves, struck his flint, and ignited a small blaze. The smoke drifted upward and his ceiling of snow began to melt, causing the fire to sizzle. Ezekial scooped his precious fire up with his wet sleeves and placed it on a dry rock. With so much deadfall around, he was able to make himself a nice, comfortable bed, up above the ice-cave floor where he could stay dry. He did a poor job of splinting his broken leg with a pair of straight branches.

Ezekial fed the fire and rubbed his hands together, trying to generate warmth as he considered his desperate circumstances. There were sure to be Indians in this valley and, with a broken leg, he would need their help to survive. If the Indians were unfriendly, Ezekial guessed he was a goner. He was not afraid of dying, but he did have regrets about the things he had planned to see and do in his lifetime. He had always wanted to sail to the

Orient, although he had never before been on the sea, and to the Sandwich Islands, where it was said that the sun never ceased to shine and the women were exotic, beautiful, and partial to tall American men.

His disappearance would not cause any great sadness back in Kentucky. He did have a mother, Beatrice, and an older and bossy brother named Edmond living in Lexington. Beatrice had always doted on Edmond and Ezekial knew that he would not be missed much by either.

There had been a fiery Mexican girl he'd met in a Santa Fe cantina and fallen for, hard. Her name was Magdelena Contreras and she had melted his heart with her smile. She had taught him the rudiments of Spanish during a tempestuous summer and fall courtship. It had taken Ezekial months to realize that Magdelena would never be completely faithful to one man. But when he thought about her sweet lips and . . . stop it, Ezekial thought angrily. Why torment yourself?

Ezekial vowed not to think of Magdelena but instead to pray for deliverance. He inched closer to his fire, comforted by the thought that he would never run out of wood and that, maybe, if the storm continued unabated for several days, he might even be able to fashion snares and trap varmints. He could hear things scurrying about the tangle of rocks and debris but the idea of eating mice, squirrels, or rats made his stomach flop.

Throughout that long first night, Ezekial sang and prayed and fed his fire, dozing in fits and starts as icy water dripped on his face. In the morning, he awoke to discover his fire almost dead and he hastily built it up again. When he was finally able to get warm, Ezekial crawled back up the crevasse to see if the storm had blown itself out. He was disappointed to discover that a cold fog now gripped the mountain valley, reducing the visibility to only a few hundred feet. The wind had subsided but snow was still falling and the avalanche field encircled him, as white and frothy as fresh milk.

Ezekial retreated back into his burrow, mood dark, splinted leg throbbing with pain. He rebuilt the fire and stared morosely into its flames, listening to the chittering of little varmints. They were probably delighted at the meal he would make if the weather did not clear and he was not found either by Joseph Walker or friendly Indians.

How long can I survive down here, Ezekial wondered.

He was already thin and weak. Surely the storm would soon pass, so that his smoke could be seen by the expedition members. Perhaps one of their sharp-eyed party would even notice the little cross marking Hugh's icy grave.

Ezekial had hooks and fishing line in his pockets and he set to work fashioning snares. He was certain that the heat, light, and dense underground smoke would activate varmints. Although he had not used snares since he was a boy in Kentucky, Ezekial saw no reason why he could not be as successful catching varmints as he'd once been catching rabbits. With this in mind, he used a precious six feet of his fishing line and made two snares.

Satisfied that he had fashioned his snares correctly, Ezekial scooted over into an area of rocks where he'd heard the most activity and set his traps, then retreated to the warmth of the fire. Had it not been for the damned melting snow that kept dripping on him, he would have been content just to sit, wait, and listen to the icy blasts of wind.

Ezekial must have dozed off again because he awoke to hear the frantic screech of a ground squirrel. He quickly dispatched the little fellow with a stick, reset his trap, then skinned and roasted the critter. It was delicious and Ezekial left nothing except the head, feet, tail, and skin. By the end of that day, he had devoured a total of four ground squirrels and a pack rat. Even so, he remained famished and spent the night setting and resetting snares but caught only two more squirrels. He picked their carcasses clean.

The next morning he went up to test the weather, but the storm persisted, so he slithered back down into his icy cavern. His traps were empty and so was his belly. He could not seem to satisfy his hunger and even roasted horse meat now sounded delicious. To raise his low spirits, Ezekial sang hymns remembered from his childhood and thought about "judgment day."

"Lord," he droned into the fire, "I ain't been too bad but I don't have to tell you that I sure ain't been too damned good, either."

Maybe the Lord appreciated his honesty because Ezekial soon began catching ground squirrels again, so many that he started roasting and saving them for the journey he knew he must take in order to find help. The squirrels weren't much for meat, but he had half a dozen roasted and pocketed the next morning when he glanced up from his bed and saw the sky lit up with the crimson promise of a bright sunrise.

"Oh thank you, Jesus!" he breathed, raising his hands toward the strengthening sunlight. "Thank you for clear weather!"

Ezekial gobbled a charred squirrel and prepared to be delivered, hopefully by Joe Walker and the party but, if not, by friendly Indians.

Exiting the slippery crevasse was not easy and, when he finally managed to reach the surface, Ezekial realized that so much new snow had fallen that Hugh's burial site had been covered. This really upset him and he spent half an hour thrashing around in the powdery snow attempting to locate the grave, but without success.

"Hugh, we'll get you planted proper in the spring," he said, shielding his eyes from the sun's glare. "Either the boys and I will do it on our way back over these mountains, or . . . or I'll do it myself when my broke leg heals."

Ezekial rolled over onto his back and, for the first time, really studied the valley. That's when he saw smoke rising through the trees from what he knew had to be a nearby Indian village. For several long minutes, Ezekial considered his extreme vulnerability. He kept looking up the steep mountainside toward the high ridge from which he and Hugh had plunged, hoping to see his friends. Ezekial wanted to start shouting, but then he would glance over his shoulder toward the smoky plumes rising out of the nearby Indian village and think that perhaps that would not be the smartest thing to do until he had a chance to investigate. After all, if these people were related to the Paiutes, they might just decide to tie him to a pine tree and roast him like a ground squirrel.

Ezekial knew that he had to do something, only he just was

not sure what. If he still had his rifle and his leg weren't broken, he'd have taken his chances with the Indians. But . . . well, now there was no hope of outfighting, outrunning or outhiding them, so he was pretty much at their mercy.

Ezekial crawled back into his ice cave, reset his traps, and fed his fire. He would think about things another day and then he'd come up with some good plan, or maybe Joe Walker and the boys would see his smoke and save his bacon. Either way, it was worth cogitating on and there were still so many damned ground squirrels under the snow that he could fatten up while he rested.

Anina was out foraging early that morning. The women of Koom-i-ne were cooking; the men were crowded in their sweat houses, purifying their bodies for an afternoon hunt. When Anina first saw the little plume of smoke rising from the snow, she was alone and simply enjoying the warmth of the winter sunshine. The snow sparkled and bluejays were flitting about pretending to object to her presence but sounding quite happy with this new, bright, sunny weather.

Anina dropped the basket of herbs she had been collecting and gaped at the smoke rising from Ezekial's underground fire. She could not imagine where it came from. Anina remembered hot springs from the dry Mono country but had never seen anything like that on this green side of the mountains. What then could this be?

Even as she asked, Anina knew the answer. The smoke was created by spirits, of course! Maybe good ones, but maybe bad. She closed her eyes and began to chant, assuring the spirits that they were welcome in Ahwahnee. She prayed for a long, long time, feet shuffling back and forth in the snow, body swaying under the warming sun. And sometimes, the lifting tendrils of smoke reached toward her as if in friendly greeting. After an hour, Anina decided that she, as shaman of the Ahwahneeche, must walk directly to the smoke and allow it to touch her. In this way the spirits would know that she was unafraid.

But as Anina moved closer, she began to hear a low, rumbling sound and thought that it was the spirits, or even the earth itself, speaking. She listened very hard and was comforted because the sound was not the least bit angry or threatening. Rather, it reminded her of . . . of snoring!

Were the spirits asleep?

Anina crept forward. She took a deep breath and prayed that, if she was about to be devoured by evil spirits, she might at last join Ouma again in the other world. Then, she looked down into the crevasse.

"Aiiiee!" she cried, jumping back and falling down, only to scramble back to her feet.

She had seen a man, or a spirit disguised as a man. He was fast asleep, snoring on a pallet of limbs and branches. He was wet and muddy and his fire was in danger of being extinguished by the steady dripping of water. The man's face was dark and sooty-looking, like the smoke from his fire.

Heart pounding, Anina wanted to run back to the village and yet . . . her curiosity was so overpowering that she again crept forward to peer back into the crevasse. The spirit was extremely dirty and ugly. It wore hair all over its face, filthy buckskins and was covered with soot.

Anina fell back and closed her eyes, mind racing. Was this a spirit, or perhaps . . . perhaps one of the feared Spaniards that Ouma had described from so long ago?

Anina bit her lip. *This is far, far worse than spirits,* she thought. *This could be the black death waiting to destroy The People. Could this really be an evil Spaniard and not a spirit?*

Anina was so upset she fell back, then scrambled through the soft snow until she found a heavy limb, which she dragged back to push into the crevasse. Working furiously, she began to haul other limbs and throw them down to plug up the crevasse and prevent the thing below from escaping.

The evilness's snoring abruptly changed to coughing. Anina heard the evilness begin to shout strange words that had no meaning. She turned to run but tripped and fell. When she scrambled back to her feet, the evilness exploded up through the debris, like a smoking torch. He looked terrible and sounded even worse as he ranted, raved, coughed, and sputtered.

Anina fled. She ran as hard and as fast as her legs would carry her all the way back to her village of Koom-i-ne. She must have looked and sounded almost as wild as the evil spirit because Tenaya and the others became very upset. Grabbing their weapons, they urged Anina to lead them back to the apparition.

"What *is* it!" Tenaya kept asking.

"I don't know."

"Is it an evil spirit?"

"Yes, yes! I think so!"

"You are our shaman! You *must* know."

"Well, I do not!"

When Ezekial saw so many armed and obviously agitated Indians streaming out of the forest, being led by the same wild woman who had tried to bury or suffocate him, he knew that he was in big, big trouble. There being no way to run with his broken leg and no way to scuttle back down in his hole without being asphyxiated, he did the only thing he could and that was to climb to his feet and offer his burned ground squirrels to the onrushing Indians. That, and pray for God's mercy.

"Oh, Lord," he said, throwing his head back and closing his eyes, "make these people friendly. Failing that, let me die quick and easy, like Hugh."

Anina stopped, Tenaya and the other Ahwahneeche right behind.

"What is he doing?" Tenaya asked, arrow nocked to bow.

Anina frowned. She was now pretty sure that the evilness was a man, but one sent by the spirits, for only that could explain how he had arrived from the underworld. And, if he were a man, he was probably a Spaniard. She recalled the Spaniards who had killed her real mother and father and the stories that Mamota had often told about how the last one had chanted his own death prayers. "I think," she said, "that he is singing his death song."

"But he came from the earth and from the fire," Tenaya argued. "How could *he* be a man? I think he must be an earth spirit."

Anina could not be sure. Ouma had never said if spirits prayed. Anina looked up at the blue sky, then all around. She could see nothing to indicate that this man or spirit had come from any place other than middle earth.

"Say something!" Tenaya urged.

"I shall find out if we can kill it," Mo-t-anzi said, drawing back his bowstring.

"No!" Tenaya cried, stepping between Mo-t-anzi and the spirit man. "We must be very careful. If this is a good spirit, it could bring others that would bring an end to The People."

"Yes," Mo-t-anzi said harshly, "but, if it is a bad spirit, it could carry the black death, or worse."

Anina could not imagine anything worse than the black death, not after hearing all of Ouma's horror stories. She was aware that Tenaya and the other people were looking to her to be the final arbiter in this matter.

Summoning all her courage, Anina stepped forward. Her eyes were riveted on this thing that had come out of the ground in the disguise of a man and, when she was less than ten feet away, she stopped.

"What spirit are you?" she asked in a voice that betrayed her fear.

Ezekial studied the tall Indian woman and thought her quite beautiful and also quite brave. He could see that his appearance had caused a great deal of apprehension and that the men of the tribe had arrows nocked to their bows. It did not take much guess-work to realize that what he said or did next might very well determine if he lived, or died.

"Ezekial Grant," he said, slowly raising his hand and forcing a grin.

His grin must have been bad because the woman's eyes widened and she took another backstep. Several of the Indians drew their bowstrings and Ezekial was sure he was about to die. Not knowing what else to do to distract their murderous minds, he squatted on his heels, drew out a varmint, and unplugged his powder horn. Expecting arrows to pincushion his body at any moment, with trembling hands he poured black powder into the carcass of the charred ground squirrel, then struck flint to steel. Mercifully, a spark ignited the squirrel like a torch and Ezekial snatched it up and jammed into his mouth.

It was a dumb, desperate move. The fiery carcass didn't burn his mouth much, but it did taste awful. Far more important, however, was the profound effect his act had on the Indians who fell back in shock and gaping amazement. Crunching little bones and blowing smoke from his lips, Ezekial chewed and then swallowed the whole horrible mess. Wiping his mouth with the back of his sleeve, he grinned and then belched loudly.

Anina could not take her eyes off this man-spirit thing. Shivering with fear, she found an amulet that might protect her and clutched it tightly to her bosom. She had no idea what would happen next. Probably, as with Ouma, the gods would take this spirit away or maybe even plunge it back down into the smoking earth.

Ezekial chewed and waited. The terrified Ahwahneeche waited. Nothing happened. Finally, the man or spirit dropped his hands to his sides and dug into his coat pockets. Anina shrank back, expecting to die, but the intruder began to extract more charred ground squirrels which he held out to Anina and grinned even wider.

"What is it doing!" Tenaya demanded to know.

"Offering us food."

"Fiery squirrels?"

Anina shrugged. How she wished Ouma were here beside her. Ouma would know what to do now.

"So, you're not hungry, are you," Ezekial said, returning the burned and greasy squirrels to his pockets. "Well, I can't say that I'm much for eating any more of 'em myself. So what happens now?"

Anina looked at Tenaya, deciding out loud. "This *is* part man, part spirit."

"What does it want?"

"I think it wants us to eat burned squirrels," Anina said.

Tenaya and the elders began to discuss this and there was much disagreement. Finally, Tenaya's voice rose above that of the other elders. "We *must* not refuse the spirit's offer! We must eat his food!"

The Ahwahneeche lapsed into worried silence when Anina said, "I will eat first."

No one objected.

The charred squirrel she took from his hands did not explode in flames, perhaps because the man-spirit did not sprinkle the black powder upon it. Anina ate squirrel and the intruder grinned broadly.

"Good, good!" he said. "Bueno!"

Anina thought the food was terrible, but she grinned, not wanting to offend this man-spirit. Soon, the others were eating shreds of the squirrel, their hands trembling with fear.

"Good! Bueno!" he kept shouting. "Now, how about some *real* meat!"

Motioning toward their village fires, he reached out and clamped his fist around Anina's forearm. It took all of her strength and composure not to submit when he pulled her close and draped his arm across her shoulders.

"Let's go," he said, looking deep into her frightened eyes.

Anina gulped. The morning air was cold but her body was covered with a film of sweat and she had never been so afraid. The man-spirit seemed to realize this for he smiled and closed his eyes for a moment, face turned up toward the sun.

Was he calling upon his gods?

Anina had no idea. All she knew for certain was that this . . . this thing felt like a man, smelled like a man but could not possibly be *all* man because he came from the middle earth and consumed fire with his food.

He started off toward Koom-i-ne, hopping along on his one leg, leaning heavily on her for support and grunting with what sounded like but could not possibly be pain. Anina recalled that Ouma had once told her spirits could not suffer. But this one did. Anina was almost certain that she could feel pain each time he was forced to put weight upon his splinted leg.

When they finally reached the village with all The People strung out in their wake, the man collapsed outside of Anina's u'-ma-cha. He was very pale and trembling.

Tenaya rushed over to stare. He leaned close and whispered, "Anina, we must do *something!* Remember the black death?"

"Yes, of course."

"Is this of that spirit?"

"I . . . I do not think so."

"You must be sure!"

"Because it feels pain, I think it is only part spirit."

Tenaya considered this. "Will you heal and send it away?"

Anina had been asking herself the same question all the way to the village. Once, dear beloved Ouma had cared for an outsider, Anina's own mother. And look what it had cost The People. But Ouma had also claimed that her kindness and mercy might have spared The People from all dying.

"I will," she heard herself reply.

"I think," Tenaya said, "that he is either spirit, or is all man but possessed by spirits. He is generous."

"Yes, very."

"But, if he is spirit, why is he suffering in the leg?"

Anina shrugged. "I do not know."

"You must sit down with him now and find this out," Tenaya ordered, turning and indicating to his men that they were to put away their weapons.

Anina sat down in the fresh snow across from the man-spirit and waited to see what would happen next. What happened next was that the man-spirit began to shiver and finally crawled into her u'-ma-cha. When Anina peered inside, he was already removing his leg splint, then his wet, filthy buckskins and preparing to slip under her warm rabbit-skin robes.

He looked very, very much like a man now as Anina studied his lean, bruised body, then his broken leg. It was huge and purplish. Anina knew of strong medicine that would reduce the swelling and the pain. Maybe, she thought, if the man-spirit was pleased with her medicine, he would allow her to help him back to the place from which he had come and then he would crawl back into middle earth and never appear in Ahwahnee again.

Seven

Ezekial lay dozing in the meadow listening to the bees gather pollen and feeling the summer sun slowly warm his skin. Nearby, mighty three-tiered Cho'-lok thundered to the valley floor, swollen with spring snow melt. Less than a mile away, Hugh Barrett lay resting in a deep, rocky tomb. Ezekial had gone off by himself and located the body only the week before and he'd dragged it out of the snow and buried it deep under the rocks where he'd first taken sanctuary from the winter storm. He did not want the Ahwahneeche to know that there had been another white man in their valley and realize that the Americans had tumbled from the high cliffs above. Whenever Ezekial gazed up at the place where they'd both fallen, he marveled at his survival.

On warm spring days like this, he found it difficult to imagine that fifty-eight men under Joe Walker had been stranded just a few thousand feet above the valley floor. Already, the killing cold and gnawing hunger he'd felt seemed like an illusion. This valley was too serene, too beautiful, to be so near death. Ezekial thought it a little frightening that a man could suffer so much and forget it so soon. But then, that was probably what kept men from being afraid to risk failure or worse.

Only in the last month had Ezekial stopped believing that Joseph Walker and the mountain men would deliver him from Ahwahnee. He thought it probable that his friends had starved or frozen to death up on the snowy summit. That would be a cruel injustice because they'd already suffered far too much in the Nevada deserts. Yes, with the sun warming his face, the perfume of flowers in his nostrils, and the music of the waterfalls, his winter ordeal seemed like a bad dream. But it *had* happened. Ezekial's right leg ached constantly and was an ever-present reminder. He walked with a slight limp, and if he covered more than ten miles in a day, he went lame.

What he really needed in order to leave Ahwahnee was a horse. And wouldn't it be fine to have back his Kentucky rifle. Damn! If he had either, he would be like a god to these simple people. He could take Tenaya's place in a heartbeat and not one Indian would protest. But why did he even entertain such thoughts? The last thing Ezekial wanted was to become chief of the Ahwahneeche and remain stuck forever in this Garden of Eden.

He closed his eyes and Anina's face floated into his vision. Ezekial could not put her out of his mind. *She* was the reason he had not already limped his way out of this valley to search for the Walker party boys. *She* was the one whose medicine and very presence now held him in Ahwahnee. She had healed him, but imprisoned him. When she smiled at him, his blood ran hot. Ezekial found that he could not stay away from Anina and had even begun to teach her some English and a few words of Spanish. The first being "yo te amo, querida," or "I love you, darling."

Did she love him? He had tricked Anina. She thought that "yo te amo, querida" was just a common Spanish greeting.

Ezekial ran the palm of his hand across his eyes, muttering. "Get her out of your mind. Think about leaving before you turn into a white Indian and want to live in a cedar hut and eat acorn mush forever."

Ezekial sat up and rubbed his bad leg, wondering if it would always ache. And wasn't it strange how things worked out? Here he was, feared and favored by these people in a valley more beautiful even than the Shenandoah and teeming with beaver he could neither trap nor shoot so that all he could do was to think of Anina, poor Joe Walker, and the rest of the mountain boys.

But perhaps they had escaped and eventually found a trail down to the central valley of California. And, if they had, were they successful in trapping beaver and then returning to Utah's Bear River Valley? Ezekial sure hoped so. He and the boys knew that Mexico had finally won its war of independence against Spain and they'd also claimed Alta California and taken over the missions.

But that didn't smooth out anything for the Americans. Joe Walker had warned everyone that the Mexicans were very unfriendly and their governor had actually thrown Jedediah Smith and his trappers in prison but had released them after receiving their promise never to return to California. Nobody gave that warning a second thought. Hell, it just made the prospect of entering a forbidden California that much more enticing. There was even talk of one day overthrowing the Mexicans and running them out just as they'd done to the Spaniards. To Ezekial, it seemed like a pretty good idea.

"Te amo, querida," Anina said, coming to join him.

Ezekial rolled over, grinning. "Te amo, Anina. You look mighty pretty this afternoon. But then, you always look pretty."

Anina did not fully understand his words, but she thought he was telling her that she looked healthy.

She nodded. "Sí."

He laughed, always ready to have fun with her. "You're getting pretty good, pretty bueno with conversation. What would you say if I asked you to marry me?"

Anina frowned. "Marry?"

"Yeah!" He leaned forward and gazed deeply into her eyes. "You could help me leave this valley and then I'd show you some fine country. I'd even take you to see the Pacific Ocean and maybe we'd sail off . . . naw, you wouldn't like the Sandwich Islands, would you."

Anina shrugged.

"I tell you what you *would* like," he said, enjoying himself. "I'd take you to see St. Louis where we'd ride a paddle wheeler all the way down to New Orleans. You'd learn to love that Cajun cookin'. And I'd show you Kentucky and some fine horses. Have you ever seen a horse, Anina?"

"Horse?"

"Sure. In Spanish, it's caballo."

When she said nothing, he said, "By jingo, I'll bet you've never even seen a horse! It'd be something to see your eyes the first time you laid 'em on a horse."

Anina watched him intently. She could pick out some of his words, but not when he grew excited and talked too fast. She had no idea what he was talking about right now, but she loved the music of his voice.

"Anina," he said, chewing on a piece of grass, "be honest with me. Don't you ever get to feeling a little cramped in this valley? I mean, it's gawdawful pretty, but sometimes I sure do feel hemmed in by all these high rock walls."

She shrugged so fetchingly that Ezekial felt a catch in his throat. His hand reached out and he would have stroked her shiny black hair, if she had not scooted out of arm's reach.

Ezekial plucked several golden poppies and offered them to Anina. She blushed and shook her head.

Ezekial had to chuckle. "Flowers, no matter how pretty, would look plumb embarrassed on someone as beautiful as you, An-ina."

When she looked away, he touched her cheek and said, "Have you ever seen a white man like me before?"

"Huh?"

"American," he said, pointing to himself. "Ever see one of us before?"

"No," she said after long deliberation.

"Mexican?"

"No."

"Spaniard?"

Anina jumped up to leave but he leaped up and grabbed her arm. When Ezekial gently turned her around, he could see that she was extremely upset. "You *have* seen Spaniards, haven't you."

Anina began to shake her head back and forth. She pulled hard but he would not let her go.

"Easy!" he pleaded, trying to calm her. "I'm sure no Spaniard. *No* Spaniard!"

She relaxed but he could see that she was still upset. "Is that why you look so different than the others? Because there's a Spaniard in your past?"

When her eyes dropped, he exclaimed, "Of course there was! Anina means 'a girl' in Spanish! You aren't any more full-blood Ahwahneeche than I am."

Anina struggled free. Angry at him for speaking of Spaniards and for grabbing her so roughly, she thought he deserved a good scolding. But it wasn't in her because he had told her she looked healthy and he had released her. When he advanced, however, Anina turned and fled, knowing that he could not overtake her because of his bad leg.

Anina was confused and upset. Why was he tempting her with what she could only describe as a desire to touch and hold him. To join with him. If he was part spirit, that was *wrong!* And surely, if Ouma were present now, she would read her daughter's troubled heart. That done, Ouma would make strong medicine to rid Anina of the yearning that she felt for the man-spirit.

I must go and purify myself, Anina thought. *In the pool under*

*Cho'-lok where the spirits of the Po'-loti lie in wait with Ouma.
I must do this now!*

Ezekial followed Anina across the meadow, knowing that he
had made a grievous error but not exactly sure if it was trying
to kiss her or bringing up her Spanish heritage. One thing for
certain, he deeply regretted the impulsiveness that had caused
her to rush away in distress.

Anina ran toward Cho'-lok and Ezekial lost sight of her in the
trees, but he hurried along as best he could, damning his bad leg.
The pain and stiffness were especially galling since he had once
taken no small amount of pride in his exceptional foot speed.

"Anina!" he called, knowing that his voice could not be heard
over the growing thunder of the waterfalls.

When Ezekial finally limped into view of the water, he was
shocked to see that Anina had waded far into the swirling pool.
In the late summer or fall, it would not have been dangerous, but
it certainly was now.

"Anina!" he cried, lurching forward.

She was oblivious to his presence. He saw her moving fear-
lessly into the thundering torrent, water rising to her chest, then
to her neck. Her black hair was a fan on the boiling water and,
with a cry of warning, Ezekial threw himself off a rock into a
long, flat dive and struck the water hard. Its icy tentacles grabbed
his chest and squeezed so powerfully that Ezekial struggled to
breathe. But he swam hard and when he finally reached Anina,
she was already starting a slow spin toward the deadly whirlpool.
Her expression bore no fear. She was chanting a single word,
"Ouma."

Terror stronger than the grip of the current filled Ezekial and
he grabbed Anina by the hair. She turned to look at him and then
she threw her arms around his neck and hugged him tightly. They
both sank.

Ezekial was a strong swimmer and the water was not yet deep.
His toes struck the slippery floor of the pool and he propelled
himself upward, thrashing and clawing, with Anina clinging to
him. He looked up and saw that they were drifting into the waterfall, which would drive them under its great force. There would
be no hope of survival under that roaring torrent. None at all.

"Swim!" he shouted into the spray and the thunder. "Swim for your life, querida!"

Anina broke from him and began to swim but, for a few terrifying moments, the whirlpool almost sucked them into its vortex. Somehow, they managed to struggle out of the water and drag themselves up on a flat, mossy rock.

"Are you crazy!" he shouted, climbing on top of her. "Do you want to die!"

Her lips moved but he could not hear. All he could hear or feel was the pounding of water and his heart. Her face was inches from his own. Her lips were parted, her brown eyes wide with wonder or fear or . . . or God only knew what.

"I love you!" he cried.

She understood. He was sure she must have understood because she pulled his face down to her own. They shivered and then he lost control and pulled Anina's wet buckskin dress up above her waist. She reached for him when he mounted her beside Cho'-lok. The sound of their passionate lovemaking was lost in the thunder of the cascade. The Ahwahneeche medicine woman's fingernails bit into his bare back and she clung to him tighter than the bark on a tree until he was finished.

"Ouma and the Po'-loti!" she challenged the giant waterfall. "See me joined with this man. Both strong medicine. Please look upon us with favor and now as one!"

He thought she was speaking to him and he rose to study her lovely face. "Anina, I'm taking you out of here with me! I ain't goin' anywhere without you!"

She nodded vigorously, hands and heels stroking his cold flesh. "Te amo, querida!"

"Te amo!" he choked.

Ezekial closed his eyes and shivered again to think of how he had almost lost her in the whirlpool. He did not pretend to understand what had been going through her mind, but he was going to do everything in his power to make sure that she never wanted to drown herself again.

"You're a crazy woman," he bellowed over the force of the water, "but, from now on, you're *my* woman. I ain't never gonna love another, Anina. Never!"

Anina kissed his mouth and then she playfully ran her tongue over his dripping beard. She knew now that his power was strong, stronger even than that of the Po'-loti. Or perhaps . . . perhaps it was Ouma who had saved them both for this moment. Either way, she had tested the spirits and they had decided to give this man-spirit to her in *this* world.

All Anina knew for certain was that she loved this American and hoped to be blessed with his children. Anina knew the first thing that they must do after they had enjoyed each other enough was to visit Chief Tenaya and asked his permission to marry. Tenaya deserved that respect.

That evening, after Tenaya had listened to her request to marry, he led her to stand beside the moon-washed river. The night was soft and beautiful, but Tenaya did not look happy.

"Anina, this is not good," he said when they were alone.

"It *is* good," she argued.

"But maybe he is more spirit than man!"

"No," she said feeling her cheeks warm, "he is mostly man."

Tenaya frowned, clearly uneasy about his doubts. "You . . ."

"I have lain with him," she interrupted. "I believe he will give me children."

"Oh." Tenaya expelled a deep breath and walked off a little. A great horned owl hooted somewhere off in the woods and bats flitted and fed over the silently running Merced River.

Anina followed. "Ezekial is good."

"Tell me," Tenaya asked, turning around suddenly, "does he have special powers given to him in middle earth? Powers that will protect the Ahwahneeche?"

"Yes, I think."

"But he is *not* a Spaniard?"

"No, he is American."

"And he does *not* carry the black death?"

"He is filled only with life," she said. "If The People were to kill him out of fear of the sickness, the spirits would avenge his death and The People would be no more."

Tenaya considered her words for a long while before finally saying, "Then he must become Ahwahneeche. He will become one of The People and his power, with your power, will be so great that nothing evil will ever come into Ahwahnee again."

"I will become wife instead of medicine woman," she offered.

"No," Tenaya said abruptly. "You will become both."

Anina bit back a protest. Always, the shaman or medicine woman had been unmarried. Never a wife or mother. But who would take her place? Anina had never given any thought to this, but that had been a mistake. She would not live forever. Someone would have to learn the old ways of healing. Someone would have to turn her spirit to the otherworld and call upon the Ahwahneeche gods and protectors to ward off sickness, famine, and death.

"Yes," she told her chief, thinking of how her own child might even be her choice as successor.

"But you must think of someone to learn your medicine," he was saying.

Anina smiled, for this was true.

There was no wedding ceremony, not even a congratulatory slap on the back by Tenaya or the men of the tribe. That did not bother Ezekial because The People smiled and politely accepted him as one of their own. Where before they had been watchful, afraid, and suspicious, now they dropped all reserve in his presence. They shared their venison and other game. The women were more than generous with their harvest of food. Ezekial ate as ravenously as a bear and soon lost his gauntness. He especially loved the wild grapes and plums, but his favorite was the berries which the Ahwahneeche women preferred to cook. They boiled the berries into nearly a syrup, which was then mixed with acorn meal and baked in an earthen oven. A fire was kept for two or three days over the oven and the result was sweeter and tastier than hard rock candy. All types of wild game except rattlesnakes and lizards were also roasted in earthen ovens called ulu and sometimes covered with a layer of grape leaves to give them a special flavor. River mussels baked in sand and turtles were considered a special delicacy and roasted in ashes. Ezekial learned that the word for this method of cooking was hupu. Larger animals were skinned and sliced with an obsidian knife and then broiled.

One very warm afternoon, Anina woke Ezekial during his usual nap and led him out to a grassy fork in the Merced where all The People were gathered.

"What's going on?" he asked.

"Wait and see," she said with amusement shining in her dark eyes.

He didn't have long to wait. At a signal, the Indians fanned out and began to march forward, the children singing, the adults looking excited and swinging branches. At first, Ezekial thought they must be trying to flush rabbits or quail but, after a few minutes, he realized that the Ahwahneeche had a very different food source in mind as swarms of insects took flight before The People.

"Grasshoppers!" he exclaimed.

When a big cloud of them exploded directly up into their faces, Anina snatched a handful, crushed them in her fist, then dropped them in a buckskin bag tied to her belt.

"Ko'tco. Grasshoppers, sí!" She laughed.

So they marched along, driving the huge swarms of grasshoppers toward the fork in the river. That was when Ezekial noticed that the Ahwahneeche had dug many trenches near the tip of the ford and that thousands of grasshoppers were now crawling or flying into these deep, narrow holes. However, swarms more began to take wing and fly back toward the marchers.

At another signal, the women lit the grass and then everyone ran into the water. Fortunately, there wasn't much grass to burn and Ezekial saw fire singe the wings off the insects that tried to escape. The smoke was thick but did not last long and soon the fire itself died out. Several hundred other grasshoppers made it to the now-placid river, where the children had a wonderful time drowning and retrieving them. It was a madhouse and Ezekial began to laugh. Up on the shores, men and women were already dashing into the smoke to snatch up the cooked grasshoppers and devour them on the spot.

"Man!" Ezekial exclaimed, "what a party! I never saw anything to match this!"

In no time at all, everyone had filled their buckskin baskets with insects, some wet, some burned, others poisoned by smoke. All together, Ezekial doubted that more than a few dozen had been lucky enough to escape.

That night, one of the women brought them a plate of the roasted insects and, although Ezekial had his reservations, he found them scrumptious. They'd been dusted with salt bought from the Monos and were also pretty crunchy.

"Bueno!" he announced to his beaming bride. "Very good."

"Very good, sí!" she exclaimed, looking so pretty and pleased that he took her into his arms and kissed her salty lips.

They didn't even bother to finish their plate of grasshoppers but made love on Anina's rabbit-skin robe. It was midsummer, too warm to travel, and Ezekial was thinking that he would wait until fall to leave Ahwahnee. Hell, besides being too warm, things were just too nice and cozy to rush off in order to show Anina the rest of America. America could wait until the fall.

Several weeks after the grasshopper hunt, Tenaya and several of the elders came to invite Ezekial to go deer hunting. Anina was delighted and clapped her hands with joy after the chief and his friends left, but Ezekial had his reservations.

"In the first place, darlin' wife, I can't walk all that far without my leg paining me. And in the second place, I'm a damned fine shot with a rifle but I never even touched a bow or arrows."

Anina failed to understand, so early the next morning before he even awakened, she slipped out of their spacious hut and went to the village bow maker and bartered for a strong bow called a kutca made of incense cedar. She also obtained a quiver full of arrows.

Ezekial was touched because the bow, short but powerful and expertly reinforced with many wrappings of sinew, was a masterpiece.

"This must have cost you a great deal," he said, drawing the bow and testing its resistance. "But I'm afraid the best bow in the world won't help my poor aim. You see, I wouldn't know how to shoot this thing well enough to even hit the side of that big rock mountain you people call Tu-tok-a-nu'-la."

Anina knew that the American had never handled a bow for he held it clumsily. But it was not so important to her that Ezekial kill a deer as it was that he participate as a member of the tribe and begin to join the men during hunts.

She decided to demonstrate. Anina had never hunted, but she had watched the men and boys practice and she knew what was required. Taking the bow in her left hand and nocking an arrow, she drew back the bowstring and fired an arrow straight into her hut. Its point dug deep in the cedar bark.

Anina grinned and slapped her hand over her mouth.

"Oh sure," he said, laughing. "I could probably hit our hut, too, if I tried a few times. But that's a lot different than shooting a buck in the woods."

Anina could tell by his voice that he was reluctant to use the bow. But she thrust it out to him anyway. After all, it had cost her much medicine and a fine shell necklace for these weapons and the American would have to learn how to hunt sooner or later.

That evening, Ezekial practiced firing arrows at a big pine tree. Mostly, he missed. But with the help of many volunteers, he began to see how the thing should be done and he did improve a little. The Ahwahneeche certainly seemed pleased with his progress and they made it clear that, poor shot though he might be, they welcomed him on tomorrow's hunt.

"I'll go as far as my game leg will carry me," he promised.

Early the next morning, he was again wakened by Anina and when he sleepily reached for her, she slipped out of his grasp and bounced to her feet. She gave him a playful boot with the point of her toe and motioned for him to look outside.

"Blast," he groaned, seeing Tenaya and several other men waiting impatiently in the semidarkness. "What's the all-fired hurry?"

As it turned out, there really was no hurry. Ezekial, like all hunters of deer, was expected to cleanse himself in the sweat house all morning so that he could better hunt with the other men in the afternoon. Ezekial had watched hunters repeatedly enter and exit the sweat house, choking and gasping for air, dizzy from the heat, and sweating like ice, and he really wanted no part of this protracted and exhausting ritual. He had seen plenty of hunters actually faint as they tried to reach the nearby river, into which they would collapse seeking a speedy revival.

"Now, now," he hedged as Tenaya and the others prodded him toward the low, dome-shaped and earth-covered structure, "can't I just pass on this? I'll be ready when you boys come out. Okay?"

But it was obviously *not* okay.

Everyone stripped and then ducked into the sweat house. Ezekial was trapped. Although there was a smoke hole at the top, it was only about six inches in diameter and not nearly big enough to keep the air clear. It was dark inside and thick with smoke. Before Ezekial could scramble back outside gasping for air, someone gently but very firmly pushed his forehead to the floor and he was able to breathe. And there he remained, for each time he tried to jump up and fly outside, his head was pushed down against the hard-packed earth.

"Dammit!" he cried. "This is a misery!"

But the Ahwahneeche ignored his lament, and, as the daylight grew stronger and shafts of sunlight penetrated the doorway, Ezekial twisted his head enough to see that Tenaya and the others each had little piles of white oak which they kept feeding the fire. It was so hot in the sweat house that it made the summer crossing of the Salt Lake wilderness seem cool.

After a while, it became obvious to Ezekial that the Indians were trying to see which of them could stand the most heat. The whole thing was pretty ridiculous but Ezekial got stubborn and decided he would play their game. Grabbing a few sticks of one hunter's oak, he tossed them into the fire pit and grinned. Unfortunately, he was seized by a coughing fit before he had the satisfaction of enjoying everyone's surprise.

It seemed like forever before the first Indian staggered to his feet and reeled off toward the river. Ezekial was right behind him. Sweat poured from his body and he thought he saw Anina off to the side of the well-used trail between the sweat house and the Merced, but his head was spinning and he could not be sure. When he flopped into the Merced, his entire body steamed like a red-hot horseshoe tossed into a water bucket.

"Lordy!" he wheezed. "Oh, Lordy!"

It wasn't over. They came out and cooled down, then they hauled him laughing and grinning back into their damned sweat house for another hellish session. The next time they tried it though, Ezekial had enough and when he cocked both his fists, the Ahwahneeche backed off and decided maybe it was finally time for the actual hunt. Almost anything except the sweat house would have suited Ezekial better.

That afternoon, they went hunting, and although Anina had already shown Ezekial how the Ahwahneeche often used grapevine nets and even traps to take deer from hiding, he knew that this was to be a real hunt. Unlike when they hunted elk in the foothills, the Ahwahneeche did not wear deer masks or hides to disguise themselves. Today they would either run the deer down by using men in teams of relay until the animal was too exhausted to flee, or they would prepare an ambush.

"What's going on?" Ezekial asked, as the hunters stopped at the edge of a large meadow late that afternoon.

Tenaya held his finger to his lips and indicated that it was better if Ezekial just watched and waited.

Ezekial stretched out on the grass as the Ahwahneeche hunters began to encircle the meadow. They were almost invisible as they slithered through the tall, brown grass on their bellies and Ezekial, who had always been a good hunter, might have paid more attention except that the sweat house ordeal had left him weak and exhausted. In fairness, though, the intense heat seemed to have relieved some of the stiffness and pain in his bad leg. Anina promised him that the sweat house had curative powers and Ezekial guessed that it did, if it didn't suffocate a man outright.

He gazed up at the cliffs, now taking on the first colors of sunset and prayed again that his friends had found a way down from the top before they starved or froze. A few moments later, Ezekial pushed himself up on one elbow and gazed from side to side. He couldn't see a single one of the Ahwahneeche hunters who had led him to this fine meadow a few miles west of their main village. The sun began to lean into Ahwahnee's towering western walls and long, cooling shadows stretched into the meadow. Ezekial turned his thoughts to Anina and he sure hoped she appreciated the sacrifices he had made for her today. He hoped that she would be in a mood for lots of loving tonight.

Ezekial awoke with a start and to a great deal of shouting. He sat up and realized that more than a dozen deer had entered the meadow while he'd slept and that they were now being attacked by the Ahwahneeche. The hunters were rushing forward, closing their ranks in order to prevent escape even as they fired at the panicky deer. Several animals had already fallen, others were up and running this way and that with arrows in their sides, legs and haunches. The hunters were jumping back and forth to block their escape and filling the air with arrows.

Ezekial figured he had better join in, for Anina's sake. The last thing he wanted to do was to have other wives gossiping about how she had chosen a worthless husband. So he grabbed an arrow and ran forward, shouting louder than any of them.

A large buck, eyes rolling in fear, charged and Ezekial stopped, drew back his bow and let fly an arrow. The arrow sailed a good ten feet over the buck's antlers and creased a hunter in the leg. The man howled with pain.

"I'm sorry!"

The nearest buck was out of its mind with fear. Even as Ezekial watched, it was struck by an arrow in the shoulder. The animal staggered, then lowered its antlers and kept running straight for Ezekial. Dropping his useless bow, Ezekial leaped forward and managed to get hold of the wounded beast's antlers. It made a loud, bawling noise and was powerful enough to swing its antlers at Ezekial's legs, knocking him to the grass.

Ezekial grunted as the buck tried to gore and trample him.

They were about of equal weight and size, but Ezekial, with his back to the ground, managed to kick his good leg up and deliver a powerful blow to the buck's testicles. It bawled again and Ezekial twisted it down, then drew his hunting knife and cut its throat. Blood poured over him and the buck died staring right into his eyes.

"I'm sorry, but it was me or you," Ezekial wheezed, pushing the handsome animal aside and then rolling over onto it to catch his breath.

The Ahwahneeche hunters were finishing off the deer that had been unable to break for freedom. When they turned and saw Ezekial covered with blood, they forgot their hunt and ran to his side. Tenaya himself dropped to his knees and began to examine Ezekial, searching for a mortal wound.

Ezekial couldn't help himself. He rolled his eyes and began to make hideous strangling sounds as if he were expiring. He twitched as if gripped by icy fingers of death. Tenaya reared back in shock.

Then suddenly, one of the hunters noticed that the stag's throat had been cut. He began to shout and point, grabbing the animal's antlers and pulling its head back so that all could see the terrible wound. Unable to carry on his charade, Ezekial began to guffaw. A moment later, they were all laughing and whooping, Tenaya as hard as the rest.

The Indians thanked each and every deer for its life, which gave food and strength to The People. Then, Ezekial wiped his hands, arms, and buckskins as clean as possible on the dry meadow grass. He used his big Green River knife to gut his buck and then, just to show he appreciated men with humor, he began to gut the rest of the kill. With his steel blade and plenty of experience, Ezekial was a marvel of efficiency compared to the Ahwahneeche using their stone knives.

He finished off all the animals before sundown and wanted to start back to Koom-i-ne, but the hunters were famished. They scooped out fire pits and emptied the stomachs of the deer and stuffed them with the heart, liver, and kidneys. They roasted the stomachs on coals for several hours and had a great feast under the stars.

There was much laughter and teasing and it was not by acci- dent that the hunters insisted that Ezekial sit beside Tenaya in the place of honor. Over and over, they teased him, twitching and pretending to make gagging sounds after which they would laugh uproariously.

And later under a brilliant canopy of stars, Ezekial joined the Ahwahneeche in songs that he did not understand but were very much in the universal spirit of all hunters. This had, he thought, been one hell of an exciting day.

Eight

Seventeen Years Later, 1850

Ezekial Grant had to admit that he could not recall when he stopped planning to leave Ahwahnee. He had certainly intended to leave that first autumn of 1834 and would have done so if Anina had not suffered a difficult pregnancy that ended with the heartbreak of a stillborn son. It had taken time for them to recover from that tragedy, but Anina soon became pregnant again and they had been blessed with a healthy son they named Kanaka. Their daughter, Lucy, had been born two years later.

Ezekial laced his fingers behind his head and admired the leaves turning color in Ahwahnee. Let's see, he thought, if Kanaka is nearly sixteen, then Lucy is now thirteen and that would mean that this is 1850. What had happened in the outside world since he and Hugh Barrett had tumbled over a snowy mountainside? Had the Texans finally gone to war with Mexico and won their independence? Were the Mexicans still in control of California or had the Spaniards come storming back to regain their missions and vast ranchos? These were interesting questions, but Ezekial could live with his curiosity.

However, there wasn't a week that passed when he didn't wonder if his explorer friend, Joe Walker, was still leading men across the frontier. And was his mother still alive? She'd be pretty damned ancient by now—well into her eighties—and no doubt techy as a teased snake. Edmond was probably worth a fortune today and as insufferable as ever.

Ezekial flicked a big wood ant off his forearm and dug out another that had worked its way into his wild shock of gray beard. Where were the other Ahwahneeche hunters, anyway? They were supposed to be driving that black bear down his way. He'd hear 'em long before seein' 'em, but he still ought to get himself ready to shoot that bear. He sat up, still scratching and thinking.

Naw, I don't miss my family but I do wonder what ever happened to that sweet Magdelena Contreras down in old Santa Fe. Probably got as wide as the beam of a boat and birthed a passel of kids, if she got lucky and married well.

But probably she hadn't. Magdelena had a flirtatious nature and Ezekial figured the odds were that she'd probably died at the hand of a jealous lover or else of the French disease. Damned shame.

Ezekial heard a bear coming.

"Here we go," he said nocking an arrow to his bowstring and climbing stiffly to his feet. A black bear burst from the trees, its head turned around as it searched for the hunting party that had driven it from the forest. The bear didn't see Ezekial until it was within forty yards of him, and then it was too late. Ezekial's first arrow cut cleanly into its body, just behind the shoulder to pierce the lungs. The bear squawled piteously and squatted on its haunches like an old fat man. It was more black than brown and began to nip furiously at the feathered part of the arrow protruding only a few inches from its side.

"I am sorry to kill you but it's going to be a long, hungry winter," Ezekial explained, expertly taking aim and firing a second arrow to put the suffering creature out of its misery.

Ezekial drew his hunting knife and walked cautiously forward, because all bears were intelligent and even known to fake death until a man was upon them and could be grabbed, bitten, and killed. But this bear was dead. He probably weighed about 350 pounds. Be good eating, but lardy.

Kian, maybe the best bowman other than Ezekial, arrived a moment later. He also asked the bear to forgive the Ahwahneeche for taking its life and ended by thanking it for the food it would provide for The People.

Ezekial tested the sharpness of his blade against the edge of his fingernail. Satisfied, he glanced at his friends and said, "Now that I've killed him, I guess you'll also want me to use my old knife and skin this fat rascal."

The Indians grinned hopefully so Ezekial set right to work. He would tan and give this bearskin to Lucy because it was thick and rich and the weather already had turned nippy at night.

Tomorrow, there was to be a council meeting to discuss and plan the upcoming acorn harvest celebration. This important tribal event would include singing, dancing, feasting, and games which Ezekial once had enjoyed but for which he was now too old and stiff. He wouldn't be able to compete in them without causing a great deal of laughter, not to mention the inevitable aches and pains.

But late that afternoon, when Ezekial and his hunting party returned to Koom-i-ne, they discovered that the Ahwahneeche had some very unexpected visitors. Po-to-en-cies. Three of them.

The arrival of their unfriendly neighbors to the west caused a good deal of excitement among The People. Ezekial had never seen Po-to-en-cies before but that was not a bit surprising since his bad leg and Ouma's dire warnings had discouraged all the Ahwahneeche from hunting elk or horses in the hot central valley.

"Something is bad," Anina said to her husband in a low, grim voice as they watched the Po-to-en-cies meet with Tenaya. "Very bad."

"Maybe they just came to trade."

"No," Anina said. "They have nothing of value and they are not young men. They are elders."

Ezekial took her assessment as gospel. Anina knew more about Indians than he ever would, although Ezekial had lived so long among them that he now even phrased his thoughts in their native language. He had no trouble understanding the conversation that began between the Po-to-en-cies and Tenaya after the visitors had been invited to enter the Ahwahneeche's great ceremonial hang-e.

When the visitors had been allowed a proper silence in order to get comfortable with their food and surroundings, Tenaya leaned forward on his robe, directed his eyes downward as was polite, and said with all the warmth he could muster, "Welcome to Ahwahnee."

They wore ragged cloth garments, old torn coats, boots, and floppy hats the likes of which the Ahwahneeche had never seen before. The eldest of the three was thin and nervous, with deep-set eyes and a prominent scar on his face that left a ridge across his nose. He returned the greeting and spoke well of Tenaya and The People before he finally came to the purpose of his visit.

"The whites have found yellow metal in the rivers to the north. They place great value on this metal, which they call gold."

Ezekial held his tongue and forced himself to listen because to interrupt would have been an insult to Tenaya.

The scar-faced Po-to-en-cie turned and glared at Ezekial, black, bloodshot eyes smoky with hatred and distrust. "There are many, many whites and they are *all* evil."

Ezekial started to defend himself but changed his mind when Anina squeezed his hand in warning.

Tenaya asked, "These whites are Spaniards?"

"No, Americans."

Tenaya considered this news for several minutes, never looking in Ezekial's direction. Finally, he asked, "What happened to the Spaniards?"

"Gone."

Now Tenaya allowed himself to looked toward Ezekial. "You know Americans."

"Yes."

"Are there good men among them?"

Ezekial had learned over the years to take time to consider important questions before speaking in council. He could not honestly say that the Americans were generally bad men, quite the contrary. But neither did he want to give his chief the impression that they were all high-minded idealists, either.

"Many good, but some bad."

"Most bad," the spokesman for the Po-to-en-cies snapped in disagreement. "And there is one worse than all the others. His name is Savage."

Tenaya looked to Ezekial, who had to shrug, for he had never heard of such a man.

"What does this man do?" Tenaya asked.

Scar-face's hands clenched in his lap and his lips twisted with hatred. "Savage has poisoned the spirits of our young warriors. He has made them work like slaves to find him more gold. For this they are given beads and many colorful things that are no good. He has cheated our people. I come to warn you that he will cheat the Ahwahneeche, too."

"Thank you for the warning, but he will not be allowed into Ahwahnee. Our medicine protects us from such evil men."

"*Nothing* can protect you," the scar-faced Indian insisted, voice thick with bitterness. "The whites will come to Awahnee and foul your waters. Then, more whites will come. They will cut down your trees, kill your deer, and all this will be no more."

Tenaya climbed stiffly to his feet because he was growing old, but now his voice was strong. "We would kill them first. We would hurl rocks down from our mountains and crush them. Our arrows would find their hearts just as they have always found the hearts of the feared uzamati."

"They will shoot all of you," one of the other Po-to-en-cies argued. "They will destroy Ahwahnee and ride all your women. The old ones will wail and your men will fight, but die. Only the ones that work for Savage will be permitted to live."

Tenaya was so upset that, when he tried to speak, words would not come. Needing help, he looked straight at Ezekial.

"I am American *and* Ahwahneeche," Ezekial began, "and it is true that the white people place great value on the yellow metal, some of which I have seen here."

"You have rifle?" Scar-face snapped impatiently.

"No."

"Horse?"

"No," Ezekial admitted.

The visitor gave Ezekial a dismissive wave of his hand. "Then you have *no* power against the Americans. They will make you hunt gold, too."

"Never," Ezekial vowed.

There was much talk later into the night, but Ezekial, Anina, and Tenaya did not listen. Instead, they came together in the meadow not far from mighty Cho-lok, whose now-muted thunder calmed them.

Tenaya finally spoke. "You must call upon all your power," he said to them both. "We do not want white people in Ahwahnee. It was foretold by Ouma that they should never be allowed in this place."

Ezekial wanted to say what he most feared, that the whites would stop at nothing to find gold. But maybe, if there were not so many of them, the Ahwahneeche could hold them at bay. It was not an easy thing to discover, much less travel, the narrow, serpentine forest trail into Ahwahnee. Maybe the whites would not desire gold enough to endure danger and hardship, especially if there was plenty of gold to be found in the many lower rivers which drained the western slopes of the Sierra Nevadas. Ezekial suspected other Sierra rivers were as numerous as the fingers on both his hands and they would all have as much gold as this Merced, perhaps much more.

"Chief Tenaya," Ezekial said, "you should thank the Po-to-en-cies for their warning and ask them never to tell the whites, and especially this man Savage, about Ahwahnee. But they should also never return here, for they could be followed."

Tenaya looked away for a moment, before saying, "My friend, they have asked to bring their families to Ahwahnee."

"But they have always been your enemies," Ezekial protested. "They would cause trouble."

"They say to me that they want to be friends now" Tenaya replied. "That the Americans are the enemies of all Miwok."

Ezekial digested this for a moment knowing that Tenaya alone must decide. "Are you going to let them come?"

"I have not decided." Tenaya looked to Anina. "You are wise and have strong medicine. What do you say?"

Anina thought of Ouma, calling upon her spirit for wisdom to advise her chief in this decision that would have great consequences, good or bad. "Chief Tenaya," she said, "if the Mono had not welcomed us, the black death would have killed all The People. Is this *white death* so different now?"

"Perhaps not," Tenaya replied, "but, like Ezekial, I am afraid that the Po-to-en-cies would cause trouble. They do not like the mountains and they have learned to hunt with rifles and horses and so could become very dangerous enemies."

"Maybe it wouldn't be so bad to have a few horses in Ahwahnee," Ezekial argued, for he dearly missed the beasts and longed for just one to spare him the grinding pain of long hunts.

"Chief Tenaya," Anina said, "I think we must help the Po-to-en-cies."

"They could lead the Americans to Ahwahnee."

"This is true," Anina conceded. "But if you turn them away, bitterness will cause them to tell the whites about this Ahwahnee and even guide them here."

Tenaya's shoulders slumped and his chin dipped almost to his chest. He suddenly looked old and vulnerable as he weighed the vital question. Ezekial would not have traded places with Tenaya for anything.

"I will think on this," he told them quietly.

Anina touched his sleeve. "Chief Tenaya," she said, "as you know, there were once many, many more Ahwahneeche before the black sickness. There were also many villages in Ahwahnee and the world was divided into two parts by Wa-kal'-la, our great river. Those villages on the north side of the river were said to live on the *land,* grizzly bear, or bluejay side. Those villages south of the river were on the *water* or coyote side. Perhaps the Po-to-en-cies could become the water or coyote people."

"They would not be happy here," Tenaya insisted. "They have their own spirits and belong near their ancestors. With the first snows, they would go where it is warm."

"Not if they fear the whites, and especially the one called Savage."

Tenaya looked to Ezekial. "What do you believe?"

"I would tell the Po-to-en-cies that they can become the coyote people but they must never cross to the north side of the river. There is plenty to eat on both sides and, if we have to fight the whites, then we will need their horses and rifles. We are few now and our bows are no match against the Americans."

"You could get rifles for the Ahwahneeche."

Anina's fingers bit into Ezekial's sleeve and he knew that she did not want him ever to leave her and this valley. She certainly did not want him to go among the whites and try to steal their weapons.

"I do not think that would be a good thing," Ezekial told the chief. "Better to stay in Ahwahnee and guard against the first whites."

Tenaya looked disappointed as he left them to wander into the cold, lonely starlight.

"My husband, what do you *really* think?" Anina asked.

Ezekial longed to tell Anina that nothing in Ahwahnee would ever change. But he knew all too well the tragic fates of all the eastern American Indians. From the northernmost tribes like the Mohawk, Huron, and Delaware on down to the deep South, with the Pensacola and Timucua, the story was the same—all those Indian peoples had been slaughtered, enslaved, or driven from their lands. The last Ezekial had heard, even the Indian tribes west of the Mississippi River were being exterminated or relocated. He could name the Winnebago, Arikara, Omaha, and Caddo, all of whom had been reduced to a pitiful few and their cultures destroyed.

How could he honestly tell Anina that the gentle Ahwahneeche would enjoy a kinder fate?

"Please," Anina said, breaking through his dark ruminations. "Tell me your thoughts."

Ezekial drew his wife close and whispered into her hair, "We must try and keep the Americans out of Ahwahnee as long as possible. We must *never* allow them to discover this deep, grassy valley."

Anina expelled a deep breath. She knew her husband very well and understood that he was afraid for The People and particularly for her and their two young children.

"I will call upon the spirits," she vowed, "to always protect The People."

Tenaya's difficult decision to allow the Po-to-en-cies sanctuary in Ahwahnee quickly proved troublesome. There were only about two dozen families, but they arrived during the acorn harvest and, although the Po-to-en-cies women were supposed to remain on the south side of the river, they crossed over because many of the best oak trees were on the north side. This caused much anger and dissatisfaction among the Ahwahneeche women, long accustomed to gathering the harvest in very specific ways from very specific trees.

The men were even more upset at the Po-to-en-cie hunters for flaunting their rifles and horses. The horses especially were a cause of great envy among the Ahwahneeche and in particular among the youngest hunters, like Kanaka.

"I don't see why we shouldn't also have horses!" he complained. "I see their hunters riding as fast as the wind. They can run down elk and bear. And their rifles . . ."

"It is *not* the way of the Ahwahneeche," Anina sternly reprimanded her son. "The old ways of hunting are better."

"They are not!"

Ezekial, who had been raised with horses, wanted to support his wife but disagreed with her on this very important issue. Like many of the Ahwahneeche, he spent hours gazing across the river and admiring the Po-to-en-cies' horse herd while dreaming of how fine it would be to saddle a horse and race the hunting hawk across the grassy meadows.

How, Ezekial wondered, had the Po-to-en-cies gained possession of these animals? Had they traded their hard-won gold to Savage for them? That was possible, but Ezekial figured the horses had been stolen. The Po-to-en-cies boasted that there were now many horses down on the plains. They said that they were easy to take from the careless whites, whose only real concern was gold.

Yes, Ezekial mused, it *would* be easy to steal horses——and rifles.

Rifles. Nothing made Ezekial feel worse than hearing the sound of a rifle shot somewhere across the river. It always stopped conversation dead in Koom-i-ne; the women's hands would freeze over their work while the men would fall silent, wondering what manner of game the Po-to-en-cies had killed. Perhaps even the mighty grizzly bear that often entered Ahwahnee and had to be either shot with many, many arrows at great risk or else chased back up into the canyons and mountains.

One evening just at dusk, Ezekial and his family were walking in the meadow when they saw two fine bucks grazing on the land side of the now shallow Merced.

"I could return for my bow and arrows," he suggested to his family. "I could probably be back before they finish grazing and vanish into the trees."

"Let Kanaka go for your weapons," Anina suggested.

Kanaka was not pleased. He was tall for his age and trying hard to become a man. "The deer will be gone before I could return. But, if I had a *horse* to ride. . . ."

"Hurry!" Ezekial urged, weary of hearing again from his son about horses. "Run!"

Kanaka had not been gone five minutes when Lucy spotted three Po-to-en-cie hunters leaving their village. The pair of fine bucks noticed them but were not alarmed because the hunters were at too great a distance to pose danger even as they advanced across the brown grass.

Lucy frowned. "Father, they will not shoot them, will they? The bucks are on *our* side of the river."

"That would be very unwise," Ezekial said.

But suddenly, one of the hunters raised a rifle so long and graceful that Ezekial knew it had to be a Kentucky. The Po-to-en-cie hunter took careful aim and fired. The explosion shattered the evening stillness and the larger of the deer collapsed while its companion dashed away to the trees.

Ezekial was furious. He left his wife and daughter and marched over to the dead buck, staring at the gaping bullet hole in its side. The Po-to-en-cie hunter with the rifle came to the edge of the river and called to Ezekial. He would cross the river and claim his kill.

"This buck belongs to the *land* people," Ezekial shouted.

The hunter stopped in water up to his knees and yelled, "It belongs to the one who killed it."

Something snapped in Ezekial. With a roar, he plunged into the water, his charge so wild and ferocious that the Po-to-en-cie was unnerved and retreated to the coyote side and the protection of his fellow hunters. Ezekial kept coming and when he breached the river, he lowered his head and attacked all three of the Po-to-en-cies. His big fist exploded against the rifleman's jaw so hard that bone cracked like the sound of a tree limb. Ezekial grabbed a second Po-to-en-cie by the arm and hurled him spinning into the river.

The third hunter managed to grab a rock and slam Ezekial on the side of his head, dropping him to his knees. Anina and Lucy threw themselves headlong into the river and Kanaka was close on their heels. The Po-to-en-cie hunter who had landed unceremoniously in the water crawled to his feet, saw the enraged Anina and her children coming, and decided he wanted nothing more to do with this fight. He staggered out of the river, grabbed his friends, and all three fled toward the Po-to-en-cie village in full retreat.

"Father!" Lucy cried as Anina bent down to cradle her husband's battered and rapidly swelling head. "Father!"

"I'm all right," Ezekial said, his voice as thick as his mind.

"I will *kill* them," Kanaka shouted, grabbing up the empty Kentucky rifle and waving it overhead.

By the time that the Po-to-en-cies reached their village, all their people as well as all the Ahwahneeche were involved in the dispute, yelling and gesturing back and forth to each other across the river. Everyone, that is, except Chief Tenaya, who stared sadly at the troubling scene.

Anina examined Ezekial's battered head and helped him back across the river to the land side. Kanaka claimed the fallen Kentucky rifle, waving it in defiance toward the Po-to-en-cie village. Then he and Lucy dragged the carcass of the bullet-shot buck into Koom-i-ne, enjoying a chorus of boisterous congratulations.

Once Anina had her husband inside their hut, she decided that this injury called for the use of the dried and pulverized root of waka'li. She would first boil it with a little water, allow it to cool and then use it as a pain-relieving poultice that would quickly reduce the swelling.

Tenaya soon appeared. He was flanked by many of the elders and they were all very angry. They became even angrier when Anina told them what had happened to start the fight.

Tenaya swore, "I will order the Po-to-en-cies to leave Ahwahnee!"

Now Anina agreed with this decision. "They will never be coyote people, just Po-to-en-cies."

This was all that the chief of the Ahwahneeche wanted to hear before he left.

"Now what did you go and say that for?" Ezekial asked when she returned to his side.

"The Po-to-en-cies are bad," she announced. "They do not belong in Ahwahnee."

"Maybe not. But if Tenaya forces them to leave, I'll guarantee you that they will tell the whites of this valley."

"Maybe they already know." Anina raised her chin. "At least now you have a rifle."

Ezekial didn't bother to tell her that he'd long ago used up all his black powder starting fires on winter trails. And there was no use in telling his beloved that the Kentucky rifle they'd just won in the fight was useless without powder and shot.

So he lay back, head throbbing with pain, and tried not to think of what the future would bring for himself, his family, and the unsuspecting Ahwahneeche.

Nine

The Po-to-en-cies burned their coyote village and hurled insults across the water. They also set fire to the meadow and, if the wind had not driven the flames into the rocks at the base of the southern cliffs, the Ahwahneeche village of Koom-i-ne itself might have been destroyed. The People were very angry and upset. Anina made much medicine asking the spirits to cause a mighty wind to sweep away the ungrateful Po-to-en-cies.

"This will bring us no good," Tenaya said, watching thick, black smoke settle in like a poisonous blanket over the valley. "I am to blame."

"No," Ezekial consoled. "You were just trying to do good things for the Po-to-en-cies."

"Ouma warned us against inviting strangers into Ahwahnee," Tenaya said, walking away.

In the weeks that followed, the sadness of their chief ran so deep that no one, not even his favorite son, could raise his spirits. To make matters even worse, the acorn harvest was so poor that the winter granaries went unfilled and there was no autumn joy among The People.

Ezekial hunted as much as his leg would allow and took pride that he had, through endless practice, become an expert bowman. His arrows found the hearts of two large uzamati as they were preparing to sleep for the winter. This bear meat would provide an extra store of winter food for The People. *We will not starve,* Ezekial vowed.

In the very coldest time of winter, a small but important and determined group of Ahwahneeche decided to leave the valley seeking horses and rifles. Ezekial, Anina, and Chief Tenaya vehemently opposed this plan but the younger men, chafing with idleness and hunger, were adamant that they would take the risk.

"This is a bad thing to do," Ezekial proclaimed at the end of one long afternoon of contentious debate in the ceremonial roundhouse. "Ouma warned The People not to let whites into the valley, or to go out among them."

"Ouma has been dead for so long most of us cannot even remember her," Kian snapped.

"She was wise!" Anina said angrily. "And both her wisdom and spirit will always protect us from the waters of Cho'-lok."

"If we had rifles and horses," Haw-kee, one of the young leaders argued, "we would never have to fear the whites!"

"But," Ezekial countered, "if they cannot find us, this talk of horses and rifles is nothing."

"They *will* find us," Haw-kee declared. "It is said that you believe the whites will follow *all* the rivers seeking gold. Is this not true?"

Ezekial was trapped. He couldn't lie and, despite the words he had just spoken, as sure as night followed day, Ezekial was certain that the whites *would* soon enter this valley of the long grass.

"We could make peace with them," he said, realizing how feeble this sounded. "I would not allow them to destroy Ahwahnee."

"Ha!" Puya, son of a prominent elder shouted with derision. "You could not stop so many. You are one of us now but maybe they would give you gold and you would become one of them."

Ezekial would have backhanded the young hothead but Tenaya already was on his feet. "Puya, you must apologize!"

There were no fewer than a hundred adults in the hang-e and Puya struggled but finally said, "Ezekial, I am sorry for those words. But we all heard the Po-to-en-cies. They numbered far more than us and the whites washed over them like a river. The whites will also come to destroy Ahwahnee."

"Then we will fight," Tenaya pledged.

"But we cannot fight without the white man's weapons!" Haw-kee stabbed a finger at Ezekial in anger. "Can our bows match the white man's rifles?"

Ezekial had no choice but to shake his head.

"Then we *must* have rifles!"

The young hunters nodded in vigorous support but the elders, among whom Ezekial was now prominent, sat in stern disagreement, thinking that it was a sad thing to see the Ahwahneeche so divided.

Things did not improve in the weeks that followed. Kanaka's sixteenth birthday brought no happiness for Ezekial or Anina because he was one of those most determined to leave Ahwahnee in order to gain possession of the white man's horses and weapons. Finally, after a month of storms, the weather turned mild and a troubled Tenaya approached Ezekial.

"Our hunters are going to follow the river," the chief began. "They say they want only to catch a few horses. But I am afraid that they will get in a bad fight with the Americans and all be killed."

The thought of Kanaka being shot turned Ezekial pale with dread. "Then tell 'em they can't go!"

"You know that I cannot do this. It is our way that each man should decide such things for himself."

"I won't allow Kanaka to go."

Tenaya smiled patiently. "Maybe you cannot stop him."

Ezekial's broad shoulders slumped in defeat. Tenaya was right. It would bring shame on Kanaka and himself if he forbade his son to go with the other young hunters. But it was also true that Kanaka was bold and reckless. If there were trouble, Kanaka would be among the first of the Ahwahneeche to die.

"Will you lead them?" Tenaya asked.

"What?"

"Go with them," the chief repeated. "You alone among us know the white men. You can talk to them if there is big trouble. You can save the young hunters if they are caught."

"When do they leave?"

"At sunrise."

Ezekial glanced over his shoulder toward his hut, thinking about Anina and Lucy. He was going to risk never seeing them again if things went to hell with the Americans. And then Ezekial thought of Kanaka. *I have to go. If I don't and my son is shot or hanged, I'd never forgive myself.*

When Ezekial returned to Anina, she had already guessed what Tenaya wanted. "You should not go," she said, stirring a fish-and-acorn soup.

"If I don't, they'll be killed just as sure as we're sitting here."

The desperation in her father's voice caused Lucy to glance up from her work, but only for a moment. She pretended not to hear this discussion and even furrowed her brow as if wrapped in concentration. She was learning to make coiled baskets, a skill that required years of practice and an infinite amount of patience. Anina, who had little interest in this work, had asked several older basket makers to teach her daughter.

Lucy was already beginning to demonstrate a talent for basketmaking and now she was proudly working on a large, flat-bottomed, willow-twined basket called a hupulu, which was used to gather foods. If Lucy's skills progressed, in a few years she would finally graduate to the weaving of cooking baskets which were coiled so tightly that they would not leak boiling water. These baskets were usually decorated with red-and-black patterns made from fibers dyed with the roots of fern and bracken.

Ezekial was sure that his pretty young daughter had no intention of becoming a shaman or Ahwahneeche medicine woman. Lucy was too sensitive and quiet to want to involve herself in the lives of everyone. Her spirit was so gentle that even the violent death of wild creatures could bring her to tears.

"Then you *will* go," Anina said, sampling her soup.

"I have to. Where is Kanaka?"

"He is preparing to leave. You *must* talk to him."

"I already have. He doesn't listen. All he thinks about is winning a horse and rifle."

"Talk louder," Anina insisted.

Ezekial grabbed his rabbit-skin robe and went out to speak once more to his son. When Kanaka saw him approaching, he left the company of the other young hunters and came over to greet his father.

"You have come to tell me that I cannot go tomorrow."

"I've come to talk about it."

"The whites have rifles and horses. If we do not have them, they will either kill or drive us away from Ahwahnee."

"What makes you so sure?"

Kanaka looked right into Ezekial's eyes. "I spoke much to the Po-to-en-cies. They even let me ride one of their horses."

Ezekial was surprised. "That's a fact?"

"Yes."

"What did you think?"

"I *must* have a horse of my own."

Ezekial knew that he was going to be wasting his words but he had try anyway, for Anina. "A horse is a fine thing, my son. It can take you to faraway places. But Ahwahnee is our home so we don't need horses."

"No," Kanaka argued, "I must have a horse and rifle."

"Kanaka, do you know what the Americans do to a horse thief?"

Kanaka shook his head back and forth.

"The white people will hang you by the neck until you are dead. That was a fact when I was living among them and it's still a fact."

Kanaka was already five-eleven, slender but surprisingly

strong. His cheekbones were Indian and he'd been spared Ezekial's high, hooked nose. Kanaka's hair was the same color as Lucy's, chocolate with red highlights. Ezekial thought he was going to be a handsome six-footer. And, like his father, he would be an exceptionally fast runner.

"They will not catch me," Kanaka vowed, turning and marching back to the others.

Ezekial wanted to rush after Kanaka, grab and shake some sense into him but that would be a mistake, so he just walked away, feeling sad and defeated.

That night, Anina went from one hut to the next offering smoke and prayers for the young warriors who would follow her husband into the hot central valley seeking rifles and horses. All of their mothers were worried; many were crying, and these Anina did her best to comfort.

It was nearly midnight when she returned to her husband's arms. Kanaka and Lucy were both still awake and the whole family lay lost in troubled thoughts. Long before daylight, Ezekial awakened to make his leaving preparations. When Anina squeezed him tightly, Ezekial said, "Anina, we *will* return. That's a promise."

"How long?

"Ten days, no more."

Anina's hands stroked Ezekial's chest and her lips found his mouth. Moments later, they were making love, as frantically as they had the very first time they had coupled under the pounding waters of Cho'-lok. Afterward, Ezekial knew there was nothing more to say to his wife. He thought about waking Lucy, but when he threw some wood on the fire and looked over at her, she was already awake and staring at him.

"Ten days, no more," Lucy said, reaching out to take his hand in her own. "Mother is not the only one who will count the hours until you and Kanaka return."

"I know, pretty one."

Ezekial awakened his son and they left with the stars above as pale and cold as ice pellets. Ezekial and his young companions traveled in silence all that first day, each wondering if he would ever see Ahwahnee again. If he'd been willing to admit it to

Anina, Ezekial would have told his wife how fearful he was to encounter white society after nearly two decades of living as an Ahwahneeche. Ezekial had never been a complicated man, his wants and needs had always been modest. But among the Ahwahneeche, he had found joy in a life uncluttered by ambition or worldly goods. Ezekial had no illusions about the kind of rugged and ruthless men that he'd soon meet as they clawed and fought for river gold. They would take what they wanted and Ezekial knew that he was neither young nor strong enough to oppose them. Furthermore, the thought of appealing to the miners' sense of fair play was absurd.

Despite all his misgivings, Ezekial also understood that there was really nothing to do but enter the world of whites and allow matters to unfold. He sadly expected that it would take only a few more years before Ahwahnee was discovered and plundered. He knew that, even after the Po-to-en-cies' warning, his own people could not begin to comprehend the inevitability of their destruction.

The character of the land changed dramatically once the Ahwahneeche dropped down to the Sierra foothills. And, for the first time since he and the Walker party had been stranded on the highest ridges of the Sierras, Ezekial saw the immense sweep of California's central valley. Since it was winter, the rolling foothills were covered with dry, brown grass, but the air felt surprisingly warm. Instead of the black oak that sustained The People, Ezekial saw the blue interior live oak. Dogwood, maple, and incense cedar disappeared and the lower, warmer hills were cloaked with an almost-impenetrable chaparral. The river itself turned slow and sluggish, its power dissipated by warmth. Instead of a roar, it gurgled like a contented infant and allowed its banks to become clogged with willow and flanked by immense stands of leafless cottonwoods. In this low, open country, it seemed as if the earth's heartbeat was muffled, its pulse slow and weak compared to the strength and power of the high mountains. Ezekial was gripped by anxiety, and without the protection of closely surrounding cliffs, trees, and mountains, he felt terribly exposed. There was nothing out here to hide a man from his enemies. And, judging from the dispirited expressions of his companions, Ezekial was sure that the other Ahwahneeche also felt naked and vulnerable.

On the third day of their travels, one of the scouts that Ezekial had sent ahead returned with the news that there was a white man's village just downriver, containing many people and horses. The Ahwahneeche became very excited and it was all that Ezekial could do to talk them into showing patience and waiting until he had a chance to visit the mining settlement.

"I can learn much to help us," he explained, "but I need some time alone among 'em."

"Father?" Kanaka asked.

"Yes?"

"It is said that I look much like a white man. Is this true?"

"No," Ezekial told his son, already guessing what was on Kanaka's mind. "And you can't come with me."

"But you might need me!"

"Later, I *will* need you. But now you'd just be an additional worry. You see, I've been away from the company of white people so long that I've sort of forgotten how they act and talk. I don't even know who is running California, although it must be the Americans since so many are here."

Ezekial clapped a hand on Kanaka's shoulder. "We'll have horses and rifles. But we must not let the whites know that it was the Ahwahneeche that took from 'em. That is very, very important."

Without any more discussion, Ezekial handed his son his bow and arrows. "Guess it wouldn't do to wander into a settlement carrying these. As it is, I expect I'll look pretty strange with my beaded moccasins and rabbit-skin coat."

At the last moment, Ezekial decided to remove his coat. "I won't be needing this," he explained. "And I have my old Green River knife to show that I have lived among the whites."

The Ahwahneeche wished him well, and then Ezekial went down to scout the mining camp. He was sweating and nervous and, if anything, his fears were heightened when he saw that the settlement easily boasted several hundred miners. Besides the expected tents, there were even a few wooden buildings. From what Ezekial could see of the main street, this was a boomtown, with hordes of miners flocking to saloons or congregating before the various storefronts. It sure wasn't St. Louis, but it was darned impressive and a clear indication of how many gold-fevered Americans had arrived in California.

"Howdy!" Ezekial called to a pair of burly prospectors who were roughing up a small, dapper man in his late forties. There was some kind of argument and the miners looked very threatening. The little man had been shoved up against a building and had no place to run.

Unable to ignore the situation, Ezekial approached them and said, "Nice day, isn't it."

The largest of the pair spun around to confront Ezekial. "We're about to beat the hell outa this little sonofabitch, so you just go along and mind your own damned business."

"What did he do?" Ezekial asked, still trying to act pleasant.

"None of your business!"

The smaller man's bowler had been knocked to the dirt. Ezekial picked it up and brushed it off, noting that it was made of something other than beaver. He didn't have time to reflect on that very long, however, because one of the miners swatted it out of his hands and growled, "Git!"

"You'd better do as they say," the little man said, his face wet with perspiration. "They don't mean to kill me."

"Just beat you, huh?" Ezekial said, retrieving the hat a second time. "What for?"

The smaller of the miners cursed and pivoted to face Ezekial. He sneered, "Why, you dress and smell like a damned Indian!"

Ezekial suddenly remembered all about bullies. He'd endured more than his share as a boy and he'd even met a few when he'd joined Walker's expeditionary force.

"You know, I'm from Kentucky," he said, struggling mightily to grin. "I guess you heard of Davy Crockett. He dressed like me."

"The Mexicans shot him full of holes at the Alamo!"

Ezekial blinked. "They killed Davy Crockett?"

"That's right! Maybe he stuck his nose into something he shouldn't have, like you're doin'.."

Ezekial was shocked at this news, for he had heard Crockett speak while campaigning for Congress. It took a moment for him to wrench his mind back to the present and realize that the miner was challenging him with a question.

"What did you say?"

"I said, what the hell are you doing wearing buckskins!"

"Why, I trap beaver!" Ezekial said. "Been doin' right well, too."

The man's eyes narrowed and he leaned in on Ezekial, expression turning nasty, breath foul with bad liquor. "Did you say you were trappin' *beaver?*"

Ezekial sensed something was very wrong but, desperately wanting to avoid attracting attention, he grinned even wider and said, "That's right, prime pelts, too!"

"Well, mister, I'd like to know who the hell is buyin' beaver anymore!" The miner glanced at his partner. "Mike, this dummy don't even know that beaver hats went out of style about ten years ago! Ain't no market anymore for pelts. Who the hell do you suppose he's trying to fool?"

Perspiration began to leak from Ezekial's armpits and he realized that he should have kept his mouth shut and pretended that he was just another miner, despite how he stuck out from everyone because he alone wore buckskins.

"Well, mister," Ezekial said, trying hard to avoid a fight and taking a backstep, "I guess that some people still like to make hats and coats and such out of 'em. Beaver is still fine fur."

"Ain't no damn beaver left to trap in these mountains!" the other man shouted. "I think you're a liar, mister."

"That's what he is, Joshua," the other agreed. "Just a damned dirty liar."

Ezekial's smile dissolved and his hands knotted into fists. He had learned at a very young age that no man ought to allow himself to be slandered and insulted. Attention or not, he was going to have to fight the both of these men, and he wanted it to end hard and quick.

"You just couldn't be friendly, could you?" Ezekial asked.

"Huh?"

Ezekial's fist traveled less than eight inches but it struck Joshua's jaw with such force that it caused his head to snap back. Mouth open, eyes blank and rolling into his forehead, Joshua rocked back on his heels as a ripping left uppercut to the heart bent him like a cheap spike. Joshua doubled over and Ezekial's knee slammed into his chin. The man hit the side of the building and slid down, quivering like a thick, exposed nerve.

"You sonofabitch!" Mike cried, attacking.

Ezekial ducked under the wild, windmilling punches and almost laughed. He was seized by a feeling of power and invincibility. His fear of white men, born of his long absence among them, dissolved and he waded into Mike with his lips pulled back in anticipation. Ezekial hammered three punishing blows to Mike's body and, when the miner dropped his hands to protect his gut, Ezekial unleashed a sweeping uppercut originating at his knees. It broke Mike's nose and, when the man bounced helplessly up against the building, Ezekial swarmed all over him, raining blows so fast and from so many angles that Mike finally covered his face, turned, and ran for his life. Had his leg been fit, Ezekial would have chased the man down, tackled and beat him senseless.

"Jeezus, mister!" the little man shouted. "Let him go! The fight is over!"

Ezekial expelled a deep breath. "Yeah, I guess it is."

"Where'd you ever learn to fight like that? I never seen *anyone* fight like you."

The man was now grinning like he'd found a dollar in the dust, but Ezekial had his own questions to ask.

"Tell me," he said, looking around at the people who had stopped to watch a fight that hadn't lasted much more than a minute, "what's the name of this camp?"

"This is Logtown and danged if I wouldn't be honored . . . just plain honored . . . to buy you a drink." The little man stuck out a chubby hand and said, "My name is Beauregard Lamont, Attorney-at-Law, and I am pleased to make your acquaintance."

"My name is Ezekial Grant," he said, studying the town and

not noticing the man's outstretched hand, "and this camp is named Logtown, huh."

"That's right! It's growin' every day. The color's real good here."

"What color?"

The attorney cocked his head sideways, birdlike. "Why, the *gold*, of course. Mister, you really haven't been around folks much lately, have you?"

"Been trappin'," Ezekial frowned, wondering who among this sorry collection of humanity would even bother to pursue a band of horse thieves. "Mr. Lamont, who's the law in Logtown?"

"Nobody," the attorney said. "I'm afraid that it's every man for himself. But we do get a circuit judge who comes through about every month or so to see if anyone needs fining or hanging."

The attorney chuckled, but Ezekial did not see any humor. He'd once seen a hanging in Memphis and it hadn't been a pretty sight.

"I represent the guilty and sometimes I get them off cheap. Sometimes not."

"That what happened with these two?" Ezekial asked, looking down at the unconscious one called Joshua.

"Yeah, they knifed a bad woman but they didn't really try to kill her. The judge fined 'em each a hundred dollars and they were fixin' to try and get it out of my hide."

Ezekial didn't care about any of that. "Who's running California?"

"Us Americans!" Lamont mopped his brow with a silk handkerchief. "Mister, where you been for the last couple of years?"

"Trappin'."

"Don't you read or talk to anyone?"

Ezekial sucked on his bloody knuckles. "How'd we win California?"

Bo Lamont shook his head but explained. "We had a revolution in Monterey, Sacramento, and a bunch of places. Called it the Bear Flag Revolution and we drove the Mexicans out. Happened just before gold was discovered at Sutter's Mill."

The little man's eyes narrowed. "You *did* at least hear of that, didn't you?"

"Sure!" Ezekial snapped. "Everyone's heard of that."

"That's right," Lamont said, looking more than a little relieved. Ezekial spotted the United States flag flying from a pole by a stageline office. Just under it was a flag with a bear painted on it. "What's that lower flag?"

"Why, that's our California Bear flag!" Lamont puffed up a little. "We were just given statehood a couple of months ago. John Fremont and some of . . ."

Ezekial was not certain that he'd heard or understood correctly. "A *state* of the Union?"

"That's right!"

Ezekial could not hide his astonishment. "Can you imagine such a thing," he said, more to himself than to the attorney. "A *state of the Union* clear out here on the frontier? Never thought it would happen in my lifetime."

Lamont was looking worried again. "Mr. Ezekial," he said solicitously, "perhaps it would be better for a man of your . . . nature and temperament, to return to the wild."

That caused Ezekial to snort a laugh. Turning back to the small man and seeing his genuine concern, Ezekial said, "Mr. Lamont, I'd like nothing better. But some things just can't be ducked or avoided."

"Such as?"

"Bein' here," Ezekial whispered, fighting off an almost-overpowering need to escape Logtown for the security of his mountain paradise.

He heaved a deep sigh and his eyes narrowed into slits as he toed the dirt with his moccasin. Ezekial was no saint and he'd done his share of sinning, but he had learned a better way to live. Everywhere he looked, this camp was rotting with filth and drunkenness, and exploding with ornery sonsabitches like the pair he'd just whipped. Logtown was an eyesore. All the trees had been chopped down and the landscape was littered with tin cans, bottles, and trash. He needed to leave in a hurry.

"Mr. Lamont, I guess I don't fit in here. I do, however, need a horse and a rifle."

"What happened? Some digger Indian steal 'em from you when you were trapping for beaver?"

" 'Digger Indian'?" Ezekial had never heard of that tribe.

"Yeah," the man said.

"Who are they?"

"Why, that's just the general run-of-the-mill California Injun. The ones who grub for roots and insects and stuff to eat."

Ezekial watched a pair of drunken, screeching miners spill out of a saloon, gouging, clawing, and punching their way across the street with a crowd suddenly materializing to egg them on.

"Mr. Lamont, this may surprise you, but grasshoppers are good eatin' when they're roasted and salted. But never mind that anyway. Who's got horses and rifles around here to sell?"

"Horses can be bought, but they're high. Best place to buy rifles is at one of Jim Savage's trading posts. The nearest one is about seven miles west of town. Horses can be bought right here at Potter's Livery."

"How much?"

" 'Bout forty dollars a head. Mules a little higher."

"Damn! That *is* high. I was thinking they'd sell for around ten dollars."

"Ten!" Lamont chuckled and straightened his tie. "Maybe they did when they were running wild, but not anymore. And when is the last time that you bought a rifle?"

"A long time ago," Ezekial admitted. "Mine was old, but it shot straight."

"New Sharps might cost you fifty dollars."

"What is that funny-looking pistol that you're packin' on your hip?" Ezekial asked, eyes dropping to the attorney's coat that he'd just brushed aside.

"Colt revolver," Lamont said proudly.

"Why didn't you drag it out and shoot them two big sonsabitches that were givin' you a hard time?"

"I'm an attorney! No one can just shoot someone over a disagreement."

When Ezekial's expression made it clear he did not understand, the attorney elaborated. "It's like this. Since there is no money for a regular constable, we employ a system of 'rope justice.' Now, I'd far rather let some big miner give me a black eye than shoot him dead and risk getting hanged by his drunken friends."

Ezekial just didn't understand. "But even little fellers like yourself got to protect themselves."

"I probably could have talked my way out of a beating," Lamont said. "And I was just about to tell them that I have some pretty rough friends of my own. They probably think that you're one of them and, in fact, you are."

"No, I'm not," Ezekial said. "I'm a man in need of a rifle and a horse. I'm just passing through, but I would like to have a closer look at your pistol."

Lamont handed it over. "Don't worry," he said, "it isn't loaded."

"Well, for crying out loud!" Ezekial exclaimed. "Why would anyone pack a gun that wasn't loaded?"

"Makes men think."

Ezekial gave up on understanding the attorney and focused his attention on the pistol, which he found most interesting. "Six shots?"

"That's right. It's a new Navy Colt," Lamont said proudly. "Ain't it a dandy?"

"Where," Ezekial asked, turning the weapon this way and that, "is the flint and powder pan?"

The attorney laughed. "That's no flintlock, Ezekial, it's a *percussion* pistol! Everything is going percussion now."

"How's it work?"

"Instead of a flintlock like the Kentucky rifle you had stolen, this pistol uses a percussion cap."

The man showed Ezekial a cap and then explained exactly how the pistol operated.

"Well I'll be! Misfire much?"

"Almost never. This isn't like your old flintlock, where you have to worry about wind and rain either blowing the powder away or getting it wet."

Ezekial was impressed. "I'll tell you, if a man can fire five or six times without reloading, he'll be dangerous even if he is a poor marksman."

"That's true," Lamont agreed, holstering his empty pistol. "How'd you come to California?"

"Overland. Do you know what happened to a fella called Joseph Walker? He brought a party over from Utah in the year of thirty-three."

Lamont shook his head. "What else did he do?"

"I don't know. I lost track of him a long time ago."

"That happens a lot in California, where nobody stays in one place very long. Word of every new strike spreads like wildfire and camps pack up and move overnight, often simply on the basis of some rumored new strike. Logtown may be gone tomorrow. You just never know."

"What would happen to the wooden buildings?"

"Their owners would tear 'em down, move 'em to the next strike, and nail 'em back up in a few hours, all ready for business."

Ezekial could not visualize that, but he believed it to be true.

"Ezekial," the attorney said, "are you interested in gainful employment? I could use someone who is not afraid to fight."

"Nope. I just need horses and a rifle."

"That's too bad——for me, at least." Lamont stuck out his hand, which was as soft as that of a baby. "I am in your debt, sir. And, if you ever need representation, I would do so without recompense. I am a graduate of Harvard and an excellent attorney, despite my present poor circumstances."

"What brought you out here to a place like this?"

Lamont smiled sadly. "Gold fever, of course."

"You came to prospect for gold?"

"That's right. I was bitten just as severely as the rest of them. You'd be surprised how many highly educated and supposedly intelligent men like myself gave up promising careers back in the East to come west and strike it rich. I threw away everything to join the rush and I've been sorry ever since."

"You could go back."

"No," Lamont said, shaking his jowls. "I've humiliated my family and friends and I've too much pride to return, hat in hand, and beg my former classmates for a position with their law firms."

"Pride goeth before a fall."

"And after," Lamont said, having to clear his throat.

Ezekial heard and saw the man's pain. "Where can I find that livery?"

"Go down to the end of this block and turn right. You'll see Potter's Livery. He usually has at least a dozen horses for sale. Some of them are good. Most are not."

"Are they skinny . . . or have they got a lot of meat on their bones?"

Lamont's sadness was replaced by amusement. He had a little mustache and now he stroked it reflectively and said, "Why on earth do you ask?"

"Just wondering."

"Some are fat, some are skinny."

"I see."

"Good day, Mr. Grant. And don't forget my offer of repayment."

"No sir."

"Oh, one more thing. Watch your back. Those two misfits you whipped might decide to get even."

"They can try," Ezekial said, hand dropping to his big-handled hunting knife, "but it wouldn't be good for their health. Next time, I'd probably have to gut 'em."

Attorney Bo Lamont chuckled, thinking this remark bluster or joke. But when he looked straight into Ezekial's eyes, he clamped his mouth shut and then turned and walked quickly away.

Ten

Because people were still staring at Ezekial, he did not linger about the mining camp as he'd intended. He did, however, pay a visit to Potter's Livery but saw only four skinny horses standing in the corral, none of them worth the risk of stealing. They were so poor that they reminded Ezekial of the starving horses that he and the Walker party once had eaten to stay alive.

"My name is Potter," an old man said, emerging from behind

a stack of hay and eyeing Ezekial closely. He was as thin and hard-used as his horses, but his eyes were clear and probing. "What can I do for you today?"

"I need some horses, but none of these suit me," Ezekial said, gesturing toward the corral before turning to leave.

The old man spit a long stream of tobacco and shuffled after Ezekial, cutting off his exit. "Hold up there! Those are just ponies that I trade to the Indians for gold. Anyone can see they ain't worth spit. But the Indians sure prize 'em."

"Them horses don't look fit enough to walk across the corral for a drink."

"Oh," the man chuckled, revealing that most of his teeth were gone, "they can do a sight better'n that! But they ain't much, that's for sure. I buy 'em cheap and sell 'em high to the Indians. Good profit in it. But if you're looking for some real horseflesh, come into the barn and have a peek."

Ezekial guessed that would not hurt anything, although it seemed much too risky for the Ahwahneeche to slip into a barn and steal horses. The "barn" was just a pine-pole frame shrouded by dirty canvas hanging over a maze of tiny stalls. Ezekial had to admit that the stalls were clean and the horses well fed and slick despite the cold weather.

"Now look at this big stud horse down here!" Potter said, hooking his talonlike thumbs into a pair of rein-leather suspenders. "Ain't he something special!"

Ezekial agreed. The horse that Potter obviously valued most was a liver chestnut. It was big and strong, with a blaze on its face and three white stockings. Its coat shone like polished mahogany and it had a fine, intelligent look to its head.

"Mighty fine animal," Ezekial agreed. "How old?"

"Just seven. Take a look at his mouth and you'll see that I'm telling you the truth. People will pay you ten . . . twenty dollars to breed their mares to this horse. You could earn your money back in stud fees the first year."

"How much?"

"I could let you have him for . . . oh, two hundred dollars."

"Two hundred dollars! Why, he'd have to be made of gold to be worth that much money!"

Potter had a little goatee and mustache and he rubbed them reflectively. "Seen you someplace, haven't I? Maybe at Sutter's Fort."

"Not a chance."

"I never forget a face and you cut quite a figure, mister. And as everyone knows, the richest man in California used to be John Augustus Sutter, but he lost everything on account of the big gold rush."

Ezekial said nothing. He didn't have a clue as to whom he might resemble at Sutter's Fort, which he'd never heard of to begin with. Also, he was having an impossible time taking his eyes off the stallion. Ezekial had seen thousands of beautiful horses, most of them in Kentucky when he was growing up, but he'd never seen a handsomer animal than this chestnut.

"Sutter had a big mountain man like you working for him. Man's name was Horace Cleaver. It is said that Cleaver walked away with thousands of dollars. I seen him once, off in the distance. Like you, he stood out. But I expect he's changed his name and would like everyone to think he's nothing."

"My name is Ezekial Grant and I never heard of Cleaver."

Potter pulled on his goatee. "Are you gonna tell me you never even heard of Jim Savage?" the old liveryman asked, eyes narrowing. "He got rich plundering the Mexican ranches. Hell of a horse and cattle thief before he gave that up to become a successful trader and learned Indian talk."

"He speaks in the Modoc tongue?" Ezekial asked, completely surprised.

"Like he was born to it," the liveryman said. He paused, then added, "A man like you arouses my curiosity."

"Too much curiosity will often get a man killed," Ezekial said quietly.

"Hell, I'm old. I wouldn't be losing much except a few years of aches and pains. And I *am* a highly curious man. I can tell a lot about people just from their looks, their manner, and the way they act, you know."

"Is that a fact?"

"Yep. I can tell that you ain't no miner, nor a mule skinner nor a farmer. I expect you're a trader like Jim Savage and that you've come to skin me out of some fine horseflesh."

"You've got the imagination of a child."

Potter pretended not to have heard the remark. "Tell you what," he said. "I can see that you're a horse trader so, if you'll pay me five hundred dollars, you can take every damned horse in this barn . . . *and* I'll throw in the four Indian traders corralled outside!"

Ezekial could not have paid this old tobacco-spitter two bits, but he did admit to feeling a powerful draw to the striking chestnut. Ezekial could easily imagine himself astride that fine animal and taste a hard wind as he galloped across Ahwahnee like a king. None of the Po-to-en-cies had owned a horse that could compare to this flashy chestnut.

Potter chuckled. "I can see that you like him. And I'll guarantee you that the other six in here are all sound and in good flesh."

"Yes," Ezekial said quietly as he began to walk up and down between the little stalls, trying to distract himself from the chestnut. "I can see that they are fine animals."

"Five hundred dollars," Potter said, rubbing his hands together. "I got me a chance to invest in a mining claim. Sure payoff. Might be, we could work something out on that, too."

"That's possible."

"Who are you really, mister? I can keep a secret."

Ezekial saw no harm in satisfying the man's curiosity. "All right, I am Horace Cleaver."

"You sonofabitch!" Potter hooted, then doing a little shuffle in the dirt. "I bet you robbed old Sutter blind before the rush came through and picked his place clean as a hen's tooth."

"I believe," Ezekial said with mock seriousness, "that the poor . . . not the meek, shall inherit the earth by fleecing the fat and the foolish."

Potter cackled and actually bent over to slap his knee. But when his laughter died, he instantly turned serious. "So when you gonna bring the money? I'm about out of hay and I have to move on that mining claim in a hurry."

"I'll bring it tomorrow, first thing in the morning," Ezekial promised, heading for the door.

"Hey! You know something?" Potter called.

Ezekial turned. "What?"

"You're a terrible liar."

Ezekial stopped, then slowly pivoted. "What do you mean?"

"I knew you worked for either Sutter or Savage. Knew it the minute I saw you walk in dressed up in those old buckskins that look like they're nothin' but lice and flea beddin'."

Ezekial's fists knotted at his sides and he wanted to rush over and throttle Potter, telling him that Anina had lovingly made his outfit and that it was warm and soft and that he wouldn't trade it for any damned old cotton or wool coat. That's what he wanted to say, but instead, he turned and stomped away.

Ezekial made very sure that he was not followed before he rejoined the Ahwahneeche, who had grown very restless in his absence. The sun was dipping into the Sierras when he arrived, and his bad leg was throbbing with pain. But despite that, Ezekial's mind was filled with the picture of the chestnut stallion as he slumped down with his friends.

"Your hands," Kanaka said, noting his father's skinned knuckles.

"Ah," Ezekial scoffed, having already forgotten his fight. "Just a little disagreement in that camp. It is nothing to worry about."

"Where can we get rifles and horses?" Kian wanted to know.

"Rifles I still don't know about," he said. "But we can get ten horses."

The Ahwahneeche leaned forward; Kanaka licked his lips with anticipation.

Ezekial told them all about Potter and the horses, making sure to add, "That stallion is going to be mine. Stallions need special handling. The four horses in the corrals are weak, but they'll bloom on Ahwahnee's long meadow grass."

"So, do we kill Potter?" Puya asked, his expression grim.

"No!" Ezekial lowered his voice. "There is no need to do that. I'll just sneak into his barn. I saw his cot in one of the stalls. I'll make sure that he *stays* asleep."

"Does he have guns and rifles?"

"Maybe both," Ezekial said. "Yeah, I'd say he probably does. But I learned that the best place to get a bunch of 'em is at one of Jim Savage's trading posts."

"Maybe," To-che, one of the most aggressive of the warriors said, "we should get the weapons first, *then* use them to take many more horses."

The very last thing Ezekial wanted was to arm the Ahwahneeche and risk a battle with seasoned marksmen. "We'll steal the horses first, then go to Savage's trading post and get weapons."

He leaned forward, voice dropping. "It is *very* important that no one see us. No one! The worst thing that could happen would be for someone to know this was done by the Ahwahneeche."

"Maybe they would think it was the Po-to-en-cies," another warrior said, looking pleased with the idea.

"Maybe," Ezekial said, "but that could backfire on us if they went after the Po-to-en-cies only to learn that they didn't have Potter's stolen horses. Then we'd be in big trouble."

"What do we do now?" Kanaka asked.

"I think that I ought to go back to steal Potter's horses alone," Ezekial said.

When the hunters started to object, Ezekial held up his hand for silence. "All I'd have to do would be to tie 'em all together. There's plenty of rope around the place and once I got 'em out of town, we could ride 'em . . . oh my Lord!"

"What?" Kanaka asked.

"Most of you can't even ride!"

But, one by one, the Ahwahneeche confessed that they had sneaked across the river and ridden the horses of the Po-to-en-cies at night while their owners slept. Sometimes they were almost caught.

"No wonder their women thought nothing of crossing to the land side to harvest our acorns," Ezekial said, quite sure that even Tenaya had known nothing of these secret night rides.

For the next several hours, the Ahwahneeche debated who should go after the horses and who should stay. Finally, Ezekial

simply allowed all of them to come along despite his grave reservations. He was in charge and, if this quest for horses and
weapons failed and his men were captured and hanged, it would
be a terrible loss. Ezekial had no doubts whatsoever that the
Po-to-en-cies would be only too happy to lead the whites in a
vengeful attack upon the Ahwahneeche.

"Remember, no sounds," he warned one last time when they
were finally assembled in thickets at the edge of the mining
camp. Logtown was still bustling despite the lateness of the hour
and its saloons remained packed.

Ezekial took a deep breath. "If anyone sees you, scatter to the
woods. We'll meet back where we started and try this again somewhere else. Is that understood?"

They all nodded, but Puya said, "Too much talk."

Ezekial knew that Puya was right. There *had* been too much
damned talk.

"That white man's music very bad," To-che said, referring to
the tinkle of piano keys that somehow penetrated the din of
laughter and shouts.

"Yeah," Ezekial said, feeling his heart begin to race. The only
good thing about all this was that they would not have to cross
any streets or expose themselves to lamplight. "Let's go!"

Ezekial's bad leg was on fire, but he hobbled as fast as he
could toward the livery. He feared that his leg could buckle at
any time and that gave him even more resolve to possess that
chestnut stallion. The last hundred yards were an agony and
Ezekial was grunting with pain when he finally hobbled up to
Potter's canvas-covered barn.

It was pitch-black inside. A horse, probably the stallion, nick-
ered and Ezekial paused for several moments, hoping his eyes
would adjust quickly and at least detect contrasts in the darkness.
Potter wasn't making a sound, not even snoring as Ezekial stumbled forward, realizing that he was going to have to have some
light.

Potter's cry broke the night. "Who goes there!"

Ezekial heard the metallic click of a rifle's hammer. It was
something that a man did not forget.

"Who goes there, I say!" the old man shouted.

Ezekial squatted down, hands groping for the side of a stall. He did not hear the others, but that was not surprising since they had an uncanny ability to move with absolute silence. Ezekial had learned that the Indians' eyes were superior in the dark, though Ezekial doubted that even they could see Potter.

"I got a buffalo rifle and I'll blow you to pieces!" Potter cried.

"All right," Ezekial said, rising to a crouch. "It's me, Ezekial . . . Horace Cleaver. Don't shoot, Mr. Potter."

A long pause, then, "Cleaver?"

A match flared and, in the sickly yellow light, Ezekial turned to see Kanaka and several of the others, all looking scared.

"Gawdammit!" Potter cried, rising into full view. "Throw up your hands or I swear I'll blow a hole in you the size of a bucket!"

Ezekial stood up but not before he motioned the Ahwahneeche to scoot back out of the tent-barn and run.

"See, I told you it was just me, Mr. Potter," Ezekial said, somehow managing a grin.

Potter swore, spittle flying from his mouth. "What the hell were you going to do, cut my throat and steal that stallion?"

"No sir! I just wanted to take another look at him to make sure that . . ."

"The hell you say!" the old man swore, lighting a kerosene lamp that hung from a support post. "Cleaver, there's only one reason that you came skulkin' around in the dark and that was to murder and rob me!"

Ezekial gulped. "Oh, no sir!"

Potter's eyes slitted. "You got the five hundred?"

"Ah . . . yes sir."

"Show it to me."

"But . . ."

Potter raised the big-bored rifle to his shoulder and sighted on Ezekial's chest. "Now!"

Ezekial didn't even have a dollar to show the man. His only chance was to dive for cover, draw his knife, and rush Potter, but that was a poor plan indeed.

Potter licked his lips with anticipation. "Guess I'll just blow you apart and take the money anyway. You stole it from Sutter,

I'll steal it from you 'cause stealin' ain't really stealin' when you do it to a thief."

Ezekial's mind raced. "Mr. Potter, I don't have the money with me right now."

"You just said you did!"

"I . . . I lied. The money is . . . is hidden."

"You probably whored and drank away all of Sutter's money and now you turned murderer and thief! Well, I think I'll kill you right where you stand!" Potter's eyes took on a strange gleam in the lamplight and he almost smiled. "Ain't no law gonna hold me to blame."

When the old man jammed his cheek down to the stock and closed one eye, Ezekial felt an icy finger of death snake up his spine. His body turned rigid with fear, but then he heard the familiar whirring of an Ahwahneeche arrow followed by a "thud" as its flint bit deeply into Potter's chest. The old man's fingers splayed and he gagged blood. His rifle spilled from his hands and he grabbed the arrow, tearing at it so violently he stripped away its feathers before he pitched forward.

Ezekial turned to see Coati, a short but very powerful hunter, lower his bow. The other Ahwahneeche rushed into the barn and began to grab ropes and halters. Ezekial went over and knelt beside Potter. The liveryman was dead.

"Father!" Kanaka cried, grabbing Ezekial's shoulder and squeezing hard. "We must hurry!"

Ezekial broke away the shaft of Coati's arrow then forced himself to drive the blade of his knife into the dead liveryman's chest and twist so that it would appear that Potter had died of a knife rather than an arrow wound. Feeling heartsick at the death of the old man, Ezekial hurried over to the chestnut stallion, snatching up a bridle on the way.

It took much longer than it should have to bridle and halter the horses. The stallion was very excited and tromped on Ezekial's foot. That pain, coupled with his bad leg, caused Ezekial to grunt constantly. He was finally able to get the powerful animal saddled, and Kanaka helped him mount.

"All right, let's go out the back way and move straight into the trees!" Ezekial ordered.

"What about the tracks?" Puya demanded. "Even a blind man could follow us to Ahwahnee."

Ezekial knew that Puya was thinking more clearly than the rest of them. "You are right, we must brush them away. And all the moccasin tracks in the barn and around the corrals as well."

Puya and two others found horse blankets to sweep away all their tracks. Meanwhile, the stallion kept dancing. It was all that Ezekial could do to control the magnificent animal and, when he finally gave the chestnut a loose rein, it shot out of the tent-barn. Ezekial could not get it under control until he reached the trees. Fortunately, no one seemed to have seen him or any of the other Ahwahneeche who fled the mining camp. Maybe everyone was too drunk or preoccupied to notice. Ezekial didn't care. All that mattered was that he and the others had safely escaped with ten horses.

They hurried through the night, keeping to the trees. The moon was round and bright, it illuminated the sky and highlighted a flotilla of silvery cloud-galleons.

When they finally returned to their original hiding place just outside of town, Ezekial's leg was so stiff that he had to be helped down from the rambunctious stallion. The Ahwahneeche were just as excited as Ezekial's horse, believing they had accomplished the impossible by entering the white man's world and taking his prized horses. Had Ezekial not been among them, the Ahwahneeche might even have celebrated by butchering one of the scrub ponies on the spot. Ezekial alone felt depressed. Potter had been an old man and not an especially kind or Christian one, but he had not deserved to die defending his property.

"When it is discovered that Potter was killed and his horses stolen, there will be trouble," he told his companions. "I don't know how many friends that old man had, but you can bet that he had at least a few that will form a posse."

"No tracks," Me-cha said.

"I know," Ezekial agreed, "but my guess is that there'll be at least some effort made to find out who killed Potter and took his horses. Even in a mining camp, murder isn't taken lightly. It just makes sense to return with these horses to Ahwahnee."

When this suggestion was met with a chorus of protests, Kanaka said, "Father, we have the horses, but we are still powerless against the whites. We *must* have guns and rifles."

"And we will have, but not this time," Ezekial said sternly. "A man is dead. News travels fast and everyone will be on the lookout for these horses during the next week or two."

The Ahwahneeche considered this as Ezekial continued. "What happened in Logtown tells me that I need to spend a little time among the whites and learn more."

"What about Savage's trading post?" Coati asked.

"Too risky," Ezekial flatly stated. "A trading post will have employees and they're not going to just open it up and let us come in and take over without a hard fight."

"So we find weapons somewhere else," Kanaka said impatiently.

"No! All of you are returning to Ahwahnee and will stay there while I check out Savage's trading post. When I see my chance, I'll steal the rifles."

"Alone?" Kanaka asked with disbelief.

"Yes," Ezekial answered. "Alone."

When the Indians began to protest, Ezekial raised a hand and said, "If a white man steals their weapons, then no harm will come to the Ahwahneeche."

"I do not like this!" Puya complained.

"It is best for The People," Ezekial argued. "I will go to the trading post tomorrow and live among the traders until I find a way to take their weapons."

There was some debate, but not much. The Ahwahneeche were thrilled with their prize of horses and soon agreed to Ezekial's plan. They were ready to leave within the hour.

"Father?"

Ezekial had been sitting, back resting against a tree, eyes closed. Now, he looked up at his son.

"Father, I want to go to this trading post with you."

"You can't do that."

"But why not!" Kanaka protested. "I look . . ." It was an effort for him to add, ". . . part white."

Ezekial heard the pain in his son's voice and he knew that Kanaka was greatly troubled, not only because he was afraid to leave his father among the whites, but also because of his mixed heritage. Up this point, it had not greatly mattered. But now, with the whites a threat to The People, Kanaka had fallen prey to some inner confusions and feelings that he had never before considered.

"Sit down a minute before you ride away with the others," Ezekial said with a smile.

Kanaka was young and impatient, but he sat.

"Listen," Ezekial said, voice low so that his son alone could hear what he was about to say. "I'm not going to be in any real danger. By blood, I am white. I made some pretty dumb mistakes in town and got in a fight, but I'll have a better story tomorrow when I show up at the trading post and I'll be just fine among these Americans. You wouldn't be. I've taught you and Lucy English and Spanish because I always feared that the Ahwahneeche would one day have to deal with whites."

"But why!"

Ezekial rubbed his barked knuckles. "The white people are just . . . well, they just aren't ever satisfied. They're always moving and gobblin' up things. I was the same way when I first came to this valley. I *wanted* more of everything. More money, land, more adventure."

Kanaka drew his knees up to his chin. "I don't understand that."

"No reason you should. And, up until the Po-to-en-cies came to Ahwahnee, there was no need."

Ezekial smiled sadly. "The first few months, I used to pray that my friends would find me in Ahwahnee. That one day, old Joe Walker and his boys would all ride in and I'd show 'em what a pretty place it was and we'd trap out the beaver, then ride away together. That's what I wanted. Until I fell in love with your mother."

"And then?"

"Then I *still* wanted to leave. You see, there was a restlessness in me that took a long, long time to smother. For years, I wanted to show Anina places and things." Ezekial shook his head. "That would have been a bad mistake. Your mother wouldn't have been happy traipsin' around the country with me, puttin' up with city people and all. It took a long spell before I decided to hell with it and that I was happy with things just as they were in Ahwahnee. With your mother, you and Lucy, the hunts and the valley."

Ezekial scratched his beard. "And that's the way I've felt for longer than I can recollect. And I'd have just gotten real old and died a happy man the way things were if the Po-to-en-cies hadn't come along and turned everything upside down."

"What about me?" Kanaka asked.

"I've given it plenty of thought," Ezekial replied. "About you, Lucy, your mother, and all the others. I couldn't come up with any answers. The whites will arrive soon and take whatever they want."

"We'll fight them!"

"Then they'll kill you to the last man, even if I do bring you back a wagonload of rifles," Ezekial said, voice heavy with resignation.

Ezekial let his son chew on this for a moment before he added, "Kanaka, seeing as how you, Lucy, and your mother are the only ones who can speak both English and Spanish, it falls upon you to help me save The People."

"Save them?"

"Yep. You'd need to strike a peace. But, if we kill and steal from more whites, the best words in the world won't save The People."

Ezekial gestured toward the others who were about to leave. "That's why I'm sending you all back tonight. You see, no matter what, we can't let the whites think of us as a bunch of killers and thieves."

Kanaka tried hard to understand.

"There's one other thing I just realized," Ezekial said. "That chestnut stallion is a horse that no one will forget. The others don't stand out and won't be remembered as belonging to Potter. But that liver chestnut horse will."

"What are you saying?"

"We'll keep him awhile to breed the mares," Ezekial said, thinking aloud and hating the road his mind traveled. "But no matter how much we admire that animal, we need to butcher and eat him."

It was plain to see that even Kanaka despised the idea of butchering such a magnificent horse.

"It's time to leave," Ezekial said, pushing himself stiffly to his feet and testing his bad leg to make sure it would support him. "I'm going to ride one of the scrub trade ponies over to Savage's trading post in the morning. That kind of horses don't attract any attention. Son, do you think you can handle the stallion?"

Kanaka rose to his full height. "Yes."

"All right then, but if anything happens to me—not that it will—but if it did, then you'd need to butcher the stallion. Is that understood?"

Very reluctantly, Kanaka nodded.

"Last thing in the world we'd want to happen would be for the whites to find that horse among The People. You can understand that, can't you?"

Again, Kanaka nodded.

Ezekial was not a man to display his affection but, standing there beside Kanaka and thinking about what he had to do in the days to come, he hugged his son and whispered, "You get back as fast as those horses will carry you. Tell your sister and your mother I'll be along before the next full moon."

Ezekial flexed his swollen fingers. "But don't tell 'em about the scrap I got into earlier. Tell your mother that I got along with the whites just like I'd never been away from 'em."

"I will," Kanaka promised.

Ezekial went over to the others feeling much better and sure that he was doing the best thing all around. "I know that everything happened real fast back there, but did anyone think to get Potter's rifle and look for any other weapons?"

Two of the Indians stepped forward, one with Potter's big hunting rifle and a six-shot revolver.

"If you don't mind, Me-cha," Ezekial said, reaching out for the pistol. "I think I'd better take this, but I'll bring it back to Ahwahnee along with a stack of other weapons."

Ezekial studied the moon and guessed there was a good three hours left before dawn. With luck, Potter's body wouldn't be discovered for hours and, by then, Ezekial and the Ahwahneeche would be many, many miles away. No one in Logtown had any reason to think that Potter hadn't just been the unfortunate victim of some murdering horse thieves.

Eleven

Ezekial slept for a few hours and dreamed of Anina, when they first met and later when they first made love under mighty Cho'-lok. His dream was so real that Ezekial shivered to touch Anina's cool, wet skin and taste her mouth. In his dream he was surrounded by mist and the pounding of water-thunder.

Anina was still in possession of Ezekial's mind when he awoke just after dawn feeling very old and afraid that someone would recognize Potter's scrub pony. He had been very careful to choose an unbranded one, but it had an odd-shaped star in the center of its ugly little head and that might be remembered. If the miners associated him *and* the pony with Potter, Ezekial was sure that he would either be shot or hanged. Bo Lamont had talked of "rope justice" and Ezekial had no doubt that it would be brought into play should he be apprehended.

And what, Ezekial asked himself over and over, would he say to Mr. Savage or his traders when he arrived at their post? What kind of imaginary past could he offer that would not expose him as either a liar or an oddity, as he had been judged in Logtown?

It was still difficult for Ezekial to believe that there was no longer a market for beaver pelts. That being the case, what had happened to all the trappers and mountain men that he'd known and called friends?

"Too damn many questions and not enough answers," he muttered to himself, as he washed his face in a stream and then chewed some dried venison. The meat was rawhide-tough but tasty. Swallowing the last of his meat in a big gulp, Ezekial wiped his hands on his breeches and spent a few minutes admiring his new pistol. It occurred to him that, if he was walking into another fight, he ought to at least make sure the damned gun fired.

So he hobbled off a little way from the scrub pony, picked a tree, and raised the weapon. It had good balance and, when Ezekial cocked back the hammer and squeezed the trigger, the gun bucked solidly in his fist. A cloud of white smoke blossomed like a wildflower. The Colt's detonation had a very different sound and feel than that of a flintlock; it was fast, cracked sharply, and the kick was harder. The pistol was also very accurate.

Ezekial examined the place where his slug had bitten into the bark of the pine and then he pried the lead out with the point of his knife. He was impressed by the gun. It wouldn't stop a grizzly, but it sure would straighten a man in his tracks. Ezekial's only regret was that he lacked the powder, ball, and experience to reload. Five shots would just have to make do. If any more than five whites tried to smoke his bacon, Ezekial supposed he'd just have to start cutting with his old reliable Green River knife.

Riding the skinny pony down to Savage's trading post later that morning was like riding the sharp edge of a saw blade. It was near intolerable but Kanaka had required the use of their only saddle to control the high-spirited stallion.

Ezekial took his time and it was almost noon before he rode into view of the trading post and reined in the pony, astonished by all the activity. The post was a huge, multiroomed log building with a long, brush-covered porch. There were six or seven supply wagons and half that many buckboards in the yard. Ezekial did not fail to note that Savage's corral held at least a dozen horses and mules.

On the west end of the post, over near the river, Ezekial saw a big table where two white men sat before a line of Indians. The whites were busily weighing the Indian's gold dust and nuggets before paying them off with worthless glass beads and trinkets. The sight caused Ezekial to bristle until he remembered that he also had traded cheap goods to the Rocky Mountain Utes for prize pelts when he'd first come West.

The miners busily trading at the post were grinning and laughing, in large part owing to the presence of brightly dressed young

Indian women who moved among them, liberally pouring free liquor from big brown jugs. The miners were whooping and slapping the girls on their rumps and trying to grab them. A huge, bearded man in a red flannel shirt watched sternly and Ezekial soon realized that it was his job to rescue the Indian girls from too amorous miners. The few miners not drinking or visiting among themselves were busy hauling goods and supplies out to their wagons.

Between the wagons, a pair of large, snarling dogs stood with teeth bared and hackles raised as several miners enthusiastically egged them to fight. Ezekial noticed three brown chickens resting on the roof of the cabin. Nearby, a fine red rooster crowed from high up in a cottonwood tree. At the far edge of the yard, a noisy collection of Indian women and children squatted in the dust, shouting orders as their men traded away their hard-earned gold.

Ezekial took all this in with a glance while regretting that he had not asked either Bo Lamont or Mr. Potter for a physical description of Mr. Savage. Among the men Ezekial could see, he guessed that the very large, grim-faced man keeping the miners from carrying off the Indian girls was James Savage. Either he, or the gent at the front table paying off the Indians while his friend weighed and poured the gold into a small oak casket.

"Well," Ezekial muttered, shifting his weight uncomfortably on his pony, "here goes."

Ezekial's heels drummed against his pony's washboard ribs and he nervously rode in to take his place among the whites, taking small measure of comfort in Potter's revolver resting behind his waistband. Despite the frenzied activity at the post, Ezekial's size and grizzled buckskin appearance did not go unnoticed. Many eyes turned to gauge him with more than a little curiosity.

"Howdy!" Ezekial called to no one in particular as he dragged his pathetic pony to a halt near the table.

When no one answered his greeting, Ezekial fished up a brittle smile. "Name is Ezekial. I'm hungry and looking for work. As you can all plainly see, my pony is in need of some hay and grain."

"No work here except pannin' for gold like the Indians," the big man in the red shirt that Ezekial had supposed to be Savage replied. "Not unless you want to pick up an ax and split logs."

Ezekial had always prided himself on his ability as a wood-cutter. Kentucky winters could be severe and he'd chopped his share of firewood.

"Might be I could do that," he said in his most ingratiating manner, hoping that his leg would not stiffen before he could earn a good meal.

"Then step down and grab a handle," the man said. "You look as thin and hungry as your pony, which, I will add, ought to be put out of his damned misery."

The other American chuckled but the Indians either did not understand the words or did not appreciate the humor.

"I've ridden a long, hard trail," Ezckial admitted, looking around for an ax and the log pile.

"There's a tall mountain of logs waiting for you directly behind the post," the man with the gold scales said. "Don't worry about your sorry pony—there's nobody here desperate enough to steal him."

"Thanks," Ezekial said over more laughter.

"Hey!" the man called from behind the table. "What's your name?"

"Ezckial," he said, leaving it at that as he tied his pony and then walked around the post to find the logs and the ax.

It turned out that the man hadn't exaggerated about there being a mountain of logs. The pile looked to be as high as the post itself and almost as big around. The logs were already sawed in ten-foot lengths, so Ezekial found a sharp ax and went right to work.

He chopped wood into late afternoon and was grateful for the hard effort because he needed something to take his mind off his own huge pile of worries. The weather was cool, his leg didn't stiffen, and the old, well-practiced chopping motion felt natural. Ezekial had forgotten the satisfaction a man could get from this kind of labor and it brought back some of his better childhood memories. He smugly recalled how his brother, Edmond, hadn't been worth a damn with an ax, a plow, or even a hoe. Edmond had also been worthless with a rifle or a tool. He'd never done enough physical labor to callus his hands and, even though Edmond was almost three years older, Ezekial had always taken pride in outdoing his brother in all things physical.

"Say, you're damned good with an ax, for a long-in-the-tooth buckskinner!" a well-dressed man in his mid-thirties called, emerging from around the corner of one of the many additions to the log trading post.

Ezekial smiled but kept on chopping. "I'm pretty hungry and so is my pony."

The man stopped a few yards away and watched the chips fly for several minutes before saying, "Ezekial, your pony is fed and you can eat all your belly will hold. My name is Jim Savage."

Now Ezekial quit chopping and had a good look at his host. Savage was not anything close to the man he had imagined. The trader was handsome and composed but physically unimposing. Of ordinary height, Savage had long, wavy blond locks that tumbled to his shoulders, hair that Ezekial thought much too clean and pretty on a man. Ezekial imagined Savage would be considered striking by women. His most dominant feature was a pair of ice-blue eyes, which Ezekial found cold. He was also clean-shaven which, by itself, set him apart from most white men on the frontier.

His suit of light brown wool was as well tailored as anything that a St. Louis man would sport. Savage wore a white silk shirt, open at the neck, and a fancy vest with a heavy gold chain and pocket watch. There was a Colt strapped on his hip and many gold and diamond rings glittered on his slender, well-manicured fingers. Ezekial decided that the former horse and cattle thief turned successful Sierra trader bore a strong resemblance to a Mississippi riverboat gambler.

"I still have a long way to go on this log pile," Ezekial said.

"It isn't going anywhere soon," Savage replied. "You did as much in five hours as most men would do in ten. Even so, it would take even a man like you weeks to get it all cut. I got Indians can do that for a jug of liquor or two. Come eat and rest."

"Much obliged."

When Ezekial followed Savage back around the cabin, he saw

that the line of Indians was gone, as were the men at the trading table. There were still quite a few miners and wagons, but no one seemed to be in a hurry and many were just sitting on chairs drinking. The quarreling dogs were gone and the three brown chickens had flown to join the proud red rooster scratching and pecking at the undigested grain found in the fresh manure yard.

"Quite a place here," Ezekial said by way of a compliment.

"Thanks. I've got several posts, but this one is the busiest." Savage spoke to one of the Indian women but Ezekial couldn't catch the words before she hurried inside. Turning back to Ezekial, Savage asked, "Are you a miner?"

"Nope." Savage would have caught him in that lie.

"I didn't think so. I don't see men in buckskins come through this gold country much anymore," Savage said, leading the way into the post. "You look like you've come from far up in the north country."

"That I have," Ezekial said, entering the cavernous trading post and gazing around, thinking that he couldn't remember a general store in St. Louis any better provisioned.

Savage stopped in the aisle and straightened a line of tin cans before he looked up and asked, "You a hunter?"

"I am," Ezekial said, knowing that he had to claim to be something he knew a little about.

Savage grinned without warmth. "Without a rifle or a pistol?"

The question was posed so casually that it sneaked up on Ezekial and slapped him right between the eyes. He said, "I've had some bad luck. Lost my good horses and weapons to the Indians who ambushed and tried to kill me. Twisted my leg runnin' for my life. Maybe you noticed I hobble a mite."

"I noticed. Where'd they attack you?"

"Up north," Ezekial said, wanting to divert the questions away from himself before they went any farther. "You had troubles around here, Mr. Savage?"

"I have," Savage said, skin tightening around his eyes. "I've had a damn sight of Indian trouble in the last few months. A couple of my posts have been raided. A couple of men killed and my livestock run off."

"Sorry to hear that."

"Not as sorry as the Indians will be when I settle with them," Savage vowed. "I always get back what I lose and I get it back with interest."

Ezekial was taller and bigger than Savage, but there was something about the man that spelled danger in spite of his boyish good looks and elegant clothing.

Savage frowned. "I suppose you've heard that we are having a bloody Indian uprising. The governor of California has authorized the formation of the Mariposa Battalion."

"Mariposa what?"

"Mariposa Battalion," Savage repeated. "It's composed of over a hundred volunteers. I'm in command as a *full* major."

Ezekial didn't know what to say.

"Something wrong?"

"No, Major. Not at all."

Savage studied him closely. "Since you've also been attacked but managed to escape with little more than that poor pony and the buckskins on your back, maybe you'd like to join us."

"Your battalion?"

"That's right." Savage looked Ezekial up and down. "You appear to be the kind of a hunter and outdoorsman who could fight Indians on their own terms. And, seeing as you've been robbed, you've got a strong reason to help us round up the hostile Indians and herd them back to a reservation where they'll be tried and brought to justice."

"I guess that I do. Sure, Major Savage. I'll fight."

"Good! Glad you'll be joining us. Now, let's get you something to eat."

"Thank you," Ezekial said, thoughts all ajumble as he followed the trader down the main aisle toward the back of the post.

"This way to my dining room," Savage said, as they made their way between long, narrow aisles stacked high with trade and canned goods that Ezekial had forgotten even existed.

As they made their way toward the rear of the store, miners and employees alike turned to stare at Ezekial, but not one of them had a smile or a kind word in greeting. On the whole, Ezekial thought them about as friendly as a box of badgers. When they passed through a door and entered a huge dining room,

Ezekial pulled up short and stared to see at least a half dozen young Indian women serving food and drink to Savage's boisterous customers and employees seated at tables flanked by rough wooden benches. The girls were all barefoot but wore clean cotton dresses. Their long black hair was brushed to a shine and tied with pretty ribbons. Each girl smiled shyly at Ezekial as they hurried about the large dining room.

"How do you like my kitchen and dining room help?" Savage asked, a playful grin touching his lips.

"They're . . . they're handsome," Ezekial said, choosing the word carefully.

Savage barked a laugh. " 'Handsome'?" he repeated, eyebrows shooting up with surprise.

Before Ezekial could say anything, Savage told the young women what Ezekial had called them in their native tongue. This caused the girls to smile and several even to blush. Feeling caught off guard, Ezekial threw caution to the wind and introduced himself in the Miwok tongue common to the Ahwahneeche as well as the Yokut, Po-to-en-cies, and many of the other local Western Sierra and valley tribes.

It was Savage's turn to be surprised but he recovered quickly and said, arm sweeping across the room, "I married them all, Ezekial. Them and at least ten more."

"Married?"

"That's right! Until a few months ago, when the Indians struck my Fresno post and killed some employees, I actually believed that the best way to keep the peace with these people was to marry their daughters, preferably their *chiefs'* daughters. As you can see, I have an excellent eye and great fondness for pretty girls."

Ezekial felt his cheeks warm. He knew that, in some tribes, men took more than one wife, but that usually happened when girls were sisters and their own husband had been killed, causing them to need a hunter and strong provider. This, however, was an entirely different matter.

"Something wrong?" Savage demanded, his voice taking on an edge. "Do you have something you'd like to say about the practice of polygamy?"

"No sir!"

Savage waited a moment, then he slowly relaxed. "Ezekial, I want you to know that I'm not a member of the Latter Day Saints. I'm just a man who is trying to make an honest dollar and give these girls a better life than they'd have on the Fresno River Reservation."

"Sounds reasonable to me." Ezekial was having trouble with the idea that California Indians were already being subjugated to the confines of a reservation. He didn't know anything about Fresno, but he imagined it would be somewhere in the hot central valley and nothing like his own beautiful Ahwahnee.

Savage took a seat at the table and motioned for Ezekial to do the same. Instantly, girls were at their side with plates, eating utensils, and pitchers of milk. "You know something, Ezekial?"

"No, Major."

"Well, you surprised me when you spoke to my wives in their own tongue. Where'd you learn to do that?"

"I picked it up after living with 'em awhile."

"Where?"

"North a ways."

Savage reached over the table and tore a big hunk of bread from a loaf. He chewed it slowly, eyes riveted on Ezekial. "The truth is," he finally said, "I find you to be a highly interesting man. Most that come through here can't think of anything except gold. That's all they talk about. Gold, gold, and more gold. I get a little tired of the subject, although I'd be the first to tell you that I am a man who keenly appreciates the better things in life."

"I can see that," Ezekial said, eyes pulled to the young women, one of whom even bore some resemblance to his wife and whom he found very attractive.

Savage's eyes tracked Ezekial's. "Her name is Eekino. Her father was an important chief of the valley Chowchillas a few years ago. Unfortunately, a farmer shot him in the back for stealing eggs out of a henhouse. Too bad, huh?"

It didn't sound like Savage cared one way or the other as he stared at Eekino, who blushed and hurried off to what Ezekial supposed was the kitchen.

"You like Indian women, don't you?" Savage asked, not looking up as he forked food into his mouth.

"I'm more interested in food right now. Mind if I just sit and eat?"

"No," Savage replied, not the least bit offended. "I believe a man ought to be allowed to satisfy his hunger—as long as he understands what is the *forbidden* fruit."

Ezekial had read the Bible and he knew exactly what Savage meant. The warning could hardly have been clearer.

Almost a month to the day after he'd arrived at Savage's trading post, Ezekial finished chopping and splitting the great pile of logs. It had been a cold and a stormy month and Ezekial knew that the people would be shivering and hungry in Ahwahnee while he grew harder and heavier working and eating his fill at this trading post. He missed Anina, Kanaka, and Lucy with all his heart but believed that he needed to live among these people in order to understand them. Particularly James Savage, who was a charmer, but who had already displayed rage and an unbridled craving for power over everyone who entered his realm.

Now, like always at their midday meal, Savage took his place at the head of the massive oak table. He alone enjoyed a fine chair, the others sat on rough benches while his Indian wives hovered close, ready to jump to satisfy his slightest whim or request. It made Ezekial seethe and he tried to ignore Savage's oration, which wasn't difficult since the food was excellent. Everyone ate prodigious quantities of beef, chicken, pork, potatoes, and bread. Savage alone drank wine, Ezekial and the other men had either water or milk. Ezekial, not having tasted milk in so many years, drank an entire pitcher at every meal. No one noticed or complained.

When men finally had their fill of food and Savage's endless pontifications, they picked up their hats and thanked their host for the bounty of his table.

"You are welcome," he replied to each of his guests with a peculiar formality that Ezekial thought must be due to some military background or training. He acted far more like an officer than a sutler.

Tonight when it came Ezekial's time to excuse himself, however, Savage raised his hand and said, "Wait."

Ezekial waited, expecting, now that the wood was all chopped, that Savage would tell him it was time to move on and find work elsewhere until he would be needed to join the Mariposa Battalion. But instead, Savage spoke to him in Spanish and, when Ezekial answered in kind, the trader smiled with delight.

"You *are* different," he said. "Ever since I laid eyes on you, Ezekial, I looked through appearances and judged you to be an educated man."

"I can read and write," Ezekial admitted. "But, while my mother tried to make me a scholar, I resisted and finally ran away."

"You speak three languages that I know of—English, Spanish, and California Indian. Any others that I don't know about?"

"No sir."

Savage raised his head and shouted, "Everyone clear out of here. I need to talk to Ezekial in private."

Ezekial watched as Savage's Indian wives scurried out of the dining room. Several employees, still eating their food, grabbed pieces of bread and hurried away. When there was only the pair of them alone in the room, Savage poured his own wine and leaned back in his chair, staring intently at Ezekial.

"Besides being educated, I have noticed that you work hard and keep your mouth shut. You don't talk about yourself at all."

"Plenty of others willing to do that," Ezekial said.

Savage blushed slightly. "Yes, that is so. But who *are* you?"

Ezekial gave the question some thought before he answered, wanting to say no more than was absolutely necessary. "Major Savage, I'm just a man who likes to hunt, fish, and roam."

"And chop wood."

"I can do that, yes," Ezekial admitted with a grin of relief.

"You can also speak the Indian language," Savage said, eyes narrowing. "I can use you."

"Sir, with all due respect, I am getting restless to travel so I'm just not interested in joining a battalion," Ezekial said, deciding that it was time to leave this place and sneak back to Ahwahnee. He placed his hands on the table and started to get up and leave.

"Here," Savage said, digging into his coat pocket and handing Ezekial a couple of large gold nuggets. "That ought to more than repay you for chopping down my wood pile. And it ought to tell you that I can be very generous to people who are willing to take orders and fulfill their promises."

"Thank you."

"Hell," Savage scoffed, "it's nothing! I'm a rich man."

"Yes, Major, I know that."

"What you don't know is that, a couple of months ago, I took two of my wives and a back-stabbin' Yokut Indian named Jose Juarez along with a full pork barrel of gold to San Francisco."

When Ezekial had no comment, Savage said, "Do you have any idea why?"

"To have a good time, I expect."

"Sure!" Savage laughed. "And to show them high-and-mighty Nob Hill folks how a poor man can make more money than they ever dreamed of makin'! We had ourselves a time in that town, I tell you! One night, I was gambling at the Plaza Hotel and lost thirty-five thousand dollars on a single turn of the card. Didn't matter at all to me."

When Ezekial said nothing, Savage leaned back in his chair. "Ezekial, I'll just bet that you never earned that much money in your whole damned life."

"You'd win that bet."

"Listen," Savage said, voice dropping. "I've got *big* Indian troubles and you just might be the man to help me solve 'em. You see, the reason I took that damned Juarez to San Francisco was so that he could see how many whites have come to California. I let him drink it up and have a good time and, when we got back, I ordered him to make sure all the other Indian troublemakers know how powerful and numerous the whites are in California. But do you know what?"

"What?"

"The sonofabitch betrayed me! Behind my back, Juarez told the Indians that the whites were far too soft and rich to bother comin' out to these hills and fighting!"

Savage pounded the table so hard glasses danced. "Can you imagine that! And he told my Indians I was cheating them! Not givin' 'em enough trade goods for their gold! That's why I'll horsewhip Jose Juarez if I don't beat him to death the minute I lay eyes on him!"

It occurred to Ezekial that Savage might have been drinking whiskey before the wine and so he stood up to leave.

"Sit down!" Savage roared. "I'm about to make you a proposition that will make you prosperous."

Ezekial didn't give a damn about money, but he knew that he'd have to pretend otherwise, so he sat. "I'm listening."

"I need a man who can act sympathetic to the Indians."

"Sympathetic?"

"Yeah, at first."

Savage removed a cigar from his coat pocket, offered it to Ezekial and, when the offer was refused, bit the tip off and lit it for himself. Puffing rapidly, he continued. "You speak their language and you're different. And though you won't say so, I think you've lived among the Indians, probably even sampled the favors of their young women, huh?"

Savage winked lasciviously but, when Ezekial showed no response, he plunged on. "That being the case, you'll have no trouble making them believe that you feel sorry for 'em and promise to strike a better deal for 'em. Maybe even a little more freedom so that my Mariposa Battalion won't drive them all down to that hellhole they call the Fresno River Reservation."

"Is it bad?"

"It's very bad," Savage said, nodding vigorously.

Ezekial thought about this for only a moment, then said, "What else are you offering in your 'better deal'?"

"I can afford to be more generous," Savage answered. "But I *won't* sell 'em guns or rifles. Nor strong spirits to whip up their courage."

The conversation had suddenly gotten interesting. "Mr. Savage, exactly what *will* you do for them?"

"Those that behave and live by my rules will enjoy my generosity. I'll take their gold in trade for more beef and even horse meat, which some of them prefer. And I'll trade for good wool blankets and clothes so they don't get cold." Savage chuckled. "Don't you see what that would mean?"

"I guess not," Ezekial said, a little confused.

"It means that *you* will look like a hero and *I* will have an ear among 'em so that I'll know which ones are stirrin' up the pot and causing the trouble. And there's something else."

"What's that?"

Savage leaned closer. "I hear that the Indians have this secret hiding place in the high mountains to the east."

Ezekial's mouth went bone-dry but he managed to stammer, "Hiding place?"

"Yes! I'm sure of it because a couple of Po-to-en-cies told me last month about this valley called Ahwahnee." Savage waved his hand excitedly. "They said it means . . . either valley of the long grass or valley of the gaping mouth or some such thing. Don't matter a damned bit as long as I find it. They call the Indians who live in this place Yosemites."

"Yosemites?" Ezekial couldn't imagine where this word had found its roots.

"Yeah," Savage said. "The Yokuts, Miwok, and others say they have always been the grizzly bear people—the word for grizzly bear is Yosemite."

"No, no," Ezekial said quickly. "It's uzamati."

"Wrong," Savage argued. "It may sound like uzamati, but it's really Yosemite. At least, that's the way we've interpreted the word grizzly bear. Besides. Who cares!"

Ezekial cared! His people were the Ahwahneeche, dammit! But, he had to admit, it was perhaps to their advantage to be wrongly thought of as Yosemites. So, not wanting to anger or educate Savage, he let the mistake pass.

"Maybe," Ezekial whispered, "this Ahwahnee is just a myth. Like the lost cities of gold that were never found in the Southwest."

"No, no!" Savage exclaimed. "Ahwahnee exists and that's where all the bad Indians are going to live and hide, among those damned Yosemites! They're as guilty as anyone for all the killing and stealing and I'm going to make them sorry they ever got involved in all this trouble. I intend to clean 'em all out!"

Ezekial did not trust his voice. His heart was pounding like a mighty waterfall and he felt as if he were drowning.

"Tomorrow, I'm going up to see the governor of California and tell him about Ahwahnee. I'm asking him for authorization to form a battalion, then to capture every last Yosemite and deliver them to the Fresno River Reservation."

Ezekial was choking. "But Major, I don't think . . ."

"Goddammit!" Savage swore, voice cutting like a bullwhip. "I'm not asking you to think! Just find Ahwahnee! Do you understand?"

Ezekial could and did nod, but his mind was too frozen to speak.

"You see, Ezekial, as long as the Indians have a secret place to hide, they'll keep on raiding, killing, and stealing. That's why I *must* find Ahwahnee and root out those Yosemites."

He *had* to say something. "But . . . but maybe the Yosemites aren't even responsible!"

"If they've given sanctuary to the murdering and thieving foothill and valley Miwok," Savage said, "then they *are* guilty!"

When Ezekial stared dumbly at the floor, Savage's voice softened. "Look," he said, "if you can get me the names of the men that raided and killed at my other trading posts, I'll see that they alone hang. But the main thing is, if the Indians have no place to run or hide, they'll give up raising Cain and keep panning gold for me without complaint."

Ezekial looked up. "Why didn't the Po-to-en-cies just tell you the way to this valley?"

"They would have," Savage answered with bitterness, "but I'd caught them stealing horses and locked them up in the back. They broke out and were shot down by my boys as they tried to escape, probably to Ahwahnee."

"I see."

"Good, then find out the best way to lead me and the battalion there," Savage ordered.

Somehow, Ezekial made his mind work. "How much do I get paid to find that hidden valley?"

Savage's eyes slitted like those of a cat. "Oh, how about an even thousand dollars."

Ezekial wasn't sure that he had heard correctly. His confusion must have been evident because Savage raised his glass in salute and said, "That's right, a thousand dollars! Hell, by your standards, you'd be rich. You could buy a ranch or set yourself up for life with a business of some kind. Any kind, long as it doesn't compete with me."

Ezekial raised his own glass. "I guess I could at that."

"As you're probably starting to figure, the *real* money," Savage said with a wink through the smoke of his cigar, "ain't in finding the gold, it's in gettin' it out of the finder's hands into your own. Savvy?"

"I do." Ezekial bobbed his head energetically.

"Then, to us!" Savage said, clashing his glass into Ezekial's almost hard enough to shatter them both. "And to cleaning out the Yosemites!"

Ezekial drank his milk-tainted wine.

"Now," Savage said, looking very pleased, "you claim to be a hunter."

"Yes."

"Who have you hunted for?"

"Myself."

Savage toyed with his wineglass. "I always like to check out a man's background before I do business with him."

"That's not going to be easy in my case."

"Well," Savage said, "who do you know that I might know? We might have friends in common; I know almost everyone in California. I came over the mountains in 1846, arriving just in time to be recruited by Captain John Fremont to help seize this territory from the Mexicans. I worked briefly for Sutter, who found me invaluable. Do you know Sutter and Fremont?"

"No," Ezekial said, shifting uncomfortably. "But I know *of* them."

"Of course you do!" Savage chuckled. "Everyone knows *of* them. Just as everyone in California knows of me."

Savage laid his elbows on the table and leaned forward. "Who do you know personally?"

Ezekial took a swallow of water. The truth was, he didn't know anybody other than Bo Lamont and Potter, who was dead and whose body was probably causing quite a stir in nearby Logtown.

"I . . . I was a friend of Joseph Walker," Ezekial finally said. "I came to California with him ten years before you got here."

"For a fact!" Savage looked delighted to hear this news.

"Yes."

"See," Savage cried, "I just happen to *know* Mr. Walker very well!"

Ezekial knew that he was being dragged into deep water but he couldn't resist asking, "I lost track of Mr. Walker after we arrived. What happened to him and his boys?"

"After nearly freezing to death in the mountains, Joe led most of his men back over the mountains and across the Great Basin along the Humboldt River. Got attacked by the same miserable bunch of Paiutes that attacked you comin' out."

"Wasn't that much of a fight," Ezekial said, remembering the brief skirmish that had quickly turned into a rout for the tough mountain men. "What happened then?"

Savage steepled his fingers. "Well, Joe trapped for the American Fur Company for a while, then he made a pretty good living guiding wagon trains and Fremont to California. When the gold rush started, he struck paydirt right away. He invested and wound up buying a ranch in Monterey. Last I heard, he sold it and was talking about the Arizona Territory."

"Joe Walker had itchy feet," Ezekial said with a smile because he was so relieved to hear that his friends had survived the Sierras and returned to the Bear River country before scattering, as would be expected of free-spirited mountain men.

There was a long pause while more wine was poured for Savage. He sipped it for several minutes, then said, "As a hunter, you must be a very fine marksman."

"I can shoot."

"Good," Savage said, wiping his lips with a napkin after tossing down the last of his wine, "so let's see how good you *really* are."

Ezekial had no choice but to follow the man out of the room, wondering if he'd be given the choice of a familiar Kentucky rifle, or some more modern weapon that would put him at a serious disadvantage. The fact that he had not fired a rifle in over seventeen years also was weighing heavily on his mind. If he had to make a guess, Ezekial supposed that his aim would be quite rusty but there just did not seem to be any way out of this predicament, so he went along.

On the way back out through his store, Savage called for two loaded rifles. Ezekial could only hope that they were well balanced and would offer him some basis of familiarity.

"All right," Savage declared, taking a stand under his front porch and gazing out across his yard. "Select a target."

"Me?" Ezekial asked.

"Sure! You take first shot and, if you miss, I'll take second. But if you do hit your target, then I get to select a more difficult one and have first try." Savage was fairly bristling with the anticipation of competition. "Fair enough?"

"I guess," Ezekial said, as a heavy rifle was pressed into his fists.

He balanced the rifle and saw that it had a percussion nipple just like a Colt revolver. The rifle was much shorter-barreled than his old Kentucky, but considerably heavier. Ezekial took a moment to study and get the feel of it.

"I gather that you haven't shot one of these new Sharps rifles before, have you?" Savage finally asked.

"No, Major, I have not."

"My guess is that the rifle the Indians took from you was a Hawken. Correct?"

Ezekial knew better than to say his last rifle was an old Kentucky flintlock.

"Yes, sir."

"Well," Savage declared, "if you liked your Hawken, you'll *love* this Sharps. It's quite revolutionary, short-barreled enough to be handy on a horse or in the brush but powerful enough to stop a grizzly in his tracks. It's also damned accurate up to seven or eight hundred yards. I've been practicing with these new paper-wrapped cartridges and I can now fire a steady four shots a minute."

Ezekial couldn't imagine such a rate. "Did you say, 'a minute'?"

"That's right," Savage boasted. "But you sound as if you doubt me."

"No, Major, but. . . ."

Savage, impatient with talk, raised his own weapon. "It wouldn't be fair for you and me to compete since you've had no experience with this weapon. Just watch."

Ezekial was more than happy to watch and Savage was equally pleased to demonstrate.

"Never liked those damned squawking chickens that are always waking me up at daybreak," he muttered as his first shot turned the strutting red rooster into a crimson smear and a cloud of feathers.

The hens scattered and Savage jerked the trigger guard down to lower the breechblock and expose the chamber. Ramming a fresh paper cartridge into it, Savage returned the breechblock to the closed position, jammed the rifle to his shoulder, and fired. A racing hen dissolved into another cloud of feathers.

"Take a shot at that lead hen before she flies!" Savage shouted.

Ezekial figured he had nothing to lose since the chicken in question was over eight hundred yards away and running so fast it was mostly off the ground. He had always been a remarkable shot and now, as he pulled the trigger, the powerful weapon belched smoke and fire. Ezekial missed but saw the dirt kick up only inches from the racing hen. A moment later, as the fear-crazed bird launched itself into flight, Savage shot her out of the air and what was left of her mangled pulp slammed into the brush.

"Damn!" Savage swore with a broad grin. "That's shooting!"

"It sure is," Ezekial said, impressed.

"Next time I shoot like that," Savage vowed, "it will be to take the head off one of them thievin' Yosemite Indians!"

Ezekial's smile went sour. He pushed his rifle at Savage and said, "I think I'd best be getting along."

Savage was caught by surprise. "You can stay the night and visit the Po-to-en-cies and the other thievin' Indians starting tomorrow."

"I'd rather not wait, Major."

Savage grinned. "Sure," he said, "I understand. That thousand dollars is already burning a hole in your leather britches!"

"How'd you guess?" Ezekial hissed, as he walked away.

"Oh," Savage called with a laugh, "I know what money can do to a man! And, Ezekial?"

Ezekial slowed but did not stop as he moved woodenly toward the stable. "Yeah?"

"I understand that your old friend Joe Walker is in Sacramento on some business. I'll be sure and give him your best regards!"

Ezekial stopped and turned. "Do that," he said.

"But," Savage added, no longer smiling, "I'll need to have your last name."

"Moses," he said, thinking about how Moses led The People in the desert all those many years. "Ezekial Moses."

"Well, Moses, I'll pass along your regards to the governor and to Mr. Walker."

"You do that, Major," Ezekial said, turning and walking quickly away.

He had not taken ten paces, however, when Savage's rifle boomed and the last hen, which had taken refuge high on a tree limb a good thousand yards away, disappeared in a swirling tempest of blood and feathers.

Ezekial did not look back. He heard some men clapping and cheering for Savage and then he heard the powerful rifle's echo dying against the far brown hills. Minutes later, when Ezekial climbed back on the scrub pony, he was nearly shaking with fear and dread. Kanaka and the other young men had been right, they *had* to have rifles, Sharps rifles like the ones whose thunder still echoed in his ears.

Twelve

Anina stood beside the river watching Kanaka and his friends as they raced the horses back and forth across the meadow. The young men were showing off and occasionally they would fall, but they had yet to suffer serious injury when they landed in the thick brown grass.

Kanaka, as always, was astride the magnificent stallion and was the center of attention. That horse could run faster than any of the others and, when the sun touched upon Kanaka and the stallion late in the afternoon, they were as rosy as the rim of a rainbow. It cheered Anina to hear her son's laughter and, with Ezekial still lost among the whites, she needed cheering. Anina had made medicine with the spirits every day and every night since Ezekial and the young men had gone to steal horses. And when the young men returned without her husband, she had suffered agonies of the mind that left her quaking far into the night.

Lucy came to stand close and she slipped her hand into Anina's hand. "Mother, I am sure that he is coming soon."

"Do you feel his presence?" Anina asked.

"No," Lucy admitted. "But he *is* coming."

"I will go find your father."

"Mother!"

"I am leaving tomorrow," Anina said.

"Have you told Tenaya?"

"No," Anina admitted.

"And what about Kanaka? He will not allow you to go alone."

"Then I will speak to him . . . and to Tenaya," she decided. "But I will not allow their words to stop me from leaving to find my husband."

Lucy's chin dipped and, without conscious thought, she said, "I will go with you."

"No."

"But I *must!*" Lucy cried. "I speak the white man's language much better than you . . . or Kanaka."

It was true. Only Lucy had really enjoyed the lessons and the company of her American father enough to become a good student of English and Spanish.

"I must give this matter some thought," Anina said, already deciding that she would allow her daughter to go, but only a little way beyond the mountain that hid Ahwahnee. No more than a day's walk—not one step farther.

That afternoon, Anina went to see the chief of the Ahwahneeche. Tenaya was unwell and had suffered much sickness during the winter but, as always, he was gracious and a good listener. When Anina had fully explained the reasons behind her decision, Tenaya surprised her by allowing her to leave.

"You must not go among the whites, however."

"Then how can I know if they have my husband?" Anina asked with great concern.

"Seek the wisdom of Ouma and the other Ahwahneeche spirits for your answers," the chief said. "And Lucy must not be allowed to go."

"I think she must," Anina argued. "She alone among us speaks the white man's tongue smoothly."

"This is so," Tenaya said, "for I have heard and seen her and her father speaking that way many times. And Lucy has even taught my grand-daughter, Totuya, some of the white man's words."

Anina knew this to be true. Totuya was Lucy's best friend and a clear favorite of their chief.

"This," Tenaya continued, "is why I think that Lucy must stay among the Ahwahneeche."

"I do not understand."

"If the whites come, who would be left to speak for us?"

Now Anina understood. Tenaya, being wise, was taking into account that Ezekial might already be dead. If that were the case, Lucy would become invaluable.

"I will tell her your words," Anina said, "She will stay."

"And Kanaka?"

"He would not stay," Anina said, wanting very much to avoid her son's having to disobey the chief's wishes.

"Take horses."

"I will walk."

Tenaya thought he should object. After all, Anina was starting to grow old and he knew from the stories told by the young men with American horses that it was many days to the white man's villages. But when he looked into Anina's face, he changed his mind and gave his approval.

The next morning, Kanaka had the stallion saddled and he even had one of the better horses tied on the end of a rope, just in case his mother grew too tired to walk. All the Ahwahneeche came to say good-bye to Anina and it was clear that they were very worried about their medicine woman.

"The young men with horses are going with you," Tenaya said. "It has been decided."

Anina was not pleased. "Too many. Too dangerous. It is better that my son and I go alone."

"They will not take rifles from the trading post until your husband has been found."

Anina knew that she could not stop Me-cha, Coati, Puya, Haw-kee and the others from going with her to find Ezekial. It had all been decided that evening before in the ceremonial round-house or hang-e while she had prayed and made strong medicine to protect herself and her son. Anina knew that her objections would fall on deaf ears.

Lucy was bravely trying to hold back tears and looked so sad that Anina gave her a hug and said, "I will be back soon with your father. You stay with Tenaya and your friend Totuya."

"If anything should happen to all of you," Lucy said in a trembling voice, "I would have *nothing.*"

"You would still have life and Ahwahnee," Anina reminded her gentle daughter. "And you would be the only one who could speak for The People. This is very important to Chief Tenaya, whose wisdom is great."

Lucy straightened and nodded with understanding as she struggled to hold back her tears.

"I *will* return," Anina promised as she set her eyes on the towering rock face near the west entrance of Ahwahnee, whose eyes saw and guarded The People from all invaders.

Ezekial used all haste toward Ahwahnee as he skirted the white man's mining camps strung along the upper reaches of the Merced River. He was gripped with anxiety knowing that, when he didn't report to back to Savage, the man would simply redouble his efforts to divine the location of Ahwahnee. The Po-to-en-cies, bitter at being expelled, could be bought or gotten drunk and they would talk. Any way he looked at it, Ezekial figured that it was a matter of only a few weeks, months at the outside, before the Mariposa Battalion entered Ahwahnee. And when that happened, blood would flow because Ezekial knew that The People would never agree to being driven from their valley and placed on a reservation. Tenaya and all the Ahwahneeche would rather die first.

Ezekial was so worried and preoccupied that he rounded a bend and ran smack into a trio of prospectors coming downriver. They were a weary, defeated lot and obviously hadn't had much luck prospecting.

"Hello there," Ezekial said, wanting to offer just a greeting and then hurry past.

"Better hold up, stranger," one of the prospectors said, blocking the trail. "You don't want to go any farther up this river by yourself."

"Why is that?"

"There's hostile Indians up ahead. They've already killed white men and they'll kill more."

"Where did you hear that?" Ezekial asked, pretending ignorance.

"Hell, man! Where you been? Major Savage and Jim Burney, the sheriff of Mariposa County, they led a party of men up into this country less'n two months ago and got whipped not more than a couple of miles ahead."

This was news to Ezekial. "Are you sure?"

"Course, I'm sure! But Savage and some of the others regrouped and went back and killed a few of 'em."

"Said they killed twenty-three, but I wouldn't believe it."

"Say," another said, "didn't I see you at Savage's trading post about three weeks ago?"

"That's right."

"Then you should have heard about that fight."

"Naw," the shortest of the three explained. "Major Savage, he don't like to remember them first gettin' whipped. That's why he didn't hear no talk about it."

"What Indians were they fighting?"

"Yosemites," the man said with a firm nod of his head. "The murderin' buggers."

"It couldn't have been," Ezekial blurted.

"Well how the hell could you know!" the third man demanded. "Oh, it *was* the Yosemites, all right. You see, they get their name on account of how the other tribes call 'em the 'grizzly bear people.' We hear they kill grizzlies for the fun of it and that they're real bloodthirsty devils."

"That's right," the first man said. "Now, mister, you can go up this river if'n you want, but you won't come back alive."

"You did."

"Yeah, but there's three of us and we only went another half mile or so. No gold up there anyways, at least, not enough to risk losin' your hair."

"Well," Ezekial said, pushing past. "Thanks for the warning, but I'll take my chances."

"You're a damned fool!" one of them called as Ezekial went on up the river wondering just what tribe had routed Sutter and the sheriff. Probably it was the Po-to-en-cies, and maybe it had happened on their way back after being expelled by the Ah-wahneeche.

When Ezekial finally entered the deeper forests miles above the foothills, beyond the last sign of any prospectors, he had the shock of his life when he was met by Anina, Kanaka, and the same young warriors who had accompanied him to Potter's Livery in Logtown.

"I was afraid that you were dead," Anina said, hugging him with all her might.

Ezekial buried his face in Anina's thick, graying hair. "I promised you that I'd return."

Anina stepped back and studied her husband at arm's length. What she saw caused her to bite her lower lip with worry. "You look tired."

Ezekial tried but failed to laugh. "That's because I've been chopping a mountain of wood."

He made a grin and showed everyone his calloused palms. "Haven't worked so hard before in my life."

"There is more," Kanaka said, knowing his father was hiding something bad.

Ezekial shoved his hands deep into his pockets. "Yeah, I'm afraid that there is."

They made camp right where they met, in a stand of cedar by a meadow only a few yards from the great river. A cold, biting wind was blowing a veil of snow over the highest mountain peaks and a storm was threatening. At this elevation, it would rain before the night was over. In Ahwahnee, it might snow and The People, with their poor supply of acorns, would be hungry again, but at least they had a scrub pony to butcher if things became really desperate.

A campfire was lit and the Ahwahnee gathered closely around it for warmth as Ezekial, face haunted by a vision of what lay in store, told them all about James Savage, the trading post, and the Mariposa Battalion that would soon form to enter the mountains in search of Ahwahnee so that they could capture and force the Ahwahneeche down to a reservation. He saw no point in telling them that the whites had even corrupted the word uzamati to become Yosemite and then attached that misnomer to The People.

"He's up in Sacramento right now," Ezekial explained. "And he's expecting me to meet him when he returns with his battalion of volunteers."

The Ahwahneeche asked many questions but, in the end, they all fell silent, stunned by this terrible news.

"Then we must be ready to fight," Puya said. "And we must get rifles now. Rifles like the one that Savage used to kill the birds."

"He's only got about three or four at the trading post and he probably took a couple of those with him to Sacramento," Ezekial said, greatly dreading the idea of returning to steal from the well-guarded trading post. "He's got some Hawken rifles, too."

"How many men are there to guard these rifles?"

"Maybe four," Ezekial said. "But they were probably drunk within an hour after Savage left for Sacramento. I don't expect they'll be much trouble. His wives, mostly Yokuts and Chowchillas, might be another story. If nothing else, they're completely loyal."

The matter of Savage's many Indian wives greatly bothered the Ahwahneeche, who had not realized that one white man could take so many young women. Ezekial could see that Kanaka in particular was troubled by this news.

That night, as they lay around a small campfire, Ezekial tried to talk Anina into returning to Ahwahnee, but she would not listen. He became exasperated and finally said, "If there is a fight and we have to run, how can you escape on foot?"

"I will ride the stallion behind you," she said, as if that should have been perfectly apparent to her husband.

"And if I'm shot!"

"Then I will kill the man that killed you."

Ezekial snapped at Kanaka. "You should not have let your mother come!"

"This was *her* idea."

"It was?"

"Yes."

"Then it is Tenaya's fault," Ezekial groused. "I thought he had more sense."

No one said anything after that. Anina thought she should act hurt, or angry. But she was so relieved and happy that her husband was alive that pretending to be upset was impossible. So, she just held Ezekial until the coals died and they fell asleep in each other's arms.

In the morning, the Ahwahneeche prepared to ride back down to Savage's trading post and steal weapons and more horses. Ezekial, as their leader, was given the chestnut stallion to ride while his son rode double with one of the others. Anina climbed up behind him and laced her arms around his waist. After that, there was little talk and they rode slowly, keeping away from the river, where they were most likely to meet prospectors or other Indians working for Savage. The Ahwahneeche were shocked at how close these people were to the entrance of Ahwahnee. It made their faces pinch with worry.

For Ezekial's part, there was little to say. He felt a crushing sense of doom and found it nearly impossible to speak to his wife, who asked him many questions about the whites and about James Savage in particular.

"He is ruthless, greedy, and determined to become rich and powerful," Ezekial finally said by way of a clipped explanation. "He will stop at nothing to achieve wealth."

"He should be killed."

"If he were, then others like him would come. It would make no difference. You do not understand these Americans."

"I understand *you,* Ezekial Grant."

"Now you do," he said. "But you didn't know my heart when I first came among the Ahwahneeche. I have changed because I have lived so long among The People."

"And there are no good people among the Americans?"

"There are many good people," he countered. "But the whites put more importance on wealth. On . . . on having things."

Anina understood greed. It was not common, but also not unknown among her people.

"For instance, whites believe in the ownership of land."

"Of land?"

"Yes."

"How can someone own that which belongs to all?"

"Well," Ezekial said, unable to answer the question, "they just do. They own land and will not allow anyone else to use it. It's kind of like when the Po-to-en-cies crossed to *our* land or grizzly bear side of the river and their women picked our acorns and their men wanted to hunt our deer."

"But that was different," Anina said stubbornly. "The water or coyote side of the river where the Po-to-en-cies were allowed to come was never ours. In fact, Ouma told me that, many, many years ago . . ."

"Listen," Ezekial said, cutting her off short. "I understand why you disagree with owning land. But you need to understand that the Americans will take what they want and put a claim on it as their own."

"They *cannot!"* Anina said angrily in her husband's ear.

"But they *will!"* he growled before lapsing into a brooding silence.

* * *

That night they waited until all the lights finally died at the post and then waited an hour longer. Unlike before, when they were preparing to sneak into Potter's Livery and steal horses, Ezekial knew exactly where everyone slept and was sure that the post could be entered and looted without great risk. The employees and their wives slept in separate cabins adjoining the post, whose doors were always padlocked at night. Ezekial figured he could pry the door hinges loose and enter with the use of a metal crowbar.

The rifles and pistols inside were also under lock and key, but their storage cabinet would be even easier to open than the front door. Given the number of employees at the post, it was obvious that Savage had not worried much about thieves. Only his gold was really safe because he kept it stored in a huge bank vault that had been shipped around Cape Horn. The vault was six feet tall, four feet wide, and probably weighed several tons—empty. No one was going to pirate it away without a small army of men and a big freight wagon.

"You stay right here and wait until we return," Ezekial ordered his wife. "Promise me that you'll do that."

"I promise."

"There will be some yard dogs," Ezekial said, "so I'll go in by myself and draw them out. When I signal, Kanaka, you and the others walk into the yard. The dogs are accustomed to strangers and they will not bark."

Anina grabbed and squeezed her husband. She could see that Ezekial carried the pistol in his waistband but that gave her little reassurance. Away in the moonlight, Savage's post looked to be huge, ominous, and very bad medicine. It was far larger than even the Ahwahneeche's first ceremonial house. Anina could also see the corrals with many mules and horses as well as a collection of wagons. She had never seen a wagon before and wondered if one of them was like that upon which her own dying but legendary mother, Jacinta, had been carried into Ahwahnee so many, many years ago. Her poor mother must have felt small and lost within such a large thing.

Ezekial did not draw his gun but walked slowly across Savage's freight yard whistling softly an Ahwahneeche song of the mountains that was Lucy's favorite. The dogs, resting on the porch, raised their head and then sleepily climbed to their feet and trotted out to meet him, tails wagging.

"Hemet. Petey. Blue. How you fellas been?" Ezekial asked, scratching each dog in turn.

The three dogs yawned. Ezekial signaled for the Ahwahneeche to come slowly out to greet him and meet Savage's watchdogs. As expected, the greeting was brief before the dogs lost interest and went back to the porch, where they flopped down to go back to sleep.

Ezekial sent half of the raiding party out to the corrals saying, "No mules. Just get the horses. There are saddles, bridles, halters, and ropes just inside that tack shop. Be quiet and take everything as fast as you can. Don't stop until you are well into the trees!"

Me-cha grabbed the front door and pulled hard, making a noise.

"It's locked," Ezekial said, knowing the Indian did not understand. "I need to find a crowbar or something to pry the hinges off the door. Wait here and don't move."

Ezekial went to the blacksmith's shop only a short distance away and quickly found a crowbar used to fix wagon wheels. He hurried back to the front of the post and went straight to work. Unfortunately, the hinges were strong and well set. He grunted and cursed under his breath, fighting the hinges and freezing with dread each time one of them shrilly protested.

"Dammit!" he swore, finally getting the hinges to yield and tear free.

The door was solid pine and heavy but they carried it aside without great difficulty. "All right," Ezekial said, stepping into the dim and cavernous trading post, "just stay close and follow me."

The Ahwahneeche had never seen anything so grand or amazing. They pushed in through the doorway and stood gaping at the ceiling-high piles of goods.

"Savage doesn't carry pistols except a few used ones that he gets in trade," Ezekial said, knowing exactly where a lantern and matches could be found. Once the lantern flared to life, he tiptoed deeper inside, whispering, "All the weapons, including the knives, are locked in this big cabinet, but it'll be much easier to pry open than the door."

Ezekial slipped the blade of his knife between the door's body and the edge of the door, then began to work the flimsy hinges free. There was a small squeak as one hinge protested, but it was followed by a loud crash as one of the Indians accidently knocked a bucket off a peg.

Ezekial's breath caught in his throat. He froze as the kitchen door swung open and pale yellow light flooded across the back section of the trading post and through the dining room. They all ducked, hearts pounding as the squeak of floorboards announced someone's cautious approach. Ezekial didn't know what to do. The glowing lantern was in his hand and . . .

"Eekino?"

The girl blinked like an animal blinded by firelight. When Ezekial stood up to reveal himself, Eekino stared, eyes round with fear.

"Eekino," Ezekial said, speaking to one of Savage's youngest wives in her own tongue as he slowly approached her. "I know that you are loyal to your husband, but we need some weapons and we *don't* want a fight."

"Go away," she said, retreating toward the kitchen.

"I can't do that," Ezekial said. "We have to have weapons."

"Yosemites," she whispered, eyes widening, voice clotting with terror. "Yosemites!"

"Eekino," he pleaded. "You know I'm a friend."

"No friend!" The young woman's lips pulled back from her teeth. "Friend of Yosemite!"

Ezekial was still a good twenty feet away when Eekino threw back her head and screamed. Her cry was shrill and wrenching; the sound jaggedly ripped through the night like the blade of a dull sword.

"Get out of here!" Ezekial shouted to his companions.

"But Father!" Kanaka cried. "We *must* have weapons!"

"There's no time for that! Run!"

Ezekial whirled and ran himself. He saw the shadowy figures of the Ahwahneeche as they crowded in a knot and struggled through the doorway, fighting to escape. Eekino kept screaming and Ezekial heard other voices yelling in sleepy confusion.

"Gawdammit!" Ezekial wailed.

Everything was confusion as they bolted outside and began to run across the yard. Even the dogs began to bark. Kian and Puya had each scooped up an armful of woolen trade blankets and these were spilling from their grasp like leaves caught in a high wind.

"Forget them!" Ezekial yelled, as he shoved both men into a hard run.

To-che, and the others sent to the corrals had successfully captured horses. Ezekial saw them leading some with halters and now stampeding the rest out of the corral toward the trees. Shots shattered the night and Ezekial glanced back to see the flash of muzzle blasts. Being the only one armed and with many of the scattering Ahwahneeche still in sight, Ezekial spun around and returned fire until his Colt was empty, purposefully drawing fire from the post. He began to turn and run when his leg buckled. Before he could straighten, a bullet punched him in the shoulder and Ezekial was knocked spinning to the dirt. He tried to get up but another shot struck him in the arm and the empty pistol spilled from his hand.

After that, he remembered nothing until a bucket of cold water was thrown into his face.

"Wake up, you traitorous sonofabitch!" a man shouted.

Ezekial opened his eyes. His arms were outstretched and he was chained to a pair of stout hitching posts. A second shockingly cold bucket of water roused him fully, which was unfortunate because one of Savage's men kicked him in the face with the toe of his boot. Ezekial blacked out only to be drenched again until he managed to raise his head. His mouth was filled with blood and he spit a stream of it between his legs.

"You were leading the Yosemites, weren't you!" a man named Taggert shouted in Ezekial's face.

"You're crazy."

"That's not what Eekino says! She *saw* the Yosemites!"

"They were . . . Yokuts," Ezekial said thickly.

"You're a damn liar!"

The man swiveled his hips to kick Ezekial again but one of the other men working for Savage jumped in to stop him. "Hold it! If Ezekial is in cahoots with the murderin' Yosemites, then he can lead Mr. Savage and the rest of the battalion to their hidden valley! You kill him, you're going to be damned sorry."

Taggert, face contorted with rage, saw the logic, but he didn't like the idea of backing off. "I got no use for a damned Injun lover! I always knew something about him was queer. I even warned Mr. Savage not to trust him."

"They got away with all the horses!" someone called.

"You kill any of 'em?"

"Hell no! It's as dark as the inside of a cave out under those trees!"

Taggert leaned in, hands on hips. "We know you didn't get any pistols or rifles. But when Mr. Savage learns that you broke into his post and the others took his horses, he's gonna skin your hide with a whip, then tack it up on the side of his post. He's gonna make you die real slow and we'll hear you scream for a week!"

"No, you won't," Ezekial said through his broken lips. "You aren't gonna hear anything out of me."

Tagger lost control again and this time he punched Ezekial in the temple and mercifully ended the night's complete debacle.

Thirteen

"Well now," Savage said as he scowled down at Ezekial. "So it turns out that you were playing both ends against the middle."

Ezekial raised his head. His face was still badly swollen and disfigured from the blows that Taggert had inflicted and his head throbbed.

"What does that mean?"

"It means," Savage hissed, "that you had planned to empty out my rifle and gun cabinet in order to arm the hostiles."

"Why would I do that?"

Savage bent down and grabbed Ezekial's shirtfront. "Don't try to be clever with me, I've no patience for it!"

Ezekial's hands were still outstretched, chained to the hitching posts. They were bluish and numb. "Major," he managed to say, "if you're so sure that you have the answers, why are you asking me questions?"

"Because I want to hear you admit your little scheme. Admit that your intention was to help the Yosemites to rob me in exchange for gold."

"That's ridiculous."

"Is it?" Savage looked Ezekial right in the eye. "I'll bet you that the rivers of Ahwahneeche run yellow with gold. My guess is that you stumbled onto the Yosemites' village, somehow managed to keep them from murdering you, then learned their language and figured out how to get them to pan gold."

"So what?"

"So, in order to save your double-crossing life, you're going to give me all the gold you've managed to steal from those Yosemite Indians and then you're going to lead my Mariposa Battalion into Ahwahnee."

Ezekial shook his head. "Not a chance, Major."

Savage reached out, grabbed a shock of Ezekial's hair, and wrenched his head back. "If you don't cooperate, I'm going to have you hanged, Ezekial whatever-your-name-is."

"Moses."

"Moses, hell! When I went to Sacramento, I looked up old Joe Walker, just like I promised. And guess what?"

Ezekial clenched his teeth.

"When I told Walker your name was Ezekial Moses and that you were with his first expedition to California, he said that the only man in that group named Ezekial had the last name of *Grant!* Joe Walker said that Ezekial *Grant* was lost in a storm along with another buckskinner named Hugh Barrett."

Ezekial shrugged and felt like grinning because he'd been remembered. "Well, how about that?"

Savage's eyes narrowed. "So what happened to your friend Hugh Barrett?"

"I don't know what you're talking about."

Savage's laughter was a cold, mean sound. "Of course you do! And I'll just bet a barrel of gold dust that he's buried somewhere in Ahwahnee."

Ezekial stared at the dirt between his legs. Savage was right about poor Hugh, but he'd be damned if he was going to give Savage any satisfaction.

"You know," Savage continued, "old Joe Walker has done pretty well for himself on a big cattle ranch over near Monterey. I got the impression that you were one of his favorites."

"You're barking up the wrong tree, Major."

"No, I'm not. You see, when I described you, Walker got pretty excited. He told me that you *had* to be Ezekial Grant and he wants you to come work for him in Monterey."

"A job offer from a rich and famous stranger," Ezekial said clucking his tongue. "Well, how about that!"

Savage buried his fist in Ezekial's beard until it hurt. "You know," Savage breathed, roughly shaking Ezekial's head back and forth. "If you cooperate, you actually might live to visit Joe in Monterey."

Ezekial didn't buy that. Savage felt betrayed and wanted him dead. "And, if I don't?"

"Your next visit will be in hell. So what's it going to be, Mr. *Grant?*"

When Ezekial continued to hold his tongue, Savage stood erect and called back over his shoulder toward the crowd of men who had been gathering to form his expeditionary assault against the Ahwahneeche. "Will somebody get me a good, stout rope from inside my trading post!"

A rope was brought and Savage squatted back down in front of Ezekial and tied a slipknot. Demonstrating the knot with a malevolent gleam in his pale blue eyes, Savage smiled and said, "Ezekial, did you ever see a man hang?"

"Yes."

"Good. Then you probably know—that, if a *real* hangman does the job professionally, his knot breaks the victim's neck, causing him to die instantly."

Savage heaved a deep, troubled sigh, but the corners of his mouth were lifted in a smile as he added, "However, when a

simple slipknot like this is used, the victim always dies of stran-
gulation. I tell you, Ezekial, it's a terrible thing to behold though
I admit there is a certain morbid fascination to watching a man
kick and buck on the end of a rope while he is slowly choked to
death."

"I can tell your soul has been seared by the experience,"
Ezekial quipped.

"Oh, it has! As you are aware, it takes a good five minutes for
the victim to fully expire. By then, his face is dark blue, purplish,
really, and grotesquely bloated. He has lost control of his bodily
wastes. There is a terrible stench. His eyes bulge, his . . ."

"All right!" Ezekial shouted, wanting to silence this demon
and buy time in order to save the Ahwahneeche.

"I'll lead your damned Mariposa Battalion to Ahwahnee!"

"Is that a promise?" Savage asked as he dropped the noose
over Ezekial's head.

"Yes!"

The noose tightened. "Just like you promised to earn that thousand dollars I agreed to pay you a couple of weeks ago?"

Ezekial felt weak and sick with fear. Savage was twisted and
the twisted part of him would revel in watching Ezekial dance
at the end of a rope.

"Major, you've got me pegged right. I *was* working both ends
of the string, you and the Yosemites."

"How much gold did they pay you to help them break into
my post while I was away in Sacramento?"

"Not much."

"I'll be the judge of that."

There was a lump in his throat and Ezekial swallowed hard.
"Mind taking that rope off my neck and getting me something
cool to drink?"

Savage removed the noose. "Talk first, then you'll get a
drink."

"The Yosemites gave me about five or six pounds of nuggets
since we didn't have pans to work the Merced for gold dust."

Savage beamed. He tore a pencil and pad of paper out of his
shirt pocket, wet the lead with the tip of his tongue, and began
to figure. "Let's say the Yosemites gave you just five pounds of

gold nuggets. That would be . . . sixty Troy weight ounces. Right now, gold is bringing eighteen dollars an ounce in San Francisco. Seventeen in Sacramento. Okay, let's use the average of $17.50. That means that five pounds—or sixty Troy ounces—of gold is worth . . . $1,050! Not bad!"

"You're sure a lot handier with figures than you are with a rope," Ezekial said drily.

His attempt at gallows humor brought a belly laugh from Savage. When the sutler's laughter died, however, he said, "That's my offer, then. One thousand fifty dollars of the Yosemite Indians' gold in exchange for your dishonorable life. I'll turn you loose in Ahwahnee."

"Agreed."

Savage's lips pulled back from his teeth. "But, this time, there will be no tricks or betrayals. I'm going to keep you under constant guard after we leave for the high mountains. And you are going to deliver those thieving, murdering Yosemites right into my hands. The ones that tried to rob this post will be hanged, the others will be herded like cattle down to the Fresno River Reservation."

"All right," Ezekial said meekly.

Savage leaned back. "If you even *think* about double-crossing me again, I'll personally loop this slipknot around your neck and haul your stinking carcass up to a tree limb. Is that clearly understood?"

Ezekial dipped his chin and whispered, "Major, it couldn't be any clearer."

"That's all I wanted to hear," Savage said, climbing to his feet. "We'll be leaving as soon as I can muster in a full battalion of volunteers. How long will it take us to reach Ahwahnee?"

"Are they greenhorns or veteran soldiers?"

"Volunteers, but good men all. They're doing it out of a sense of duty," Savage snapped. "The men supply their own horses, arms, ammunition, and equipment."

"And their provisions?"

"Paid for by the State of California."

"That's what I figured, Major. You see, I've been watching the ones already here as they file into your post and spend government paper for their provisions." Ezekial winked. "I'd say that you're making a pretty hefty profit outfitting all those 'volunteers,' huh?"

Savage's fists doubled and Ezekial figured that he had pushed the trader too far. But Savage regained control of himself. "How many days to Ahwahnee?"

"Two days' hard ride, Major. Maybe two and a half."

"What about supply and artillery wagons?"

"They'd never make it," Ezekial flatly stated. "The trail is too narrow and washed out by the rain and snow."

Savage's brow wrinkled. "All right then," he decided. "The Mariposa Battalion will enter on horses. I also expect to recover the livestock taken from my corral, along with others that have been missing from all over this foothill country."

"It's been a hard winter up in Ahwahnee, Major. And, as you well know, the Indians like horse meat."

"They'll pay for it by the ounce," Savage said with a chilling smile, "as if stolen horse meat were equal to the value of pure gold."

After the former cattle thief and now appointed major of a battalion of California volunteers marched away, Ezekial figured himself a dead man. The very best he could hope for was to somehow alert the Ahwahneeche to the approach of the Americans and their intention to drive them down to a valley reservation where they would no doubt sicken in the unaccustomed summer heat and die.

If I can just warn them somehow, Ezekial thought, *then I will die a satisfied man.*

That night, to everyone's surprise and displeasure, federal Indian commissioners arrived and assumed full command of the Mariposa Battalion and instructed Major Savage to immediately put his campaign on hold until the Yosemite and other mountain Indians could be offered a peaceful surrender on the condition that they would be relocated to the new Fresno River Reservation.

"Damn!" Savage could be heard to scream in frustration.

For his own part, Ezekial just waited and prayed for an opportunity to get word to the Ahwahneeche that they must not fight but instead must run. He was convinced that their only hope of survival was to escape over the Sierras and rejoin their neighbors, the Mono Indians. If they remained exiled from Ahwahnee until the white men had panned all the gold from her rivers, disfigured her meadows with sharp plows, and chopped down the finest of her timber, perhaps then the whites would move on to ravage another mountain paradise.

In the days that followed, the federal Indian commissioners used coastal mission Indians to seek out the Yosemites and the other Indians who had escaped to the Sierras. These mission Indians had a very simple message: surrender and accept treaties which would subjugate them on the new valley reservations or face certain annihilation.

Ezekial did not know if the Indian messengers actually entered Ahwahnee. He did learn that one messenger reported to the commissioners that the Yosemites threatened to roll great boulders down from their high cliffs to crush any whites foolish enough to enter their valley. The rumor among the Miwok was that the Yosemites also had many witches who would help them destroy the Americans.

The federal commissioners responded by declaring that the Yosemites and any other mountain Indians would have to surrender within eight days, or be attacked.

"The grizzly bear Indians won't come," Savage predicted almost gleefully. "Them feds will see."

Savage was proved correct. Eight days passed without any sign of the Yosemites or their allies.

"All right," Savage railed at one federal Indian commissioner, "you've tried it your way, now we'll do it *our* way!"

Ezekial marked the day he was unshackled and thrown on a horse as being Saturday, March 22, 1851. That's when the so-called Mariposa Indian War began, the day that Savage's damned battalion headed into the Sierras to kill or capture the Ahwahneeche. Each of the volunteers was given fifteen rounds of ammunition with strict orders not to waste it on animals, but instead to use it only to kill Indians.

* * *

Ezekial worried because he did not fully regain sensation in his hands and fingers. The chains had bitten deeply into his wrists and had interrupted the flow of blood, so that his fingers worked but felt stiff. It was all he could do to make a fist. That, coupled with his bad knee, made him think that he couldn't escape even if they gave him a full day's head start.

"It's gonna storm and drench us," one of the volunteers, a soft, heavyset man riding a big draft-type horse complained as he looked up at the sky. "Look at them black thunderheads. I tell you, it's gonna rain and we're going to be slogging through mud soup by this evening."

"Then turn around and go back where you came from," Savage snapped without a trace of sympathy. "Purvis, you volunteered because you wanted some adventure. Well, you're old enough to know that adventure has its discomforts."

Several of the other volunteers chuckled and the heavyset man on the draft horse muttered something uncomplimentary into his beard but kept quiet.

All that day, they followed the South Fork of the Merced out of the low foothills and into the mountains. The terrain grew increasingly steep and, when the rain began to fall, it was cold and drenching. Within an hour, their mountain trail became a gutter of mud, causing both horses and mules to struggle in an effort to stay on their feet. When the rain turned into a driving sleet that punished the faces of Major Savage and his Mariposa Battalion, Ezekial smiled, for it seemed to him a sign from God. It was as if the Creator were angry at these invaders and warning them to turn around.

But the Mariposa Battalion stubbornly pushed on over Black Ridge and Chowchilla Mountain. Sleet turned to snow but they stayed in the saddle and rode late into the night. About three o'clock in the morning, Major Savage finally called a halt and the volunteers, too cold and exhausted even to grumble, pitched their soggy bedrolls down right on top of the fresh snow. Those who could, slept; while those who could not, built small, smoky fires and tried without any success to get warm.

"My scouts have told me that there is an Indian village just up ahead," Savage said, coming over to squat beside Ezekial, who could not stop his teeth from rattling. "We're going to stage a surprise attack at dawn."

"Why are you telling me this?"

"I want to know if the Yosemites are armed with stolen guns and rifles and will put up a fight," Savage explained.

"I don't know," Ezekial said honestly. "Major, this area is called Wawona and is marked by a stand of giant trees. My people don't have a village here so, if there are Indians up ahead, then they're visitors to Ahwahnee."

"I'm sorry to hear that," Savage replied, unable to hide his sharp disappointment. "But it doesn't matter. This is just the first bunch and, after we capture them, maybe your Yosemites will see that resistance is futile as well as fatal."

"What are you going to do, Major, charge in there with guns and rifles blazing and shoot them all down?"

"Hell no!" Savage swore. "I'm not that kind of man. We're going to try and take them alive. I gave my word to Governor McDougal and the federal Indian commissioners that we'd not fire unless fired upon."

"If you round up The People and herd them down to a valley reservation, you might just as well shoot them," Ezekial said with deep resentment.

"I'm going to tell you something, Grant. I know that you don't think much of me."

"That would be an understatement."

Savage's eyes tightened. "I don't have much use for someone who would support the treachery, murder, and thieving of your Yosemites."

"All they want is to be left alone, Major."

"That's not possible!" Savage lowered his voice. "Don't you see what is happening? Have you no grasp of history? I'm the one and *only* chance that the Yosemites have to even survive!"

Ezekial snorted with derision. "You're going to enslave them and you have the gall to tell me you're their salvation! What kind of fool do you think I am!"

"A big fool," Savage said. He waited a moment and then added, "I also believe that you're a murderer."

"What!"

"I think you murdered your friend, Hugh Barrett a long, long time ago and found a trail down from the cliffs. Rather than get into trouble with Joe Walker and his men, you just entered Ahwahnee and made yourself a big man among those poor, ignorant people. You'd have had a rifle and the power to become a chief among them. You see, I know that to be true because of my own personal experience."

"You're crazy!"

"Am I?" Savage leaned forward, eyes boring into Ezekial. "I believe that back during the winter of 1833 you murdered and then buried Hugh Barrett. And now I am convinced that you intend to warn the Yosemites, which will result in getting most of them killed. And I think you then plan to gather up the survivors and become their undisputed leader. Like a Moses, leading them out of the wilderness."

"You're insane!"

"Really? Then why did you first tell me that your name *was* Moses?" Savage clapped his hands together and laughed out loud. "You see! My theory fits!"

Ezekial just shook his head. Savage, perhaps even while leading his battalion through most of this long, freezing night, had concocted a truly bizarre theory. Being a man who craved fame and power, he suspected everyone else of having the same obsessive and destructive ambitions. Talking to him now would be useless. The man was poisoned by his own ambitions.

"So," the major said with a maddening grin of triumph, "you have nothing to say about that, huh?"

"Nothing."

"Good! I *knew* that I had you figured."

Savage bounced to his feet and began to issue orders to prepare for a dawn attack on the sleeping Indian camp just up ahead.

* * *

The attack was amazingly uneventful. The Mariposa Battalion caught the Indian village by surprise and, true to his word, Savage did not allow a single shot to be fired. Instead, the forty or fifty freezing Indians who had deserted the valley and the subjugation of the whites in hope of hiding in the mountains surrendered meekly. To Ezekial, their predominant attitude seemed to be that of gratitude for the food and extra blankets that Savage provided and which were paid for by the Unites States government.

"Bring Ezekial Grant over here!" Savage called when the sun was fully up and the Indians were all huddled together in the snow and surrounded by the battalion.

Ezekial was grabbed and roughly prodded over to Savage who said, "Take a good look. Do you recognize any of these people as being Yosemites?"

"No," Ezekial said. "You realize as well as I do that they're Yokuts, Po-to-en-cies, and other valley Miwok peoples."

Savage asked the Indians in their own tongue if any of them knew Ezekial. When they all shook their heads, Savage looked very disappointed. He next asked the captive leaders where the Yosemites' village was located.

"Ahwahnee," a shivering chief said as he pointed northwest. "Over there."

"How many?"

The chief was an old, helpless-looking Indian now wrapped in a new blanket. "Many peoples," he said, eyes turned down to a pair of sandals that were totally inadequate to protect his feet.

Savage turned to Ezekial. "How many are there, really, Ezekial?"

"About three thousand warriors, all heavily armed," Ezekial said, surprising himself at how smoothly the lie came to his cold lips. "And, if you enter Ahwahnee, they're going to cut you and this bunch of Sunday soldiers to ribbons. Major, I promise you it will be a slaughter!"

His loud warning caused every bit of the anxiety and alarm that Ezekial had hoped.

"Don't listen to him!" Savage called, pivoting to face his volunteers. "I'm sure that there won't be more than a couple of hundred Yosemites and they won't have guns or rifles."

"Don't bet on that!" Ezekial challenged.

Savage, in a fit of rage, grabbed Ezekial's coat front and hissed, "What is the name of their head chief?"

"Damned if I know."

Savage drew back his fist but the captured Indian chief said, "Ahwahneeche Chief Tenaya."

Savage lowered his fist, forgetting Ezekial. The anger drained out of him as fast as quicksilver and he even clapped the pitiful little Miwok chief on the shoulder and said, "Tenaya, huh?"

The chief nodded, as eager as a child.

"Chief, I'm setting you and several of your young men free. Go find the Yosemites . . . or Ahwahneeche, if that's what you call them, as well as any other Indians hiding in these mountains. Tell them to come to me and surrender. If they do this, we will give them warm blankets, food, clothing, and a safe place to live down in the valley, where it is never cold."

The Miwok chief understood. In a few minutes, he selected some of the youngest and strongest among his people and hurried off into the snowy forest.

"I hope they're smart enough to come in peacefully," Savage said after they were gone.

"I'm hopin' those Yosemites are real dumb and want to fight," Purvis said, looking excited. "Major, I know you got your orders, but me and my friends didn't come up here to freeze just so we can nursemaid a bunch of digger Indians back to the Fresno Reservation."

When this sentiment was echoed by many of the others, Ezekial clenched his teeth and grew even more determined somehow to foil Savage and his men, most of whom were just itching to shoot some "diggers" as they called them.

The storm passed that morning and the afternoon became clear and sunny. Members of the battalion took advantage of the chinook to nap and recover from the ordeal of their long and bitterly cold night. The Indians they'd captured had no food, but Savage had plenty and the Indian women were more than happy to cook great quantities of beef, mutton, and potatoes. Guards were posted on the perimeters of the camp but no one, not even Ezekial, seriously expected the Ahwahneeche or any other of the tribes who had taken sanctuary in the mountains to attack.

In the late afternoon, Indians began to appear from the forest in twos, then threes, and finally in large numbers, All of them were shivering and hungry. Savage greeted them in their own tongue and was effusive in congratulating their headmen for their wisdom. He presented them all with new woolen blankets, perhaps a shirt and, finally, hot food. The smell of roasting meat was as tantalizing as bait and Ezekial did not blame the poor Indians for ending the suffering of their families.

Only the Ahwahneeche did not arrive until, just before sundown, several of Savage's Indian scouts rushed into the camp in a flurry of excitement. Before they could even be understood, Tenaya himself appeared.

"Oh, dear God, no!" Ezekial groaned, raising his hands and waving his old friend away.

"Tenaya, run!" he shouted. "Run!"

But Tenaya wouldn't run and Savage, witnessing Ezekial's great distress, threw back his head and howled like a timber wolf serenading a cold winter moon.

Fourteen

When Tenaya recognized Ezekial's battered face, the chief stopped in his tracks and might even have turned and darted into the forest if Savage had not rushed up to grab and then pump his hand in greeting.

"Chief Tenaya, I'm honored that you have seen fit to come and join us!" Savage exclaimed, speaking in the Miwok tongue.

Tenaya's face was a mask showing no emotion. But even at a distance, Ezekial could see that his friend was extremely upset as his gaze surveyed the Americans' camp and then came to rest on the sad collection of fugitive Indians who already had surrendered. They would not meet Tenaya's eyes and kept theirs turned downward.

"Chief," Savage said, leading Tenaya over to Ezekial, "I understand that you and this man are friends."

"What have they done to you?" Tenaya asked, voice shaking with anger.

"I am all right," Ezekial replied. "It is The People who are threatened."

Savage began to protest, "Now that's just not . . ."

"You are Savage?" Tenaya interrupted.

"*Major* Savage. I assume that you are here because one of our Indian messengers has given you my orders to surrender."

"He said we must go down to the valley," Tenaya said. "That the Americans have a place there for the Ahwahneeche to live."

"That's right," Savage replied. "It's a good piece of land with buildings and there won't be any of this damned cold weather. You'll have food and . . ."

"Why are we to be herded to that place like horses?" Tenaya asked. "We do not want to leave Ahwahnee."

"I assure you, it's for the protection of your Yosemite people."

Tenaya's questioning eyes flicked to Ezekial who understood at once the chief's confusion over the foreign word, "Yosemite."

"Chief Tenaya, these whites call us Yosemites," Ezekial said, seeing no point in explaining that they had hopelessly corrupted the Ahwahneeche word, uzamati, meaning grizzly bear.

Tenaya turned back to Savage. "The Ahwahneeche people do not want your protection. We have all we need now. We do not want anything from the white man."

"I'm afraid that what you want is not important," Savage told the chief. "White men will come for your gold, timber, grass, and wild game. This valley belongs to the State of California and you are subject to its laws."

Tenaya's voice sharpened. "Let my people remain in the mountains where they were born, where the ashes of our fathers rest. My people do not want to go to the low country. The Indian peoples who live there will make war on the Ahwahneeche. We cannot live with them. We must stay in the mountains to protect ourselves."

"That's just not possible," Savage said, without a trace of regret.

He turned and made a sweeping gesture with his arm. "Chief Tenaya, look around and see all the Indian people who have come to me for protection. They are now warm in our blankets and no longer hungry because I put food in their bellies. If you bring your people to this place that has been saved for them, they will be happy."

"They are happy *now.*"

Savage was getting impatient. "Ezekial, why don't you talk to your chief in private? Make him understand that I'm not *asking* him to surrender, I'm *telling* him to surrender his people."

"He knows that."

"Then make him cooperate or we will wash the canyon walls of Ahwahnee with Yosemite blood!"

Tenaya stiffened and drew back. He started to turn and leave but Ezekial caught his arm. He had agonized over what he would say at exactly such a moment as this and decided that resistance was futile and that negotiation was the only hope for The People. Maybe . . . maybe his old friend Joseph Walker could even be convinced to intercede on behalf of the Ahwahneeche. Walker had always been a fair and reasonable man and now he was successful, with a good deal of money and influence.

"Tenaya," Ezekial said, believing that some way might be found to cut a fair deal for The People, one that would at least allow them to continue to dwell in Ahwahnee, "it is true that the whites will kill all The People, if they do not surrender, but . . ."

"Will they beat us first," Tenaya interrupted in anger, "as *you* have been beaten?"

"Now wait a minute!" Savage yelled, storming over to confront them. "I didn't kick Ezekial in the face. Taggert acted without authority."

"Chief Tenaya," Ezekial said, ignoring the man's outburst, "The People will not be beaten and this was not done to me according to Savage's wishes. But *your* words are also true when you say that our enemies might try to kill us in the low valley."

"Dammit!" Savage raged, pushing Ezekial aside. "Chief, I don't want to kill anyone, but either you and the Yosemites surrender by treaty or your entire tribe will be destroyed; not one of them will be left alive. Is that clear?"

Tenaya turned his back to everyone. Ezekial could feel his chief's agony as he weighed this terrible decision, one that would determine the fate of the Ahwahneeche. Finally, Tenaya's shoulders slumped and he pivoted to say, "I will surrender The People and bring them here."

"Excellent!" Savage was all smiles now. "Tenaya, you're doing a wise and courageous thing. Truly, you deserve to be respected as the leader of the Yosemites."

Ezekial thought he was going to be ill. He sat back down in the snow, drew his knees up, then rested his head upon them. He heard Savage introduce Tenaya to the volunteers and then say, "And I won't tolerate any shooting or killing of the Yosemites. Is that understood? Old Chief Tenaya here has agreed to bring them in peacefully."

There was some grousing and open disappointment expressed at this news among the young bachelors, but most of the older and married volunteers looked relieved because they were ready to end this brief but eventful campaign and return to their homes and families.

For his own part, Ezekial could not bring himself to raise his head and speak to Tenaya. He agreed with his chief's difficult decision to surrender, but he simply could not imagine his wife or either of his children being rounded up like cattle and penned up on some hot valley reservation, a reservation where they could not breathe the scent of pines or hear the thunder of Cho'-lok and that of the other waterfalls. A valley reservation where they could not even take part in the fall acorn harvest or celebrate the changing of the seasons.

When Ezekial finally raised his head, Tenaya was gone.

"He went to bring in his Yosemites," Savage said. "Is Chief Tenaya a man of his word?"

"Of course!"

"He'd better be and I'll expect your gold when this is over. Afterward, you can go free, but I don't ever want to see you again in these parts."

Before Ezekial could reply, Major Savage turned and marched off through the melting snow.

It was late the next day when Tenaya, visibly exhausted, returned alone from the mountains and explained to Major Savage that the Ahwahneeche had agreed to a surrender. However, because of the recent snowstorm and the deep drifts, his people would not be able to reach the camp for several days. Tenaya said that it was very difficult for the old people and the children to walk out of Ahwahnee.

Savage was disappointed and impatient. Losing his temper, he said he was sure that Tenaya was lying but he could not be certain of this so he had no choice but to wait. Two anxious days passed without the appearance of the Ahwahneeche. Early on the morning of the third day, Major Savage ran out of patience. Convinced that Tenaya had lied and tricked him, he selected fifty-seven of his best volunteers to accompany him into Ahwahnee.

"Chief, you and Ezekial are both coming along. If we're ambushed, you'll be the first to die."

Savage ordered his quartermaster to issue fifteen days' rations and extra warm clothing for everyone going into Ahwahnee.

"We're going to smoke them Yosemite grizzly bears out of their holes," he bragged.

Ezekial tried to convince Tenaya to ride a horse back up the mountain but the chief of the Ahwahneeche stubbornly refused. Right from the start, the trail grew more precipitous and the snowdrifts deepened. On the second day of their struggle, the Mariposa Battalion traversed a deep gorge and fought their way back up through heavy forest to a ridge.

"Look!" one of Savage's Indian scouts cried soon after they cleared the ridge. "Yosemites!"

The sight of the Ahwahneeche was enough to break Ezekial's heart. He saw a long, ragged line of women and children. Anina was out in front helping to break through the deeper snowdrifts while his daughter Lucy struggled along close behind. The weakest of The People were taking advantage of the freshly packed snow trail but were still having a great deal of difficulty.

"How many?" Savage called out to his volunteers even as he raised his finger and took his own quick accounting.

"Seventy-two, Major!" one of the men shouted. "But I think they're all women and children . . . and real old people."

Savage twisted around in his saddle and glared at Tenaya who was gazing down at his displaced and suffering people. "Chief!" he roared. "Where are your warriors! Where are the young fighters!"

"There are no more," Tenaya said, voice hoarse with emotion.

"Bullshit!" Savage screamed. "There *are* more and they damned sure better show up or we're going to hunt them down and kill 'em to a man!"

Savage whipped his horse and sent it plunging forward through the snow. "Come on, men!"

They all went racing ahead, whooping and hollering. Ezekial's greatest fear was that one of the fools would start shooting and the Mariposa Battalion would slaughter Anina, Lucy, and all the others. But, to his immense relief, not one shot was fired as Ezekial dismounted and walked with Tenaya down to greet the Ahwahneeche people.

"Anina! Lucy!" he shouted, hobbling into a run and then embracing his wife and daughter.

When Anina saw her husband's battered face clearly, she struggled to attack the nearest volunteer but Ezekial held on until he calmed her down. Lucy, gentle Lucy, began to cry.

"It's all right," Ezekial said, comforting her.

Right about then, Anina noticed Ezekial's dark and swollen hands. She immediately began to rummage around in her medicine basket.

"You're wasting your time," Ezekial told his wife. "I think that I've lost a few fingers and . . ."

"Shhh!" Anina's own fingers trembled badly as she opened a little wooden bowl wrapped in damp leaves and then began to rub a greenish ointment into Ezekial's hands and fingers.

"What medicine are we using this time?" he asked.

"Buena mujer," Anina replied. "I mixed its ground seeds with the fat of a fox."

When Ezekial kissed the top of Anina's head, she looked up and her eyes glistened with tears. "Very, very strong medicine, Ezekial."

"I love you, Anina, but I sure wish you'd taken our daughter and The People over the mountains to live in safety among the Mono."

"Too many would die in the deep snows."

"Yeah, I guess you're right," Ezekial agreed as he surveyed the old and the very young, all worn down by a hard winter and a poor acorn harvest. It hurt Ezekial to imagine what would become of his people on a reservation with valley Indians, many of whom had become thieves and beggars because of the loss of their own lands and cultures.

"Anina, I hate to say this, but maybe death would have been a blessing for all of us."

"No!" Anina whispered angrily. "You live! We *all* live. Go to this reservation. Return to Ahwahnee next spring. You'll see!"

Ezekial saw no point in telling his wife that, even if Joseph Walker did intercede for the people, it was very unlikely they would ever be allowed to return to Ahwahnee.

"Father," Lucy said, reading his dark thoughts, "We *will* come back. Just like Ouma after the black death."

"You're right, darlin'," he said. "We'll all come back."

Late that afternoon, a camp was hastily made on the exposed slopes of the mountainside. No fire was allowed, but provisions were given to the surrendering Indians. Savage was convinced that Tenaya and the Yosemites were being deceitful and that there were many more Indians still hiding in Ahwahnee.

"He's lying!" Savage growled, not caring who heard him. "But I'm no fool and we *are* going to capture every last one of his murdering warriors! And you're coming with us, Ezekial! You're going to show us their village and talk the young men into a peaceful surrender."

"I'm not their chief," Ezekial argued. "They'll never listen to me."

"I think they will," Savage replied. "And if they don't, then you can show me where you murdered and then buried your old friend Hugh Barrett."

Ezekial chose to ignore the remark. "I just want to know your plans for Chief Tenaya."

"I'm sending him along with the rest of these ragged women and children to the Fresno River Reservation."

"I want to stay with my own wife and daughter, Major."

"Not a chance," Savage snapped. "You'll see 'em again though—if you cooperate and deliver Tenaya's warriors—and that Yosemite gold. Otherwise . . ."

Savage didn't have to elaborate, but Ezekial just couldn't bring himself to leave Anina or Lucy.

"But, Major . . ."

"Mount up, Ezekial, or by God I'll have you hanged in front of the bunch of 'em!"

Ezekial knew that the man wasn't bluffing. He gave Anina and Lucy a quick hug and said, "I'll be all right. Just take care of yourselves."

"You come back, Ezekial," Anina whispered, giving him her little wooden bowl of greenish ointment.

"Father?"

"Yes?"

Lucy leaned close and whispered, "Kanaka, Puya, Haw kee, Me-cha and all the others will *never* surrender and you'll be killed by those men!"

"I'll find a way to escape and join Kanaka. You just stay close to your mother, Lucy. Stay very close!"

Major Savage rode at the front of his men but only until the snow became too deep, and then he relinquished that position and rode near the back of the long column that snaked up the Sierras. And finally, on the morning of Friday, March 27, the Mariposa Battalion suddenly emerged from heavy forest and stood transfixed on what was later to be called Inspiration Point. In the distance ahead, they saw domes, spires, and sheer granite cliff faces dappled with lichen, brush, and snow. Low clouds floated just over the deep, silent valley, their gray shadows sweeping darkly across the heavy blue-green forests and long, golden meadows. The Merced River was a twisted bead of silver that flowed black in some places then foamed white over long stretches of churning rapids. The very air of Ahwahnee was strangely translucent, diffusing sunlight so that it appeared as if the entire valley was surreal and viewed through a sorcerer's veil of frosted glass. Mighty cascades of water thundered hundreds of feet to the rocks below, forming multiple rings of dancing rainbows.

"My God!" Dr. Bunnell whispered with awe. "Just look at it!"

Even Ezekial, who had now lived most of his life in Ahwahnee, stood transfixed by the scenic wonder of the great valley guarded by monolithic cathedrals of snow-dusted stone.

"Ezekial," Savage asked, apparently subdued by the grandeur, "is *this* where you have lived all the years since 1833?"

Ezekial saw no point in further denial. "Yes, and where I'd expected to grow old and die among my grandchildren."

"Why in heaven's name were any of you so foolish as to ever leave this place?"

"The Americans were coming," Ezekial explained. "You would have entered this valley within another year, two at the most. Prospectors always follow a river. It was the river that formed Ahwahnee and it was the river that I knew would finally betray her."

Savage considered this quietly for a moment, then said, "I suppose that is true. Where is the Yosemite's main village?"

"Straight ahead past that great rock and just up the valley."

"I've never seen such a huge block of granite," Dr. Bunnell said, scribbling notes in a pocketbook. "What is it called?"

"We call it Tu-tok-a-nu'-la. To the Ahwahneeche, that means the 'measuring-worm stone.' "

"Bad name," one of the volunteers said. "It deserves something more important sounding."

"That's right," another volunteer readily agreed.

"Like what?" Savage asked.

"El Capitan," someone blurted. "I'll just bet that *is* the captain of all the great rocks of the world!"

There was laughter but, when the battalion rode on, Ezekial noted that the name El Capitan stuck. He didn't care. These invaders could name the great natural treasures of Ahwahnee whatever they wanted. That would change nothing, mean nothing to The People. Each thing here, every rock and tree, cliff and waterfall, had a name and a living presence for the Indians.

"Let's get down there and find those Yosemites!" Savage ordered. "Ezekial, you lead us down to the valley floor."

Ezekial dismounted and led his horse down the steep, narrow trails, which were deep and slick with snow. Many times his horse fell or had to be whipped to force it through the deepest drifts and it took them until late in the afternoon to finally reach the meadows of Ahwahnee. By then, everyone was far too exhausted to appreciate the sunset and how it made the faces of the cliffs blush like shy maidens. Savage ordered his men to dismount and make camp. That night, they built a fire in clear defiance of the Yosemites, but Ezekial saw that they still kept a guard.

At the end of the evening, a lively discussion ensued as to what they should call this valley.

"It has a name," Ezekial said. "Ahwahnee."

"I say we call it Yosemite, after the Indians who live here," another man argued.

"And I say damn the Indians! We should call this Paradise Valley!"

The argument went on for nearly half an hour and finally, someone suggested that a vote be taken.

"How many for Ahwahnee?"

To the accompaniment of laughter, only Ezekial raised his hand.

"You don't even count, Indian lover!" a man groused.

"How many for Paradise Valley?" Savage asked.

Several dozen raised their hands but, when the name "Yosemite" was posed, it was easily the favorite.

"All right then," Savage decreed. "Yosemite, it is! Now post the guards around the camp and the horses. Everyone to their bedrolls because we got a long day ahead of us tomorrow."

Ezekial was bound, the rope cutting into his already abraded wrists and ankles.

"Why this?" he demanded to his guard.

"The Major ain't about to take any chance of you slipping out and helping your friends ambush us, or maybe even just escape."

Ezekial eased back upon his bed of pine boughs and gazed up at the heavens. Were the Ahwahneeche aware of their presence? Would they attack the Mariposa Battalion with nothing but bows and arrows? Such an attack would be suicidal, but Ezekial knew that his son and the other young men were desperate enough to do anything.

All night long, Ezekial fretted about what tomorrow would bring. He tried hard to sleep, to listen to the familiar sounds of Ahwahnee that should have brought some comfort. But now, those sounds were muffled and what he heard instead of crickets, owls, and waterfalls were the sounds of soldiers snoring and of their picketed animals stamping their hooves.

At first light, Savage was up and rousing his tired men. They ate a cold and hurried breakfast, then mounted and started up the valley even as the sun was peeking over the eastern rocks. No one spoke. The men had their guns and their rifles in their cold fists and their faces were stretched and drawn with fatigue and fear. There should have been deer feeding in the meadows but there were not. Even the birds had no song for the advancing Americans.

Despite the chill of the early morning, Ezekial was covered with sweat and his heart was racing. Koom-i-ne, the principle village of the Ahwahneeche was just up ahead at the end of the long meadow.

"Look!" Savage hissed. "Smoke!"

The smoke was so faint that even Ezekial had trouble distinguishing it against the slate gray of the cliffs.

Savage raised his gloved hand and then made a forward slashing motion. The Mariposa Battalion booted their weary horses into a trot and rifles were raised and ready.

Ezekial threw back his head and bellowed a warning. He

kicked the flanks of his horse and would have charged forward except that one of the volunteers pistol-whipped him across the back of his skull. Lights flashed before Ezekial's eyes and he clung to the neck of his galloping horse as Savage and his men raced past and into the village.

It was deserted. Ezekial, dazed and with blood streaming down his neck, raised his head, looked around, and began to laugh hysterically as the volunteers galloped back and forth through the camp, looking for someone to shoot. But the Ahwahneeche had escaped.

"Godammit!" Savage bellowed in frustration. "We must have just missed them! Their campfires are still smoldering."

He rushed over to Ezekial and dragged him from his horse. "Where did they go!"

"How would I know," Ezekial spit. "Up into the mountains."

Savage threw him to the ground and began to order out small patrols. "I want ten men to follow the river, five men to go up into that canyon and more details to search for tracks. Now!"

The volunteers broke into search parties and went galloping away. Hours later, however, they returned empty handed.

"We saw tracks," one of the leaders admitted, "but we couldn't follow them."

"Why not!"

"They were up above us on trails so steep and narrow we would have been picked off like pigeons!" the man swore. "I volunteered to bring in the hostiles, not get wiped out, Major."

Late that afternoon, they did find *one* Yosemite. She was an old woman named Yetani. Yetani was so old that she claimed to have known Jacinta, Anina's mother and wife of the Spaniard. She was one of a very few who could describe the time of the black sickness to The People. And, like Ouma, she had hated her exile among the Mono Indians and had vowed never again to leave Ahwahnee.

"Who are you and where are your people hiding?" Savage demanded, after being led into a small cave where Yetani had taken up her lonely vigil.

Ezekial thought Yetani's cave at the base of a rockslide very much like the one where he'd taken refuge after his nearly fatal plunge into Ahwahnee.

"Old woman, who are you?"

Yetani did not even raise her head in reply but kept stirring a thick acorn porridge. Savage whirled on Ezekial. "Is she deaf or crazy?"

"Neither. She understood you, Major."

"Then why won't she speak?"

"She doesn't like your tone of voice," Ezekial said. "I think you're going to have to be nicer."

Savage blushed with anger, but lowered his voice and even made a feeble attempt at smiling. "Old woman, I must know where the others are hiding. If you tell us, I will give you much food and many gifts. Blankets and beads."

Yetani whispered something and Savage leaned closer. "What did you say?"

Yetani finally looked up from her porridge. "I said you must go out and *hunt* for them."

"But . . . but where?"

Yetani shrugged. "This is my home and I am too old for climbing rocks so I stay and eat."

"She *is* daft!" Savage growled, pushing out of the rock cave and placing his hands on his hips as his eyes raked the landscape. "She's not going to be any help."

The brutish man named Purvis had a ready solution. "We could drag her out of that damned cave and persuade her to . . ."

"No! Just leave her alone. Nothing could make her tell us anything. Isn't that right, Ezekial?"

"Yes."

Savage shielded his eyes and studied the rock cliffs. "They're up there and they're watching everything we do," he said. "I can *feel* them watching us."

"So how do we get 'em?" Purvis asked.

"I don't know," Savage replied. "It's a waiting game now, but time is on our side. We have their village, their stores of food, and their shelter. Maybe we'll get another late winter storm and they'll either freeze or starve to death up on those cliffs."

Savage turned to Ezekial. "You remember how that feels, don't you."

"I remember we slaughtered horses and roasted them," Ezekial said, unwilling to give this man even a little satisfaction. "And that's also what the Ahwahneeche will do. But there's one big difference, Major."

"What's that?"

"They *like* horse meat."

Savage's hands knotted but he did not strike Ezekial before he turned and marched back toward the Indian village.

"I don't know why he just doesn't have you shot," Purvis groused, following along behind.

"Maybe," Ezekial answered, "he just admires my style."

"Ha!"

"Then you figure it out," Ezekial said before he said goodbye to old Yetani and followed the major back to camp.

Each day Savage sent his scouts out to hunt for the Ahwahneeche but each day they came back with the same report: no sign of the Indians.

After several more days, the approach of another storm left Savage with no choice but to leave the valley and hurry back out of the mountains. His rations were almost gone and he knew that he had lost.

"Tomorrow morning, just before we leave, we're going to raze this entire village," he vowed. "We're going to burn every damned acorn, piece of leather, reed basket, hut, and granary and leave them nothing. If we can't draw them out with the promise of peace, then, by God, we'll *starve* them out!"

Savage marched over to Ezekial. "I want that gold you're hiding and I want it now."

"Not until I'm back with my family and about to be released."

"Maybe," Savage said, hand falling to the gun on his hip, "I should just put a bullet in you and be done with it."

"That's your choice."

"I was sure that gangrene would kill you by now," Savage told him. "You'd be dead, if not for your woman."

"Anina's medicine is powerful. Dr. Bunnell thought I was a goner, too."

"Well," Savage said, "now or later, it really doesn't matter, because we both know that you *are* a dead man."

It snowed hard that night in Ahwahnee. The wind howled and the volunteers were forced to take shelter either in u'-ma-chas or in the ceremonial house where they kept fires blazing. Ezekial was tied outside and it was clear that he was expected to freeze to death before morning.

Ezekial knew cold. He'd suffered it before and he was quite sure that its death was merciful, far better than being strangled by an improperly knotted noose. He was not afraid, but he could not stop shivering until long after midnight when he grew drowsy and then felt a deadly warmth seeping into his body and spreading to his outer extremities. The sensation was very much like that which occurred when a man consumed too much strong liquor, only freezing to death did not cloud the mind. His eyelids grew heavy and Anina came into his dreams once more.

"Ezekial!" an urgent voice called. "Ezekial! Wake up!"

Ezekial's head rocked back and forth and he felt force but not pain as Dr. Bunnell slapped his face over and over.

"Leave me alone," Ezekial muttered.

"Dammit, wake up, man!"

Finally, Ezekial opened his eyes. The snow was still falling and a long rut through it marked where the doctor had dragged him out to the very edge of the camp.

"What do *you* want?" Ezekial asked.

"You're getting out of here," the man said. A few quick slices with a knife freed Ezekial's hands and feet.

"Why?" Ezekial asked. "Why . . ."

"I regard life as sacred and, as a boy, I grew up in Michigan and had a number of friends among the Chippewa Indians. I've had a bellyful of what's happening here."

The words formed slowly on his tongue. "You . . . have?"

"Indeed I have!" Bunnell dragged Ezekial to his feet. "Can you stand and walk?"

"I . . . I think so."

"Here," Bunnell said, giving Ezekial badly needed support, "I'll help you over to a horse that I've saddled for you. I'm not sure that escape is even possible on such a bitterly cold night."

Ezekial could scarcely get his limbs to operate and he was having difficulty forming any kind of thought. But when they reached the saddled horse and he laid his forehead against its warm shoulder, he really began to understand that he was about to taste freedom.

"Thank you," he mumbled thickly.

"You're welcome."

Dr. Bunnell hoisted Ezekial into the saddle and said, "By the way, what *was* that greenish ointment that saved your hands and fingers from gangrene?"

"My wife said it was buena mujer, I think it's a flower."

Bunnell frowned. "I doubt it's called that in my botanical books."

"Anina mixed its ground seeds with the fat of a fox."

"The . . ."

"Yes, the *fat* of a fox. It's very powerful medicine, Doctor Bunnell."

"After seeing what it did for you, I can't dispute that claim." Bunnell handed Ezekial the reins and even bent his fingers around them so they would not drop away. "Mr. Grant, I'm sure that you realize Major Savage will order you to be shot on sight."

"Yeah."

"When I was a boy in Michigan, they killed almost all the Chippewa too," Bunnell said, stepping back from the horse. "I couldn't do anything then. Maybe I can, in some small way, do something now. But, if you are captured, please . . ."

"I'd die before telling 'em about this."

"Thank you and . . . good luck."

The doctor spanked Ezekial's horse on the rump and it lowered its head into the driving snow and began to walk up the valley, toward Pai-wai'-ak which, to the Ahwahneeche meant "white water" and which was already being called Vernal Falls by the Americans. And beyond it was the great Yo-wei'-yee or "twisting water," renamed Nevada Falls.

Ezekial clung to his saddle horn, head bent down, eyes closed. He knew that the horse would travel only far enough to find shelter in the heavy trees until the storm passed. That was enough for now if he could just hang on and make it through this night. Because, somewhere up above, Kanaka and his friends would be waiting, and Ezekial knew that he could find them.

Fifteen

Three days after her escape from the Americans, Anina still could not believe that the nine guards assigned by Major Savage to escort The People to the reservation had been so careless. Almost all the Ahwahneeche had been able to slip away into the foothills one dark night and then make their way back to Ahwahnee. And now, with thundering Cho'-lok suddenly in view and with the perfume of the pines and incense cedar filling her senses, Anina and The People were almost home again. It was good because they were all very weak from the cold and hunger. The only thing that kept Anina from being filled with joy was her constant worry about Ezekial, Kanaka, and all the other men who had never consented to surrender and who had left this valley to hide in the higher mountains, where Savage and his volunteers could not catch them.

The grass of this last meadow was deep and brown, but Anina could see the tiny green shoots of grass and wildflowers straining up to feel the warmth of spring. In another few weeks, a month at the longest, this meadow would be transformed into a giant bouquet of grass and wildflowers. There would be a colorful profusion of lilies, daisies, azaleas, and mountain violets, all ready to sway with the warm breezes of a Sierra spring.

Lucy suddenly stopped, grabbed her mother's hand, and cried, "Look what they did to our village!"

Anina jolted to a halt. She stared at the desolation, finding it impossible to believe her eyes. She even wiped her forearm across her face but there was no mistake, Koom-i-ne was no more. There was nothing standing, not their sacred hang-e or their u'-ma-chas or precious granaries.

Women who had been too weary even to speak moments before now threw back their heads and began to wail. Their high keening filled the deep mountain canyon with echoes of sorrow.

"Mother?"

Anina forced herself to start walking again and even to say, "We are home, all will be well."

"But without food . . ."

"Ouma and the spirits of our gods and ancestors are all around us. We *are* protected."

Anina glanced over at Chief Tenaya, who also had escaped with his family. He appeared to be in shock as he stared at what had been their ancestral home. All the people were staring, some with tears on their faces, others in a daze.

"Come," Anina said, pulling Lucy along toward the blackened and silent site of the village.

Soon, they were sorting through the charred rubble, picking up barely recognizable objects burned beyond any practical usefulness. Lucy sobbed when she discovered a few piles of spiderweb ashes that marked the remains of her baskets. Old women gnashed their teeth and knelt in the snow and blackened ash to weep with bitterness. Every last hut, as well as their beloved ceremonial house, had collapsed into piles of ashes. Only a few bone awls and needles, stone knives and grinding bowls were salvageable.

Anina's granary had held her last precious store of acorns. Like all the women, she had carefully husbanded her hoard to last through the final days of winter until more food could be found. Now, all were gone. Her cylindrical chuck-ah had been about eight feet tall and constructed of slender poles of incense cedar. A large, round rock had served as the floor of the granary so that the acorns at the bottom did not spoil with dampness. Inside the chuck-ah had been a basketlike web of deerbrush tied at the ends with willow stems and fastened together with grapevine. Anina had taken much pride that the interior of her chuck-ah had been lined with dry pine needles and wormwood, the latter to repel mice and insects. Now, however, the chuck-ah was just a low mound of char and ash.

"What are we going to do?" a woman cried, tears streaming down her round cheeks. "My children are *hungry!* They are cold and tired. We have no food!"

Anina had no answer. She looked to Tenaya, but his face was slack with exhaustion and defeat. For the moment, even Tenaya seemed unable to accept this latest tragedy.

Fighting down her own panic and despair, Anina sought comfort in the beauty of Ahwahnee, turning to gaze up at the cliffs and peaks, the sun and the blue sky. Where, she wondered, were Ezekial, Kanaka, and all the others now so desperately needed to help feed The People.

Anina listened for their voices but heard nothing. Her eyes touched every little crevice and rock, but saw nothing. Anina fought back her own bitter tears. The thunder of Cho'-lok pulled at her and Anina turned to stare at the waterfall. Suddenly, Ouma's beloved face appeared on the mist and Anina's chin snapped up and her lips moved with a question for her mother.

Where have they all gone? she asked. *Do my husband and son yet live? Did Savage and the Americans slaughter them all with rifles so that their spirits are buried now by deep snow? Where are the men, my mother?*

The waterfall spoke loudly, but Ouma's misty vision melded into a pale glimmer of rainbow.

"Mother, look!" Lucy cried, her voice cutting through Anina's reverie. "Roasted acorns!"

Anina shook herself, then turned to see her daughter madly digging into the mound of ashes that had been her granary. Hearing her excited cries, everyone rushed over to surround Lucy and watch as, from under a hard, black crust, Lucy began to scoop out big handfuls of scorched and roasted acorns.

"Mother!" Lucy said happily as she collected a great pile of acorns into her lap, "there are still many, many!"

The other families clapped their hands with joy and then hurried away to their own charred granaries. Dropping to their knees, whole families began to dig furiously and were soon scooping out the last of their own precious stores of acorns.

Anina began to crack the cold but well-roasted acorns and eat them. She was so hungry that she had trouble separating out the bitter but nutritious acorn meat. "See," she cried, pounding Lucy on the back and giggling like a girl when her mouth was stuffed full, "my mother still protects us and we will not starve before spring!"

During the next few days, the air warmed and the snow melted while The People worked hard to accumulate food. The salvaged acorn harvest, which had been poor to begin with, would not by itself sustain them. More food must be found before the spring harvest of bulbs, wild greens, and berries. Tenaya and his sons, as well as the old men, worked hard to fashion crude bows and arrows. To no one's surprise, they soon managed to kill several deer. The youngest boys and girls successfully rigged snares for birds and rabbits. Nothing went to waste.

Anina had an even better way to feed the people. She and Lucy went down to the river and worked three days from dawn to dusk in order to construct a series of small fishponds. At night, they brewed a strong concoction of soaproot, which they added to the water of their ponds. Within hours, fish began to float belly-up in the water and were easy to retrieve.

"We must steam them well to draw out the poison," Anina warned the hungry but much-encouraged people.

At the end of the first week, starvation was no longer a threat to the returning families. And then, like a gift from the Ahwahneeche gods, Ezekial and Kanaka appeared, riding double on their proud but now thin chestnut stallion, galloping and whooping across the meadow, with the other men charging behind.

That night, a thin, sickly horse was slaughtered, but there was enough meat on its bones to make a good feast. Around an immense bonfire, The People sang, danced, and offered their thanks to the spirits for reuniting the Ahwahneeche.

"You have suffered," Anina said, clasping Ezekial's hands in her own. "But your hands have healed."

"Because of your medicine," he assured her.

"How did you get away?"

"There was a doctor among the Americans who helped me escape. On that night, the spirits brought the snow to fill my tracks. Savage and his men could not find me although I was only a short distance away, watching them hunt and burn our village. It was very hard to watch, but there was nothing I could do to stop them."

"My husband, now that Savage and his men have failed, will they leave us in peace?"

"No," Ezekial said quietly. "They'll come back as soon as the weather warms. They won't give up."

"Why!"

"They just can't."

"Then what can we do?"

"Steal rifles and fight them to the death. It's either that, or gather all the food we can carry and leave Ahwahnee."

"To go . . . where?" Anina asked, trying to smother her rising desperation.

"I don't know. Over the mountains, I guess. But we both know that it's hard living in the desert after living here so long."

"I will *never* go back among the Mono!" Anina vowed.

"It may come down to that, or the Fresno River Reservation, or . . . or death."

"Then death," Anina proclaimed.

"And what about Lucy and Kanaka?"

Anina tried to speak, but couldn't. Instead, she used her forearm to wipe away unbidden tears.

During the early spring of 1852, the Ahwahneeche worked furiously to prepare themselves for the return of the Americans. The women and girls collected food, smoked fish and meat, and searched for edible greens.

The men hunted and fashioned new weapons. Late into the

night Lucy wove baskets that would carry food out of Ahwahnee if The People were forced to escape back into the high mountains.

The days grew sunny and the meadows filled with flowers but, even so, there was no joy in Ahwahnee.

The whites returned two moons later. Tenaya's three sons, who had gone hunting together to the entry of Ahwahnee, were captured by Captain John Boling. One of them managed to escape but the two youngest were tied back to back in the middle of camp. Fleet-footed Yokut messengers were sent into the mountains to find Tenaya and demand that he give himself and his Yosemites up or his sons would be shot.

"I must surrender," Tenaya said when he learned of the capture of his sons.

"Maybe I can help," Ezekial offered.

"How?"

"I could speak to Savage. He still wants my gold and . . ."

"No Savage," Tenaya said. "Yokuts say he did not come this time."

"That's odd. I guess there must have been another strike or another raid on his trading posts to keep him from invading Ahwahnee again," Ezekial said. "But I know this Captain Boling. He's a reasonable enough man. I'll speak with him."

"No!" Tenaya insisted. "It is my place to go to my sons, not yours."

"Then we should *both* go," Ezekial said in a tone of voice that left no room for argument.

When Anina heard that Ezekial was going down to try to reason with the Americans, she became very upset. "You escaped them once," she said. "They will kill you this time."

"Not if I can help it."

"Please," Anina begged. "Don't do this."

"It'll be all right," Ezekial pledged. "Tenaya doesn't speak their language and, if Savage isn't there, how will he be heard and understood?"

"The Yokut will translate his words for the Americans."

"He does not trust them," Ezekial said, "and with good reason. They will say whatever the Americans want to hear."

"Then *I* will go with you."

"No." Ezekial placed his hands on Anina's shoulders. "Please, trust me. The Americans *need* to make a treaty with the Ahwahneeche. They will not kill me and risk losing the chance for a peaceful surrender. I expect they know that we can go up into the mountains, where they'd have a devil of a time capturing us. That's the last thing they want."

"It seems like we are always saying goodbye," Anina said. "And each time you go among the whites, I am afraid. . . ."

"Don't be. I understand them. I can take care of myself and Tenaya."

Anina held her husband and whispered her goodbye.

On the way down to the valley, Ezekial and Tenaya heard rifle fire, and shortly after that, one of Tenaya's teenaged sons raced breathlessly up to intercept them. A bullet had furrowed a deep crease across his scalp and he was almost incoherent with grief.

"They have killed Muaga!" he cried. "They have killed my little brother!"

Muaga had been Tenaya's youngest and most favored son. When the chief heard this news, he broke down and wept. Ezekial didn't know what to do or say so he waited. When Tenaya finally composed himself, the chief ordered Ezekial to escort the wounded boy back up to Anina, who would make medicine for his wound.

On his way back up to Ahwahnee, the wounded boy, whose name was Ein-ee, told Ezekial how he and Muaga had been captured and tied to an oak tree. Shortly after that, the guards had pretended not to notice that they loosened and then untied their bonds. When Muaga and his older brother had broken and run for cover, the guards had enjoyed their murderous target practice. Ein-ee, older and a faster runner, had escaped with the scalp wound, but Muaga had been shot in the back.

When they returned to the Ahwahneeche with this sad news, The People became very upset. They could not agree on what to do. Everyone looked to Ezekial for leadership, but he did not want to make the important decisions. However, he alone understood the Americans and so he was the obvious choice to decide what should happen next.

"I will try to free Tenaya," Ezekial finally announced.

"At what price?" Kian asked. "They want us *all* to surrender."

"I know that," Ezekial said as he prepared to leave. "And I also know that, if we refuse, they might decide to kill Tenaya."

When the Mariposa Battalion saw Ezekial's familiar face, they wanted to shoot him. But Captain Boling, perhaps under orders from Major Savage, spared his life. He was dragged into the camp where Tenaya was being held and then bound to an oak tree.

"I guess that you know what's in store for you, huh?" Boling said.

"What about my gold?" Ezekial was thinking about a slipknot. "I can't believe that you'd hang me without getting paid first."

Boling was a tall man with a thick beard. He made a face. "Savage talked to the Yosemites, who admitted that there was no gold in Ahwahnee. "While he was there last time, he had some of his Indians pan for gold and they came up with nothing."

"Maybe they just looked in the wrong places," Ezekial said.

"Maybe, but Savage doubts it. The truth is, the major is convinced you lied about that, too."

"And so," Ezekial said, "I suspect that he's ordered you to strangle me on the end of a rope."

Boling looked surprised. "Did Major Savage threaten to hang you?"

"In so many words, yes."

"Well," Boling assured him, "you can relax. We are under orders from the governor and being closely watched by federal Indian commissioners. We are not a mob of vigilantes. We operate according to law."

Ezekial's bitterness spilled out. "And the law says that you can shoot an escaping boy in the back?"

Boling flushed with anger. "That was an accident!"

"But I'll wager it will happen again."

Boling drew a deep breath to compose himself. "I can't promise you that it won't. But you are an intelligent man who should be able to understand that we are trying to *protect* the Yosemites."

"You can do that best by leaving them alone."

"That's unrealistic and we both know it," Boling snapped impatiently. "There are fortunes to be made in Ahwahnee. Nothing can stop progress now that this valley has been discovered."

Ezekial knew this was the sad truth. And if Ahwahnee was lost, then so were its people. "Captain, confining the Ahwahneeche to a valley reservation will destroy them."

"Better they die warm and fed on a reservation than shot down by a horde of gold seekers." Boling cocked his head a little to the side. "Wouldn't you agree?"

"No," Ezekial said, "I would not."

"Let me put it this way," Boling said, trying hard to be patient. "So far you have aided the enemy of the State of California. However, we are now offering you a rare opportunity to become a *peacemaker*. And who knows, maybe the Yosemites or Ahwahneeche, as you call them, will one day be allowed to return to this beautiful valley."

Ezekial scoffed at the notion. "Captain, be honest. Even you don't believe that."

"It's not likely," Boling admitted, "but anything is possible."

Ezekial glanced over at Tenaya, who seemed lost in his grief and disinterested in any conversation. "What happens now?"

"Help us and you'll save the Yosemites as well as yourself. We're giving you a chance to walk away clean."

"Until James Savage catches and hangs me?"

"He's out of the picture, at least for now," Boling said bluntly. "The governor himself is aware of you and what is going on here, so use your head and cooperate. I don't see how I can put the matter any plainer."

"Captain, killing our chief's son makes everything much more difficult. Tenaya now has every reason to hate you and your volunteers."

Boling sighed with resignation. "Don't you think that I know that? I can't restore the boy's life, but I have asked my best interpreter to convey my deepest apologies and regrets. The individuals who fired upon those two escaping boys will be reprimanded."

"They ought to be put before a firing squad!"

"It is not for me to say. I'll present the facts to the Indian commissioners and they will make recommendations to a judge, who will decide if the guards in question are to be brought before a court. They are *not* soldiers, Mr. Grant, but civilian volunteers."

Ezekial was outraged and shaking with anger. "We both know that they'll get off with nothing but a damned slap on the wrist."

"Be that as it may," Boling said, "it is the best that I can do. Would you please again tell your chief that we did not mean to kill his son, whose name I understand was Muaga."

"It would be a waste of my breath."

"Tell him!"

Ezekial told the chief what Boling had said. As he spoke, Tenaya's face grew dark with fury and, finally, he exploded, shouting as Ezekial translated his exact words, "Kill me, sir captain! Yes, *kill me,* as you killed my son; as you would kill my people! Tell your soldiers to kill this old chief because you have killed the child of my heart."

Boling started to turn but Ezekial grabbed his arm and held him. "It was one of *your* guards who shot that man's boy in the back, at least hear him out."

Boling nodded with reluctant agreement and forced himself to listen as Tenaya regained his composure and continued, his voice thick with hatred. "Captain, sir, you may kill me, but I will follow in your footsteps. I will not leave my home but will always be with the spirits among the rocks, the waterfalls, in the rivers and in the winds; wherever you go I will be with you. You will not see me, but you will feel the spirit of this old chief . . . and you will grow cold."

Boling glanced sideways at Ezekial. "I guess your chief has put a curse on me, huh?"

"That's right."

"Very well then. So be it. We will forever be enemies." The captain turned to leave but checked himself. "Where *exactly* are the rest of the Yosemites hiding?"

"In the high mountains."

"You're going to lead me to them or I'll have no choice but to have you shackled and escorted to the reservation where you will be kept in confinement. Now, which is it to be? Cooperation, or imprisonment?"

Ezekial weighed these bitter options. He had no doubt that Boling's orders were to capture the Ahwahneeche at any cost. And, if surrender of The People was inevitable, then Ezekial wanted to be sure that he was with Anina and Lucy when it happened so that he had some hope of protecting them.

"All right," he said, *"you* win."

"No," Boling corrected, *"you* win. Where are the renegade Yosemites?"

Ezekial pointed up a deep canyon they called Py-we-ack. "That way."

"Then let's march," Boling said, turning to issue orders to the battalion.

Several hours later, they came to a small, quiet lake. "What is this little lake called?" Dr. Bunnell asked as they rested their horses beside its shores.

"Ah-wei'-ya," Ezekial replied.

"And what does that mean?"

"It means 'quiet water.' "

"Pretty name," the doctor said, "but no one will remember it. "I think we will call this one Mirror Lake. Is that all right with you, Captain Boling?"

"That's fine," he answered. "I don't care. Name everything, if you will. All I'm interested in is capturing the last of the Yosemites and getting back to my own family."

"Mirror Lake it is," Bunnell said, scribbling in his ever-present writing pad. "And that big half rock, Mr. Grant. What is it called?"

"Tis-se'-yak. It means 'woman turned to stone'. There's an old Ahwahneeche legend that says that . . ."

"Half Dome." Bunnell mused, not listening. "We'll call it Half Dome."

Ezekial clenched his jaw in silence.

"Captain!" one of the Indian scouts called as he hurried into camp. "Captain Boling, the Yosemites are surrendering!"

"Where!"

"Look!"

Everyone looked up to see the Ahwahneeche appear from the trees. Anina and Lucy were near the front and Ezekial was sure that they had surrendered in order to see him again. But Ezekial also noted at once that Kanaka and many of his friends were not among these people.

Where had they gone? Over the high, snowy mountains to the dry side to live free among the Mono? Ezekial had a million questions to ask his wife and daughter.

"Anina!" he bellowed from beside the tree where he was chained. "Anina, Lucy!"

They shouted his name and came running with arms outstretched. For the first time since he had surrendered, Ezekial was glad that he was still alive.

Sixteen

Ezekial would never forget his first impression of the Fresno River Reservation. He was riding his chestnut stallion, with Anina hanging on behind and, had the circumstances been different, Ezekial thought his wife would even have enjoyed being astride a horse. Lucy was content to walk with the rest of The People being escorted by the soldiers across the lower foothills.

"The Fresno River Reservation is just over that rise," Captain Boling said quietly. "I'm afraid that it isn't as pretty a place as your Ahwahnee, Chief Tenaya. But it'll be warmer in the winter and you won't go hungry, the federal Indian commissioners will see to that."

When Tenaya made no response, Boling reined his horse over to ride beside Ezekial. "I suppose you're wondering what's to happen to you, huh?"

"The question has crossed my mind."

"Well, I don't know the answer myself," Boling admitted. "You'll be brought before Major Savage and the commissioners who will decide your fate."

Anina, who knew a good bit of English, hugged Ezekial tightly and cried, "No hanging!"

Ezekial regretted he'd told his wife about hanging. "Don't worry, darlin', I'll never let them hang me."

A few minutes later, they topped the rise and drew rein. The volunteers, saddlesore but eager to celebrate bringing in the greatly feared Yosemites, wearily grinned at each other as everyone stared at the crowded reservation situated alongside the slow, muddy Fresno River.

"There it is," Boling said, pointing, "the new Fresno River Indian Reservation. We've got Yokuts, Chowchillas, Po-to-en-cies, and many other tribes living together in peace with the white man."

Ezekial couldn't bear to look at Tenaya, Anina, or any of the Ahwahneeche because he knew that their reaction was one of shock and despair. The reservation confirmed his worst fears. It consisted of only a few cabins and supply shacks, along with a half dozen dirty canvas tents. Crowded haphazardly around these structures were several hundred brush and timber huts where Indians families huddled in languid squalor. There were no horses to be seen other than a few that belonged to the whites, and someone, most likely an Indian commissioner, had ordered about twenty acres of river bottom to be plowed and planted with corn. But whoever had ordered the fields planted had failed to supervise the digging of workable irrigation ditches. The uneven rows of yellowing cornstalks had already been abandoned to roaming cattle, which had eaten and trampled all but a few withered stalks. Had this been an Ahwahneeche village, the women would have been working and even singing, the men talking and the children playing. But here, almost everyone sat quietly and mostly alone.

Boling lifted his reins and said, "I know it doesn't offer a good first impression, but, at night, those people gather around their campfires and seem to enjoy themselves. And, Chief Tenaya, things will seem better after your Yosemites get accustomed to the ebb and flow of this reservation life. I'll even try to get you a piece of land with shade trees along the river. I know your people like trees and we want to make this transition as pleasant as possible."

Ezekial thought the comment so ridiculous as to not even warrant a reply.

"Come on," Boling said, giving up his attempt to make this seem better, "let's get this over with. Your people are tired, cold, and hungry. They'll be fed and issued new clothing. They'll be far happier after they're situated on their own ground."

"No," Ezekial said, "they won't."

Boling opened his mouth to speak, then changed his mind. His company of men, as if sensing the growing outrage of The People, drew in tighter around the Yosemites to prevent any from suddenly deciding to make a run back to Ahwahnee. But Boling had been right, The People were too exhausted and weak from hunger and their forced march to resist being herded down to the already-hated Fresno River Reservation.

When those in the camp saw the approaching Yosemites, people came to their feet to watch stoically while scores of dogs charged up the hill, barking furiously at the new arrivals. Some of the dogs were big and ferocious, causing several of the Ahwahneeche women to snatch up their children and hold them protectively aloft, screeching at the pack of howling mongrels.

Boling shouted at the dogs but, when they kept coming, he twisted around in his saddle and bellowed, "Volunteers, drive those dogs off from these people! They're scaring them!"

"How we supposed to do that, Captain?"

Boling lost his composure. "Shoot the leaders! That ought to teach them a lesson."

Purvis, always ready to use his gun, shouted, "Yes sir!"

Purvis and about twenty of the men drew their revolvers and spurred on ahead to intercept the charging pack. When the Indians from the camp realized that their dogs were about to be shot, they also began to charge out of the reservation camps. Ezekial thought the sight of all those onrushing Indians and barking dogs was enough to unnerve even seasoned soldiers.

The volunteers, finally realizing that everything was about to be thrown into a state of absolute chaos, spurred toward the dogs, firing their guns but mostly missing. One dog, however, a huge, shaggy black-and-white fellow, was struck in the foreleg and began to somersault across the grass.

"Stop it!" Lucy cried, breaking from the rest of her people and running into the melee. "Don't kill him!"

"Lucy!" Ezekial shouted, sending his stallion racing forward with Anina hanging on for dear life. "Lucy!"

"Hold your fire!" the captain shouted. "Hold your fire!"

The dogs scattered and retreated except for the one that had been shot. When Lucy reached this huge animal, she threw herself down by its side and hugged its neck.

"Lucy!" Anina exclaimed, jumping off the stallion, falling hard, but then getting up and hurrying to her daughter's side. "Lucy, get away from that animal!"

But Lucy had no intention of abandoning the wounded dog, which had already begun to lick her bare knee.

"Dammit!" Boling shouted as both he and Ezekial rushed over to the pair. "Girl, you could have gotten yourself killed just now!"

Lucy glared up at Boling. "This is bad!" she cried. "All bad! No good will come of this. No good!"

Captain Boling flushed with anger. "Grant, you'd better teach your daughter some common sense if you expect her to survive on this reservation."

Ezekial joined his wife and daughter. Lucy's cheeks were wet with tears and Anina was pale and shaking.

"It's going to be all right," he assured them. "Everything is going to be all right. But Lucy, darlin', the kindest thing we can do for this suffering animal is to put it out of its misery."

She looked up at him, brown eyes pleading. "No, Father, please!"

"Shhh!" Anina hushed as she placed her hand on the dog's leg and squeezed hard enough to stop the hemorrhaging. "Husband, you don't know anything."

Ezekial was stung by his wife's rebuke. "I'm no medicine man, but I do know that this big fella's leg is shattered and there are already far too many vicious dogs on this reservation."

"Get my medicine bag," Anina ordered. "Hurry!"

Ezekial couldn't believe it. "For this . . . this wolf?"

"Now."

"Damn," Ezekial cursed as he went over to his horse and untied his wife's precious store of herbs, bandages, and medicines.

"What is she doing?" Boling demanded.

"They're going to fix the damn dog's leg, Captain."

"Why?"

"Because that is what their hearts tell them to do," Ezekial said, realizing he sounded like an Indian rather than a white man.

Boling's hand dropped to the pistol strapped to his hip. "This is foolishness! That dog is vicious and has caused trouble before. I'm going to shoot it!"

Ezekial's hand clamped on the captain's wrist. "I don't think my wife and daughter can take any more heartaches today. Just let 'em nurse the dog, Captain. It won't hurt and it might make things easier for their minds if they've both got some healing work to do."

Boling finally nodded and pulled free. "Very well," he said. "I see your point. But don't blame me if it takes a bite out of them."

"Captain, it's *licking* them." Ezekial dredged up a tolerant smile. "Now, I suspect you've got a lot more to worry about than a three-legged wolf-dog, haven't you?"

"Yes," Boling admitted, "I'm sure that I do. But stay in plain sight with your friends. Major Savage and the others are very anxious to have words with you."

"I'm not going anywhere without my family and the Ahwahneeche people," Ezekial promised.

An officer galloped out to meet the newcomers and, after riding off with Captain Boling and having a long, animated discussion, the man hurried away. Boling, actually looking pleased, spurred back to rejoin his men and their captives.

"We've got a place for the Yosemites beside the river, only about a half mile west."

"But there is already a group there," one of the men said.

"I know and that was the point of our discussion," Boling said. "The people there now are in the process of being moved."

"That's not going to make things easier."

"To hell with it," Boling snapped. "We're to wait here until those people are out of the trees, then go in and take over their camp."

Ezekial was upset, but there was nothing to do except watch as the Indians who had taken up a choice piece of ground amid some cottonwoods were displaced. It was almost four hours before the order came that the Ahwahneeche were to be brought forward.

"Who were they?" he asked the captain as they rode into the trees and the Ahwahneeche collapsed in exhaustion near the abandoned but still-smoking campfires and the usual discards left by people when they are forced to break camp and move quickly.

"I don't know," Boling admitted. "Some branch of the Miwok. Maybe you can go ask them but my guess is that they are a collection of peoples. There's been a lot of . . . well, displacement and turmoil the past month or so."

"Yes," Ezekial said, helping Anina down from their stallion, "there has been."

He was about to dismount himself when a pair of soldiers came galloping into their new camp. "Captain, orders are for you to remain here with your men and help these Yosemites to get settled in and fed while we escort Mr. Grant to headquarters!"

Boling wearily climbed down from his horse. "You heard him."

Ezekial took a deep breath. He looked down at Anina and said to his wife and daughter, "Don't worry. I'll be back soon."

"I want to go with you."

"Sorry," one of the guards said. "Just him."

Anina grabbed his hand and held it tight. "I will pray to Ouma now," she said. "She will protect you."

"I know that." He shifted his attention to Lucy and the big wolf-dog, with its front leg swathed in bandages and splinted with sticks. "How's his leg?"

"Mother says that it will heal."

"Good. He's a fine-looking dog and would probably be good eating."

"Father!" Lucy scolded.

Ezekial forced a thin smile. "Only kidding, darlin'. Just kidding. Don't let him eat *my* supper, though. I'm as hungry as he looks."

"Mr. Grant," the older of the guards, a man with a round red and freckled face said. "They're waiting."

"Sure."

Lucy rushed up to touch his hand and then Ezekial reined the stallion away and the two guards flanked him as they headed back toward the big gray tent.

"Boys, do either of you know what they have in mind for me?"

The two guards shook their heads.

"No awards, money, or citations, I'll wager," Ezekial said, twisting around in his saddle and gazing back at the pathetic and smoky little Ahwahnee camp under still-barren cottonwood trees.

The sight of his wife and daughter standing alone at the edge of the hated camp filled Ezekial with despair. He fought back the sting of tears and leaned forward in his saddle, eyes shut and gripping the horn as they walked their horses across the reservation.

"You all right, Mr. Grant?" the younger of the two asked.

"No," he answered, "but there's nothing that either of you can do to fix what ails me."

"They got the prize camp," the older guard said. "We thought they'd look a whole lot happier."

"Sorry that you're so disappointed," Ezekial said acidly.

The pair of guards turned away and said nothing as they rode along.

Ezekial tilted his face up to the sky. In another hour, darkness would fall. He decided that this valley sky was not to his liking. Its color was too pale and washed away. The sky over Ahwahnee was a far darker color, sometimes almost indigo at this hour.

"Mr. Grant!"

Ezekial's chin snapped down and he saw the little attorney that he'd befriended only a few months earlier in a mining camp.

"Mr. Grant!" the attorney said. "I wanted to have a word with you before you met them."

"Mr. Lamont." The sight of the attorney caused a glimmer of

hope to spark in Ezekial's breast. It was obvious that the man had come to befriend and counsel him in this crisis.

Bo Lamont approached the sweat-crusted stallion and extended his plump hand. They shook and the attorney said, "I am sorry that we meet again under these circumstances."

"Me, too."

"You know," Lamont said, stepping right up to the stallion, "I have always prided myself as a man who is willing to repay a kindness."

Ezekial leaned over and whispered, "I can't tell you how glad I am to hear that. I'm going to need your services, Mr. Lamont. You see . . ."

"Please," the little man said. "Mr. Grant, I've come out here to tell you that you are beyond legal counsel."

Ezekial straightened in his saddle. "I don't understand. I thought you . . ."

"This is an exceptionally handsome stallion," Lamont said, stroking its muscular neck. "A very striking animal but one that will be easily recognized." Lamont's voice fell to a confidential whisper. "Do you *understand,* Mr. Grant?"

Ezekial *did* understand. The attorney was telling him that he was going to be judged a killer and a horse thief and there was absolutely nothing that would save him from a hangman's noose or a firing squad.

"Let's go!" the senior guard ordered. "Now."

Ezekial did not trust his voice but said in his softest voice, "Mr. Lamont, I see that you are still wearing that very fine revolving six-gun. Can I examine it again?"

"I'm afraid that would be out of the question," Lamont said, with a resigned shake of his head, "but I do seem to remember hearing that this animal possesses exceptional speed."

Ezekial glanced back at the Ahwahneeche camp and he could still see the outlines of his wife and daughter. He felt the attorney touch his pantleg and he turned to say, "That is true."

"Well, then?"

Ezekial's hand shot forward and he snatched Lamont's new Colt revolver from the man's holster. In the next instant, he righted himself and booted the stallion forward into a hard run.

He clamped a hand around the saddle horn. He glanced back and saw that the two guards had drawn their own revolvers and were firing at him. The stallion, weak and weary, seemed to be running in deep sand but Ezekial liked his chances until a bullet struck him in the back and almost knocked him out of the saddle.

"Ezekial! Ezekial!"

He turned sideways and saw Anina running toward him. He started to rein toward her but then realized that would put her life in jeopardy, too. So he sawed on the reins until the stallion's head was pointed toward Ahwahnee and he yelled at it to run faster.

Another bullet bit into the cantle of his saddle and a third struck Ezekial just below the rib cage and he sprawled forward across his chestnut's neck. He lost consciousness for a moment but, just as he started to fall, Ezekial roused himself as the stallion charged into the middle of another Indian camp.

People scattered, screaming and shouting as Ezekial clung to the chestnut. The stallion's ears were laid back and, with the sound of its fiery breath filling Ezekial's ears, the great horse ran like a demon, trampling anything in its path. The gasping animal clipped and toppled a hut and then sailed over a campfire before it finally reached open space and ran away from the sunset toward distant, purple mountains.

Ezekial clung to the horse and tried to think. If he were in normal possession of his mind, he would hide his tracks. But what good would that do? Savage, Boling, all of them knew Ezekial was going home to Ahwahnee.

Like everyone else on the reservation, Anina had been startled by the sudden volley of rifle fire. Her head had snapped up from the great dog whose leg she believed still could be saved.

"Mother!" Lucy had cried.

They had seen Ezekial bent over, practically lying across the stallion's neck as it charged through a neighboring Indian camp. They both had begun to run after him but the Americans overtook them quickly and forced them back to their new river camp. That very hour, as the land was turning dark, they were marched to the tent and brought before Major Savage and the white officials.

"I will speak to them," Savage announced to the other officials. "I speak their language."

Boling stepped forward. "That is not necessary, Major. We are both well aware that Grant's wife and daughter both speak *our* language."

Savage glowered at Boling but the three Indian commissioners stepped between them and ordered Anina and Lucy to take seats.

"No," Anina said.

Behind a long table, three Indian commissioners leaned forward, their faces tired and sallow in the lamplight. The oldest of the trio smoked a pipe and Anina found its tobacco not to her liking. The man said, "First, I want to make very sure that you are Ezekial Grant's wife and that this girl is his daughter."

"Yes."

"Are you aware that your husband killed a man for the horse he was riding?"

Anina clamped her jaws shut. She did not know what to say to these men. All she could think about was the last vision of her husband, back colored crimson with fresh blood, hanging to the neck of his horse.

"You must answer the question," Savage growled.

In response, Anina located a big stain on the side of the canvas tent and tried to draw herself into the very core of its darkness.

"What about the girl?" one of the commissioners asked. "Ask her!"

"But she's only a child," Boling protested. "No more than fourteen or fifteen."

"Ask her!"

Lucy could feel their eyes and she was frightened but filled with hatred. She let the hatred rule her mind even as her hand reached out and gathered in the hem of her mother's dress.

"Girl, where is your father going?"

Anina saw that her mother was lost in a trance, or maybe she had even become one with the spirit world. Lucy desperately wanted to do it, too.

"Your father was a horse thief," someone was saying. "He

killed a man. Your people have killed and robbed many innocent white men. Your father was no good. He was . . ."

Lucy could not do it. Mind whirling, wanting to scream and run, her thoughts batted around and around the room and then she closed her eyes and thought of her new dog. She could see its face. The wolf-dog smiled and then Lucy felt the wetness of its tongue licking her hand. Wolf-dog had such strange and beautiful eyes. Maybe, Lucy thought, Ouma had come to this terrible place in the form of the dog so that she would again be near The People. Lucy almost smiled, for it would be good to tell her mother of this thought.

Or maybe the dog was her father. Wolf-dog had a bad leg, her father had a bad leg. The dog was big and seemed ferocious at first, but when it had been hurt, goodness along with the suffering had radiated from its brown eyes.

That is it, Lucy thought, *my father, not Ouma, has come to be with us in Wolf-dog!*

"Is she crazy?" one of the commissioners asked more in shock than concern. "The child is smiling!"

"I don't know," Boling answered. "She is a *strange* child. She almost got herself killed running to save a dog. Maybe she *is* crazy."

"Get them both out of here!" the oldest commissioner ordered in disgust. "We'll learn nothing from either of them."

Savage stepped forward. "This is the Yosemites' *medicine* woman, their shaman. She must be guarded constantly and not allowed to escape."

"This woman is important?"

"Very," Savage assured the gathering. "Perhaps even more important than Tenaya himself."

"But why?"

"Because," Savage explained, "if we keep her here and under constant guard, the Yosemites will have no more medicine and their spirit will be broken."

The commissioners exchanged thoughtful glances. The senior one said, "But this is assuming that all of the Yosemite have surrendered."

"Yes," Savage admitted.

Everyone turned to look at Captain Boling, who finally dipped his chin and said, "I . . . I believe that is true."

"If that's the case," one of the other commissioners argued, "then why are there hardly any young men of fighting age?"

"They probably went over the mountains into Nevada to join the Monos," Savage said when Boling had no answer. "At least, that's what some of my faithful Indians have told me. And I say, good riddance!"

"Yes," the senior Indian commissioner said after a long pause, "we barely have enough food and money to take care of those we have now. So yes, good riddance indeed!"

"Then you agree that we should keep this pair locked up and a constant guard posted on them," Savage said, clearly wanting to establish the point so there could be no doubt about it later.

"Yes, yes," the commissioner said, looking as if he were suddenly bored with the whole business. "At least keep them both locked up for the next couple of weeks."

Savage slapped his hand down on the table hard enough to spill water from several of the glasses. "They must be kept under constant guard for several *months,* sir."

"All right, Major! Now, has a company been formed to run down that killer and . . ."

"That won't be necessary," Savage said. "I was watching his escape through my field glasses. There is no doubt that Ezekial Grant was mortally wounded."

"Then send out a patrol to retrieve the body, Major."

Savage grinned wolfishly. "With great pleasure, Commissioner. With *great* pleasure."

Incessant waves of nausea and dizziness crashed into Ezekial like rolling ocean waves striking rock. He had had enough presence of mind to jam Lamont's six-gun into his coat, and then he clung to the stallion and just let it follow its own lead as long as it was racing back to the mountains. Ezekial was struggling to breathe. It was as if *he* and not the stallion were running.

On and on they galloped until even the stallion could run no more. Ezekial let it walk, and, in the last moments of sunset, he finally took the time to study his wounds. Blood was oozing from his chest and, since the pace had slowed to a walk, he could hear the sucking sound of air moving through a punctured lung. His side was numb, his pants and saddle soaked with blood.

"I'm going to die," he said, feeling rather detached and without much pain. "Oh, sweet Mary, Jesus, and God, have mercy, for I've been killed."

Ahwahnee . . . Ahwahnee . . . Ahwahnee.

That word took possession of Ezekial's mind as he climbed familiar trails leading ever higher into the Sierra foothills and then passed into the cool, quiet forests. Ezekial, fearing that he would die before he reached his beloved valley, tore off his bloody leather shirt and managed to cut off the sleeves, which he then used to bind his legs to the stirrups.

He frequently slipped in and out of consciousness while being carried down the last steep trail into Ahwahnee, but the stallion was as determined to return to its pasture as Ezekial was to reach what remained of the charred village of Koom-i-ne.

Ahwahnee.

"Father!" Kanaka cried.

Haw-kee leaned close. "He is happy on a journey to the spirit world."

"No."

Ezekial could really hear Ouma now. She and Anina and Lucy. And they were all speaking in one voice to him. And now . . . now he heard Kanaka.

"Father!"

His eyes fluttered open. "Kanaka."

"What happened?"

Ezekial's voice was so faint that Kanaka had to press his ear to his father's lips, but he was not sure he if he could hear his father's dying words because mighty Cho'-lok was so very loud.

And then, Kanaka could not even feel the warmth of his father's breath. Kanaka lifted his head and gazed at the last of the free Ahwahneeche warriors.

"What did he tell you?" Puya asked.

Kanaka gazed at his dead father and thought very hard before answering. "Ezekial said . . ."

Kanaka took a deep, shuddering breath and slipped Bo Lamont's bloody revolver from his father's coat pocket. Looking at his few remaining friends, he told them, "Ezekial said that there could be no peace with the Americans and that we must fight them until we are all dead."

The Ahwahneeche nodded, then each warrior went off into the meadow and began to sing his death song.

Seventeen

Anina and Lucy were home once again in Ahwahnee but were filled with sorrow over the death of Ezekial, whose ashes had been spread to the wind. Last summer had been a nightmare on the Fresno River Reservation and many of The People had died.

Tenaya himself had begun the exodus of the remnant of the Ahwahneeche by requesting permission to return to his valley to bury his dead son properly and to have a traditional "cry" for the boy's departed spirit.

Almost miraculously, the request had been granted by the American officials. And once Tenaya had been given leave to go, the last of The People soon followed. There was no planned escape; rather, in small groups, quite independent of each other, The People ventured farther and farther into the upper foothills in order to avoid the punishing valley heat and to forage for game and acorns. And once again among their beloved pines, they had simply kept walking until they were back in Ahwahnee.

They returned to nothing and, for the second winter in a row, life among the Ahwahneeche had been extremely difficult. Somehow, The People had survived until the spring had brought good hunting and the promise of continued survival. Now, they greeted each sunrise with prayers and bid farewell to each sunset with praise and thanks.

But on this very day, Tenaya's high-valley sentinels had returned to say that more whites were coming. Just eight men. Tenaya and others discussed this matter at great length but no agreement could be reached. Kanaka and the younger men believed that these new interlopers were independent prospectors and should be killed. Others were more conciliatory and believed they should first be warned to leave. The last of the tribal elders suggested they ignore the prospectors and hope that they did not find enough gold to stay in Ahwahnee.

Finally, when everyone had had his say, it came down to Tenaya to speak and he made it clear that he preferred the middle course. "We will tell the whites that this is our home and they are not welcome. We will ask them to leave."

"But they will laugh in our faces!" Kanaka exclaimed, gripping his father's revolver.

"Perhaps," old No-taka said, "but if we spill their blood and the soldiers find out, they will kill us all as punishment."

"They will kill us anyway!" Kanaka shouted angrily. "My father's gun holds six bullets and each will find a white man's heart."

Tenaya waved off that remark and declared, "Kanaka, Coati, and your friends will stay away from the gold seekers. I will send other, wiser men to ask the Americans to leave."

Kanaka flushed under this clear insult. "And when they refuse to leave Ahwahnee?"

"Then we will consider this as an act of war," Tenaya said after long deliberation, "and it will be the end of The People in this place."

Kanaka went to see his mother and sister. He told them what Tenaya had said and Anina listened until her son had finished. "Tenaya is wise. This is the best thing to do."

"But . . ."

"You must *not* go among the whites," Anina warned. "Your heart is filled with poison."

"They *killed* my father!"

"And my husband," Anina said, "and Lucy's father. But he would not want them to also kill us. Don't you see this?"

Kanaka was so filled with hatred for the whites that he did not care what his father would want anymore. What mattered was revenge.

"Go into the mountains and hunt," Anina said, looking old and haunted with sorrow, "Do not come back until this thing is finished."

"But I have a *gun!*"

"I know. Bury it. Or throw it away in the river."

Kanaka shook his head and backed away from his mother. "No."

"Then do not," Lucy said, surprising them both. "But go away, my brother. Do it now."

Kanaka drew in a deep breath and expelled it slowly. "And what if there is trouble and you both are killed, or taken back to the reservation?"

"If Savage or more of the American soldiers come," Anina decided, "then Lucy and I will run to the high mountains and find you in Tuolumne."

Kanaka did not want to leave his family and he had no faith at all that the whites would leave without first making big trouble. When that happened, he alone had a gun and his father's stallion, which Kanaka was sure was the finest animal in all of California. With such a gun and such a horse, Kanaka believed that he could be very important and gain great stature as a fighter among the Ahwahneeche.

"Kanaka," his mother pleaded, "listen to me! If there is trouble, we will find you and go away together."

Kanaka pulled his attention back to his mother. "What if the Americans follow you into the high mountains? What shall we then do, lose ourselves in the far desert? Would you return to the Mono? Would it not be better to fight and die?"

Anina lapsed into a troubled silence because she had often declared that she would much rather die than be exiled to the dry side of the mountains among the Mono, where she had been raised as a child.

"I will pray to Ouma and the spirits that the whites go away."

Kanaka shook his head. "Father knew that they would never go away. Remember?"

"Just go," Anina told him, her voice hardening.

Kanaka went to get his horse. His friend Coati came hurrying after him. "Where are you going?"

"Away."

Coati, the one who had killed the old man named Potter, glanced back at the camp for a moment, then he returned his gaze to Kanaka and made his decision. "I will go with you."

Kanaka was grateful for the company. Coati was brave and also hated the white men. An excellent bowman, Coati had always shared Kanaka's reckless sense of adventure and lack of fear.

"Take the gray horse," Kanaka said. "Next to my own, it is the best."

Coati agreed. "I will tell my family that I am going hunting with you."

"Hunting for what?" Kanaka asked, fingers caressing the butt of his gun.

"That depends on the white men, doesn't it?"

"Yes," Kanaka said, knowing that he would not be able to go to the high mountains until this thing with the whites was settled.

The very next day, Kanaka and Coati watched from the cover of trees along the river as Tenaya's chosen elders went to meet the prospectors and respectfully ask them to leave Ahwahnee. The Americans were camped in the deep, grassy meadow just to the west of Po-ho'-no, the "puffing wind" falls. Kanaka noted how the whites had bound the ankles of their horses with leather straps so that, in order to graze, the animals had to move with short jumps. Kanaka was puzzled by this and thought that his stallion would never tolerate such a thing.

Kanaka could see that, when the whites greeted Tenaya's hand-picked elders, they held on to their rifles tightly, even though the Ahwahneeche were old and unarmed. Kanaka and Coati could not hear what words passed between the two groups, but they knew that their elders were attempting to persuade the whites to leave the valley. From the angry gestures of the whites, Kanaka could see that the warning was greeted with anger and contempt. One of the prospectors even pointed his gun at the feeble and half-blind elder named Mis-tika, making it clear he would shoot if they did not go away. The elders left, heads down in defeat.

"I knew that the Americans would not leave," Kanaka declared. "They *must* all be killed."

Coati looked closely at him. "When?"

"Before they come any farther into Ahwahnee."

"We will need the others."

Kanaka considered this. He did have a gun, but the whites would have many guns. And, in truth, Kanaka had not dared to fire the gun even once and was not entirely sure how it worked.

"Kanaka," Coati said, looking very worried, "we cannot fail this time!"

Kanaka knew that his friend was right. "Go get Puya, To-che, Kian, and Haw-kee. But say *nothing* to Tenaya."

Coati nodded with understanding and disappeared.

That night, Kanaka sat alone among the big rocks that had tumbled down from the cliffs. He could hear and see the silhouettes of the eight white men as they laughed and talked around their campfire.

They were such confident fools. Probably, they thought that the Ahwahneeche already were running away to hide in the highest mountains. Probably, they were talking about how they would also burn the rebuilt Indian villages and steal anything of value, perhaps find some young Ahwahneeche women for their pleasure. The whites sounded very happy; their sharp laughter cut like a blade at Kanaka's heart.

He did not sleep at all that night but spoke to the mountains, the stars, the rocks, and especially to Cho'-lok, for he did believe that Ouma was watching and would approve of what he had decided to do to these bad whites. On two occasions, Kanaka went over to stand beside the chestnut stallion and scratch its ears. The horse had become his friend just as Wolf-dog had become Lucy's true friend. The only difference was that Lucy believed that their father's spirit now lived in Wolf-dog. Kanaka found that amusing, but it was characteristic of Lucy, who had always been a dreamer and whose imagination spun her thoughts about like a feather in the wind.

Coati arrived just before dawn with their young warrior friends. All were excited and eager to kill the invaders, but they were not sure how this could be accomplished since there were eight Americans and only six Ahwahneeche.

"Maybe they will split up in the search of gold and then we can kill them one by one," Haw-kee suggested.

Kanaka and his friends agreed that this was likely to happen, and that they should bide their time.

The whites were in no hurry to begin their day. They cooked meat and sat around their morning fire while the sun rose to drive away the great shadow behind Ko-su'-ko, the stones which the whites now called Cathedral Rocks. Kanaka watched a doe and her fawn wade into the shallows of the river. Both were fragile, like so much of this valley, and both watched the Americans, ready to vanish instantly into the trees. Kanaka felt disturbed when he could not help but compare The People to the anxious and watchful deer.

"Look!" Puya whispered. "Some of the Americans are leaving."

"Yes," Kanaka said, counting five who had risen from their places, gathered packs, and were tromping upriver toward the new and partially rebuilt village of Koom-i-ne. "We should kill them first."

Kanaka was not the oldest nor even the acknowledged leader among his friends, but he had the gun and so they agreed because they were eager to also win guns and more horses.

Very quickly, the Ahwahneeche laid their ambush along the river. Kian, the best bowman, had an important place with a good angle of fire down on the river. Haw-kee was near him and Coati chose to hide behind a rock beside the water. Two of the five prospectors were armed with rifles, all had pistols, and one even carried an ax. The prospectors also carried their large flat metal pans to scoop up their precious gold.

As they neared their hiding place, Kanaka could hear the whites laughing and talking just as if they were in their own villages instead of walking into the home of their sworn enemies. Kanaka gripped the pistol in his fist. He had seen such weapons fired and he knew how it was done but, at this very last moment, he lost faith in the white man's gun and laid it aside while he drew his father's Green River hunting knife. Killing a white man with his father's knife would be a sweeter revenge anyway.

"I'll just bet you," one of the prospectors said, "that none of them Mariposa Battalion boys had any idea how to prospect for gold or even thought to bring a gold pan. I'm expectin' to find color in this river and maybe even some nuggets."

"We should be watching out for those Yosemites," another grumbled. "They seemed pretty upset last evening."

"Upset!" another laughed. "Why, they were just a collection of hungry old men hopin' we'd give 'em something to eat. They're all nothing but a bunch of dirty, gawdamn beggars."

Kanaka alone among the Ahwahneeche understood these cruel words and, when he heard them, he lost control and sprinted silently forward, angling toward the last man in line, with his father's knife clenched tightly in his fist. He would be the first to draw blood and maybe the first to die this day.

The prospectors were totally absorbed in finding a likely stretch of river to start panning gold and their backs were to the trees where the young Ahwahneeche lay waiting. Kanaka was almost upon them when one of the men happened to turn and see him. The prospector's eyes bugged with fear and he stammered, "George, look out!"

The warning came much too late. Kanaka's knife blade flashed in the morning sun and then sliced into George's shoulder. The white man cried out in pain and Kanaka's momentum carried them both into the swift river. Kanaka felt the man struggle as the current rolled them over and over through a stretch of rapids. Kanaka slammed up against a mossy boulder, tore his knife free and buried it deep in the prospector's chest. The heavy blade stuck between bones and Kanaka could not tear it free. George's dying scream was lost as he sank beneath the boiling water. Kanaka heard gunfire and shouts. He twisted around, already a hundred feet downriver, to see the Americans running toward their camp with the Ahwahneeche giving chase.

Kanaka struggled to avoid being impaled on the broken branches of a tree lying half across the Merced. George's body surfaced and struck the log first. The powerful current tried to drag him under but his coat snagged on one of the branches. The dead man's feet were tilted up in the air and his head plunged back under the water. Kanaka aimed for a place on the log where there were no protruding branches and made a desperate grab. His fingernails bit into the soggy bark and he clung to the log for a moment even as George's body was ripped loose by the roaring torrent. Kanaka felt his body being sucked underneath the tree. His fingers scraped at the bark but could not gain purchase and then he also was dragged under the log.

Hidden branches raked his body, shredding his clothing as well as his flesh like a mountain lion's claws. For one terrifying instant, Kanaka was pinned deep under the log by its branches. He momentarily lost all reason and beat at them, breaking wood until his buckskins tore free. With lungs ready to explode, he was rolled along the bed of the river and tossed up to the surface. Gasping, Kanaka threw back his head and gulped for air. His feet touched the bottom and he realized that the Merced had widened. He looked downriver in time to see George's body being swept around a bend. Kanaka swam hard and finally reached shore. He lay there choking and spitting up water and it was several minutes before he could rise to his hands and knees, oblivious of the fact that he was naked and covered with blood.

"Coati! Puya!" he shouted, crawling up upon the warm grass and hearing the distant crackle of rifle and pistol fire. "Kian! Haw-kee!"

Kanaka climbed to his feet and ran back to the place of the ambush. His lungs were on fire by the time he burst into a clearing and skidded to a halt. There was only one dead white man lying in the clearing but when he gazed back downriver, Kanaka saw all of his friends running toward him.

"What happened!"

Coati was furious. "What did you do that for? They would all have walked into our trap!"

Kanaka knew that his friends had every right to be angry and he wanted to salvage a victory. "We can still catch and kill them."

"Where is your gun?"

Kanaka hurried over to the place where he had placed it carefully aside. He picked it up and ran to get his horse, determined to atone for his stupidity. At least two whites were dead and the others were running and perhaps even badly wounded. Was that such a terrible failure?

"Let's go!" Kanaka shouted.

They did go but killed no more whites that day. The three who had remained in camp had time enough to open fire and beat back the Ahwahneeche while being joined by their friends. Minutes later, they all scrambled onto their horses and managed to escape the valley.

"They will never return," Kanaka said, mustering up a fair measure of satisfaction. But neither Coati nor any of the others would meet his eyes or say anything good, and they certainly did not appear ready to celebrate.

Kanaka grew angry. "What is the matter!"

"We needed to kill them *all,*" Puya said quietly. "Now, they will tell the soldiers who will return and kill all of *us.*"

Kanaka opened his mouth to argue, but then he changed his mind because he was sure that Puya was right. If only he had waited instead of acting crazy and killing one white while allowing most of the others to escape.

"What do we do now?" Haw-kee asked sullenly.

"We must tell Tenaya what we have done," Kian said.

Kanaka expelled a deep breath. He did not want to face Tenaya but, even more, he dreaded facing his mother, after promising her he would ride up to Tuolumne.

"Kanaka?"

It was Kian. "Yes?"

"You had better wear that man's clothes."

Kanaka had forgotten that he was naked. He did not want to put on the white man's clothes but knew that he had to wear something and there were no clothes back at their poor village.

"You can't go back that way," Coati said, eyes shifting back and forth between Kanaka and the dead prospector.

Kanaka walked over to the dead man and, biting back his revulsion, began to undress him.

* * *

Tenaya had listened calmly while Puya, son of one of the most prominent elders, had explained what had happened that morning. When the young man was finished, Tenaya simply walked away to be alone to think. His granddaughter, Totuya, followed their chief across the meadow.

Anina was furious. "Kanaka, you lied to me and you disgraced your father!" she shouted. "And even worse, you let those bad whites get away so that they will tell Savage and all the soldiers will come again and, this time, there will be no peace . . . only death."

Kanaka had nothing to say in his own defense. Dressed in the prospector's clothes, he felt much less than a man, so he went to his stallion and rode west toward the place of the fight. Maybe, he thought, one of the running prospectors had dropped a gun or rifle in the grass that could be found. If so, he would present it to Tenaya and plead for his chief's forgiveness.

Kanaka searched for hours, but found no lost weapons and had to content himself with studying the bodies of the two white men, one of whom he'd stabbed to death. George had washed up on a sandbar and one of his arms was twisted so grotesquely that Kanaka knew it had been broken. The stallion snorted and rolled its eyes when Kanaka tried to force it into the water and close beside the body. So Kanaka dismounted and let the horse graze while he waded across a waist-high narrow channel to reach the corpse.

He squatted on the sandbar in his scratchy wool pants and shirt, his boots squeezing bubbles between his toes and studied what little he could see of George's face because the man was lying facedown against the sand. The American was wearing a heavy, red woolen coat with a brown fur collar. George had been young, not much older than Kanaka himself. His hair was yellow, the one eye that Kanaka could see was blue. Peppered with grains of sand, it stared at the river.

Kanaka climbed to his feet and grabbed George's arm, then rolled him over to discover that Ezekial's knife was still embedded in the prospector's chest. Kanaka worked it free and could not retreat from the corpse fast enough. George's face was clotted with wet sand and his mouth was distended, as if he were screaming in silence.

Kanaka gulped and felt his stomach roll. What should he do now? The river would be offended by the presence of this dead white man. He approached the body again and grabbed George's boots, noticing that the right sole of the boot had been patched. It pulled free of the man's foot as Kanaka began to drag the body toward the channel. Kanaka backed into the river. The body, suddenly caught by the current, swung away and nearly dragged Kanaka back downriver. For a moment, it was all that he could do to fight the body and the surging current. But he finally prevailed and dragged George across to the meadow, where he stopped to catch his breath.

It was then that Kanaka decided that the meadow did not want this body either. Kanaka gazed all about Ahwahnee. There was no good place for the white man's body to rest. Unable to decide what to do, Kanaka abandoned George, glad that he had at least retrieved his father's precious knife. He started to walk away, but halted out of curiosity and went back. George was now completely matted from head to foot with dirt and grass. He hardly looked human. Kanaka wondered what a young man such as this would have in his pockets, so he searched them and found a knife, some coins and . . . most troubling of all, a small, framed likeness.

Kanaka stared and stared at a daguerreotype of a young woman. She was pretty, if a white woman could be considered pretty. Her likeness was in two colors, one the color of the reddish brown rocks, the other of dry sand. Kanaka decided that her hair would have been yellow, like George's, and that her eyes were probably dark blue. She was smiling, but the colors had run and her lips were a small, pink stain.

Kanaka stared at the picture for a long, long time. Was she George's woman, his sister, or someone he loved? For reasons Kanaka did not try to understand, he wished that he knew. He also wished that he could somehow find and tell this girl that he was sorry that he had killed George without giving him a fighting chance. Kanaka doubted that the youthful prospector had even seen his face before they had plunged into the river.

"It was not the way that *you* would have done such a thing, Father," Kanaka whispered. "It was not at all honorable."

Kanaka slipped the water-stained picture back into George's shirt pocket, near his heart, then walked away. The stallion watched him for several minutes and then it snorted at the body and followed its master.

On the following day, Tenaya banished Kanaka and his friends to the west end of the valley, where they were to remain, keeping guard against the whites. Anina was devastated by her son's rash failure. Everyone knew that it was Kanaka who had foolishly ambushed the prospectors and the blame would be his for whatever else happened to The People. Even now, most of the Ahwahneeche were already preparing to climb the mountains and live once again on the dry side with their eastern neighbors, the Mono Indians.

Every night for the next week, the elders met in their now very small and temporary ceremonial hang-e to discuss what should be done. Anina, Lucy and the other women and children listened to arguments instead of talk, as it had been in the old days.

It was terrible to hear so much anger and fear among the elders. To make matters even worse, a cold and constant rain began to fall. The People were not prepared for such weather in May. Many had left their government blankets, baskets, and most of their warm new clothing at the Fresno River Reservation. Now, they huddled in misery under trees or up on the slopes among the talus caves located at the base of Washington Column which they called Lah-koo'-hah, meaning "come out" place. Here, they waited, shivering and wet like frightened, hunted animals.

Kanaka had lost all respect. He slept apart from the others, near the mouth of the great valley. And, on the stormy night when the soldiers came and discovered Puya, Coati, Haw-kee, Kian, and To-che sleeping, Kanaka alone witnessed their early morning execution by a firing squad. He despised himself for being alive while his friends all stood straight and showed no fear of death.

"We must go," Tenaya told the last of his people. "The whites are coming."

Anina, Lucy, and all the others were prepared this time and it took only minutes to gather their few belongings in baskets. Many of the women and children cried. The old ones were sure that they would be overtaken and killed. As Kanaka watched the chaos and prepared to stay behind and probably die so that his people could have a chance to escape, he felt relieved because this day would prove the end of his disgrace.

He mounted the stallion and watched as Tenaya began to lead The People swiftly away from the valley floor, following the stream that led past what the whites now called Half Dome and then Mirror Lake. Kanaka knew that, if they could climb beyond Py-we-ack of the glistening rocks, they would reach a blue lake and then achieve the high mountain meadows of Tuolumne. Once there, Kanaka felt certain that nothing could stop the Ah-wahneeche from retreating down to the dry side and into the desert, which he had heard the white men feared and avoided.

The stallion was excited. It kept whinnying over and over to its absent mares, some heavy with his offspring. Precious food was being left behind, but that could not be helped. The white soldiers were in Ahwahnee and they were coming.

Anina and Lucy, with Wolf-dog, hurried over to say goodbye. Looking down at his mother, Kanaka felt an almost overpowering despair. Anina looked so old, now that Ezekial was gone.

"You had better hurry," he told them both.

"You come with us," Anina pleaded. "Come with us *now!*"

Kanaka shook his head. "I will come, but not until everyone is safe . . ."

"The old ones will never make it," Anina interrupted. "They are too weak from age and hunger. There is no reason to die with them."

"This is a good day to die," Kanaka said. "And a good place."

Lucy stepped close to the chestnut. "Please," she said, "Mother needs you now. You are the man of our family."

"I hope that will change and you live to have a husband."

Tears filled Lucy's eyes. "I have no plans," she said, "except to come back to Ahwahnee."

Kanaka could take no more of this. "I will meet you in Tuolumne," he pledged. "I will be there! Hurry away now!"

Wolf-dog, sensing danger and anxiety, barked loudly. The huge beast limped, but he was still the king of his kind in this village and this past year had chased off several uzamati. His presence alone gave Kanaka comfort about the safety of his mother and young sister. Wolf-dog would protect them from all dangers. Maybe Wolf-dog really did possess Ezekial's heart and spirit.

Kanaka wheeled the stallion away and let it run to the river. He dismounted and turned his face up to Cho'-lok. Kanaka screamed like an eagle. His cry would be heard by the advancing Americans and it would cause them to shiver with dread. It would also be heard by the last of the Ahwahneeche and give them the courage to climb the mountains.

Kanaka's chin dipped and he smiled at the shining water. At this bittersweet hour of his death, he felt much, much better.

The Americans did not come at once but spent most of that day locating and then burying their dead. By this time, Kanaka's voice had grown hoarse from screaming. Thinking that perhaps his battle cry had given the invaders cause to turn back, he decided to ride after his mother and sister. The stallion was ready. While he had stood beside the river hurling his challenges, the chestnut had grazed through that long morning and afternoon. It was well fed and well rested and it wanted to be with the mares.

Kanaka rode through the late afternoon, past Half Dome and around the still and beautiful Mirror Lake. The trail of the fleeing Ahwahneeche was easy to follow and he rode without looking back over his shoulder until he came to a rocky slope where a few of the old and weak ones had taken refuge in exhaustion.

Kanaka dismounted. "You *must* go higher," he urged.

"Are the whites coming?" an old man asked, his hands shaky as he held a bow.

"I do not think so."

"Then why do we run?"

Kanaka realized that this was a very good question. "Maybe I am wrong," he said. "When I reach the top of Wei-yow, I will be able to look down and see if the whites are coming."

"They will *never* stop coming," the old man said. "And anyway, it does not matter if we die. We are old. Go now!"

"I will stay."

But the old man with the bow and no arrows became enraged. "You have been foolish and brought all this upon The People! Go away!"

Kanaka, who had been in the act of dismounting, rode on up into the mountains. It was a good day to die, but not to throw his life away. Better, Kanaka thought, that he should give his life to save his mother and his sister.

Eighteen

Mono Lake, Eastern Sierras, 1853

Kanaka slumped listlessly on a rock just outside the Mono village. Clad again in buckskins tanned by his sister, his back was turned to the dead lake, his attention absorbed by a deep layer of billowing storm clouds that had foundered on the highest Sierra peaks. Beside him sat Anina and near her was Lucy, scratching Wolf-dog's ears. It had been over a year since they had fled Ahwahnee and Kanaka still could not believe that all his closest friends had been executed by an American firing squad. Right now, however, he was trying without success to ignore the loud and excited shouts coming from the center of the village telling them that the game of "hand" was still being contested between the Ahwahneeche and the Mono Indians.

Anina turned her head to listen. "Tenaya and our elders have won much so far."

"They should quit," Lucy said, starting to look very worried.

"The last time that they played, our people won so much that the Mono were angry for weeks."

"They are *still* angry," Kanaka said.

"That is true," Anina agreed, her contempt for the Mono a poor secret. "They are boastful winners and poor losers."

Kanaka said, "The Mono should know better than to bet with our elders. Tenaya is nearly impossible to beat at 'hand. ' "

"The Mono cannot accept that," Lucy said. "Their young men are very proud and do not accept defeat or refusal."

Kanaka pulled his eyes away from the storm clouds and gazed for a moment at his sister, aware that Lucy had been under intense pressure to marry into the Mono tribe but had stubbornly resisted. Kanaka supported her because he did not like these people and had made it known that he would protect his sister's right to remain unmarried, even to the point of spilling blood. Wolf-dog also seemed to have formed an intense dislike for all things Mono and had torn the throats out of two of the leaders of their mongrel dogs.

Lucy's Mono suitors had not been eager to risk a fight with the tall, angry Kanaka who, alone among them, had a six-shot gun. And yet they continued to scheme and to watch her because Lucy was sixteen and exceptionally beautiful. Like all of Kanaka's family, she had inherited height as well as a fair skin from her Spanish and American ancestors. Lucy was already several inches taller than her mother, and Anina had been considered exceptionally tall among the Ahwahneeche people.

Faintly, Kanaka could hear Tenaya and his current playing partner, old Yo-mina, as they chanted their gambling songs, waiting for their Mono opponents to try to guess in which hands they held the "man or unmarked" bones as opposed to the "marked or woman" bones. Each side took turns hiding the four small cylindrical bones in wads of grass while chanting their luckiest gambling songs and moving their hands very quickly before their chests as they deftly switched the bones back and forth in order to confuse and then trick their opponents into picking "woman" bones. The "woman" bones were always distinguishable by a middle groove wrapped with black string. Each correct pick of a "man" bone allowed a neutral person to award the winning side a "counter." Each incorrect pick resulted in the loss of a counter. There were ten counters in all and they passed back and forth until one side finally won them all and the game was ended.

Kanaka and the young Ahwahneeche men long ago had realized that they were poor "hand" players because they became too excited. Tenaya and the elders were far more skillful in reading their opponents' facial expressions as well as masking their own. Also, the elders were skilled enough to make it seem that choosing the "man" bone was easy, therefore tricking their younger, inexperienced opponents into choosing the wrong hand. "Hand" was the favorite game among all the Miwok as well as the Mono peoples and required intense concentration, a quality that few young men had developed or could maintain hour after hour in order to win all ten counters.

"It sounds like the game is almost over," Lucy said, fingers absently stroking Wolf-dog's mane. "I thought I heard someone yell that Tenaya and Yo-mina had nine counters and only needed one more to win."

"Win what?" Kanaka asked, for it was his understanding that the Mono already had lost everything.

"Their horses," Lucy explained. "All the ones that the Mono captured on their last raid far to the south."

Kanaka's eyes widened in amazement. "But there are more than forty of them!"

"I know," Lucy said. "That is why I am so worried."

Lucy's meaning was clear. The Mono already were bitter and this loss would be more salt in an already-festering wound. Mono pride as well as plunder was very much at stake.

"I still hope the Mono lose," Lucy said, eyes continually shifting toward the nearby village as Wolf-dog's gold-and-black-flecked eyes kept glancing up toward her.

"So do I," Anina decided. "If the Mono lose all their horses, we should drive them over the mountain passes into Ahwahnee. Maybe with the ones we do not eat this winter we could buy peace with the Americans."

When neither of her children said anything, Anina looked at Kanaka and said, "Don't you agree?"

Kanaka shrugged. He had his chestnut stallion, which he rode constantly in search of good foothill grass and in order to avoid spending time among these Mono people. Kanaka simply did not care about any other horses. One great horse was enough for any man.

"Well," Anina persisted.

"It might work," he finally hedged.

There were more shouts, this time of joy and from the Mono. Lucy sighed with relief. "Maybe their luck will turn and they will get to keep their horses."

"Maybe," Anina replied. "But Tenaya and Yo-mina would never lose on purpose. Like the Mono, they *must* always win."

"Sometimes," Lucy said, "it is better to lose so that you can win."

"Explain that to old Tenaya," Anina said with a look of amusement. "And just hear what he has to say."

The afternoon, as well as the tense game of "hand," wore on, and Kanaka supposed he and his family were the only ones not watching the crucial contest between the Mono and the Ahwahneeche. There were far better things to watch and dream about in Kanaka's estimation. Up on the peaks, the foundered clouds were growling like dogs and Kanaka watched bolts of lightning flash from their torn underbellies. The westerly wind was picking up and, out on Mono Lake, the water began to boil with whitecaps. Seagulls, squawking and angry, beat at the wind, wheeling and calling, then beating hard for the shelter of the salty islands. A flock of coots took wing, calling back and forth as they flew low and straight across the angry water toward a dark green marshland hidden just to the south.

The wind carried the scent of pines down from the high mountains and that brought the sharp and painful memories of Ahwahnee. It was autumn and Kanaka yearned intensely for his beautiful valley of the deep grass, knowing that its maple, spruce, dogwood, and aspen trees would be awash with colors more brilliant than any rainbow and that the last gooseberries, elderberries, and wild raspberries would be sweet.

Back in Ahwahnee, the acorns were ripe for the harvest, but there would be no Ahwahneeche women to collect them, laughing and scurrying about and always saying prayers for the bounty

of their harvest . . . even when it was not good. Also, the deer
would be fat like the bear and most wonderful to roast and eat.

Great, noisy flights of southern migrating birds would stream
like wind-torn clouds over the valley while the sunsets had a
glow unrivaled by any other time of the year. Once mighty and
thundering Cho'-lok, and Po-ho'-no would have long since withered into misty, floating veils and all of Ahwahnee would be
hushed in anticipation of the first frost, the first thundering cascades of melted snow.

"Listen," Lucy said, interrupting Kanaka's dreams, "The People are shouting now. Tenaya and Yo-mina must have won back
the ninth counter bone."

The two women cocked their ears to the sound, but Kanaka's
thoughts were lost in Ahwahnee. "I do not think that the Americans would brave our winters," he mused aloud. "I think that it
would be safe to spend this winter at home."

But Anina shook her head and turned to her son. "We must
wait until spring and then . . ."

"But Mother," he protested, "that is when the prospectors will
return!"

Anina's fingers, once slender and graceful, were now thick,
with most of their joints knotted and twisted. When she became
upset and thought of whites in Ahwahnee, her fingers worked
against each other, twisting and fighting. To calm herself, she
liked to tell the old stories. "I remember when Ouma, who also
hated this place, declared to Chief Mamota that she was going
back to Ahwahnee. Ouma was *very* wise and believed that Ah-
ha'-le, the Coyote, was calling."

Lucy and Kanaka knew better than to ignore their mother when
she was about to launch into her favorite story of the earth's
creation.

"You see," Anina was saying, "long ago the earth was covered
only with water."

The angry voices in the Mono village subsided for a moment
and Lucy relaxed. "Was the water even higher than these mountains?"

Anina's eyes rolled up to the peaks. "Oh yes! Even higher

than Tuolumne. It was then that Coyote told Frog he would create The People and many good things for them to eat."

"And Frog said?" Kanaka asked, deciding to enjoy himself.

Anina ignored her son's amused smile. "Frog asked how The People could live without land."

Anina's fingers stopped fighting because this story brought peace to her heart. "Well, Coyote knew that this was a very good question and so he thought about it for a long, long time. Finally, he went to see Hi'lkuhnai, the small blue duck, and asked him to dive under the water and find some earth."

"But he could not," Lucy said, blocking out all the shouts and commotion from the village.

"That is so," Anina replied, "and neither could two other kinds of ducks, or even Watersnake. So, at last, Coyote asked Frog to dive to the bottom of the water and bring him up some earth. Frog did this, and when he came back up to the sky, Coyote was very pleased, for he had great powers and could use this earth to form all the land."

"He must have brought up a lot of dirt," Kanaka teased.

"Shhh!" Anina's eyebrows knitted in disapproval. "Do not be disrespectful. Coyote is *always* listening."

"I am sorry, Mother." Lucy's head turned sharply. "Mother! Did you hear that cry?"

Anina heard nothing for her eyes were closed and she rocked gently back and forth. "After Frog brought up the earth, Coyote then planted all kinds of seeds, especially pine nuts and acorns. But he still could not yet see in his mind how to fashion The People so he gathered the wisest animals and asked them about this big problem."

"You mean, how The People should look," Lucy said, one eye on her mother, the other cast toward the noisy Mono village, which was mostly hidden from view by the outlying Ah-wahneeche huts.

"Yes, that is what I said," Anina replied with a hint of annoyance.

When Kanaka opened his mouth again, Lucy clamped a hand over it and scolded, "Be quiet, Brother!"

Anina continued. "Coyote wanted to start making The People

from the ground up. With their feet. He thought he would give The People feet just like his own. All the animals agreed but Pe-ta'-le, the Lizard, told everyone that Coyote's feet were too round. He argued that The People needed feet exactly like his, ones with five toes."

"And why would Coyote agree to this?" Lucy asked, having learned the answer before she could run.

"Because," Anina said, raising her own five thick and bent fingers, "Lizard said that, with *five* toes, The People could pick acorns, gather seeds and bulbs, and even shoot a bow when they needed to protect themselves against the terrible uzamati."

Anina clapped her hands together with pleasure. "Coyote decided that this was very smart of Lizard. So he made The People with five fingers on both their feet as well as their hands. And their feet were so strong he sent The People all over the world, after giving each man a wife so that each pair should have a child every year and increase their numbers."

"Coyote," Lucy said, "was wise."

"Yes," Anina agreed. "It was very wise to create The People with hands and feet like those of Lizard and then to send them to places in every direction. It is just sad that the white men had so many more children than the Indians."

Lucy's soft laughter died and her head twisted toward the village. "Mother," she cried, arm encircling Wolf-dog's throat, "I think I heard Tenaya cry out in pain!"

Anina listened, but she could hear nothing besides the squawking seagulls and the hum of the strengthening wind. "No, no," she assured Lucy as she turned her daughter's lovely face in her direction so that she could finish her best story.

"Now then," she continued, "when this work of Coyote was done, he told Frog that he could live and play in the water forever. And he told each of the animals where they could live, too. And last of all, Coyote said that he alone would live everywhere and travel the world mostly at night. And this, he has always done."

The story was over but the noise from the Mono village had become a terrifying din. Kanaka jumped to his feet, also hearing Ahwahneeche screams. He pulled out his gun.

"No!" Anina begged.

But Kanaka ran back toward the Mono village and what he saw chilled his blood. The Mono, in a fit of rage, had picked up stones and had used them to beat not only Tenaya and Yo-mina to death, but also three other tribal elders.

Knowing he too would be slaughtered if he ran headlong into the Mono village, Kanaka skidded to a halt and raised his gun. He cocked back the hammer and, not sure of what else to do, he pulled the trigger. To Kanaka's amazement and to the shock of the rampaging Mono, the gun fired and a sharp explosion echoed up and down the mountainsides.

The Mono stopped crushing Ahwahneeche skulls with rocks and turned to face Kanaka, who began to yell, "Get away from them!"

"We will kill you, too," Maito, chief of the Mono declared.

Kanaka took an unsteady aim at the chief but he could not tear his eyes from what was left of the crimson mush that had been the skulls of Tenaya and four other Ahwahneeche elders. His hand shook with fury and he again cocked back the hammer of the gun. "But not before *you* die too, Maito!"

"They cheated!"

"Tenaya *never* cheated!" Anina raged, as she and Lucy overtook Kanaka. "You are all bloody dogs! Murderers!"

Maito grabbed a spear and shook it until the shell necklace around his neck rattled like a snake. He was a squat, powerful man and wore a sleeveless rabbit-skin coat and deerskin pants. Like many of these people, his long black hair was matted and twisted.

"Go and never return to this land!" Maito ordered. "Go and take nothing! I give you your lives."

Kanaka was willing to accept this offer. Without taking his eyes or his aim off of Maito, he said, "Mother, Lucy, gather your things. We are leaving!"

Lucy started to move but Maito shouted, "The wolf-dog, he stays."

"No," Lucy said, voice cold and hard. "He won't stay. You'll kill and eat him!"

Maito shook his spear again. "And the tall yellow stallion. He stays too!"

Kanaka took a backstep. "I'm taking my horse and Lucy is taking Wolf-dog. I'll kill you if you try to stop us."

Maito whispered something to one of the Mono, and the man dashed from sight. Kanaka dared not shift his attention to the runner because Maito would hurl his spear and kill him in an instant.

Anina began to chant. Her words sent a chill up Kanaka's spine because she was laying an ancient curse upon Maito as well as the other Monos responsible for the death of Chief Tenaya and the last of the Ahwahneeche elders. Suddenly, Kanaka heard the stallion whinny. He had picketed the animal to a tree and now he turned to see four Mono attacking it with their sharp stone axes and steel-tipped spears.

"No!" he bellowed, crazy to protect his beloved horse.

At that very moment, Maito raised his spear to make his throwing motion. Twisting away from the terrible slaughter of the stallion, Kanaka took aim on Maito's chest and his finger squeezed the trigger of his gun even as Anina's words crashed against his ears.

"Kanaka, if you kill him, you also kill *us!* The last true Ahwahneeche."

Kanaka began to shake under the spell of this appalling dilemma. He wanted nothing more than to kill Maito, who now stood poised and unafraid of dying.

"I am old," Anina pleaded, "and you are filled with hatred. But what about Lucy, who will not be put to death quickly, but will suffer at the hands of these people?"

Kanaka's eyes shifted momentarily sideways to his sister's face. Lucy's fingers were buried in Wolf-dog's coat and the huge beast was crouched, the hair standing up on its back and a low rumble filling its throat.

"All right," he choked with fury. "All of the Ahwahneeche, come and gather beside me. I am chief of The People now and I will deliver you from this accursed place!"

None except Tenaya's granddaughter, Totuya, rushed forward to join them. The rest were too young, too old, or too afraid.

"Come with me!" Kanaka yelled.

But they shrank away and disappeared.

"Let us go," Anina whispered. "Quickly!"

There was nothing else to do. Together, they retreated from the Mono village, taking only a moment to grab a few precious things from their huts and then hurrying upslope with the Mono closing in behind, jeering and hurling their own curses.

They scrambled up the canyon trail leading toward Tuolumne, straight into the bitter wind, still hearing the Monos' whistles and taunts. A thousand feet above the Mono village, Kanaka's composure broke and he turned to look back, yet instantly regretted it. The Mono were throwing brush and dead-wood upon the bodies of Tenaya and the other murdered Ah-wahneeche to create a huge funeral pyre. And, farther out, they were already quartering the great stallion and preparing for their feast.

In an uncontrollable fit of fury, Kanaka emptied his gun at the Mono. Gunshots like broken bits of thunder rained down upon the Mono, who scattered like quail.

Kanaka shook his empty gun and then he threw his head back and laughed, his laughter and the echoing gunfire resonating up and down the dry slopes of the Eastern Sierra. But at last, when Kanaka could laugh no more and when the echoes had died, the Mono torched their funeral fire and began to dance and to celebrate in an orgy of burning and butchery.

Kanaka led the way, stopping often so that Anina and Totuya could catch their breath. He knew that they were climbing directly into the fury of the storm above, but there was no other choice. Near the summit, the dark storm clouds that Kanaka had watched with interest from below now closed around them like a fog, and the wind intensified, mist turning to a chilling rain. They pushed on as fast as the old medicine woman and Totuya could climb, aware that, if it snowed, they had no robes or blankets and would likely die of the cold.

Totuya was inconsolable with grief at the death of her grandfather. Her mother had died only a few years after her birth and she had lost the rest of her family to the whites. Now, she had lost Tenaya, too. There was no one left for her except Kanaka and his family. Lucy stayed very close to the girl. While crossing the alpine meadows cupped in the highest hands of the mountains, the rain became especially hard and the winds washed tears across their faces. Totuya slumped down on a lichen-covered rock and buried her face in her hands as Lucy dropped to kneel by her side.

Because of the keening howl of the wind, Kanaka could not hear but the two young women spoke together for a long time while thunder and lighting clashed like gladiators in an arena of dark, swirling clouds. A gnarled, century-old pine took a jagged bolt of lightning and crackled with smoke and fire. An instant later, a freezing rain pelted the flames until the pine steamed and hissed at the angry sky. Lucy pulled the girl to her feet, and they hurried on.

They took shelter under some familiar rocks, where the Ahwahneeche had camped in other times of bad weather. That night they huddled together for warmth, each lost in misery and shivering with cold. Just before dawn, the storm spent itself in a wild and earth-shaking blast of thunder and lightning. Kanaka eased out to the entrance of their shelter and watched as the sunrise began to sneak across the desert and then over the nearby peaks. It came in a rush, turning darkness into a glowing salmon sky that quickly turned gold and then indigo.

"We will survive," Anina said, coming over to join him while the two girls at last slept. "We are the Ahwahneeche and we will *not* die."

"We will die," he argued, watching as the icy blanket laid across this high country began to glisten and melt.

"No, Ouma watches."

Kanaka would have laughed with disdain had this not been his own mother.

"Listen," she said, "I have been thinking much about you."

"Why?"

"You have no more bullets and no fast horse on which to escape. You will be killed if the whites see you again."

"It does not matter."

"It *does* matter!" Anina gripped his arm with surprising strength. "There is only one way for you, the last chief of the Ahwahneeche, to live."

"To make a peace with the whites! Never!"

"No," she said, "to make peace with yourself. To forget about hatred and to go off alone and learn to be like the spirits of the forest. To become so much like them that the whites cannot see or ever find you."

"Why?" he asked in a hushed voice.

"Because," Anina told her son, "as long as we live, the Ahwahneeche live. This is a most-important thing."

Kanaka laid his chin upon his bent knees and watched the crown of the Sierras glisten and sweat under the warming sun. He saw a golden eagle sailing on the rising breeze.

"What," he asked, "is your protection?"

"Ouma," she said. "And the spirits that have always protected the Ahwahneeche."

"That have *failed* to protect the Ahwahneeche!"

Anina sighed. "I am old, so I do not matter. But there are Lucy and Totuya. Maybe others that we do not know about. If you live, we will find a way to live."

He raised his head and looked deep into his mother's eyes. "Among the whites?"

"Yes," she said. "There is no other way to live in Ahwahnee."

"And what am I to do when you are rounded up and taken to the Fresno River Reservation?"

"We are just three women," Anina said. "We are not important enough for them to bother with soldiers. They will take pity on us and expect us to die, but we will survive and remain. But so, too, must *you* remain."

Kanaka took a deep breath. It was so incredibly beautiful this day on top of these mountains. There were nothing but snow-capped mountain ranges unfolding one after another as far as the eye could see. Could he survive alone and avoid the whites? Could he become more spiritual and one with all that Coyote had created for The People?

"Kanaka, please. In the spring and in the fall, we will meet together."

"Where?"

"Here," she said. "In Tuolumne. Promise me that you will try to live as one with the earth and the spirits."

He saw a pair of coyotes suddenly appear from behind a twisted old pine and trot into a meadow some distance away. They were young, but not pups. As Kanaka and Anina watched, the coyotes began to play, chasing each other's tails, wrestling and biting and yipping with joy. Suddenly, one of them saw a movement in the rocks and it froze. The other froze, too, and they began to stalk their prey.

"What do you think they are hunting?" Anina asked her son.

"Ground squirrels, Mother."

"Yes," she said. "The squirrels will feed the young coyotes just as they once fed your father. And so, Ouma has shown us a circle that you cannot break. Kanaka, you *must* survive!"

Returning to the timberline, they took some shelter in the western slope forests. Once again, they smelled the incense cedar and saw wild game and quiet ponds surrounded by grassy meadows. But, farther on, they discovered the desiccated corpses of the old ones, who had been caught by the whites and hanged from trees. Kanaka turned away from them. Their faces were unrecognizable but their hair was silver and he knew they were the people who had spurned his offer of help and then had chased him away. At least, Kanaka thought, they had died close to Ahwahnee.

And finally, Kanaka and the women broke through the trees and stood on the dizzying edge of the same cliff from which his own father once had tumbled. Before him stretched their great valley, awash in colors even more brilliant and beautiful than they had remembered.

Kanaka stood at the very edge and took a deep breath, then he smiled, vowing that he *would* survive and become like a forest spirit and never be lost to Ahwahnee again, even if it meant that he would stay on the cliffs and only watch the deep valley.

Anina came to her son as he stood alone and touched his arm. "You must go. I will take Lucy and Totuya on alone. Go! Let the mountains and the rivers and the Great Spirit heal your heart."

Kanaka touched her cheek and then pulled her close to his

chest. "Goodbye, Mother," he whispered a moment before he broke free and hurried away.

Nineteen

Anina, Lucy, and Tenaya's daughter had fared very well in Ahwahnee that first lonely winter of 1853-54. They had arrived just in time to discover that the autumn acorn harvest, after several poor years, finally was bountiful. They had also used the soapweed to poison more fish. Wolf-dog had thrived, mostly on squirrels and rabbits. He had driven a bear and a mountain lion away from their separate kills and gorged himself for weeks.

Lucy thought the work of survival very easy because many of the ponds that Anina and Lucy had constructed the previous year to save the Ahwahneeche people were intact, requiring only minor repair.

The next spring, two gaunt and dispirited Ahwahneeche men returned the ashes of Tenaya and the other murdered elders to their final resting places and to have a long "cry." Afterward, Totuya, still grieving, had gone with those Ahwahneeche to the Fresno River Reservation, hoping to find a few of her surviving relatives.

But Anina and Lucy were so busy gathering food that they had little time for grieving over the loss and exile of their people. As the weather improved, a few prospectors arrived to test the icy waters of the Merced for gold. But what they found was hardly worth their time and, when they did come to visit Anina and Lucy, they were made so nervous by Wolf-dog's growling that they never stayed for more than a very short while.

Occasionally, that first winter, Anina and Lucy had seen a thin spiral of smoke that told them Kanaka sometimes approached Ahwahnee to hunt along the clifftops.

"The snow is much deeper up there," Lucy always fretted. "I hope he is not cold and hungry."

"He is strong and this time alone will be good," Anina assured her. "Kanaka will make a bow and arrows. He will hunt and he will not starve."

"I wish that I had been able to make him a warm rabbit-skin coat."

"He will grow strong with the cold and one with the spirits of Ahwahnee," Anina had predicted, never doubting that her only son was more than equal to the severest of winters.

As spring melted the snow and the valley was reborn again, Anina and Lucy gathered fresh greens and made many acorn dishes for Kanaka. Finishing their large, conical "burden baskets," they loaded all the food they could carry and followed what the whites had renamed Tenaya Creek, past Tenaya Lake and Cathedral Peak on their way to Tuolumne Meadows, where they planned to spend time with Kanaka. Wolf-dog, as usual, stayed near Lucy, and there was no fear between them that they might meet the dreaded uzamati.

"Look!" Lucy exclaimed, when a man appeared, trudging across a vast belt of snow. "Is that Kanaka?"

"Yes," Anina said, beginning to hurry forward.

"He looks like a *white* man!" Lucy said, rushing after her mother. "And I thought he would be very thin after such a winter."

"It was an easy winter," Anina puffed as Wolf-dog barked and pranced around, exhorting her to hurry, "because Ouma and the spirits knew that we had little to protect us from the cold."

Lucy dropped her burden basket and began to run across the snow. When she reached Kanaka, she threw herself into his arms and hugged him tightly. "My brother, we have missed you!"

"And I have missed you," he said, dropping his bow and the rawhide bag he carried to protect his empty gun and necessities. He picked up Lucy and whirled her around in a full circle.

When he set her down again, Lucy laughed and rubbed her brother's cheeks, making a face. "Kanaka, for shame! You have grown a *white man's* beard!"

He blushed, then bent and gave Wolf-dog a playful cuff behind the ear, which caused the beast to roll over onto its back, tail whacking the earth like running feet. "I know. I could not pluck it and it keeps my face warm."

Lucy turned to her mother. "Look, Kanaka has a white man's beard!"

Anina came and hugged her son. She studied his face and saw that all his boyishness was gone. "Now when I look at you, I see your father when I saved his leg and healed his wounds."

Kanaka felt honored by the comparison. "What have you brought that is green that I can eat?"

"Are you hungry?"

"Starving for something besides deer meat and roasted ground squirrels."

Anina took her son's arm and led him off toward a place out of the wind. "Here," she said, finding a rock to sit upon, "we have many good things."

Kanaka ate ravenously, his particular favorite being the bulbs of the brodiaea and the camas, which Anina had already baked in an earthen oven. He also enjoyed the lupines that Anina had moistened with manzanita cider as well as the tender shoots of the young brake fern.

"I have dreamed of this," he said, mouth full. "But, Mother, where is the acorn mush?"

"Here," she said, unwrapping leaves and spreading it out on a rock.

"And you must be hungry for venison," he said, laying before them his own offerings. "And smoked fish."

"What meat is this?" Lucy asked, pointing.

"That of the bighorn sheep."

Lucy knew how difficult it was to hunt the sheep with the large, curling horns. They were extremely wary, with the eyes of the eagle. "You killed a sheep?"

"I did," he said, unabashedly proud of this accomplishment. "After living among such animals for so long, they almost accept me as one of their own. Now, I use the skin and the decoy head of one to hunt others."

"As your forefathers used to do when hunting elk in the great warm valley."

Kanaka frowned as he struggled to remember. "Was that long ago, in the time before the black sickness?"

"Yes," Anina said. "It was during the time of Mamota and my mother, Ouma."

Kanaka nodded and continued to devour the greens and his mother's acorn mush until he could eat no more, and Wolf-dog meandered away to explore these new hunting grounds.

That afternoon, Kanaka led his mother and sister to a cave high up in the mountains. It was a hard, steep climb and they had to cross a snowfield but were soon rewarded by a little hidden valley cupped by tall, snowy peaks where spring melt fed a deep alpine lake.

"The fish are good here," he told them. "And there is much game climbing to this high place now that the snows are beginning to melt."

Kanaka led them through thickets and rocks until he arrived at the base of a small hillock. "Do you see a cave?" he asked.

"No," Lucy said.

"No," Anina repeated after they had looked all around.

"Over here," Kanaka said, pointing out the shadowy entrance to a cave. "It is very well hidden."

"I have never seen this cave before," Anina said with amazement. "And we have been up here many, many times."

"I know," Kanaka said, taking their hands. "Come, follow me!"

The cave's entrance was just large enough to allow the entry of a horse but Kanaka had made the opening smaller by piling large rocks around its base so that you actually had to climb over them in order to crawl inside. At first, the cave appeared small, but it soon opened out into a large cavern naturally illuminated by lancing shafts of sunlight squeezing through fissures in the high, rock ceiling. Lucy tiptoed around a pool of water fed by melting snow that dripped down from above. Behind the pool was a bed of pine boughs and animal skins. A small fire crackled in a fire pit, its smoke filtering upward through a pair of ceiling cracks.

"I do not think that The People *ever* knew of this place," Anina said, gazing all around.

"Long ago they did," Kanaka said.

"How do you know this?"

"Come," Kanaka urged, lighting a pine bough and holding it aloft to reveal an entire wall of ancient drawings. "Mother, I was sure that this would greatly please you."

Anina's breath caught in her throat and her eyes widened as she gazed at the pictures of men hunting and killing a variety of recognizable game. The pictures were drawn in black and vermilion. They were primitive but magical and Kanaka was pleased to see that his mother's emotions were powerfully affected.

"Mother," he asked, "do they speak to you?"

"Oh, yes!" she whispered.

"They speak to me as well," Lucy said. "And to you, Kanaka?"

"Often," he admitted. "They protected me through this winter. I have named each one and they are like friends."

Anina revolved completely around, eyes surveying every inch of Kanaka's secret Tuolumne cavern. "This is a *very* spiritual place."

"I know. Ouma must have led me to it one afternoon in a blizzard when I was freezing and thought I would die. But then, my feet carried me inside. I found other things," he said, becoming even more excited about showing them to his mother and sister. "Old stone tools and many bones and . . ."

Anina's hand flew to her mouth. "Kanaka, don't *touch* the bones!"

Kanaka froze, then turned. "Mother, I didn't," he assured her, "except to move those where I walk and make my bed. Is that all right?"

"I . . . I will make sure that it is," Anina promised.

Lucy laid her burden basket down and then she found a rock upon which to rest. She studied Kanaka and then turned to her mother, nodding. "Mother, you were right, he *is* different."

"I told you that he would no longer be poisoned by hatred," Anina said, looking very pleased.

That afternoon it rained, but Kanaka and his family did not care. There was a store of dry firewood in the cave and they made good use of it, resting on beds of fresh meadow grass and pine boughs. Wolf-dog brought in a fat marmot and devoured it with obvious relish.

"Eat well," Kanaka told them. "As long as I live, there will be no more hunger in this family."

Anina and Lucy were both in a mood for feasting and they did little else for the next two days except to tell Kanaka stories of their winter experiences until the storm broke and the sun washed down upon the Sierras again.

A few days later, when Kanaka, Lucy, and Wolf-dog were out walking and Anina took an afternoon nap in the cave, Lucy said, "You have not asked about Totuya."

Kanaka glanced sideways at his sister. "I think she must have gone down to the Fresno River Reservation."

"Yes. Totuya was hoping to find a few of her cousins."

Kanaka inhaled the perfume of wildflowers and pine. "Will she stay there?"

"I don't know," Lucy admitted. "It was very sad when she left after Tenaya's ashes were buried. Totuya went with Be-nay-hei and Ca-bea."

"I saw them pass through here," Kanaka said. "But I did not let them see me."

"Why?"

Kanaka shrugged. "They stayed among the Mono and now they go to the reservation to live under the heel of the Americans. I have nothing to say to them anymore."

"Totuya spoke of you constantly. I think that she was strongly attracted to you, Kanaka. I thought that you might also be attracted to her."

Kanaka's cheeks warmed. "She is the granddaughter of Chief Tenaya and deserves my respect."

Lucy could not suppress a smile. "Is that why you kept looking after her so carefully?"

Kanaka started walking across the meadow, his eyes fixed on the ever-ranging Wolf-dog. The animal did have a limp, but it was not very noticeable. He would have expected that, given it had been Anina who had splinted and healed the animal's bullet-shattered leg.

Lucy caught up with her brother and struggled to match his long, swift stride. "Do not be angry with me! I was just thinking that it must be lonely up here."

Kanaka stopped in his tracks. "If you want to say something, then say it."

Lucy squared her shoulders. "All right," she said, "I am worried about you being alone all the time. Mother thinks that it is good for your spirit, but I think it is bad. If you live alone too long, one day all this sky and the mountain will swallow your mind. You will forget how to speak and feel among people."

"The People are dead."

"As *you* will be, if you live too long alone."

Kanaka would not have taken this talk from anyone but his mother and his sister. He thought to run after Wolf-dog, but he knew that Lucy would not leave him in peace until he satisfied her.

"I will not always be alone," he said quietly, as he knelt and plucked a tiny yellow flower. "Someday, maybe I will take a wife."

"Good! Because, someday, maybe I will take a husband."

"Ahwahneeche?"

Lucy shrugged. "I cannot say. And you?"

He had to smile. "There are not many left."

"There is Totuya."

Kanaka had thought often about this but his mind always came around to the same disappointing conclusion. "No," he told his sister. "Totuya would die up here. Either of cold . . . or loneliness. She would not be happy."

"Kanaka, are *you* happy?"

"I miss all my friends," he confessed, voice quiet like the low, summer mountain breezes, "and hunting with them, as well as my beautiful golden stallion. I miss Ahwahnee, and sometimes I go down to the cliffs and spend days watching the great river far below and the rocks which the whites have all renamed. I close my eyes and listen to Cho'-lok and all the falling water. I mourn to think of how Ahwahnee no longer is the home of The People but, most of all, I remember my father and how he died to return."

Lucy was silent for several minutes, then placed her arm across her brother's shoulders and said, "Kanaka, those are such bad thoughts. You must not think about such things."

"It is hard," he confessed. "I am filled with sadness. What about your heart? How could it be happy?"

Lucy expelled a deep breath. "The sun is always inside of me. I cannot be sad very long."

Kanaka knew this was true. Lucy had always found the best of everything. Even when she was sick as a child, she had been happy not to be dead. It was just her way.

"I am sorry about Totuya," Lucy said after a long silence had stretched between them. "But I am afraid that you are right. She would not be happy up here."

"Maybe," Kanaka said, "someday I will come down to live in Ahwahnee. Or one of the prospectors will see and remember that I killed their friend, a man called George. Then they will capture and shoot me like they did Puya, Kian, and the others. If this happens, you must see that my ashes remain in Ahwahnee."

"I would do that," Lucy promised. A moment later, she brightened and pointed. "Look, Kanaka! Wolf-dog has found a fox to chase!"

They both jumped up and hurried after the big dog. The red fox was hopelessly outmatched in the open but it quickly dived under an ancient and twisted pine, whose roots were as hard as granite. After a few minutes of digging, Wolf-dog gave up and the fox was forgotten, but Lucy would never forget this talk.

Saying goodbye to his sister and mother a few weeks later was very hard for Kanaka. He even extended their parting by escorting Anina and Lucy into Ahwahnee along a different and considerably longer route, leading past Nevada and then lower Vernal Falls. He would have taken them all the way into the old village of Koom-i-ne except that Anina objected.

"Maybe there will be prospectors camping at the village and one among them would recognize and decide to kill you."

"Then I would have to kill him first," Kanaka said with a dismissive wave of his hand, as if killing were of no consequence.

"With what, your empty gun?" Lucy asked testily. "Or with your bow and arrows?"

Kanaka was not amused. "I killed a bear this last winter with them."

"But the Americans are far more cunning and dangerous than uzamati," Anina reminded him. "I can say that, even if your father was one."

"He was *different*," Lucy said.

"Yes, in *most* ways."

Lucy and her brother exchanged questioning glances but neither cared to pursue the issue. Kanaka stood just beyond the cold spray of the falls, hearing its great roar.

"In the autumn, when the leaves are red and gold, I will come here to meet you again," he promised.

The canyon air below Vernal Falls swirled with mist and shimmered with rainbows that masked Lucy's tears. She hugged Kanaka and then set her path down to the valley, holding Anina's arm to guard her from falling on the slippery stones.

Kanaka watched them disappear downriver, with Wolf-dog taking the lead back to his familiar haunts. Once they were lost to sight, Kanaka slumped down on a bed of moss and closed his eyes, feeling very sad. Their short family reunion in Tuolumne had passed much too quickly. He had even begged them to stay with him, but Anina had refused, simply stating that the Tuolumne snows were too deep, the winters too hard for the likes of an old medicine woman. And Lucy would never leave their mother alone in Ahwahnee.

Several hours passed. Finally, Kanaka roused himself from his lethargy and circled to the west behind Half Dome and Clouds' Rest. He had a vague intention of perhaps shooting some fish with his arrows in the cold waters of Tenaya Lake or taking an unwary mule deer. He was walking along, feeling morose and lonesome when suddenly he heard a rifle shot.

Kanaka threw himself to the earth and froze, heart racing as the single echo rattled against the mountainsides. He waited a half hour, with only his eyes moving. When he was sure that he was not being hunted, he stood up and began to sprint forward at a crouch. Like his father, Kanaka had inherited exceptional speed, and his long winter travels in search of food had left him lean, fit, and sinewy.

He was sure that the rifle shot had originated a little higher up this canyon. Kanaka had been over this country many, many times since his boyhood and he visualized every square foot of it now as he ran, trying to imagine how many whites had already invaded this high country and what they were now hunting.

When Kanaka reached the crest of a ridge, he flattened and crawled the rest of the way, slithering through thick tangles of manzanita. What he saw when he crested the ridge created more questions than answers, for there was a lone rifleman balanced precariously high up in a big tree.

Kanaka crouched and watched as the large, bearded man finished reloading his rifle with more than a little difficulty because, every time he let go of the tree's trunk, he nearly toppled to the earth. It would have been a serious fall. Kanaka could not help but wonder what kind of foolish hunter would deliberately put himself in such an awkward position.

When the big man finally finished reloading his rifle, he jammed his arm through a sling and then began to try to extricate himself. He wasn't very successful. Tree limbs snagged his coat and pants so that he had a terrible time descending to the lowest limb. Kanaka could hear his grunts and cursing as, ponderous as a big porcupine, the American eased down, finally reaching a point about ten feet above the earth. The man's difficulties were not helped by the fact that he had a large pack on his shoulders that also kept snagging on branches.

Kanaka watched the American grip the lowest stout limb and then lower himself until he dangled for a moment over the ground at full arm's length before he dropped. The man struck the earth and tumbled sideways.

"Dammit!" he muttered, ducking around behind the tree and then poking his head back around with his rifle at the ready.

Kanaka followed the American's eyes, which were totally focused on the entrance to what Kanaka immediately recognized as a grizzly bear's den.

"Come on out, Mrs. Grizzly!" the hunter bellowed, as he took his firing position. "I'm ready for you!"

Kanaka's hand tightened on his own bow. He found it impossible to believe that a single man, even one with a rifle, would be foolish enough to challenge a grizzly bear. But here it was and, even as the American waited, Kanaka heard the unmistakable roar of a grizzly from inside the cave.

"What a fool!" Kanaka whispered, attention totally absorbed by this bizarre drama that was being played to a deadly finale.

Kanaka could not figure it out. This canyon and its surrounding mountainsides were crawling with deer and even black bear, all of which were better eating and a lot easier and less dangerous to kill.

"Come out!" the man bellowed, as he hobbled across the ravine until he was only about forty yards from the mouth of the den. Stopping to snatch some twigs off a manzanita bush and stuff them into his cap, the foolish American again fired his rifle. He immediately took cover behind another tree and began to reload.

Suddenly, the mouth of the cave was all grizzly bear, and she was mad. Snarling and gnashing her teeth, the mother bear charged outside, big head swinging back and forth, looking for something to attack. But the man was now still as a stone and, after a moment, the bear hurled a last empty challenge, turned, and began to reenter the den.

"Hiii-yew-eiii!" the man screeched like a wounded panther. "Eiii-yip-yee!"

The cry filled the ravine and brought the huge grizzly spinning back around, quick as a cat. Surrounded by the eerie echoes, the bear raised on its haunches and roared again, her little eyes revolving like beads in a gourd.

The man took very careful aim and then his rifle barked flame, smoke, and thunder. Kanaka saw the bear stagger back against the entrance to her den. She bit at the terrible hole in her chest and then she saw the man running toward her, screaming like an evil, avenging spirit.

Kanaka could hardly believe his eyes as man and bear each charged forward. The man whipped out his pistol and, with every bound, began to fire bullets into the onrushing grizzly whose charge began to falter. When the man emptied his pistol, he threw it aside and yanked out a big knife. Kanaka bounced to his feet and reached for an arrow, but the grizzly's front legs buckled and it spilled to the earth to die at the American's feet.

The man threw back his head and howled like a wolf over a fresh kill. Kanaka had become so excited during the fight that he had forgotten himself and did not even think to drop back down into hiding. The American saw him and froze for a moment before he shouted, "Does sneaky Indian like the taste of strong bear meat!"

Kanaka blinked to make sure that he was not imagining things. He did not fear the crazy white hunter because he was out of bullets. But then Kanaka remembered how miserable he'd felt after stabbing George to death in a dishonorable way so he just stood rooted in silence.

"Hey!" the American called again as he began to reload his pistol. "Come on down and cut yourself some fresh bear meat! There's more'n plenty for everyone."

Kanaka found himself walking on down to meet this big man and wishing that Ezekial could have been here to tell him if he was about to be shot . . . or just fed.

"My name is James Capen Adams," the man said, finishing his reloading and shoving his pistol into a holster. "I'm a hunter, an explorer, adventurer, and wild animal trainer. Most people just call me Grizzly. **Grizzly Bear Adams.** Who are you?"

"Kanaka."

"Part Yokut or maybe Po-to-en-cie?"

"No, Ahwahneeche," Kanaka said proudly.

"Well then, you must know this country like the back of your hand." Adams leaned forward. "You're a half-breed, aren't you?"

It wasn't a question but Kanaka had never heard the term before. "What do you mean?"

"I mean you're part white . . . like me. It's clear enough for anyone to see because of your beard, height, and color. What'd you say your name was again?"

"Kanaka."

"Well," Adams said, "I'd just as soon call you Nak. Okay?"

"Okay," Kanaka said, turning to look at the riddled grizzly. "Why did you kill her if you give the meat away?"

"Good question. Like I said, I train animals. My favorites are grizzly bears."

"What do you mean, 'train'?"

Adams walked back to get his rifle, which he then began to reload. "I mean," he said, as he worked, "that I take a baby bear cub and train it like a cat or a dog. They make fine, loyal pets."

Kanaka had thought he understood English very well, but apparently he did not. "Pet?"

"Sure. You feed and take care of a pet and they give you some company and amusement. In my case, with these grizzly cubs, I expect to profit. But never mind all that," Adams said, finishing his reloading. "Cut and carry off all the meat you want, Nak."

Kanaka nodded to indicate his thanks and gratitude. The huge sow would be tough and gamy, not nearly as good as a deer or even a fat black bear, but Kanaka knew that he could smoke the meat and it would keep in his cave and serve him well this winter. He drew his own Green River knife, which he kept sharpened with a stone.

"Ha!" Adams said, drawing his own knife. "I'll just bet that knife was a gift from your white pappy, wasn't it?"

Kanaka dipped his chin and knelt to start cutting bear meat, deciding that he had never before met a man like Grizzly Adams.

"Tell you what," Adams was saying. "I think that there's either another big grizzly in that den, or some cubs. You want to help me out a little?"

"Kill another bear?"

"Probably not. But if there are cubs inside, I'd like you to help me when I bring 'em out. There's no sure way of tellin' exactly how big they'll be or how fast the little buggers can skitter around, but they sure can be a trial."

"Yes," Kanaka said, not understanding what "trial" meant.

"So," Adams was saying, "just watch yourself that a cub doesn't bite the bejeezus out of you. I got some leashes and little muzzles; it takes a few minutes to get 'em under control."

Kanaka had no idea what to expect next but, when Adams crawled up to the opening of the den and howled, Kanaka stepped back and put an arrow to his bowstring, expecting the very worst. Instead, he heard the mewing of cubs.

"They sound pretty young," Adams assured him as he gathered a wad of dry branches and put a match to them to use as a torch. A moment later, he disappeared into the den and calling, "I'll be right back, Nak!"

The tunnel's entrance was about three feet across. Standing next to the huge mother bear, Kanaka found it difficult to believe that she could have fitted through that small opening.

Kanaka knelt beside the dead sow and whispered softly so that Adams could not overhear and perhaps scoff at him. "Mother bear, you were brave and strong. I thank you for your meat and promise that I will not let your cubs be killed or mistreated. If that should happen, I would steal and set them free."

He replaced his arrow in his quiver and dropped to his hands and knees and peered into the den, seeing nothing. The man had totally disappeared into the cave and must have turned a corner. Suddenly, Kanaka heard the sharp growls, hisses, and screeches of the young cubs.

"Ouch!" Adams shouted. "Dammit, take it easy, I'm not going to hurt you! Ouch!"

It was a good ten minutes before the strange American inched back out of the cave with two squirming cubs clutched in his big bleeding hands.

"They're a couple of little hellers," he announced with a wide grin. "Here, Nak, hold this one while I get the leash and muzzle on the other."

Kanaka had never held a grizzly cub. The People had always thought of the grizzly as the most sacred among the animal people. But The People were gone and Adams was already fitting a noose and a little leather muzzle over one of the cub's heads. The cub was squealing and fighting but Adams was careful and very determined until he had the job finished.

"Here," he said, giving the muzzled one to Kanaka, "now the little scrapper can't bite your fingers off."

When both of the cubs, which were about the size of small

raccoons, were muzzled and leashed, Grizzly Adams was well pleased, but Kanaka grew increasingly aware that he was caught in a dilemma because he now felt responsible for the welfare of the cubs. And yet, if that turned out to be the case, what could he do? Without their mother's milk and protection, they would either starve or be killed by wild animals before they could grow big and strong enough to protect themselves. So, he could not just set them free, for that would be sentencing them to death. So what *was* he to do in order to protect the cubs?

"This is a real nice pair," Adams said, fitting the muzzle and leash over the second one and then examining them both very carefully. "They're just the right age, too. You see, in just a few more weeks, they'd have bitten my head off when I went in that cave. But now, they'll be easy enough to train."

"What do you mean, 'train'?"

"Listen, Nak. Have you had much to do with the white man yet?"

He shook his head.

"That explains why you're all by yourself up in this wild country instead of living the easy life down on the reservation. Well, that I admire. I see all those Indians sitting around looking forward to free everything and I really feel sorry for 'em. Now you, on the other hand, are too proud to sit around expecting life to be so easy. Am I right?"

"No," Kanaka said stiffly. "Indians are forced to live on the reservation."

"Some, yeah," Grizzly conceded. "But it appears to me that a lot of them want to be taken care of, with nothing to worry about."

"No!"

Adams sighed. "There's no point in us arguing what can't be changed anyway. Our opinions don't mean nothing. Damn! These little buggers are crawlin' with lice. We'll get rid of most of 'em, though. So, Nak, how would you like to help me out? I can't pay you much of anything, but you'll learn lots and I will figure out something to trade."

"Bullets," Kanaka said, for he well understood the word "trade."

Adams scowled. "Bullets, huh?"

"I have gun. No bullets."

He stared down at Kanaka, bushy black eyebrows meeting like the point of an obsidian arrowhead. "You aren't going to use the bullets on me, are you?"

"No."

"Or *any other white men,*" Adams said firmly. "I won't have that on my conscience, along with all my other past sins. Agreed?"

Kanaka was not entirely sure what the man was talking about, but he was wagging his chin again so Kanaka followed his example.

"Fair enough," Adams said. "Now, let's cut all the bear meat we can pack and get on down to my camp so you can meet the others."

Kanaka stiffened. "Others?"

"Sure! I got a couple of friends. You'll like 'em. They're both Indians and hate the reservation life just like you. One is named Solon and the other is a kid named Tuolumne."

Kanaka's chin snapped up. "Ahwahneeche?"

"No, Yokut. But he's a good kid and gets along with everyone. You'll see."

Kanaka felt drawn toward the high country. Toward Tuolumne. But then he gazed down at the struggling little bear cub in his hands and knew that he must somehow keep his promise to their dead mother. Besides, the absence of Anina and Lucy still weighed heavily on his mind and Kanaka was not eager to return to his lonely cave with only the pictures of the ancients to keep him company.

Twenty

Grizzly Adams hardly seemed to notice Kanaka's anxiety as they made their way toward his camp. The large, animated American was eager to display his knowledge of the grizzly bear.

"They're the most ferocious but also the most interesting damn beasts on the face of the earth, Nak. They breed in the summer and their cubs are born in midwinter, about a month earlier than black bear cubs. Do you know their size at birth?"

"No."

"They're hairless and so small that you might mistake 'em for skinned squirrels! There's usually two, but sometimes three and, once in a while, even four. They'll suckle as long as their mother allows but are soon able to eat damn near anything, including grass."

"They are already strong," Kanaka said, keeping a tight hold on his cub.

"You bet they are, Nak. They'll double in size every month or two and a full-grown male will weigh up to a thousand pounds of pure mean and muscle. They can easily outsprint a horse over rough ground. I've seen 'em break the neck of a horse and even a Spanish fighting bull with a single swipe of their paw."

"I have killed grizzly."

"Not likely with just a bow and arrow," Adams said. "But, if you did, I'll bet you had plenty of help. A grizzly is a hard, hard thing to bring down. You saw how tough these cubs' mother was when I shot her, first with my rifle and then when I emptied my pistol into her. The thing is, Nak, most men aim for the head but that's often a fatal mistake. I've skinned their heads and found out that there's far too much bone for a bullet to pass through between the eyes. And every other part of the head is slanting back from the muzzle so that bullets just ricochet away. Nothing tougher than to kill a chargin' grizzly."

"The Ahwahneeche call them *uzamati*."

"Well, you may have called 'em that, but we call 'em grizzly 'cause they've got that grizzled or silvery kind of mane where the tips of their longer hairs are white, or gray. I've seen 'em all sorts of colors, including yellow, light brown, red-brown, dark brown, even black. More'n one mountain man made the fatal mistake of thinkin' a black grizzly was just a large black bear."

Adams was just warming up. "They're afraid of nothing and the first mountain men had a hell of a time with 'em 'cause their puny flintlock rifles didn't have enough killin' power. But my

Sharps rifle can usually stand 'em straight up in their tracks. Remember, Nak, aim for the heart."

Kanaka realized that. Grizzly Adams had an amazing knowledge of bears, yet was completely ignorant of their great spiritual importance. To the Ahwahneeche, bears were the most peoplelike of all animals and possessed special gifts. But Kanaka did not think that Adams wanted to know about these things, so he held his tongue and just let the man talk.

"So, Nak," Adams was saying, "did you really have the rare privilege of growing up in this paradise?"

"Until a man named Savage and his soldiers came," Kanaka answered, unable to hide his bitterness.

"Well, in case you haven't heard, there was some disagreement between him and the boys over at the King's River Reservation. Savage made the mistake of going over there. He knocked some fella down and then turned and started to walk away. Fella he knocked down grabbed a gun and shot Major Savage to death. And the murderer got off scot-free because he was friends with the judge who ruled the shooting was in self-defense!"

Kanaka could not believe this. "Savage is dead?"

"Deader'n a doornail."

"I am glad," Kanaka said without hesitation.

Adams gave him an odd look. He opened his mouth, then closed it and walked on. About an hour passed before Adams said, "Nak, I'm going to keep this cub for myself and name him Ben Franklin. The other one I've promised to give to Solon, who is going to name his cub General Jackson. I told him that the general was wise and a great warrior. So, I'm holding Ben and you're holdin' General Jackson."

"Jackson," Kanaka repeated, his mind still dwelling on the unexpected death of James Savage.

"*General* Jackson, Nak."

Kanaka pulled his mind back to the present. "*General* Jackson," he repeated.

"Now you got it. Let's set 'em down and teach 'em how to lead on a leash."

Kanaka followed Adams's example and placed General Jackson on the ground. Both cubs immediately took off running but hit the ends of their leashes and did flips before they recovered and took off running again, with the same unpleasant results.

"Just hold on tight, Nak," Grizzly instructed. "They're pretty smart and it won't take them more than four or five of these hard spills before they figure out they aren't going anywhere."

The cubs were dashing in all directions, hitting the end of the leash, falling, choking, and getting up spitting mad, only to make another charge.

"Won't they break their necks?" Kanaka asked.

"Nope. They're as tough as boot leather. You'd have to hit 'em over the head with a blacksmith's hammer to do 'em any real damage."

Kanaka discovered that Adams was right because the cubs quickly learned that it was impossible to escape.

"Okay, now that we've taught 'em *that* lesson," Adams said, "we can now teach 'em to lead."

"How?"

"It's easy. We just drag the little buggers for a half mile or so. They'll squeal and raise hell, but finally, they'll get the idea. Watch."

Kanaka watched as Adams marched on ahead. The leash was only about ten feet long and, when it jerked Ben Franklin forward, the cub let out an angry screech and dug in its heels, straining with all its might. But Adams didn't break stride.

"Come on, Nak! Don't be worried, just drag General Jackson along."

Kanaka put General Jackson down and began to drag the cub who squalled like an infuriated baby. But Adams knew bears and, in less than a mile, both cubs were worn-out and had submitted to being led. In fact, they sometimes tried to race ahead. Kanaka would have given anything if his mother or father could have witnessed this peculiar sight. Lucy, however, would definitely not have approved because of her great love and respect for all animals.

When they finally neared Grizzly Adams's camp, the American let out a holler. Solon and Tuolumne and a very unusual-looking dog with puppies came running. Solon was in his twenties, squat and bowlegged, with two front teeth missing.

Tuolumne was taller, older, and much quieter. Kanaka had met few Indians besides Po-to-en-cies, Mono, and a few Miwok, but he found that this pair was friendly and spoke good English. The dog had very short hair and was exceedingly thin. Kanaka had never seen anything quite like her.

"She's a greyhound, Nak, and she's going to be the bear cubs' new mother. Her own pups are old enough to be weaned. Here," Adams said, handing the leashes to the two Indians. "Walk them down until they're ready to go to sleep, then we'll see if we can get the greyhound to let them suckle. She'll growl and probably bite 'em at first, but she'll soon come around. If not, we'll just have to think of some other way to feed those two cubs."

Kanaka would have liked to watch what happened when the two famished cubs were presented to the skinny greyhound, but Adams led him away, saying, "What I'm about to show you takes a little getting used to, so just don't get all lathered up and excited."

Kanaka had no idea what the strange American was talking about until the man led him into a clump of manzanita and showed him a full-grown, sleeping grizzly bear.

The instant that Kanaka saw her, he whirled and started to run.

"Whoa!" Adams called, grabbing his arm. "She's my friend and she wouldn't hurt anybody unless they hurt her first. Her name is Lady Washington. Come on over here and let's wake her up and get acquainted."

Kanaka shook his head and pulled back.

"Aw, come on! As you can see, when I'm not around to give her company, I keep her chained to a tree."

But Kanaka refused. He had never been this close to a live grizzly and could not imagine one that would not suddenly awaken and charge despite being chained.

"Okay," Adams said, "then I'll do the honors myself."

And he did. Adams went up and squatted beside the bear. He began to scratch Lady Washington behind the ear and the grizzly's eyelids quivered, then opened. It gazed at the American for a few moments, then, to Kanaka's utter amazement, she licked Adams's hand.

"That's my girl!" Adams said, scratching the bear under the chin and allowing it to lick his beard. "Ain't she a beauty, Nak!"

"She is . . . is very big."

"You bet she is! I caught her in eastern Washington a couple of years ago. Taught her to lead and to carry my supplies on her back in a special pack that I designed. Why, once she even fought off another grizzly until I could reload and end the affair."

Kanaka, fueled by his boyish pride, inched forward and touched Lady Washington's coarse mane. The bear licked his arm and her tongue was so rough that it tickled and caused Kanaka to smile. "She *is* friendly."

"Like a dog, only bigger," Adams said. "And speakin' of dogs, we'd best get back to camp now and see how my greyhound and those starvin' bear cubs are getting along."

Kanaka frowned. "Why do you keep her chained?"

"Because, if I let her go, she'd most likely wander off and maybe fall in love. If that happened, I'd never see her again and she's a pretty valuable animal. Better'n any packhorse or mule. Let's go see about the cubs."

When they returned to camp, Kanaka could not believe his eyes. The greyhound had decided to accept the cubs as replacements for her own pups, which Solon and Tuolumne had taken and hidden from her view. Now, the greyhound was already letting the cubs suckle.

"Boys," Adams told them that night as they feasted on roasted bear meat, "you need to remember that, with a lot of hard work, a fair measure of patience, and a big dose of faith, most everything in life works out fine."

"Not for the mother bear that we're eating," Kanaka said, chewing hard on the tough meat.

Grizzly Adams thought that Kanaka was making a joke so he laughed, then Solon and Tuolumne laughed, too.

Grizzly Adams and his Indian friends were gone from the Sierra Nevadas for several months, traveling to another place of high mountains called the Rockies. But they returned late that summer with all their bears, dogs, and horses. The American was eager to have Kanaka guide him around the Sierras. Because Kanaka was so familiar with this country and the habits of its wild animals, he soon helped Adams catch a pair of wolf cubs in an area thick with manzanita, high up behind what Grizzly Adams insisted on calling El Capitan.

"As big as this rock is, that's a fitting name," Adams said as he fitted leashes onto the wolf cubs in preparation to teaching them to lead. "What'd your people call it?"

"Tu-tok-a-nu'-la."

"Well," Adams reflected, "that kind of Indian name don't mean anything."

"It means 'measuring-worm stone.' "

Adams made a sour face. " 'Measuring-worm stone'?"

"Yes."

"Hell of a name for a rock that big and impressive," Adams opinioned. "El Capitan is an improvement."

Kanaka knew that it would be a waste of time to argue the point, so he remained silent.

"Nak, why won't you come down into the valley with us when we leave and spend the winter where it's a lot warmer? Our log cabin is small, but there's always room for one more."

"No."

"You got a woman hid up here somewheres?" Adams asked, eyes narrowing with suspicion. "If you do, you're welcome to bring her along. We're all gentlemen . . . at least I am!"

Adams laughed at his own joke, and then Tuolumne and Solon laughed, right on cue. Kanaka, however, failed to see the humor.

"Then go ahead and freeze to death up in the high mountains," Adams groused. "But first, we'll see if we can catch us another big bear . . . or maybe a panther. I can sell the adults to the traveling circuses and sideshows for top dollar. The bigger and more ferocious the wild animal, the bigger the price. City folks—especially Easterners—will pay most anything to see a full-grown grizzly or mountain lion."

Adams pulled thoughtfully on his beard, as was his habit when his mind was especially active. "Kanaka," he said, "I'd like to trap a really big male grizzly before they all go into hibernation.

If you help me do that, I'll not only give you more bullets, but I'll give you my Sharps rifle, ball, and plenty of powder. What do you say?"

After hunting with Adams and even being allowed occasionally to shoot, a rifle was no longer a mystery to Kanaka and was now something he could very much use and appreciate. And so, despite his better judgment, he said, "Yes."

"Good! Then where should we start looking, Nak?"

Kanaka knew of a box canyon off Tenaya Creek that was frequented by a very large grizzly. And, although he hadn't actually seen this giant, Kanaka once had accidently chanced upon tracks so immense that he had never gone back to that canyon. When Kanaka told Adams of this bear, the American became excited.

"It's getting pretty late in the season, but maybe he's still fattening for winter. So, let's see if we can trap this big devil before he dens up."

Tenaya Lake was already ringed by early morning ice when they passed it and entered the box canyon. The aspen were as brilliantly colored as spring flowers and their leaves billowed in the breezes.

"I dunno," Adams said, looking doubtful as he gazed up at the high, broken cliffs surrounding them. "Even if we can locate his tracks, he might already have taken to his den because it's colder up here. We're going to have to be careful or we might get caught by an early blizzard."

But Kanaka was not worried because he alone knew the way of the high mountains and that winter was still several weeks away. Besides, to earn a good rifle was an opportunity not to be missed, so Kanaka's search was tireless until he again found the great pawmarks.

When Adams saw them, he danced with excitement. "Nak," he exclaimed, "these are the biggest paw prints I've *ever* seen! We're going to have to build a huge trap and bait it with venison. Then, we'll just have to hide and hope that this monster takes our bait."

Kanaka had never worked so hard in his life as he did the next few days with Adams and the two Indians. They chopped down trees and then used horses to drag the logs near the giant grizzly's tracks. It took nearly four days to build a trap they felt would be impossible to destroy.

"This thing would hold a herd of stampeding buffalo," Adams pronounced after the trapdoor was lifted and the fresh carcass of a four-point buck laid far back inside the cage. "Now, all we have to do is clear out and see what happens."

Two days later, they returned to find that the trap had been entered by the giant grizzly but the door had failed to drop. The carcass was gone.

"Damn!" Adams swore. "Now we're going to have to do it all over again. Let's hike off a ways so that the sound of our shot can't be heard. We'll try to get another buck, then haul its carcass back and put it in our trap. I'll set the door spring lighter this next time and we'll catch him for sure."

Kanaka and Adams went hunting, and, when they spied a fat buck downwind in some alders, Adams extended his rifle, whispering, "Nak, you drop this one. Just do as I've taught you and don't hurry your shot."

Kanaka had fired the Sharps before, but only at stationary targets. Adams had told him a number of times that it was a .45 caliber, breech-loading, single-shot, the very same one that he had fired from up in the tree when he'd mortally wounded the cubs' mother. It had two triggers and, after thumbing back the hammer, the rear trigger was pulled, which "set" the front or "hair" trigger.

Kanaka did all these things and then he took aim, finger still not touching the hair trigger.

"Just take a deep breath and hold it, then slowly squeeze," Adams instructed.

The big rifle roared and slammed back into Kanaka's shoulder, there was so much noise and smoke that, at first, he could not even see his quarry.

"Nice shootin'!" Adams exclaimed, pounding Kanaka on the back. "Got him right through the gizzard!"

Kanaka was well pleased. When he approached the buck, he saw that the ball from Adams's powerful rifle had killed the deer instantly. Kanaka knelt beside the animal, grateful that he had not caused it to suffer.

"Aw, go ahead and say your prayers for the thing," Adams allowed, "then let's pack it out of here."

Because Adams insisted that the buck be unmarked, it proved difficult to carry. They finally cut a long pine pole and ran it between the buck's tied ankles. By placing the pole on their shoulders and walking in a straight line, they managed to carry the buck all the way back to the trap just as dark was falling.

"Whew!" Adams sighed as they hiked off down the canyon. "I'm plumb worn-out. But, if we get lucky, the next few days could prove exciting."

Four freezing nights later, they awoke in the dark, hearing a terrible commotion. Jumping up, Adams yelled, "Come on, boys! We got him!"

Lighting torches, they hurried through the darkness and, when they drew near the cage and raised their torches, the trapped monster went insane, biting and clawing at the logs so savagely that Adams yelled, "Everyone move back! Just . . . just stay back and we'll see if he won't settle down before he rips those logs apart!"

Kanaka wished he or Adams had thought to bring rifles. They weren't even armed. Tuolumne and Solon were equally frightened because they had never before seen such a huge grizzly. The greyhound whined and paced restlessly back and forth in the frosty moonlight while Lady Washington and the cubs, who had also been curious enough to investigate, now hid and watched from deep in the thickets.

When dawn finally arrived and the light grew strong, they were all astounded at the great size of the beast. Adams approached the cage and the monster charged him, striking the side of his prison violently enough to splinter thick timbers. Tuolumne turned and fled but Solon and Kanaka remained.

"Let's get more logs and reinforce this thing!" Adams shouted. "Hurry!"

The next hour was hellish, with the grizzly ripping apart logs almost as fast as they could be replaced. Kanaka's blood ran cold whenever the beast charged him, its crimson-streaked eyes rolling with rage. One by one, the replacement logs were braced and set until it became obvious that they had won and the bear was not going to escape. Long before that, Tuolumne, looking more than a little sheepish, had returned to help.

"We'll make our camp here for the next few days and then we'll decide what to do next," Adams wheezed, mopping perspiration from his brow.

"He will starve to death," Solon predicted.

"You will not train this one to walk on a leash," Tuolumne added.

But Adams was too exhilarated to listen. "I'm going to call him Samson! He's the largest and most ferocious captive bear in the world and he'll earn me a fortune."

At that moment, Samson smashed into the logs again, ripping away new hunks of bark and pine with his teeth and claws. Adams was delighted. "Yes," he said, moving dangerously near the shaking cage, "a fortune. And all we have to do is keep him alive until spring, when I'll return with an iron cage that he cannot possibly tear apart."

Adams rubbed his hands together in brisk anticipation. "For starters, I'll exhibit Samson in San Francisco. After that, I'll take only the best bookings and accompany him to the East. If he stays angry and acts ferocious enough to keep exciting the crowds, in two years, I'll be rich."

"Will you then allow the great bear to be set free?" Kanaka asked, feeling uneasy about the bear spirits that might seek to avenge the fate of this animal.

"Oh, Lord no! When I've finished milking the cities and their curious crowds, I'll sell this one to a circus or a sideshow."

Kanaka could not hide his sadness at this thought, for such a great animal deserved to roam free.

"Don't worry," Adams assured him. "Samson is more valuable than any Kentucky Thoroughbred racehorse and he'll earn far more money although he's considerably more expensive to keep. But being so valuable, I promise you that he will be well taken care of."

Adams placed his hand on Kanaka's shoulder. "Say," he declared, "I just had an idea. Nak, why don't you winter in this canyon to feed and watch over Samson? I'll have to find a good blacksmith to build an iron cage and we won't be able to haul it back up here until next spring."

"You want me to hunt meat all winter for that grizzly?"

"Sure! You'll have my rifle and plenty of ammunition. I'll also see you are well paid."

Kanaka shook his head because he did not feel good about any of this.

"Look, I know that you could use a good horse and I'll find you a top animal as long as you promise that you won't eat it. You wouldn't, would you?" Adams asked, only half in jest.

"No."

"What color do you favor?"

"One who shines like gold," Kanaka said, remembering his stallion, which had been sacrificed to the treacherous Mono.

"A palomino!" Adams nodded with approval. "Nak, you sure know how to pick them. All right. I'll see what I can do and we'll return next spring with an iron cage loaded on a big wagon."

Kanaka gazed at the great bear and decided that he might allow it to escape. But then, he thought about the horse and how wonderful it felt to race the wind.

"All right, then," Adams said, grinning. "We've got a deal."

Kanaka, despite himself, nodded. He would take care of poor Samson all this winter and become an expert hunter with his new Sharps rifle. "There is only one thing."

"Name it."

"I want you to tell my mother and sister that I am here and not to go up to Tuolumne to meet me."

Kanaka had never spoken of his mother and sister, or for that matter, much of anything concerning his past.

Adams was surprised. "You have family living down on the Fresno River Reservation?"

"No," Kanaka said. "In Ahwahnee. You will find their camp near Cho'-lok, or what you now call Yosemite Falls."

"Well, I'll be! Why didn't you ever say anything about them?"

"You didn't ask."

"No," Adams said, looking a little sheepish. "I guess I'm a lot better talker than listener. Right?"

Kanaka just smiled.

"Listen, Nak. If you prefer, I could leave Solon and Tuolumne here to watch over Samson and you could accompany me down to the valley and see your family. Everyone gets lonesome."

When Kanaka shook his head, Adams frowned. "Mind telling me why you won't go down there?"

"Too much trouble now."

Adams studied his face. "My guess is that you fought against the Mariposa Battalion when it was led by Major Savage. Am I right?"

Kanaka dipped his chin to tell Adams that this was true. He saw no point in adding that he had also stabbed to death a white prospector and might be recognized by George's friends.

"Well," Adams said, "from what I've heard of things, my people were just as much at fault as yours. The Yosemites started it by stealing valley horses and cattle, but that shouldn't have caused us to shoot and then herd the last of 'em off to the reservation."

When Kanaka said nothing, Adams toed the ground. "Listen, if you killed a few of those Mariposa Battalion volunteers—or any other whites—that could be a serious problem. *Is* that the problem?"

"Yes."

"Okay," Adams said, "we'll never talk about this again. What happened took place in war. They're even calling it the Mariposa Indian War. Good men, red and white and some half-breeds like yourself, killed or got killed. That's history. You shouldn't feel guilty but someone could recognize and shoot you. So . . . so, don't tell anyone else and you're probably smart to stay out of the valley for a few years, until the hatred dies."

Adams turned and started to walk away, then changed his mind. "Nak, remember, you promised you'd not kill anyone with my bullets or rifle."

"I promised."

Adams was relieved. "I'll find your mother and sister and tell them to come here instead of heading all the way up to Tuolumne. It's a lot closer, anyway, so they'll be glad."

Kanaka went over to sit on a rock and watch Samson. The bear had settled down and was no longer trying to destroy its cage. Now, it just crouched in wait, eyes smoldering with hatred.

Lucy was up in an oak tree gathering the last of the season's acorns to prepare acorn mush for Kanaka when she spotted a big, bearded man dressed in buckskins with a raccoon-tail cap ride into view. A moment later, she saw Lady Washington flanked by two walking Indians, a thin dog, and two bear cubs.

Lucy was so startled that she almost fell out of the oak tree. "Mother!" she called down to Anina, who was collecting fallen acorns. "Mother, look!"

Anina followed her daughter's pointing finger. Her reaction to the strange entourage was no less dramatic and she sat down hard.

Lucy flew down the tree. She helped Anina to her feet and they quickly gathered up their scattered acorns and then began to run toward their bark-covered u'-ma-cha. Wolf-dog ran with them but he was barking loudly, hackles raised at the sight of the huge, advancing grizzly. When they reached the old village of Koom-i-ne, Lucy and Anina collected their most precious belongings but then could not decide whether to run or to stay.

"He might have the uzamati attack and eat us!" Anina exclaimed. "We must hurry into the forest and hide!"

"There is nowhere to run that they could not find us," Lucy argued, as she grabbed Wolf-dog by the mane and ordered him to stay and not to go out and fight.

Anina threw back her head and began to chant and pray to all the spirits that had always protected her and the Ahwahneeche, especially to Ouma and the witches of Cho'-lok. Lucy, meanwhile, went out to meet whatever fate might befall her.

"Hello there!" Adams called, booting his mount into a trot and waving.

Lucy's knees were knocking but she stood her ground and even managed to wave in return and smile, knowing how these gestures of greeting were important to whites.

Adams drew up his horse and doffed his fur cap. He twisted

around in his saddle and pointed at Lady Washington and the rest of his company. "Now, Miss, don't you be alarmed by that bear or them cubs. They're all grizzlies, but gentle as kittens. I'm the wildest thing in this bunch and I come as a friend."

"Then my mother and I greet you as a friend," Lucy replied, willing herself not to look at the huge grizzly.

"I saw we caused you quite a start," Adams said. "You nearly fell outta that big tree yonder. As pretty as you are, it would've broken my heart if you'd broken your neck."

"Are you hungry?"

"No, thank you," Adams said. "We're just passin' through and there's still enough daylight to travel a spell. You'll be Lucy."

"How do you know this?"

"I'm a friend of your brother, Nak."

"Nak?"

"Kanaka."

"Is he well?"

"Sure is! He's guarding a grizzly even bigger'n this one up near Tenaya Creek. Said that's where you can find him instead of up at Tuolumne."

Lucy did not understand what this "guarding a grizzly" meant, and puzzlement must have shown on her face because the man dismounted and explained, "I trap and tame bears. That's why we've got a couple of cubs. Kanaka helped me catch and tame 'em. Now, we've caught a monster and I can't move him out of a big log cage until next spring. Do you follow?"

Lucy shook her head in confusion.

"Don't matter." Adams looked over at Anina, who was peeking fearfully around a maple tree. "Does your mother speak English, too?"

"Yes."

"And she's all right in the head?"

Lucy resented the question. "My mother is a great Ah-wahneeche medicine woman. She is very wise and . . ."

"I didn't mean no insult. She just looks a little . . . well, rattled."

Lucy motioned her mother to come and join them but Anina resisted, hanging back, eyes fixed on Lady Washington, who had begun to dig up the meadow in search of wild onions and bulbs. The two cubs joined her and the earth really started to fly.

"I'd better get my bears out of here before they dig you a lot deeper valley," Adams told them.

But Lucy had noticed that Adams had a badly infected hand. When she held it up, he blushed and said, "Ain't nothin' that won't heal in time, Miss Lucy."

Lucy disagreed. The hand was quite red and swollen. "Come," she said. "My mother will give you something to heal this quickly."

"Are you sure?"

"Yes."

When Anina realized that her services were needed, she forgot about being afraid. She ducked into their hut and soon reappeared with a dark green salve which she rubbed into Adam's infected wounds.

"Kinda stings," Adams said, face screwed up with pain. "What is it you've got in that stuff?"

"You whites call it 'gamble weed' but the Ahwahneeche call it 'rattlesnake medicine.' "

"But I didn't get bit!"

"No matter," Anina said. "Strong medicine. Leave on hand for two days and poison all gone. Hand feel good again. You see."

Adams looked over at Lucy who said, "My mother is a great Ahwahneeche healer."

"In that case," Adams said, shaking his injured hand and making a face, "I'll leave it on for two days. Kanaka told me that his mother had great powers and that his sister was the best basket maker in Ahwahnee."

"The *only* basket maker," Lucy corrected without humor.

"I'd like to buy one," Adams said. "If you make lids for 'em, maybe I could put them cubs in one for the night."

"No lids."

Adams bought two of Lucy's finest baskets anyway, trading away fifty pounds of jerked venison. "I've seen a lot of Indian baskets, but none as fine as these," he said, as he remounted his horse and prepared to leave. "You've got a gift, Miss Lucy!"

Lucy was very happy with the dried meat and secretly flattered by the American's lavish praise. She realized that she was not yet nearly as skilled as her old mentors, mostly women who had either remained on the dry side of the mountains with the Mono or died. But, in time, Lucy was sure that she could be a very respected Ahwahneeche basket maker.

"That's some dog," Adams said. "Big devil, ain't he? I'll wager he's mostly wolf."

"His name is Wolf-dog," Lucy said proudly.

"Well," Adams said, raising his reins, "I guess we'd better hurry on."

He tipped his hat to Lucy. "I got a cabin in the foothills two days west of this valley where we'll be wintering. If you have any trouble with anybody, try to get word to me and I'll come runnin' to help. Kanaka and I have gotten to be good friends."

Lucy watched as Adams galloped out to rejoin his entourage and then they all turned and went downriver through the trees.

"Crazy man," Anina muttered.

"Kanaka is waiting for us in the canyon of the glistening rocks," Lucy told her mother. "He is guarding another uzamati."

"Then *he* has become crazy, too!"

"No," Lucy said. "He has made a friend of a good white man and so I think he is growing wise."

Anina hurried away to make acorn mush for her crazy son.

Twenty-one

Grizzly Adams's cabin,
North Fork Merced River, 1855

Lucy and Anina had gone to see Kanaka up in Tenaya Canyon once that fall and several more times during the winter and spring. On two of those occasions, they had met Grizzly Adams and had finally grown comfortable with him. They even enjoyed visits by the strange man and his equally strange pets. But now, guided by Solon, they were riding horses up a small valley west of Ahwahnee, perhaps to save Adams's life.

"That is Mr. Adams's cabin," Solon announced.

Anina looked very uncomfortable on horseback and this had been a difficult trip. It had been raining most of the two full days they had traveled and the rivers were deep, wide, and treacherous to cross. But somehow, they had made it safely and now Adams's cabin was finally in sight.

"Ben Franklin is hurt, too," Solon told them once more. "Both man and cub bear, hurt bad."

"I'm not touching the bear!" Anina repeated once more.

Lucy already had made up her mind that *she* would minister to the young grizzly if only her mother would prepare the medicines.

As they grew near the log cabin, the greyhound, whose name was Rambler, spotted them and began to bark. Wolf-dog galloped on ahead. A moment later, Tuolumne and a tall, clean-shaven white man appeared from inside the cabin and hurried forward. Lady Washington, chained to a tree, raised her head for a moment to yawn, then dropped it back to rest on her huge paws. The cubs were nowhere in sight and Wolf-dog quickly dominated the much smaller Rambler who tucked her tail between her legs and rolled over on her back.

"Thank heavens you made it," the American said, taking the reins of Anina's horse and then offering to help her dismount. "My name is Dan Marble and you must be Anina."

"Yes."

"Here," he said, "I'll help you down."

"No." Anina pushed his hand aside and climbed down under her own power. She had two buckskin baskets of herbs and medicines slung over her shoulder and Lucy carried a burden basket filled with food and extra things that they might need during their stay.

"What about you?" Dan Marble asked, smiling up at her Lucy. "Can I help you down?"

"I can climb down for myself."

He had blue eyes and they mirrored amusement. "Suit yourself."

* * *

The American returned his attention to Anina and said, "Mr. Adams is feverish. He was chewed up pretty badly. If it hadn't been for Gentle Ben jumping into the fray, the mother grizzly would have killed Mr. Adams. I'm afraid he may still die if we can't break his fever."

Anina gave no indication that she understood. Neither she nor Lucy had ever been inside a white man's cabin and now, poised in front of this one, Anina hesitated with obvious dread.

"It will be all right, Mother," Lucy assured her, taking Anina's arm and urging her inside.

The square interior of the room looked very strange and the floorboards under Lucy's feet squeaked like quarreling mice. She saw a stove and many other things whose names and functions were complete mysteries. Then she saw Adams lying on a pallet and beside him rested the yearling cub they all called Gentle Ben. Both were in obvious distress. Someone had shaved bare places in the young grizzly's thick coat and applied salves.

Anina hurried over to the badly injured pair. She touched the American's forehead. The poor man's scalp had been ripped from the front part of his skull and then smoothed back across his upper forehead in the hope that it would reattach. A vile smelling poultice sweating a greenish ooze rested on the wound. Anina pitched it across the room and it stuck to the log wall.

"Bad fever," she said, ignoring the mauled bear cub that now whimpered pathetically at her feet.

Adams opened his eyes and, when he spoke, his voice was shockingly weak. "My own damn fault. I was in heavy thickets, where I had no business being, when I stepped between a sow and her cubs. I raised my rifle but she knocked it away with one paw and laid my skull open with the other. After that, she jumped on top of me and began to chew. I yelled for help, so Ben and Lady Washington attacked that mother bear and drove her offa me. They saved my life."

Anina glanced over at the poultice weeping down the wall. "What is that?"

"Tree and river moss," Dan explained, when Adams was at a loss for words. "Tuolumne said that his people use it to draw out poison. I've been applying it night and day but it doesn't seem to be doing much good. Those wounds are still festering."

"Make fire. Boil water. Hurry!" Anina urged, pulling down Adams's blanket and studying the bite wounds on his chest and upper abdomen.

Lucy could see that Grizzly Adams had suffered a terrible clawing and biting. But, as she gazed over her mother's shoulder, she did not see any sign of rotting flesh nor was there the sweet, sickening stench of decay. Rather, all the wounds looked red and angry.

"I sent Solon because I was hoping that you'd bring some more of that 'rattlesnake medicine' that cleaned up my hands," Adams whispered. "Did you bring some of that stinging salve?"

Anina nodded, then, as a fire was being made and water set to boil, she closed her eyes and began to chant because, in addition to her medicines, much of her confidence was based on the belief that sickness is brought on partly by bad spirits while healing takes place much faster when good spirits are invoked.

When the water was ready, Anina added the leaves of the plant she called hotcotca, also known to the whites as "mule ears."

"What is that I'm supposed to drink?"

"No drink," Anina said. "You die if you drink."

"Then what . . ."

Anina dipped a soft piece of buckskin into the steamy liquid and said, "Lie still. No complain."

To her daughter, she said, "You go outside. All go. Now."

Lucy had already started for the door with Solon, Tuolumne, and the American following. A moment later, they heard Adams gasp and then yelp, "That's too damned hot! You're scalding me!"

"What's that stuff your mother is boiling Mr. Adams alive with?" Dan asked when they sat down on a log outside the cabin and prepared to wait out the treatment.

"It makes him sweat," Lucy explained. "It will break fever and is also good for cleaning wounds. You'll see."

"Ahhhh! I'm on fire!" Adams howled.

Solon started to jump up from his seat but Lucy grabbed his arm. "Don't worry. My mother learned everything from Ouma. She fix. She heal Adams good."

Solon exchanged worried glances with Tuolumne and then they both looked to the American, who said, "We've had our turn and Mr. Adams is getting worse. All we can do now is trust that Anina knows what she's doing."

Lucy, who had seen her mother use this medicine many times before, was not worried, and she kept offering reassurance to Adams's friends. "This medicine very good. Mr. Adams be much better soon. You wait and see."

"I sure hope so," Dan fretted. "That man has been in terrible pain. There's no real doctor between here and that new city they're calling Sacramento. By the way, Miss Lucy, I own a blacksmith shop in Sonora. That's where I built a huge iron cage for that giant grizzly bear that your brother is watching. That cage is strong enough to hold an elephant. . . ."

"Elephant?"

Dan laughed and Lucy thought she had never seen better teeth on a man.

"I'm sorry," he apologized. "I forgot that there's no way that you'd have heard of an elephant. It's a huge animal that lives in Africa and has a great long nose."

Dan made a downward swooping motion with both hands curled to indicate what a great nose the elephant possessed. Lucy had to smile. "I never see animal with a nose so long."

"Well," he said, "there are many crazy-looking animals in this world. I saw an elephant in Alexandria, Virginia, when I was a boy. Biggest thing you could imagine. And when they get upset, they trumpet."

Lucy shrugged her shoulders and stared down at her lap.

"You're quite beautiful, you know," Dan said. "Mr. Adams warned me that you would be and that I should watch myself or I'd get smitten. And he was right."

She looked up. Yes, his eyes really were as blue as the winter sky over Ahwahnee. "Smitten?"

Dan stood up and extended his hand but Wolf-dog, who had been lying behind the rock, climbed to his feet and growled.

"Whoa!" Dan said, backing away. "Is he your protector?"

"He is my best friend," Lucy explained as Wolf-dog trotted around the log and came between them with his fangs bared.

Dan backed away. "He's big enough to give even that mother bear a fight."

Lucy dropped her hand to the Wolf-dog's mane and shushed him, then said to Dan, "What's this word 'smitten' mean?"

"Never mind," he said, eyes glued warily on the wolf-dog.

Lucy didn't have any idea what the handsome young American wearing the red flannel shirt was talking about but he suddenly remembered other things to do. She watched him go to a small corral and saddle a horse. In a very few minutes, he was riding across the yard.

"I'll be back soon," he called to her. "Nice meeting you, Lucy."

"Nice meeting you, Dan," Lucy said, feeling a curious warmth touch her cheeks.

When Lucy turned and looked at Solon and Tuolumne, she could see amusement had replaced anxiousness in their eyes. "What does this word 'smitten' mean, please?"

The two Indians giggled like children and hurried away. Lucy shook her head, deciding that these were all very strange people.

The next two weeks were very busy and Lucy had not had such an enjoyable time for as long as she could remember. The main thing was that Grizzly Adams was improving rapidly and the American could not say enough about Anina's powers and medicines. Anina obviously was flattered by this rare and enthusiastic praise, which was a revelation to Lucy. This was especially significant considering that, only a few years ago, both Anina and Kanaka had hated all the whites and thought of them as devils. And, while it still was true that they were responsible for the destruction of The People, Lucy could not help but like Grizzly Adams and his handsome young blacksmith friend. Every day, Dan accompanied her and Wolf-dog on their daily walks to gather more herbs and to search for greens. The tall American with the laughing blue eyes said the reason he came was to protect her against grizzly bears like the one that had attacked Adams.

"I need no more protection," she told him, glancing toward Wolf-dog.

"Well, that might be true, and it might not," he said. "Sometimes, grizzly bears run in packs like dogs. If a pack of them should find you, even Wolf-dog would not be much help."

"I never heard of them being together that way," Anina said with a frown. "Uzamati hunt alone."

"Well, sometimes even the uz-a-what-you-call-'ems get lonely. Lucy, *all* things get lonely." He moved closer until Wolf-dog began to growl and then he stopped and said, "Don't *you* ever get lonely?"

"No. I have my mother and Wolf-dog. Not lonely ever."

"Too bad," he said, looking genuinely sorry.

Lucy was very grateful for Wolf-dog's loyal protection, as much from Dan as from any grizzlies. And often, when she bent to pick a plant for her basket or to dig up a tasty bulb or reach for a wild plum or berry, she saw Dan watching her intently. His eyes caused her to shiver, though she was not sure why.

"What do you Americans call this?" she would ask whenever she found a plant that the Ahwahneeche collected as food.

Dan surprised her because he knew a great deal about plants. In addition to his blacksmithing, he raised cattle and sheep on pastures down near a big river called the San Joaquin.

"Let's see," he mused. "That plant is called . . . rose lupine."

"Tulmi'ssa," she said, giving him the Ahwahneeche name.

"And this?" she asked, holding up a very green plant with small white blossoms."

He plucked it from her fingers. "Lucy, that's easy! It's nothing but plain old clover. Are you really going to eat that stuff?"

Lucy began to chew the clover. "Ahwahneeche name is pumusayu. Very delicious. If steamed in basket, then dried, good to save for winter."

Dan grimaced until Lucy boldly walked up to him and stuck the clover in his face. Still chewing, she said, "You try, Dan."

And, to her surprise, he actually nibbled a little, then grimaced. "Ugh! It tastes like vinegar!"

"Good for Ahwahneeche, good for Dan, too," Lucy said, biting back her laughter.

Dan swallowed the clover and, when Wolf-dog growled, the American dashed off, probably to rinse his mouth in the river.

One day, three more Americans arrived, one on horseback and the others sitting in the front of a big wagon that carried Samson's new iron cage.

"Well," Dan said, when they helped Adams outside to look at his new acquisition, "what do you think? Is it big and strong enough to hold that monster that's going to make you a fortune with a traveling circus?"

Adams looked much better and, because Anina also had been treating Gentle Ben, the yearling cub was going to survive its own previously infected bite wounds.

Although still weak from his mauling, Grizzly Adams inspected every bar of the cage, pulling and then pounding on each with a hammer until he was satisfied. He took particular note of the trapdoor and pronounced it satisfactory.

"You've earned your fifty dollars and then some," he announced to Dan. "And I wish that I could pay the balance upon delivery as I agreed. Unfortunately, I cannot at this time because I had intended to capture some animals to sell but was prevented by my accident."

"Never mind," Dan said. "You're good for the money and I've had a fine time here. Fact of it is, I'm willing to call it square if you'll give me a horse so that I can accompany you into Yosemite. I'd not only like to see this monster that you've been bragging about, but I'd like to see the valley. I've heard that it is nothing short of spectacular."

"It is," Adams agreed. "Unfortunately, I've heard that a man named Hutchings along with several other tourists, are planning extended visits to Yosemite this summer. I expect that they will only be the first of many more to follow."

Lucy's head turned toward Anina and she clasped her mother's hand tightly. "It will be all right," she whispered in her ear. "We knew this would happen. We've talked and prayed about it for years."

But apparently their prayers and talk had not done much good. Tears began to slide down Anina's brown and wrinkled cheeks.

Dan, seeing this, stepped forward and gently asked, "Can I somehow be of help?"

"No," Lucy said quietly, before she led her mother off so that they could be alone. "There is nothing that you or anyone—not even Ouma—can do now for Ahwahnee."

Several days later, after a very heavy rainstorm, they all left Adams's winter cabin and headed for Yosemite. Progress was slow because of the wagon and its heavy load. When they reached the best place to ford the Merced River, the water was high and Lucy's main concern was for her mother, who had never felt confident on horseback.

Adams, Yokut, and Tuolumne all climbed onto the wagon and Dan told Anina that she should do the same. But Anina became stubborn and refused.

"I stay on horse," she declared.

"Then I will, too," Lucy said, determined to remain close to her mother.

"You *both* ought to get onto that wagon," Dan warned. "We can tie your horses to the back and they'll swim along behind."

"No," Anina snapped.

Adams looked down from the wagon. "She's made up her mind, Dan. Might as well stop the arguing and let's get this thing across the river. It'll be all right. I know every inch of the footing."

Preparations were made. The ropes and chains that secured the massive iron bear cage were inspected and tightened. The horses were tied behind the wagon and Dan checked the cinches under Anina and Lucy, as well as his own.

"All right," he said when he was satisfied that everything was in order. "We'll go across first on horseback and the wagon can follow when we're on the other side."

Dan positioned himself upriver of Anina and Lucy, saying, "The river bottom changes, especially when the water is high like now. Lucy, Anina, if either of your horses steps into a hole, don't panic. Just give him his head and let him swim out of it. All right?"

Lucy nodded, but Anina just stared at the surging white water. "Let's go!" Dan said, spurring his own horse into the rain-swollen current.

Lucy and Anina had to force their horses into the river and the moment they were in the grip of its current, Lucy knew that the Merced was much faster and more powerful than it had been when they'd crossed it several weeks earlier. Dan yelled something but Lucy couldn't hear him over the booming of the angry river. When they reached the center of the North Fork of the Merced, the water was beginning to boil around their horses' bellies.

Suddenly, Lucy's horse dropped into a hole and rolled completely over. Lucy had no time to kick free of her stirrups and she felt herself being turned upside down. An instant later, the weight of the horse crushed and then ground her against the river bottom. Lucy's mouth flew open and water filled her throat as she whipped back up to the surface and her horse struggled to reach the opposite shore.

She could hear Dan yelling as she clung to the animal, trying to clear her lungs. Everything was a watery distortion. Lucy collapsed, pitching out of the saddle. An instant later, Dan was dragging her across the neck of his own horse and she was vomiting water.

Lucy lost all focus. The next thing she knew, she was lying facedown in the mud and Dan was pressing down hard between her shoulder blades, hard enough to break even more ribs.

"Stop!" she gagged.

He eased her onto her back, brushing away all the wet, muddy hair plastered to her face. "Lucy, it's gonna be all right!" he promised, as Anina whipped her own horse to shore and then threw herself out of the saddle to scramble to her daughter's side.

After a very hurried examination, everyone relaxed when Anina held up four fingers to indicate that her daughter had four cracked or broken ribs but no life-threatening injuries.

"If you had drowned," Grizzly Adams said, "I'd never have forgiven myself. You should have stayed in your valley."

Dan squeezed Lucy's hand tightly. Wolf-dog began to growl but Dan ignored the beast and said, "She's going to be all right,

Mr. Adams. She's going to be just fine. In fact, maybe *now* they will finally consent to ride in the back of the wagon."

Lucy managed to nod her head and Anina did the same.

The rest of the trip back to Yosemite was uneventful until they reached the great meadow near Yosemite Falls and saw a large party of tourists. Anina became so upset that they made an early camp. Dan Marble and Grizzly Adams rode their horses across the meadow and visited with the group for a while, then came back about sundown.

"The party is under the leadership of a Mr. James Hutchings," Dan Said. "Mr. Hutchings has hired a wonderful artist named Thomas Ayres and he showed us some excellent sketches of the falls and the valley. Together, Mr. Hutchings and Mr. Ayres plan to publish an illustrated monthly devoted entirely to the natural wonders of California. They are very excited about doing one of their very first features on Yosemite."

"That's the *last* thing we want," Adams said. "First thing you know, this valley will be crawling with summer tourists."

"I'm afraid you're right," Dan agreed.

Lucy was heartbroken at the thought of tourists moving in so close to the old village of Koom-i-ne, where the Ahwahneeche spirits had forever dwelled. Anina was so disturbed that she went into mourning, as she had when Ezekial died.

Early the next day, they left Anina to rest in the valley while they hauled the cage up Tenaya Canyon to meet with Kanaka and transfer the giant grizzly. Spending the winter in a log trap had done nothing to improve Samson's nasty disposition. When he saw the new visitors, he attacked the logs in a biting and clawing frenzy.

"I can see he's been upset a few times since last I was here," Adams said, noting how Kanaka had added new logs and bracing.

"He is better," Kanaka said, not bothering to tell them that he and Samson actually had reached a state of peaceful coexistence. In return for being fed and left alone, Samson finally had stopped attacking the logs. Now, however, with all these new people milling around, the giant grizzly was becoming very agitated again.

Adams also was becoming alarmed as the bark and pine shards began to fly. He feared that Samson, in spite of all his previous unsuccessful attempts to break free, might finally become so crazed that he actually would be able to destroy his cage and attack his captors.

"Let's get the new cage unloaded and the doors matched and then chained together!" he ordered.

Both cages had dropping trapdoors, and Adams had made sure that they were of the same dimensions. In that way, by pulling and then chaining the cages tightly together, both doors could be raised or dropped in near unison, preventing any possibility of the grizzly's escape.

"Watch it!" Dan shouted when the two cages were slammed together and Samson threw himself at the men, huge paws stabbing out, with long claws desperately reaching to catch and pull a man into his jaws. "Stay back!"

Even Tuolumne and Solon, accustomed to working with grizzly bears, were so intimidated that they refused to risk their lives chaining the cages together and then raising the trapdoors.

"Lure him away!" Adams yelled over Samson's fearful rampage as he struggled with the heavy chains necessary to bind the cages together.

Adams's men circled around to the other side of the cage, drawing Samson to them in a snarling rush. Dan pulled the chains away from Grizzly Adams yelling, "You can do this next time!"

"There won't be a next time!"

But Dan already had the chains and, even before Samson knew what he was doing, he had the two cages chained together. Not stopping there, the agile young blacksmith leaped up onto the log cage and strained on a pull rope to raise the trapdoor. The grizzly whirled and raced back, then reared up and took a swipe at Dan's feet. His right boot peeled open and blood began to spurt as Dan lost his balance and fell to his knees. Lucy cried out as the bear lunged with his bared teeth but Dan rolled across the top of the log cage and threw himself onto the iron one, just ahead of the grizzly's attack.

"Come down!" Lucy cried.

Instead, Dan pulled the iron door up and set a safety brake on so that it could not drop by accident. Samson, smelling blood and frantic to get his quarry, rushed into the iron cage, reaching again for Dan, who dived from the cage and rolled beyond the grasp of the grizzly's outstretched claws. Kanaka alone had the presence of mind to drop the iron door just as Samson whirled and prepared to charge back into his more familiar log prison.

"We did it!" Adams cried. "Now we've got him!"

But Lucy was rushing to Dan's side and kneeling to grab his torn and bloody boot. "You're crazy!"

Anina also hurried over. She calmly unlaced his boot and squeezed the wound tightly.

"Get my medicine bag," she instructed her daughter. "Hurry."

Lucy did hurry because she now realized that Dan was not only brave but also very dear to her.

Samson went berserk in his new cage. He threw himself at the heavy bars and bit them without leaving a mark. Frustrated, he lunged again and again until he looked dazed and defeated. Grizzly Adams heaved a deep sigh of relief. His monster was now impotent and no longer posed a danger. And soon, he would be drawing huge crowds and raking in the money.

The next day, goodbyes were said all around and the most important one for Lucy was when Dan folded her hands in his own and said, "I'm going back to Sonora and settle my affairs. And then do you know what I'm going to do?"

Lucy shook her head.

"I'm driving my livestock up from the San Joaquin all the way to Yosemite and I'm going to homestead, raise livestock, and watch over *you*."

"All because you are 'smitten' with me?"

He laughed, then pulled her close and kissed her mouth. Lucy was not sure if she minded or not. She looked around for Wolf-dog but he was taking a nap.

"Lucy," he said, "you be real careful around men and everything. I know that you've got Wolf-dog, but he easily could be shot."

"I will be good," she told him.

Kanaka came over to join them and said, "You be good with my sister."

"I will always be good to her, Kanaka. But what will you do?"

Kanaka turned to the high mountains, eyes reaching toward Tuolumne. "I will go up to live with the eagles."

Just before they separated, Grizzly Adams took Kanaka aside. "I'm broke," he admitted. "Kanaka, I'm sorry that I didn't have either the time or the money to get you that golden-colored horse that we agreed on in return for your wintering with Samson. But I'll bring him next trip."

Kanaka was not so sure. Adams, while sincerely wishing to meet his obligations, found many excuses. Besides, Kanaka was unsure that a horse could survive through the Tuolumne winters without a great deal of hay and trouble. Maybe it was better if he remained afoot.

After that, they went their separate ways. Grizzly Adams, Dan Marble, and the rest of the whites back to the valleys, Kanaka to the mountains, and Anina and Lucy to Ahwahnee.

Lucy had known too many sad, even tragic, farewells. But this time, even with the new settlers in Ahwahnee, she felt happy and believed that the future held great promise.

Twenty-two

Old Village of Koom-i-ne
Eight years later, Spring 1863

Anina was dead. Less than a year after Wolf-dog's quiet passing, Anina was dead. Lucy had expected that her mother would live to enjoy yet another summer and fall acorn harvest. But a sudden spring snowstorm had caught them gathering food far from the shelter of their u'-ma-cha. Lucy had tried to help her feverish and chilled mother back to Koom-i-ne, but they had been forced to endure a wet, bitterly cold night without shelter. There had been no fire and no food in a bone-chilling wind. Anina had become delirious with fever and, by noon, she had slipped into the spirit world.

Lucy scrubbed her red and swollen eyes as she sat alone beside their hut. With her mother's ashes still warm from the funeral pyre, Lucy knew that she would need to summon every last bit of her strength if she were to faithfully execute Anina's final wishes. But first she would fulfill the Ahwahneeche traditions of mourning by chopping off her long, lustrous hair so that all would know that she grieved.

She did this with a knife obtained from a white man in trade for two of her small beautifully woven dipper baskets. She then took a few generous pinches of her mother's ashes and went to a pine tree, where she used the blade of her knife to squeeze out some of its golden pitch. Rubbing Anina's ashes into the pitch, Lucy smeared the sticky grayish black mixture across her forehead and then down her cheeks so that the marks resembled the trails of tears. This was the old Ahwahneeche way of showing respect for the dead. Lucy returned to the hut that she had shared with her aged mother ever since Grizzly Adams and Dan Marble had departed from the valley of Ahwahnee, neither man ever to be seen again. Their u'-cha-ma was sad and silent. According to The People's customs, Lucy had included all of her mother's prized belongings in the cremation, so that Anina could have them in the spirit world. Only Anina's "mourning necklace" remained. Lucy admired it, blinking away fresh tears. The mourning necklace consisted of seven small buckskin bags filled with Anina's most precious medicinal powders linked on a string of twisted plant fibers. Lucy tied the mourning necklace around her neck, where it would remain either until the string wore out or until autumn, when she could observe the traditional Ahwahneeche mourning ceremony.

When the necklace was secured around her neck, she went over to the river and found a small pool of water. She leaned over the pool and barely recognized herself because of her shorn hair, streaked face, and swollen eyes. *I still do not look worthy to properly mourn the death of a great medicine woman and mother,* she thought, hand going to her knife, which she now raised with the intention of slashing her cheeks.

But a voice called from across the meadow. "Hello!"

Lucy whirled around, knife clenched in her fist. She recognized James Hutchings, who now operated a guest lodge in the valley. It had once been known as the "Upper" Hotel, but now he was calling it the Hutchings House. There was another hotel called the "Lower" Hotel, which had been built several years earlier, at the base of Loy'-a, which meant "long water basket" to the Ahwahneeche but which the whites had renamed Sentinel Rock. Lucy and her mother had never visited either hotel.

Mr. Hutchings was in his mid-forties and seemed kind, but Lucy wished he would go away. He never had shown any great interest in Anina. True, they had waved at each other many times, but this man had never come to visit nor had his pretty young wife, now heavy with child. Why, Lucy wondered, was Mr. James Hutchings here now?

The man carried a crude and very inferior Miwok wicker basket. It was without symmetry or design. Halting about fifty feet away, he stared at Lucy, then slowly removed his hat.

"I come to say that Elvira and I are very sorry that your mother died. We kept meaning to come visit, but we'd heard that Anina was in poor health so we put it off, hopin' she'd get better."

Lucy allowed the knife to slip from her fingers and spill into the pool. "I thank you, Mr. Hutchings."

"Me and the Missus, as well as my mother-in-law, Mrs. Sproat, all heard that your mother was a great Yosemite healer."

"Ahwahneeche healer," she corrected.

"Yes, Ahwahneeche. Anyway, Elvira and her mother cooked up some things for you to eat."

"I am not hungry."

"You will be later," he said, setting the basket down beside his feet. "So, I'm just going to leave the whole basket. We're really sorry about your mother. I understand that you are now all alone."

"Not alone," Lucy said, glancing up at Cho'-lok and thinking of how her mother's spirit would soon join Ouma's. And how, someday, her own spirit would join those of her mother and grandmother in the water where the legendary Po'-loti, or spirit witches, dwelled.

"Miss Lucy, I really wish I had known your mother," Hutchings said. "I heard about her healing Grizzly Adams after he was mauled."

"Yes, she did that."

"I never knew Mr. Adams. Wish I had, though. He and that big bear that they called Gentle Ben."

"He was a nice bear."

Hutchings smiled. "I heard stories of them opening that Pacific Museum over in San Francisco. I'm told that, a few years later, Mr. Adams sailed around Cape Horn with several more grizzlies, some pet wolves and mountain lions, an elk, a buffalo, and even an old sea lion he called Neptune. I heard that, when Grizzly Adams arrived in New York, thousands of people were waiting on the docks and they weren't disappointed. I wish I'd seen his show. Grizzly Adams joined up with the P.T. Barnum's circus. The whole country was devastated when Gentle Ben and then Grizzly Adams himself died only a couple of years later."

Lucy had not heard this and was taken aback. "Mr. Adams is dead?"

"You didn't know?"

Lucy shook her head, then dared to ask the question that still burned in her mind. "Did you ever hear of a man named Dan Marble?"

"He was with Adams, wasn't he?"

"Yes," Lucy whispered, feeling her throat painfully constrict.

"What is that stuff you smeared on your face?" Hutchings asked.

"The ashes of my mother joined with the blood of the forest trees."

Hutchings blinked but quickly recovered and pointed to a basket. "Miss Lucy, did you weave that?"

"Yes."

He smiled. "It's a beautiful basket. May I examine it?"

"No," Lucy said. "It holds my mother's ashes."

Hutchings wiped his chin whiskers with the back of his hand. "Can I go get a shovel and dig a hole for you to bury them ashes?"

Lucy shook her head.

"You know," the hotel keeper said, "it ain't safe for a pretty young woman . . . and you are pretty, even with that stuff smeared on your face and your hair all chopped short . . . to live alone. More'n' more strangers are coming into this valley. Most are good, but some might not be. Elvira and I was wonderin' if you would like to live with us. Be safer. You could also make a fine income demonstrating basket weaving and then selling your baskets to our guests, many of whom are quite well-to-do."

"No, thank you."

"It'd be perfect," he said, not hearing her. "You could also educate folks about your Ahwahneeche people. You'd be a real favorite and . . ."

"No."

Hutchings heard her this time. Troubled, he wrung his hat brim and glanced back over his shoulder toward their box-shaped, two-storied hotel before returning his attention to Lucy. "My timing is very bad. And, while I don't mean to pry or to tell you what to do, I sure hope you don't cut yourself with that knife."

When Lucy turned away, Hutchings blurted, "I am sure that God or your Great Spirit didn't create beauty for us to deface, even during times of sorrow. That's all that I know, Miss Lucy. I just . . ."

"Goodbye, Mr. Hutchings."

"Goodbye," he said. "I still want you to think about coming to live with us. Elvira is expecting a baby soon. She and Mrs. Sproat could use some help and . . . well, you'd be safe. You'd be a real special treat for the Hutchings House guests. You could talk about the Yosemite . . . I mean *Ahwahneeche* . . . ways and even sell our guests your baskets. I know you'd be real popular. So would that brother of yours, if he would ever come down and live in the valley."

"He never will."

"People change. Anyway, just think about the offer and pass it on to your brother. He could be our native high Sierra guide. Kanaka speaks good English, too, right?"

Lucy nodded.

"So long," Hutchings said. "Hope you enjoy the food. We'll talk again when you're feeling better, okay?"

Lucy nodded again even as she let her tears flow. Hutchings could not see her face turned toward the cliffs. Later, she gathered up the basket holding her mother's ashes and went to offer them to mighty Cho'-lok.

It took Lucy until sundown to climb to the top of the lowest of the three-tiered waterfalls. With the sky ablaze and her body damp with rising mist, Lucy poured her mother's ashes into Yosemite Creek, where they were swept over the falls and joined Ouma in the deep witches' pool. It had been Anina's prayer that some of her ashes would continue to float downriver so that her body would touch all of Ahwahnee.

"Goodbye," Lucy whispered to the thundering water. "Goodbye, dear Mother and Grandmother."

Lucy remained above the falls all night, staring up at the glittering heavens and thinking about Ouma, Anina, Tenaya, and all of The People who once had lived in Ahwahnee but now were dead or living somewhere they did not belong. Nothing would ever be the same again.

And what of Dan Marble, the man whose face she remembered more than all other Americans? Mr. Hutchings had told her nothing. Was Dan dead, or alive? Lucy had come to believe that her Dan had found a better woman and taken her to wife. A woman who could read and write English. A woman who would be happy living in the white man's cities and believing in his Christian god. A woman who had already given him beautiful children and could do far more than weave pretty baskets.

Sometime just before first light, in the darkest, loneliest hour of night, Lucy stepped to the very edge of Cho'-lok. She gazed at the bright North Star and felt the cold, swift water tugging at her feet and ankles. She listened for Ouma and the Po'-loti, willing them to call her to join them in the deep pool far below. But try as she might, Lucy could not hear them so she opened her eyes, stepped out of the water, and waited for the first feeble light of dawn.

Soon, it burst across the highest Sierra peaks as red as the blossoms of the mountain snow plant. Its crimson glow spilled across Clouds' Rest and haloed the crown of Half Dome. Lucy raised her hands over Ahwahnee to greet the rising sun and decided to go visit Kanaka, the last living link with her family and the Ahwahneeche.

Lucy followed Yosemite Creek around the great mountains until she finally reached Tuolumne and found her brother's cave. She waited two days before Kanaka's return and, during that time, ate nothing. When her brother finally arrived after a long hunt and saw the pitch and ashes on Lucy's face as well as his mother's mourning necklace and Lucy's chopped off-hair, he knew without words that his mother was in the spirit world.

"Four days ago, after the last snowstorm, I felt my bones grow cold," Kanaka confessed to Lucy that evening as they roasted venison over his campfire. "I heard the wolves howl and a great sadness overcame me. I knew that our mother had died. Did you bring ashes for me?"

"No. I gave them all to Cho'-lok."

Kanaka pulled his knife from a leather sheath and leaned over close to Lucy. "Hold very still," he ordered.

With his knife, Kanaka gently peeled off a thin strip of ashes and pitch from Lucy's cheeks, then he pressed it to his own face. But it did not stick, no matter how many times Kanaka tried, it would not stick to his own cheeks. So he placed the hard, gray mixture on his tongue and swallowed.

"Do you want to stay here with me?" he asked his sister the next morning, as they walked across an alpine meadow following the trail of a large mountain lion.

Lucy tracked Kanaka's eyes toward a stand of weather-beaten rocks and whitebark pine, where the big cat lay waiting, creamy coat melding perfectly with the rock, tail swishing back and forth ever so slightly. Kanaka held his rifle but had no interest in killing the magnificent cat.

"I belong in Ahwahnee," she said.

"Ahwahnee is no more for us! But up here you can feel the spirit of earth, pure and clean like air and water."

"I could not be happy here," Lucy tried to explain. "Like our mother and her mother, I will always belong in Ahwahnee."

Kanaka finally dipped his chin in acceptance. "When will you return?"

"When the aspen turns red and gold," she said, deciding right then that she would spend all of this summer with Kanaka, the last true Ahwahneeche hunter.

Kanaka was very pleased, so pleased that he threw back his head and howled, causing the mountainlion to spring to its feet and dash away.

Summer was almost over. Lucy had done little other than pick flowers, watch clouds, and sometimes join Kanaka in chasing their dark, flowing shadows across the meadows. Other days Lucy spent accompanying her brother as he explored the wonders of the alpine glaciers and meadows that were strung like colorful jewels across the Sierras. Kanaka had become one with these mountains. There was no peak, valley, snowfield, or lake with which he was not intimately familiar. Kanaka also knew where the Bighorn sheep fed in the early morning and where they went to sleep at night. He knew where the mountain lions ranged and where the eagles made their nests and where a pure vein of gold could be seen threading through a broken thrust of quartz rock. He alone knew where the wolverine passed to leave its scent on a lightning-burned old bristlecone pine. Kanaka showed her the places where bobcats, foxes, lynx, wolves, grizzlies, and elk lived and hunted during the brief but spectacular Sierra summer.

Kanaka also demonstrated extraordinary eyesight and once, when poised atop a towering, granite dome, Kanaka pointed eastward toward the desert and found a lake smaller than the point of the farthest star.

Lucy sensed a newfound strength and tranquility in her brother. Sometimes, however, Kanaka was so remote that he did not speak to Lucy for days at a time, but she always knew that he took great pleasure in her company. One indication of this was that he often braided her a headband of the rarest, most beautiful of all the alpine wildflowers.

When Tuolumne nights grew cold and aspen began to fill the canyons in a blaze of color, Lucy felt Kanaka's growing sadness at the thought of her leaving. On these occasions, she would again seriously reconsider her decision to return to Ahwahnee and she almost decided to stay in the high country. But then,

Lucy's mind would reach toward Ahwahnee and know that it was where her own heart and spirit belonged.

"Grizzly Adams died a few years ago," she told her brother one morning as they began to go in search of game. "And so did the bear they called Gentle Ben."

"His *real* name was Benjamin Franklin," Kanaka said after a long silence. "And his brother was *General* Jackson. I taught the general to lead on a leash. And what happened to Lady Washington and to Samson?"

"All dead, I think. It was many years ago."

Kanaka's brow furrowed. "Maybe Adams set them free before he died."

"Maybe," Lucy said, doubting it.

On a cloudy morning several days later, while crossing a valley surrounded by snowcapped peaks, they heard a sharp, cracking sound. Lucy thought it was thunder but Kanaka dragged her down beside him behind some rocks.

"What is wrong!"

"It was a rifle."

Kanaka listened to the noise rolling off the surrounding peaks. It was impossible to locate its origin but, suddenly, a horseman appeared, waving and shouting as he galloped toward them.

"It is Dan Marble," Kanaka said, first to recognize the approaching horseman. "He has come for you, Lucy! After all these years, he has finally come for you."

"It cannot be!"

"But it is," Kanaka insisted as he shaded his eyes. "He is much changed. His hair has turned to the color of snow and his face is now thin. He has suffered much."

Lucy jumped to her feet and began to run toward the man and the horse.

Dan reined in and quickly dismounted. His horse trotted off to graze but no one noticed as the two lovers embraced. Kanaka's lips formed a smile. He turned and hurried away to hunt a fat bighorn sheep for the marriage feast, the first ever in Tuolumne.

Lucy drew back and looked at her Dan, thinking that Kanaka was right, he *had* changed a great deal and not all of it was physical. Lucy noticed the deep sadness in his blue eyes almost at once. She saw it again when he smiled and knew that his heart also was broken.

"When I left you eight years ago," he explained, as they stood entwined together under billowing thunderheads and hearing the rumble of distant thunder, "I promised to sell my blacksmith shop in Sonora and return with my livestock, which I'd left under the care of friends living beside the San Joaquin River. Selling my blacksmith shop was easy, because it was a good business. But when I went to collect my sheep and cattle, they had all been stolen by Mexican bandits."

Lucy said nothing. Kanaka and the Ahwahneeche had stolen horses. She knew that this was not the loss that accounted for Dan Marble's great sadness.

"I tracked the thieves and my cattle to San Diego but my cattle had been sold and the bandits had fled into Mexico. I followed them across the border and eventually tracked them to a small fishing village down in Baja California. As you may not know, the Americans wrested California away from the Mexicans, who had themselves taken it by force from the Spaniards. Down below the new border between Mexico and California, they hate Americans. When I got into a gunfight over my cattle sale money, I was wounded, imprisoned, and sentenced to life at hard labor in a silver mine for killing the men who had robbed me."

"I never felt that you were dead," Lucy whispered. "I could not understand *why* you didn't return. I thought you had found a better woman."

"Never!" he said, before kissing her passionately. "And not a day went by during all the bitter years of my wrongful imprisonment that I didn't ache to claim you for my wife. But I was kept shackled and working, always under heavy guard."

Dan took a deep breath. "Lucy, the guards were very cruel. There was never enough to eat. Each day was hell. I was never allowed to write letters to anyone in Sonora who might have come to tell you of my fate. I was filled with despair until, finally, there was a riot and many guards were slaughtered by the prisoners. The soldiers chased and executed many of us in the weeks that followed. I fooled everyone by fleeing into the mountains, where everyone said there was no water or chance for life. But there were a few hidden springs. Peasants found and rescued me. They were very kind, and, when I was strong again, I walked to the Pacific Ocean and then down to another fishing village. After two months, a ship came and I became a stowaway bound for South America. It was then that I heard about the Civil War, pitting Americans against Americans."

"Why did they fight each other?"

"They are *still* fighting," Dan said. "I remember you once telling me that Ahwahnee has two sides, the one on the north side of the river is called the land, or bluejay or grizzly bear side. The one south of the river is called the water or coyote side."

"Yes, but . . ."

"Where the sun rises on America, we also have two different peoples living on a north and a south side, just like they once did in Ahwahnee. Only, instead of the Merced River separating them, they have what they call the Mason-Dixon Line."

"But the Ahwahneeche never fought between the sides."

"Well, the Americans did," Dan said quietly, his eyes becoming distant. "And *my* people lived in the south side. I *had* to go and fight for my side, Lucy. To try to protect my mother and father, sisters and brothers. I wanted to come back here, but I could not do it and respect myself."

"Which side is winning?"

"The North," he said bitterly. "I fought and was badly wounded at a place called Shiloh. I was transported by wagon to a northern hospital and was due to be sent to a federal prison. I knew I could not endure any more imprisonment, so I managed to escape and I have not stopped running since I left Boston. I have nothing left to offer you."

Lucy brightened. "You have a good horse, a gun, and a rifle."

"All on loan from old friends still living in Sonora. If you agree to marry me, Lucy, you must realize that I have nothing else to offer. Nothing but dreams."

"Dreams are sometimes enough."

"I mean to make ours come true," he vowed. "I went to find you in Ahwahnee but Mr. Hutchings told me that your mother had died and you had disappeared. He thinks you might have . . ."

"Have what?"

"Killed yourself," Dan said, brushing the wetness from his eyes with the back of his tattered coat sleeve.

Lucy reluctantly nodded. "I thought of joining my mother and grandmother in Cho'-lok," she admitted. "With Kanaka up here, I was all alone in Ahwahnee."

"What happened to Wolf-dog?"

"He died, too. He was very old and suffering. It was a good thing that he died."

"I see." Dan took a deep breath. "Mr. Hutchings has offered me work at his hotel, building and repairing. What do you want me to do?"

"Never leave me again, Dan Marble. *That* is all I want."

He kissed her again. "I will not leave you until death."

"Speak no more of death," Lucy whispered, holding him tightly. "I have seen too much of it in my twenty-seven years."

He pulled back a little and his face split into a wide grin that washed away the trials of these past years. "I always wondered how old you were. I am thirty. Now, how long will you wear your hair cut short and this stuff on your cheeks?"

"Until I become your wife, then I will no longer be in mourning."

"Then scrub your pretty face clean," he said, scooping her up and carrying her to a place where they could lie alone together, sheltered and out of the gathering storm.

Twenty-three

Lucy would never forget how she and Dan had spent the first winter living in a log cabin near the Hutchings House. They had become a part of the Hutchings family as well as getting acquainted with a growing stream of tourists. Elvira Hutchings was about Lucy's age, slender, pensive, and quiet, with hazel eyes and soft brown hair. Unlike Mr. Hutchings, who reveled in the company of their guests, Elvira greatly preferred solitude. De-

spite the gift of her beautiful new infant, Florence, or "Floy," as
they called her, Elvira was happiest when she was immersed in
the solitary pursuits of composing music on her guitar, reading,
or painting. Lucy might have found her completely aloof except
that Elvira had a deep interest in the lost Ahwahneeche culture
and ancient legends.

"Please tell me another Ahwahneeche story," she would ask
Lucy many times that winter as they sat in front of the fireplace,
taking turns holding the baby while Mrs. Sproat and Mr. Hutchings attended to the guests.

"Which story would you like to hear?" Lucy would ask in the
pleasant ritual they shared. "The one about the birth of Wek'-
wek, the Falcon, or of his contest with Ki'-lak, the birdlike monster?"

"Today," Elvira might decide after due deliberation, "I would
like to hear the shorter version of how The People finally managed to kill U-wu'-lin, the giant."

"All right. Long ago, when the first bird and animal people
lived in Ahwahnee, there was much food and everyone was
happy. But then Giant appeared from someplace bad. He was
always a very hungry giant and the people were his favorite food.
Giant walked all over the world and ate so many of the bird and
animal people that there were almost none left."

"And exactly how big was Giant?"

"Oh, very, very big!" Lucy would say, opening her arms wide
and raising them overhead. "As big as a pine tree. His hands
were so large that they could hold ten people at a time. He even
carried a great leather hunting sack to hold all his victims."

At the time of these stories, Lucy would close her eyes and
she could almost see her mother's face; Anina had so enjoyed
telling old Ahwahneeche and Miwok stories. During her last
years, she had worried that they would all be forgotten.

"In those days, the bird and animal people tried every way to
kill Giant, but nothing worked. Arrows glanced off his body and
even spears broke against his sides."

"And why was that?"

"Because Giant's only weakness was his heart, and it was
hidden in a tiny place on his heel. The bird and animal people

did not know this, but they were all sure that Giant must have some weakness, like all living things."

"And so what did they do?" Elvira would ask.

"They asked Fly to bite Giant while he slept. Fly did this, starting at Giant's head and then biting all the way down to his feet. Giant just slept until Fly bit Giant's heel, causing him to kick out in pain. Then Fly knew that he had found Giant's heart."

"And this was *very* important to the bird and animal people?"

"Oh yes!" Lucy would say as if this were a big surprise. "Very important. Now all the people that Giant had not yet eaten got together and decided to make sharp awls and stick them into the earth. They placed these awls along Giant's favorite trail and arranged them so that Giant could not walk the trail without his feet being pierced."

"That really must have hurt!" Elvira would say, making a painful face.

But Lucy would shake her head. "Giant did not feel anything until one of the awls finally pierced his heel and then his heart. When that happened, Giant howled like Coyote and fell to the ground so hard that all the earth shook . . . and sometimes shakes even still. Giant died quickly and the people became very happy."

"One of these fine days, I am going to write down your Ahwahneeche legends. In that way, they will live long after both our times. Now, would you please tell me the story of the greed of His'-sik, the Skunk?"

Lucy would tell this story and others. She knew a great many Ahwahneeche legends, for it was part of the medicine woman's role to be a good storyteller, and she had learned them from Anina almost since birth.

When Elvira's mother, Mrs. Sloat, heard these stories, she would snort with impatience. "What a bunch of Indian poppycock! You girls ought to have better things to do than sit around swapping musty old Yosemite tales."

Elvira would not say much to her mother, who, Lucy soon realized, was the real authority in the Hutchings House. It was Mrs. Sloat who did most of the cooking and cleaning while Mr. Hutchings saw his role as being a genial and entertaining host. Most of the strenuous work fell to Dan, who soon recovered and became very fit and robust, thanks to Mrs. Sloat's good cooking and Lucy's love and her late mother's traditional Ahwahneeche medicines.

Dan was a good and gentle husband. He worked hard every day and talked about saving enough money to return to Sonora, to buy more livestock, which he hoped to drive to Ahwahnee so that they could multiply until the time when he could again work for himself. Quite often, in addition to working for Mr. Hutchings, Dan made extra money shoeing the horses and pack mules of visitors to Hutchings House.

Their cabin was small but warm and cozy, so that Lucy never really missed the old log and bark-covered u'-ma-cha that she had abandoned on the far side of the meadow. Dan scraped up enough money to buy a fine glass window and he placed it so that Lucy could gaze outside during bad weather and watch Cho'-lok. But, with spring turning into summer, Lucy spent most of her free time outdoors, gathering food or working on her baskets.

One afternoon, when the meadows were shiny with morning rain and the waterfalls thundering, Dan walked up quietly behind Lucy who was humming an old song. When she finished, he touched her cheek and said, "You *are* happy now, aren't you?"

"I am very happy," Lucy told him. "But someday I want to have a baby, like Floy."

"She is a beauty," Dan said. "But I think she's going to be very stubborn and independent minded. I say that because of the way Floy decides who will hold her and who will not."

Lucy agreed. She had seen many babies in her time, but Floy was easily the most strong-willed.

In addition to wildflowers and high water, this springtime brought a new influx of guests to the valley, more than ever before. Sometimes, Lucy would see them walk out to explore the old Ahwahneeche village of Koom-i-ne and a few of the curious tourists even sifted through the ashes of the fire that long ago had been set by the Mariposa Battalion in order to starve The People.

When the visitors returned and questioned Lucy about the burned-out village and the one remaining u'-ma-cha which she and Anina had shared the previous eight years, Lucy would begin to tell them the tragic story of The People. But only a few cared to really listen. Lucy would hardly ever get past the black death which caused The People to run over to the dry side of the mountains. Seldom did she get so far as the tragic times of Ouma and Tenaya.

But Elvira and a few others, like Mr. Galen Clark of Wawona, listened and even remembered. There was also much talk that year about how something called Congress had granted Yosemite Valley and the nearby Mariposa Grove of redwoods to the state of California for something called a public park. Some people, like Mr. Clark and others who visited, acted very happy about this. Mr. Hutchings and his wife worried that the state might decide to drive them away and close their hotel.

Lucy understood nothing of this park business and Dan did not trouble himself with it either, saying, "I do not recognize the American Congress, because it is not representative of the South and it makes a big mess of everything."

In the autumn, almost a year after Lucy and Dan had been married in Tuolumne, three very rich and important men appeared at the Hutchings House and they wanted to go hunting in the high Sierras.

Mr. Hutchings came to Lucy and said, "They remember Grizzly Adams telling an audience back in New York that it was your brother, Kanaka, who found and helped him trap that great monster grizzly bear named Samson. They want your brother to help them find another just like Samson."

"To kill?"

Hutchings, aware of Lucy's dislike for pleasure hunters, was honest. "Yes," he admitted. "They have come far and will hunt with . . . or without . . . your brother as their guide. But, if he is willing to do this, they will pay us all a great deal of money."

Lucy did not care about the money but knew that Dan wanted it very much so that he could build them a larger cabin and then buy livestock. Dan had big ideas, and, even though Lucy did not necessarily share them, she knew how important they were to her husband. Furthermore, she did not like how hard Dan had to work while Mr. Hutchings stood around as his overseer.

"I will go up to Tuolumne right now and find Kanaka," Dan

said when Lucy told him what Mr. Hutchings wanted. "I'll try to talk some sense into him."

"Kanaka is already wise. He will not listen."

Dan's temper bubbled to the surface. "Are you trying to say that making money is not wise? That spending all of our time and talent working for Mr. Hutchings is better than working for our own futures?"

"No," Lucy said, hurt by his sharpness. "I just mean that . . ."

Dan placed his hands on her shoulders. "Listen," he said, voice gentling, "I'm sorry that I snapped at you. But you're spending all your time either helping out at the hotel or weaving baskets to sell to the tourists."

"I enjoy that."

"Sure you do! But I promise that you'll like taking care of our *own* baby and weaving baskets for *us* even better."

Lucy decided her husband was right. And while the value of her prized baskets was going up very fast, she was becoming tired of working long hours just to make and sell them, never to be seen, enjoyed, or admired in Ahwahnee again after the tourists carried them far away.

"All right," Lucy agreed, "but *I* must go to find my brother and speak to him."

"Not alone," Dan said. "There are still a lot of wild grizzlies up in the mountains and, since you don't have a Wolf-dog to protect you anymore, I'll do it."

Lucy knew that her husband's mind was firm. "But I must speak to him *alone* about this thing."

"Very well. But, if Kanaka won't listen to you, I want to at least have a chance to speak to him myself."

Lucy thought this was fair and so they decided to leave for Tuolumne early the next morning.

From atop a high, windswept granite dome on which a stand of ancient bristlecone pine clung tenaciously, Kanaka could behold all of his mountain stronghold. He could gaze east to the vast basin desert and feel its hot, dry winds rising all along the

Sierra mountain range. To the south and to the north marched spiked peaks whose summits glistened like columns of silver-helmeted giants. And, to the southwest, Kanaka could see the shiny blue disk of Tenaya Lake, and farther out, a section of rugged Half Dome.

But, at this moment, he was lying on his back watching a pair of golden eagles wheel and soar, carried by an invisible hundred-mile long corridor of heated updrafts. Kanaka wished he were an eagle who could rise above the troubles of the world and see things far beyond man's limited vision. The great birds could hang, almost motionless, then, with a mere dip of a wing, glide effortlessly to the very edge of the earth.

One of his mother's favorite stories had been how Kah'-kool, the Raven, long ago had complained to Evening Star and to the Mountain Lion because his feathers were white, making it too easy for his prey to see him and escape his talons. The Raven had used charcoal to color his feathers, and thus had become a fine hunter. But to Kanaka, Eagle was the greater hunter, even greater than the small and deadly Falcon. Yes, Kanaka thought, it would be much better to be Eagle because his long, golden wings could carry him easily across the face of the world.

Kanaka closed his eyes and dreamed of the old days when he was a boy and his father had been a great hunter among the Ahwahneeche. He remembered Ezekial's unbridled joy when he had been invited to join the tribal elders despite his white man's blood. That had been a momentous day for their family.

Sometimes, Kanaka also thought of Totuya. There had been a time when he had considered taking her as his wife, but she had chosen to leave Ahwahnee, probably to live on the Fresno River Reservation. Totuya, Kanaka long ago had decided, would not have survived so many lonely winters in this high country. Women needed the company of other women and children to be happy. Kanaka had seen this in even his own mother.

Kanaka often thought about Grizzly Adams, and again he considered the idea of capturing a bear or wolf cub of his own to tame and be his constant companion. Adams had proved it could be done. Kanaka thought that he would prefer the cub of the wolf to that of the bear. Perhaps next spring. He knew where a wolf mother denned and birthed her pups. It would be easy to capture the wolf, but Kanaka desired only one cub and so he would have to figure out some method to avoid killing the mother and starving her other cubs. To kill animals without good reason ran against the very nature of all Ahwahneeche.

Kanaka was thinking of this very thing the following day when he returned to his cave to find Dan and Lucy waiting. Kanaka had never seen his sister look so joyful. But when they told him of the hunting party and what it wanted, Kanaka was strongly opposed to the idea. However, Lucy and Dan were very persuasive.

"These men will pay us all very well," Dan argued.

"But I have no need for their money."

"They have new rifles," Dan said. "Much better ones than your single-shot. There are now rifles that will fire fifteen shots without reloading."

To illustrate this amazing fact, Dan raised his hand between their faces and began to snap his fingers every two seconds and said, "Think about it, Kanaka. These men have rifles that will fire *this fast*. They use metallic cartridges. You can't believe what an improvement this is until you observe them in action."

Kanaka had been using loose powder and balls and he could not imagine firing at such speed.

"If you'll agree to serve as their guide, there will be enough money for you to buy one of those new rifles," Dan said. "And your sister and I also will make enough to build a better cabin. We will have many children, Kanaka. We'd like them to have a good life in the valley."

"U'-ma-cha is good," Kanaka argued, shooting a quick glance to his sister. "Good enough for Ahwahneeche."

Lucy walked away and Kanaka knew that he had disappointed his sister. Had she tried to change his mind about this thing, Kanaka's resolve would only have hardened. But now . . . now he suddenly felt bad for Lucy.

"How much money?" he asked, thinking about the gold-bearing quartz rock.

"These are rich men, Kanaka. If they are well satisfied with the hunt, they would pay enough so that your sister and I would no longer have to work for the Hutchings family. Lucy would like to keep some of her baskets instead of feeling as if she needed to sell them all so that we could do better someday."

Kanaka reached a difficult decision. "What if I told you that I had found gold?"

Dan's surprise registered clearly. "Up here in Tuolumne?"

Kanaka nodded, eyes boring into this man to judge his honor.

Dan took a deep breath and walked off a few paces to gaze out across the meadows with their crystal-clear streams. He shook his head, clucked his tongue, and then returned. "If that news ever got out, it would start a gold rush and hordes of miners would destroy this place. They'd rip up the streams, root up the meadows, and tear apart the mountains. Kanaka, don't ever mention discovering gold in Tuolumne again."

Kanaka had already reached the same conclusion but now Dan had passed a test. "I will help you guide these hunters," he decided. "But winter comes early this year. You must bring them up at once."

"They hunt only very large animals," Dan said. "They heard about you helping Adams find Samson and they are looking for *big* game. Really big mountain sheep, elk, mountain lion, and bear. Mr. Hutchings said they won't be happy with anything less and they will pay us extra if they are successful."

Kanaka didn't understand why these hunters wanted only the largest animals, but he did know where to find them. And since it seemed so important to Dan and his sister and there was the promise of owning the new kind of rifle that could shoot as fast as a man could snap his fingers, Kanaka nodded and said, "Lead them up here."

Dan frowned and shook his head. "I'm afraid that's one of the problems, Kanaka. They want to meet you first. Mr. Hutchings said that they wouldn't budge on that point."

Kanaka's first instinct was to walk away. But he knew that he could not do so. After a moment's hesitation, he nodded his head. "I will leave with you for Ahwahnee tomorrow."

"Good!" Dan exclaimed. "And don't worry about that trouble you got into with those prospectors. That was over ten years ago and both sides recognize that wrongs were committed, more so by the Americans than by the Ahwahneeche. No one will remember you, Kanaka. You were just a kid then . . . what, seventeen?"

Kanaka nodded.

"All right," Dan said. "And, remember, never mention that Tuolumne gold you found. If I ever ask about it, tell me you were just making a joke. Okay?"

"Okay," Kanaka said, wondering what he had gotten himself talked into.

Kanaka had taken a strong and immediate dislike to all three Eastern hunters. Two of them were big, blustery men in their late thirties, Allan and Phillip Pierce. The third was their financier, an older and even more overbearing fellow named Stewart Knox. All wore fancy clothes and boots. They rode excellent horses and had rented many pack mules to carry tents and expensive foods. At least, Dan had not exaggerated about the new repeating rifles. Each one was armed with a Henry rifle, also called a "yellow boy" because of its shiny brass breech. These weapons were a marvel, and when Kanaka saw how fast a man could fire the new metallic cartridges, he very much wanted one.

The Pierce brothers and Mr. Knox did not deign to speak to Kanaka, but conveyed their every wish to Dan who ground his teeth but tried his level best to please them. He made their campfire, erected their tents, cooked their meals, washed their dishes and cooking utensils, and tended to their mules and horses. He even did all the packing and unpacking. Kanaka helped with the fire and the horses, but he refused to assist the hunters when it came to doing their menial tasks.

"You're mighty damned independent for an Indian," Allan complained their first evening after reaching Tuolumne and following Kanaka out of their camp.

Kanaka glanced back at the man without interest. They were of the same height, but that was where their similarities ended. Allan Pierce was heavyset and jowly, his face now burned red by the sun and the wind. He was dressed in the finest hunting outfit money could buy and his hands were slim and without calluses.

When Kanaka said nothing, Allan pressed harder. "We could have hired a more *sociable* guide. There were plenty that wanted our money. We even heard of a man named Brown who has the reputation of being an excellent grizzly bear hunter. I'm sure that you've heard of him."

"No," Kanaka said.

"He lives like a hermit up on the North Fork of the Merced. Brown promised he could find us a bear to shoot as big as Samson."

Kanaka raised an eyebrow. "Samson was the biggest."

"Brown says there are still some bigger in these mountains. He told us all about how he and his little dog would stalk grizzly, making sure they got downwind. Brown said that bears have poor eyesight."

"That is true."

"He said that killing them was safe because he always did his shooting near a tree big enough that he could climb . . . but not big enough for a wounded bear. Brown said that a wounded grizzly will almost always run away and then he'd track them down and finish them off. The way he explained it, hunting grizzly didn't sound at all dangerous."

Kanaka, who had been gazing off at some mountain peaks, turned to the Easterner. "Do you like the taste of bear meat?"

Allan blinked with surprise. "I don't know. We've never eaten any, but I've heard that it's tough and gamey."

"Then why do you want to kill a big grizzly?"

"For the sport of it! What else?"

Kanaka turned on his heel and start to walk away.

"Hey!" Allan called, hurrying after him. "What the hell did I say wrong?"

"You do not understand," Kanaka said tightly. "About the spirits of animals, the land, everything."

"Well there's a whole world out there that *you* don't understand either!" Allan shouted in anger, as he pursued Kanaka. "I'll bet that you can't even read or write. And I've heard stories about how you live up here by yourself all year around. What's the matter with you? What kind of a man would cut himself off from everyone and . . ."

"Leave me alone," Kanaka warned, coming to a stop with his hands knotting into fists.

Allan stepped back and tried to bluster. "Indian, you're working for *us*, not the other way around. And you had better deliver on the Bighorn sheep. Your brother-in-law made all kinds of promises about how good a guide you'd make but, so far, we haven't been a damn bit impressed. I been watching you and I think all this solitude has made you crazy."

"Crazy?"

"Yeah!" Allan used a forefinger to wag circles around his right ear. "You know, loco? Not right in the head?"

For some reason, Kanaka found this so ridiculous that he laughed loud enough that the sound of it echoed eerily off the rocky peaks.

"See!" Allan exclaimed. "You *are* crazy!"

Kanaka resisted an impulse to grab this fool by the front of his coat and shake him. Instead, he took a deep breath and hurried off to find some peace and quiet.

Allan was still angry the next morning at breakfast and said, "Mr. Marble, your brother-in-law is bad-mannered and unstable."

"Kanaka?"

"That's right!"

"You couldn't have found a better guide than Kanaka," Dan said, trying to be diplomatic. "He knows where all the largest animals are in this high country. I keep saying that, before we are done, you'll be glad that you hired the best."

"I hope so," Knox grumbled. "So far, we haven't seen much of anything but rock and sky."

"But isn't it beautiful?" Dan asked. "Where have you ever seen such . . ."

"Is he going to take us out hunting for Bighorn sheep this afternoon, or are we going after grizzly first?"

"I don't know," Dan said, clamping his mouth shut.

"Well," Knox said, "find out. We want to get this hunt over soon. The weather could turn sour on us at any time."

"Yes," Dan said, before stomping away.

Kanaka knew where a band of Bighorn sheep could be found and he knew that several of the rams were very large and handsome. Furthermore, Kanaka wanted this hunt to be over even more than the three rich Easterners.

"Tell them we will go hunting now," he told Dan when informed of their impatience.

"On horseback?"

"No," Kanaka said. "They will have to walk or the Bighorn will see them and run away."

"I was afraid that's what you were going to say. Kanaka, those men aren't used to this altitude and they are not in good shape. They're going to have to ride to within a mile of where they can shoot or this just isn't going to work."

Kanaka understood but, to ride partway from this camp would mean that they would have to double the distance to the high, rocky ridge where the mountain sheep could still be found. Yet, if that was the only way that this hunt could be finished, then Kanaka supposed there was little choice.

"All right," he said, snatching up his own rifle and marching off.

Dan and the three Easterners caught up with him on horseback after about a mile. Knox was infuriated. "Dammit!" he bellowed. "You can't just walk off and expect us to come running! Who is paying whom!"

Kanaka ignored the man and kept walking.

"What he needs is a good . . ."

"Don't say anything more," Dan warned as Kanaka turned, his rifle coming up a little and his eyes burning with fury. "Just let this pass, Mr. Knox."

"We're not paying him *anything,*" Allan hissed. "Not one damned cent. Whatever he gets comes out of *your* fee."

"All right," Dan said, swallowing hard.

Kanaka forced himself to turn and march away. Two hours later, he motioned for everyone to dismount and tie their horses, then to follow him in silence. The Easterners tired quickly as they struggled for oxygen up a steep game trail.

"How damn far are we going to have to walk?" Phillip gasped.

"Shhh!" Dan ordered.

After a difficult thirty-minute climb, Kanaka flattened near the crest of a ridge. He knew that the herd of Bighorn sheep would be hiding in a slight depression below, affording a relatively easy shot. When the hunters saw Kanaka drop, they followed his example. Kanaka had skillfully positioned them downwind of the small band of rams, all of whom were within easy killing range. There were seven, four of them very large old rams with great curling horns.

Kanaka signaled for the three men to remove their hats, then pick their targets and fire. There was a quick, hushed conference and then the hunters took aim. Stewart Knox fired a split second before the brothers and Kanaka was relieved that the largest ram of the bunch died instantly with a bullet through its heart. Allan's bullet missed entirely and Phillip shot his ram in the belly, the animal going down but then rising and trying to hop after the fleeing sheep.

"Dammit!" Phillip shouted, levering another bullet into the breech of his rifle as he jumped to his feet and began to work the lever of his Henry, firing wildly at the wounded, bucking and bawling ram.

Stunned, Kanaka just stared for a moment as bullets peppered the rocky depression, a few nicking the dying ram, but most ricocheting into the sky. Something snapped inside Kanaka when one of Phillip's bullets finally struck a hind leg and spilled the animal so that it had to start dragging itself.

"Stop!" Kanaka yelled at Phillip. When the excited man chose to ignore him, Kanaka tore the Henry from Phillip's hands.

"Give it back to me!" the hunter shouted, grabbing for his rifle.

Kanaka swung the weapon like an ax. The powerful, chopping blow missed Phillip's head but struck his shoulder. Bone cracked and Phillip screamed.

"Look out!" Dan cried as Allan spun and fired at Kanaka, missing by a good yard.

Dan jumped at the man, knocking him down. They rolled and came up together. Pierce was bigger and maybe even stronger, but he was slow and winded. Dan's fists were a blur as he sent a flurry of crisp, crunching punches into the heavier man's face and stomach. Allan collapsed and covered his face, sobbing.

"You crazy bastards!" Knox shouted, backing away with his rifle and looking panicky.

Kanaka ignored the man. He used Phillip's rifle to put the dying ram out of its misery. He marched down into the bowl, feeling sick in his stomach. Kanaka could hear the three Easterners shouting and screaming. Then, Knox came puffing down the hill shouting, "Indian, you stay the hell away from my ram! I shot him clean! Don't you dare touch that animal!"

Kanaka drew his knife and began to dress out the one that had suffered many bullets. He was so angry that his hands were shaking.

"You broke my brother's shoulder!" Allan shouted, as he helped Phillip down to inspect the fallen rams. "You broke it!"

Kanaka didn't trust himself to speak to the three hunters.

"Damn!" Knox cursed. "This ram is just worthless!"

"Worthless, Mr. Knox? What do you mean?"

Knox took another measurement with his cloth tape and cursed again before saying, "I mean that his horns are almost an inch short of the record. This isn't a *trophy* animal!"

Kanaka and Dan exchanged glances and, before Kanaka could jump up and attack, Dan drove a sweeping right uppercut to Knox's ponderous belly and the man folded.

"Let's get out of here," Dan said, pale and shaking. "This hunt is over."

"Hey Indian!" Phillip wailed. "Bring back my rifle!"

Kanaka turned, raised the rifle and took aim on the man whose shoulder he had broken. Phillip and his brother wheeled about and started running.

"Now they won't ever come back," Kanaka said, lowering his new rifle and walking away with Dan close on his heels.

"I'll have you *both* arrested!" Knox shouted, waving his fists. "You haven't heard the end of this! I'll be sending the law after you!"

"It'll be all right," Dan said, trying to offer assurance. "I'll get Phillip to a doctor and then we'll settle this without the authorities."

But Kanaka didn't believe a word of it.

Twenty-four

Tuolumne Meadows, 1869

It was five years since Kanaka had broken Phillip Pierce's shoulder and taken his repeating rifle. After that, Kanaka had vowed to have nothing more to do with hunters. Nor would he return to Ahwahnee, where he was certain that he would be arrested by the whites, who were filling up the valley with their hotels, cabins, and homesteads. Kanaka found the sight of so much activity and building profoundly depressing, so he resolved to remain in the high wilderness country. Even there, he was beginning to see white hunters and adventurers whom he always avoided.

But one day in late summer, Kanaka heard the loud barking of a dog and, when he went to investigate, he saw that the animal was slow and clumsy but enormous, with a long brown-and-white coat and large, red-rimmed eyes. Beyond the dog was a flock of sheep tended by a tall, slender man wearing a full beard. As Kanaka watched, he felt a growing sense of anger and alarm. Anger, because he saw that this could be the beginning of an invasion of even more sheep, as well as cattle and horses. The idea of livestock trampling and devouring the fragile mountain meadows was something that Kanaka found extremely objectionable.

Remaining hidden from view, he watched the man, the dog, and the flock of grazing sheep and knew that he at least had to try something to drive them away. So, two nights later, when the moon was just a silver sliver, Kanaka crept up near the bedded down flock and fired his rifle. The flock sprang to its feet but did not stampede into the darkness as Kanaka had expected. They simply began to bleat.

The huge dog was another matter entirely. Roused from its slumber, it barked twice with the deep, throaty sound of a full-grown bear, then demonstrated surprising speed as it rushed at Kanaka with a low and ominous growl. Kanaka probably could have dropped the ferocious animal, but it would have been a difficult shot and he was not prepared for the consequences if he missed. So he turned and sprinted to a tree. Slinging his rifle over his shoulder, Kanaka just managed to leap and grab a low branch, and pulled himself to safety before the beast's fangs snapped, inches below the seat of his pants.

Kanaka scrambled up through the branches to safety but the shepherd, barefoot and clad in red flannel long johns, appeared to crane his neck and peer up at a very embarrassed Kanaka.

"What are you doing?" he asked in what Kanaka was later to learn was a Scottish brogue. "Why did you fire that shot? Did ya see a bear, or a lion?"

Kanaka made sure that the sheepherder was unarmed and that he offered no threat. He could feel wood ants crawling up his sleeves and the legs of his pants and realized that he needed to get down in a hurry.

"I don't want to shoot that dog," he said, pointing his rifle downward in the dog's general direction.

"Then don't!" The shepherd smiled. "Carlo is a St. Bernard, trained to protect these sheep with his life. But he won't hurt you, Kanaka."

"How do you know . . ."

"I met your sister, Lucy," the man interrupted, "and her husband, Dan. My name is John Muir and they said that I'd have about as much chance of catching sight of you as I would a wolverine. But here you are. What a pleasant surprise!"

Muir seemed delighted and not the least bit self-conscious about standing under Kanaka in his long underwear, or even annoyed that Kanaka had awakened him with a sudden rifle shot.

"I'm sorry that Carlo chased you."

"That's all right," Kanaka said, batting away the ants and dropping down into the cold starlight.

"Would you care to come over to my camp and have something to eat?" Muir offered.

"No, thank you."

"Then let's just talk awhile," Muir said, folding his arms across his chest. "You know, from the moment I heard your story and how you smashed that rich Easterner after he repeatedly wounded that bighorn sheep, I said to myself, 'Muir, there is a man I would like to meet and congratulate.' "

"You did?"

"That's right," Muir said, very earnestly. "You see, Kanaka, I have absolutely no patience with anyone who would despoil nature's most precious gifts, be they plant, animal, or mineral."

Kanaka had never met anyone quite like John Muir. "I ought to be going," he said, scratching at a few of the ants that had invaded his buckskins.

"Please, Kanaka. I do want us to become friends because there is a great deal that I can learn from you about this mountain magnificence. I'm sure that you, more than any other living human, know this high country."

"It is my home now."

Muir tugged reflectively at his thick beard. "Have you ever wondered how it was formed?"

"Formed?"

"Yes," Muir said, reaching out to take Kanaka's arm and lead him back through the flock toward his camp. "You see, God made all, that is true. But His work is constantly evolving. Floods and winds alter the shape of even the hardest granite mountains. Snow and ice, in the form of glacier fields, carve rock. Rivers are constantly furrowing valleys and gorges, whose rich mineral deposits form alluvial plains."

Muir briskly rubbed his hands together. "And when you add the effects of earthquakes and volcanos, well . . . there is simply so much geological change occurring that it defies the human capacity to comprehend!"

Kanaka didn't understand half of what this man was saying, but he rather liked him and thought that he would find a few hours with John Muir interesting. So, ignoring the huge dog that clearly mistrusted him, Kanaka allowed himself to be led over to Muir's Spartan camp. The man pitched wood on the glowing coals of his campfire and placed a pot of coffee on to boil.

"Your sister's two young children are quite a pair, aren't they," Muir said with firelight revealing the mirth in his eyes.

Lucy and Dan had produced two fine children. William was now three and Mary was almost a year old. Kanaka had never seen either child, though Dan had promised to bring his son up to Tuolumne to finally meet his infamous uncle next spring.

"I look forward to meeting them some day."

"I understand that you have lived alone up here for more than fifteen years, since the death of Tenaya at the hands of the Mono Indians."

"Lucy has told you much," Kanaka said, not sure that he entirely approved of a stranger knowing his family's difficult past.

"She told me the story of Ouma and Anina. Of Tenaya and his favorite granddaughter, Totuya, who now lives down on the Merced with her husband and children."

Kanaka felt a sting of sadness because hearing this news brought an end to his fragile dream that he and Totuya might have raised a family up in these mountains.

Muir poked at the fire. "You cared for her."

It wasn't a question and Kanaka wasn't going to lie. "Yes," he admitted. "After the death of Chief Tenaya, when we were fleeing the Mono Indians and coming back to Ahwahnee, there was a time when I thought . . ."

Kanaka could not continue.

"I know," Muir said, ending the awkward silence. "If it helps, Totuya also remembers you with great fondness."

"You met her, *too?*"

"Certainly! Before I came up here, I worked as a general ranch hand for a fella by the name of John Connel, then later for Pat Delaney, the one who owns these sheep. Both are fine men with livestock operations down on the lower reaches of the Tuolumne River. Totuya and I met quite by accident. We began to talk and she told me all about the Ahwahneeche and of Yosemite . . . and you."

"I see." Kanaka stared into the flames. "Is she happy?"

"Yes, when she doesn't dwell on the past."

"And she isn't living on the Fresno River Reservation?"

"Totuya left there quite a few years ago."

"Good." Kanaka was pleased to learn that Totuya was living free and had her own family.

"Kanaka?"

He looked up from the campfire. "Yes?"

"About this trouble with that man whose shoulder you broke and whose rifle you took," Muir began. "I wouldn't be greatly concerned about that. The man and his brother did file charges and there was an arrest warrant issued, but that was several years ago and I doubt that anyone would try to come up here and arrest you. The authorities certainly must have better things to do, and your brother-in-law was a witness and would testify on your behalf."

"If I were brought in, would I then be set free and left alone?"

Muir had long, graceful fingers. He steepled them and brooded over that question for several moments before he said, "I honestly don't know."

"Then I take no chances."

Muir nodded in agreement. "It is much better living up here surrounded only by nature. I grew up in Wisconsin. I decided to see the Amazon River, which is the great river of South America. But I became deathly ill and never made it that far. When I finally ended up in San Francisco, what I saw in that city made me want to run to these mountains. I cannot abide places where people gather in large numbers. Like you, I much prefer the solitude of the mountains. That's why I knew that we were kindred spirits, Kanaka."

"I could not live elsewhere."

"I understand."

After a while, Carlo, the dog, sighed and fell back asleep, as did the sheep. Muir poured cups of strong, steaming coffee and they sat quietly until dawn, saying nothing and utterly content to watch shooting stars and listen to a Tuolumne night.

* * *

In the days that remained of summer, Kanaka learned there were both depth and beauty dwelling inside this quiet man who one day confided that, "When I was a boy in Scotland, I was fond of everything that was wild and, all my life, I've been growing fonder and fonder of wild places and wild creatures."

Then, looking right at Kanaka, he added, "And you, my friend, are like a wild creature. One who never can be tamed by our so-called advanced civilization."

Such frankness, coupled with such unabashed love for the outdoors, was something that Kanaka never had thought to share with an American. To discover this friendship after so many years of loneliness was both a delight and a revelation. Many an afternoon, Kanaka and Muir would leave the flock of sheep in the care of the big dog and wander off to explore the high country. John Muir always had a ready notebook and a sketch pad. He was fascinated by everything, but especially by the geology of the high country.

"The prevailing experts believe that the Yosemite Valley which, I must tell you, has been receiving more and more print since it was given the status of a state park, was created by the Tuolumne and the Merced Rivers. But as I study the sculpture and lateral scars etched deeply into these high rocks, I am convinced that the valley and the great monuments of stone comprising Half Dome and all of the hanging cliffs were created—not by rivers—but by glaciers."

"Glaciers?"

"Moving oceans of ice," Muir explained, talking loudly against the wind one afternoon as they stood atop a high vantage point that afforded them a view in all directions. "Kanaka, it seems most evident to me as I study the moraines, these mountain meadows, and alpine lakes. If a man will but look, he can see irrefutable evidence of glaciers that formed all we now behold."

And then, Muir traced the valleys with a long forefinger, expounding how the glaciers had moved down the slopes. He ended his lecture by saying, "In the springtime, we actually can measure glacial activity with wooden stakes. I am going to start writing about all this, Kanaka. I am going to tell the world how beautiful and majestic this country is and how it *really* was formed."

Kanaka believed that the earth was formed when Coyote ordered Frog to dive to the bottom of the seas and find mud. It had happened as explained by the Ahwahneeche legend. But he did not think that Muir would believe this story, so he held his tongue.

As the summer slowly evolved into autumn, Kanaka learned much about plants and nature that he previously had not known. And for his part, he told Muir about the things that he alone had seen during the long years of his lonely exile. Every few weeks, Muir had visitors, often Pat Delaney who brought up provisions and checked his flocks. Whenever Kanaka was with Muir and someone was spotted approaching from a distance, Kanaka would disappear. Muir seemed to understand and even approve of his behavior.

One day, Lucy and Dan came, which was surprising. They usually waited until the aspen were turning colors. Expecting to see his little niece and nephew, Kanaka was very disappointed to learn that Lucy's two children had been left behind.

"We have a problem," Dan said soon after their reunion. "Allan Pierce was in Sacramento. It seems his brother, Phillip, whose shoulder you shattered, never completely recovered and has finally suffered a complete physical breakdown."

Kanaka shrugged. "I am not sorry."

"He deserved it," Dan agreed. "But, Allan claims the injury caused a grave nerve disorder. He is insisting that you be hunted down and brought to trial. And . . . he's offering a very large reward for your arrest."

Kanaka turned to reassure Lucy. "Don't worry, they will never find me up here."

"But they *might*," Lucy replied. "Mr. Pierce has offered a *thousand*-dollar reward for your arrest!"

Kanaka did not know much about money, but he did know that a good horse was worth only twenty or thirty dollars, and a repeating rifle worth twice that much. Therefore, a thousand dollars would be more money than he could even imagine.

"Listen," Dan said. "I think the best thing would be for you to come down to Ahwahnee with us and we'll get this thing settled. They could have filed assault charges against me, too, but they didn't dare. I'll testify that you did not intend to harm Mr. Pierce."

"I tried to break his head."

Dan winced. "Listen, you must never say that. When you tried to get him to stop firing, Phillip Pierce became enraged and turned his rifle on you and . . ."

"No, he didn't," Kanaka said. "I hit him with it."

"In my opinion," Dan said, determined to make his case, "he would definitely have used it on you if you had not taken it away. And I'll say that in any court."

"I'm not going down to face them," Kanaka said, making his decision.

"But if you did," Lucy said with pleading in her voice, "then you wouldn't always have to worry that someone would be coming here to arrest . . . or, worse yet, kill you. They did that to a Mexican named Joaquin Murieta some years ago and he was only accused of crimes. They shot him down in the great valley and then they cut off his head and . . ."

"Lucy," Dan interrupted. "I see no point in telling your brother that grisly story."

"The point is that it *could* happen to Kanaka! You weren't here when they killed Chief Tenaya's youngest son for trying to run away. Muaga was just a *boy!* "

"Kanaka," Dan said, "I really think that you should go back down with us. I've been talking to Mr. Hutchings, a fella named Galen Clark, and another settler named James Lamon. I've explained exactly what happened on that hunting trip and they all have agreed to write letters on your behalf. They'll be powerful voices in your behalf."

"No."

Dan's shoulders slumped and he turned to Lucy, saying, "I told you he was too stubborn to listen."

"Kanaka," Lucy said, "please do as we ask."

"I can't," he told them. "I could have killed that man. Many of my old friends *would* have killed him. But I just struck him once and took his rifle."

"You should get rid of the rifle," Dan said. "Allan Pierce has its factory serial number and it could be evidence against you."

Kanaka gazed off toward the mountain peaks and then he said, "Tell me about William and Mary again. How big are they now? How much have they grown?"

Dan and Lucy stayed only two days. They told Kanaka much about what was happening in the valley and beyond. Kanaka already knew that, since Yosemite had been made a state park, private ownership of land in Yosemite no longer was recognized by California. Therefore, Mr. Hutchings had been ordered either to accept a ten-year lease on his hotel and cabins, or else vacate them entirely.

"Mr. Hutchings, along with the other homesteaders, are going to fight that all the way to the United States Supreme Court, but it will take years and the outcome is uncertain."

"I hope they all lose," Kanaka declared.

"Mr. Hutchings and his family are good people," Lucy argued. "They deserve better."

"To *own* Ahwahnee and to cut down its trees?" Kanaka challenged.

Lucy looked away.

Kanaka was sorry that he had snapped at his sister but he thought Lucy must have forgotten her ancestors who had known that no man could ever *own* the land but only live in harmony with nature for a time before their ashes joined it forever.

"I heard from my family," Dan said, breaking their silence. "The South is being looted by carpetbaggers and the North, as expected, shows neither mercy nor honor."

Through John Muir and his frequent visitors, Kanaka knew that the War between the States had been over for several years but that the South was still being punished. He also had heard about President Lincoln being assassinated. None of it meant anything to Kanaka and neither did the latest news Dan was telling him now, about how a great transcontinental railroad had just been completed linking the East to the West at a place called Promontory Point, Utah.

"It will bring more and more people westward," Dan predicted, "especially those coming to California and to these mountains."

This was not good news. "Why?"

"Because there is still a lot of land for the taking in the West. Thank heaven that Mrs. Fremont and some others were able to get Yosemite designated as a state park. Otherwise . . ."

Kanaka could guess what "otherwise" meant. He had always felt a mounting concern about more and more people moving in to destroy Ahwahnee with ax and plow.

"Mr. Hutchings asked Dan to build him a sawmill," Lucy said, quietly changing the subject.

Kanaka could read his sister's disapproval and he turned to Dan. "What is that?"

"It cuts trees into flat boards that can be used to build things," Dan explained. "But, frankly, I haven't the mind for the job. I can follow written sketches and directions, but I can't imagine trying to design a working sawmill. When I told Mr. Hutchings about my reservations, he hired a man to do the job but he fell way short. Last I heard, he's going to ask John Muir to design and build it. John has a brilliant mind and is a proven inventor. He'll build a proper sawmill."

"Maybe he won't want do something that will eat up trees," Kanaka said.

"Maybe," Dan said. "But with or without John Muir, a mill will be constructed. Mr. Hutchings wants me to keep fixing up the hotel. With a sawmill, we'll finally be able to partition the upstairs guest rooms with solid walls instead of muslin, and even build some kind of a boardwalk across the meadow so that his guests can stroll to Yosemite Falls without getting their feet dewy or dirty."

Kanaka did not want to hear any more. Unlike every previous visit, this one was disturbing. Not only had he learned that the Pierces had not abandoned their quest for revenge, but Kanaka had not seen his little niece or nephew. And now, it sounded as if his friend, John Muir, was going to build a sawmill.

When Lucy and Dan left again for the valley, Kanaka fell into a deep sadness and avoided John Muir for almost two weeks. But, one day, the man appeared near Kanaka's cave and called his name. Kanaka tried to ignore his friend's voice, but finally gave in and went out to see what Muir wanted.

"You have been avoiding me," Muir said, himself looking depressed.

"I have," Kanaka admitted. "But I am not angry with you."

"Then what is it?"

Kanaka invited the Scot into his cave and showed him the ancient drawings. Muir was very interested, but remained subdued until they both sat down with Kanaka's fire between them. It was then that Kanaka told his friend about the thousand-dollar reward being offered by the Pierces for his arrest.

When the story was over, Muir looked across at Kanaka and said, "There is one thing that I hate with a perfect hatred—cruelty to anything or anybody. And when that man began to riddle that poor, suffering bighorn sheep, he was being very, very cruel. You did what I might have done myself, if I had possessed the courage."

"You have more than enough courage," Kanaka said. "I have seen you climb a tree on top of a mountain during a lightning storm and heard you call to the gods. You have no fear."

Muir chuckled. "I have *many* fears, my friend. One of the greatest being that someday I will have to live in a city."

"I do not expect that to happen to either of us," Kanaka said.

"What are you going to do about this Pierce business?" Muir asked.

"Nothing," Kanaka said.

"A thousand-dollar reward *will* attract bounty hunters."

"They cannot find me."

"But if they do?"

Kanaka reached over and picked up his rifle. "Then I would kill them rather than be shackled like my father and locked in their iron cages like Samson."

Muir, for once, had no words to say about this. But, now, he looked as grim and morose as Kanaka.

A week after John Muir drove the sheep down to their winter

pasture, a lone horsemen appeared at Tuolumne. At first, Kanaka
thought the man was a hunter, perhaps of bear or elk. But, after
several hours, Kanaka became convinced that *he* was the man's
sole prey. This impression deepened when the horseman somehow detected one of Kanaka's faint foot trails. He dismounted
and slowly tracked it in the direction of the hidden cave. Kanaka
always had used extreme caution when approaching his cave and
had used many routes, but this man was a professional and kept
moving in the cave's direction. Watching him, Kanaka drew an
uneasy parallel between this stranger and a mountain lion tracking its prey. When Kanaka saw him tie his horse, check his rifle,
and then seem to pinpoint the vicinity of the cave, he knew that
something had to be done at once. Because the intruder's full
attention was fixed ahead, Kanaka found it easy to slip up behind
the man.

"Hello!" he called, his own rifle cocked and ready to fire.

The horseman spun around in surprise. He was dark com-
plected, with black brows and a long, unshaven jaw. Of medium
height, he wore a heavy leather coat, brown woolen pants, and
black leather boots. When he saw Kanaka standing not fifty yards
away, he relaxed and even smiled.

"Hello yourself, Kanaka!"

Kanaka's fingers tightened on his rifle.

"You *are* Kanaka. I know that," the stranger called as he started
forward. "You see, I got a good description of you from the
wanted poster that's hangin' down in Sonora. Says you're a half-
breed. That's definitely what *you* are, sure as sunshine."

"What do you want?"

"You *know* what I want," the man said, unbuttoning his coat
and brushing it back to reveal a holstered six-gun. "I'm taking
you in for the reward."

"I only broke that man's shoulder."

The smile died. "Tell it to a judge, Breed."

Kanaka heard contempt and sensed deadliness. There would
be no quarter given in this fight.

The man continued to advance. "You better throw down that
rifle. Drop it and reach for the sky. Do it easy and you may live

to reach Sonora. Be foolish and you're just another dead digger Indian."

Kanaka's heart began to pound and his mouth went dust-dry with fear. He did not know how fast a man could draw and fire a pistol, but he did know that this man wanted to fight close.

"Get on your horse and go away," Kanaka called.

But the bounty hunter kept coming. Kanaka had no choice. He swung the barrel of his rifle around, levering in a shell.

The stranger's fist streaked to his gun and it came up fast. Kanaka saw the blur of the pistol and threw himself sideways for the cover of a rock as the pistol broke the mountain's silence. A second slug whined, blasting shards of granite into Kanaka's face. He raised his rifle, fired, missed, felt a bullet burn his cheek, then fired again. Kanaka ducked, then rolled sideways between the rocks, as the man cursed and fired two more shots.

Scrubbing blood from his cheek with the back of his sleeve, Kanaka sucked in a deep gulp of air, then popped up and fired, his slug striking the man's hatband and knocking him over backward. Kanaka wiped his face again, listening to the receding echo of shots rolling off the rocky peaks. He knew he was very lucky to be alive. His knees were shaking when he rose and went over to study the dead gunman. This was no George. This man had deserved to die.

Kanaka searched the bounty hunter's pockets and found a knife, matches, and money. He stuffed the money back into the man's pockets and dragged him under the lip of a boulder. Then he went to unsaddle the horse.

"Easy," Kanaka said, stroking the horse's neck before uncinching the animal and removing its saddle and blanket. "Easy."

The bay was strong and clean-legged. It had a white star and two stocking feet. The animal was not beautiful; its head was too large and its neck too skinny, but stroking its soft muzzle brought back a rush of good memories. For a passing moment, Kanaka entertained a notion of keeping the horse and saddle, but then he changed his mind. He buried the man and his equipment under a heavy layer of rocks so that they would never be found.

Kanaka took the reins in his fist and spoke to the horse. "I'm leading you back to Py-we-ack, the place the whites call Tenaya

Canyon. That's where I'll remove your bridle and set you free. From there, you can find your way down to the sweet, green grass of Ahwahnee."

The bay nuzzled Kanaka's shoulder and then followed him down from the mountains.

In the days that followed his hurried return to Tuolumne, Kanaka watched anxiously for the first snow of winter. Snow, ice, and blizzards were now his only real protectors from the avenging whites. Where could he run? To the Mono Indians, where his ancestors had run twice before in the last seventy years? To the people who had murdered Chief Tenaya and other Ahwahneeche elders?

Never!

Then where? Certainly not to the west, for that was filled with enemies and hot, valley reservations. That left Kanaka's only escape routes to the north or the south. But what good was life without a heart or a spirit?

No, Kanaka thought as he huddled in his dim Tuolumne cave in the company of the ancient animal drawings. Better to die in this place and trust that Lucy would cremate and spread his ashes among his ancestors.

And so, as the days passed and Kanaka waited for either deadly whites or winter, he remembered many things and believed that his life had finally come full circle. He was not afraid to die, only of being imprisoned. He had seen what that had done to both his father and Samson. Remembering, Kanaka embraced his death and spoke to the cave paintings which had become his only friends and protectors. There was Hunter, tall, angular and fierce as he stood unafraid before a great uzamati with his spear ready to thrust. Before his own hunts, Kanaka always spoke to Hunter, asking for his courage, skill and acceptance of death. Kanaka was sure that none of the sacred bones in his cave belonged to Hunter who would have preferred to die fighting in the jaws of uzamati. Hunter once confided that he wished his flesh and bone to feed the animals that had always fed The People.

There were many other figures on the walls but one in particular spoke to Kanaka in times of his greatest sadness. He was
a smallish figure, bent and thick with age. Kanaka called him
Hope. Hope had never been fleet, or particularly strong but he
possessed great wisdom. He entered Kanaka's mind most often
in the lonely evenings out of the flames of the fire, and sometimes, during the bad dreams which he dispelled like sun the
rain. Hope understood all of Kanaka's sufferings. He never ventured outside in good weather when Kanaka felt most happy and
alive, but instead remained staunch and faithful in the shadows
of the cave, always coming forward then to give wise counsel.

In their many long conversations, both waking and in dreams,
it became clear to Kanaka that Hope could see all the way back
to the beginning of time. Like Coyote, Hope understood many
things of the earth and spirit world. He spoke of the sufferings
of long dead Peoples, of birth and cold and blood but also of sky,
earth and wind. Hope told Kanaka that he must live to carry on
the traditions of the Indian peoples so that their ways and wisdom
would not be forgotten. Hope spoke of all things being one thing,
each with a destiny. Hope said that Kanaka's destiny was yet to
be fulfilled and that the gift of death was sweet only unto those
who lived their destiny, despite their sadness and suffering. Hope
never failed to appear to Kanaka when he was most needed.

When the blizzards raged outside and the world was dark and
cold, Kanaka liked to huddle by his fire, wrapped in smoke,
mesmerized by the flames whose shadows danced with the rock
figures. As the heavens outside clashed with thunder and the
enduring mountains roared with defiance, the cave figures
danced in the firelight. Animals took flight from the stone hunters and Kanaka watched the history of the world swirl and circle
around and around filling the cavern with all the history of creation. At the center, he saw Woman, strong, suffering and yet
fulfilled and possessing of great patience.

Kanaka searched for the missing children and wondered about
the fate of The People as the seasons of centuries passed. And
then, music and light filled the universe of his cave and Kanaka
would awaken whole again.

But one day John Muir arrived, pursued by a cold and blustery wind. "A sheriff and posse are gathering to hunt you," Muir said without preamble.

"I am ready to fight and die."

"Your sister and brother-in-law want you to live," Muir said. "And so do I."

"A man came to kill me."

"Tell me about it."

Kanaka started to refuse, but something in Muir's eyes made him change his mind. So, in great detail, he explained how the manhunter had come and should have killed him. "Ouma and the spirits were watching over me," Kanaka said, as he fed his cave fire.

"The ones coming now are even more deadly," Muir said. "And they are bringing bloodhounds. If you stay in Tuolumne, they will kill you."

"I am not afraid to die."

"Nor am I," Muir said quietly. "But I believe we both have much work left to do before we are called to the hereafter."

"What work?"

Muir reached out and touched Kanaka on the shoulder. "Your people are almost all gone, but Ahwahnee remains and needs our help. Yours and mine, Kanaka! If we do not fight to save this wilderness, even our souls are lost."

"You speak eloquently, John Muir. I do not understand much of what you say but I know that your heart is good and you love Ahwahnee."

"Then help me *save* it!" Muir laced his fingers together. "Kanaka, we all need to work together if Ahwahnee and so many cathedrals in the wilderness are to be preserved. I am determined, with all my heart and soul, to save what is best and most beautiful in nature. I will write and speak and work tirelessly until all of this is held forever in trust for the people."

"I am a hunted man. I cannot speak well nor can I read or write. I can do nothing."

"Oh, but you *can!*" Muir became excited. "I have a gift . . . no, a great opportunity for you," he gushed, opening his pack and producing a large package wrapped in brown paper.

"What is this?"

Muir chuckled. "Open it and see."

Kanaka opened the bundle. Out tumbled a book, some paper, and pencils as well as a complete new set of clothes, right down to long woolen underwear.

He looked up in confusion. "What is all this for?"

"For *you*," Muir said, eyes dancing. "I borrowed this book from Elvira Hutchings. It is a beginning reader and speller."

Kanaka thumbed through it, seeing many pictures, including those of a man, woman, child, dog, cat, house, and horse, along with letters.

"I have a friend," Muir explained, "who is a hermit living alone in a wilderness cabin to the northwest in a beautiful canyon along the Tuolumne River. He is a good and well-educated man. Perhaps just as important, he sympathizes with the plight of the Indian, loves nature, and deplores its destruction. Now, your sister, brother-in-law, and I have decided your only chance is to cut your hair short, change into those clothes, and go live with my friend."

"I ran away from Ahwahnee, I will run no more."

Muir ignored the remark. "The Miwok name for this canyon is Hetch Hetchy. It is like a small Ahwahnee. You will even *feel* at home there and the winters are gentle. So go away until this trouble passes. I will give you a letter of introduction. Your sister and brother-in-law have given me funds to help with your keep."

Kanaka pushed away everything Muir had brought.

"I cannot do these things!"

"You must!" Muir's blue eyes grew hard. "Kanaka, when I was barely twelve years old, I was plowing my father's fields, splitting rails and working from dawn to dark. I was ignorant and unschooled but I burned to become educated. Nothing could stop me, not even my first year at the University of Wisconsin when I was so poor that I almost starved to death. I promise that you will not suffer those same hardships. And after you can read and write, we will fight together to save the land of your people."

"I will be arrested, imprisoned, then shot or hanged like the other Ahwahneeche men."

"No!" Muir took a deep breath. "Lucy and I have talked this

out. The *only* people who can identify you are the Pierces and
Stewart Knox. No one else has *ever* seen your face!"

Kanaka thought of George and his friends. "Those prospectors . . ."

"That happened more than *fifteen* years ago! And while you
and your friends did kill, it was a war of survival! Sins were
committed on both sides. But it is very unlikely that anyone would
remember your face, Kanaka. Only those three cruel trophy hunters, and they live in the East! Don't you see what is as clear as
the Tuolumne River itself? You can become a *new* man."

Kanaka rose to his feet and walked away to stand by the ancient
animal drawings. He idly brushed them with his fingertips, thinking hard about Muir's words and weighing them the way whites
weighed nuggets of gold.

Muir came to stand beside him, his voice soft but urgent. "Until a few years ago, I had no thought of ever leaving the East. I
was doing very well working at a factory that made carriage parts
in Indianapolis. I had produced a number of successful inven-
tions, and had taken it upon myself to improve the factory's efficiency. My employers were very happy with me but, one day, there
was an accident and a machine file pierced and blinded my right
eye. My left eye, in sympathy I suppose, also became blind."

Muir shook his head and closed his eyes, remembering. "And
so there I was, Kanaka, twenty-nine years old . . . about your
own age I would guess . . . and thinking my world had come to
an end. Just as you are thinking."

"I am not blind."

"You are," Muir said, eyes open and probing, "if you cannot
see that our lives are relatively unimportant compared to the work
that must be done in order to save nature's most precious gifts,
places like Ahwahnee . . . and Hetch Hetchy."

Kanaka still did not understand what Muir thought he could
do to make his life have any importance.

"My eyesight gradually returned, Kanaka. And with it I saw
clearly for the first time that I was not given sight in order to
study industry, but instead to study and marvel at the workings
of creation. So, I left everything, including a chance to be a part
owner in that factory, and I set out to discover all the glories of

nature. I found its crown jewel right here in Ahwahnee. And, now, I need your help."

"Doing what?" Kanaka whispered.

"Learn to read and write!" Muir shouted, waving his arms overhead at the cavern walls. "Change your name and work tirelessly against all those who would destroy nature."

"But . . ."

"Stop," Muir interrupted, raising his forefinger. "Kanaka, I know that you are going to ask me exactly what you could do to help, and I don't have the answer. I know only that every living thing has a purpose and ours is yet to be realized."

Muir returned to the fire, where he collected Kanaka's pencil and writing pad. Kanaka listened as his friend began to explain the route he must follow south in order to survive.

"You will follow the Tuolumne River to Hetch Hetchy."

"How will I know which one is your friend's canyon?"

"You will know it by its beauty," Muir assured him. "And by its hanging waterfalls and lush meadows. You will know it because you will think you finally have come home."

"How many days' walk?"

"Three, maybe four." Muir shook his head. "I don't know, because I have never followed that river. But you must stay in water whenever you can in order to throw the bloodhounds off your scent."

"Yes," Kanaka said, his mind already taking him from Tuolumne. "I know."

"My friend's name is Caleb. He is even homelier than I am, and his beard has much more red in it than mine. Caleb only has one arm, the left one was shot off during the Civil War. I am writing him a letter to explain everything."

"Will you tell him that I am a hunted man?"

"Of course. He is also unjustly hunted." Muir looked up from his writing. "You will like my friend Caleb. If you are a willing pupil, he will enjoy teaching you to read and write. After you learn, write letters to your sister, but use a new name."

"And can I also write to you?"

Muir nodded. "I would very much like that."

It was night when John Muir exited the cave and breathed deeply of the frosty air. He turned to Kanaka and said, "The bloodhounds will find this place very quickly. You must go at once and, if you must return, do so only when the snow is very deep."

Kanaka had so much left to say. Things that should be passed on to Lucy, things that he needed to tell this man he had come to love like a brother. But, even as he struggled to find the right words, with his long, swift stride, Muir was flowing across a backdrop of twinkling stars as quiet as Owl.

Twenty-five

"Guess who finally wrote!" Dan exclaimed as he barged into their cabin waving a letter that had just arrived on the new stageline into Yosemite Valley.

"Kanaka?" Lucy asked, looking up from her half-finished cooking basket.

"Yes!" Dan cried, opening the letter which had been addressed to: Mrs. Lucy Marble, Ahwahnee. "John Muir told you that Kanaka would write you his very first letter."

Lucy was so excited that she had to sit down. The letter had been written on brown wrapping paper, neatly printed and folded.

"Here goes," Dan said, slipping on his reading glasses.

OCTOBER 18, 1874

DEAR LUCY, DAN, WILLIAM AND MARY:
    I HOPE YOU GET THIS LETTER. JUST CLIMBED TO THE TOP OF MT. SHASTA WITH JOHN MUIR. I AM FINE. BACK LIVING WITH MY FRIEND CALEB IN HETCH HETCHY. READING EVERY NIGHT. FEEL GOOD. DON'T WORRY. COME VISIT ME SOME DAY. HOW ARE YOU FEELING? GOODBYE.

                                        MUAGA

Lucy very much approved of the name her brother was using to hide his true identity. "It is good that Kanaka would remember and adopt the name of Chief Tenaya's favorite son. May I see the letter?"

"Sure. You're good enough now to read it yourself."

"Maybe I was afraid of what it would say," Lucy mused as she carefully read her brother's letter. When she had finished, Lucy smiled. "Every time that John Muir came to visit, he told me that Kanaka was doing well."

"There was never any doubt in my mind," Dan said. "Do you want to tell the children about this letter from their long-lost Uncle Kanaka . . . or should I say Muaga?"

"I think it would be better if they did not know about this yet. They might accidently say something to cause Kanaka harm."

"Not much chance of that," Dan said. "There hasn't been a bounty hunter asking about Kanaka since that first one rode up to Tuolumne and vanished. And last summer, the sheriff and his posse couldn't find anything, even using a pack of bloodhounds. Besides, there are so many tourists coming and going in Ahwahnee now that no one remembers anyone's name for more than a few weeks at a time."

Dan's remark about the tourists was true. James Hutchings had done his part by extolling the beauty of Ahwahnee in an article published in the widely read *California Magazine*. He also was constantly inviting prominent artists, photographers, and writers to come and witness Yosemite's grandeur. The completion of the transcontinental railroad five years earlier, and the Central Pacific Railroad's recent extension line down to Merced, had generated a dramatic increase in the number of tourists coming from outside the state. Even more important had been the completion of the Coulterville and Big Oak Flat stage roads into the valley, finally making it possible for tourists to visit without either having to walk or ride a horse. The opening of the Wawona Road also was responsible for delivering hordes more summer visitors.

A family named Snow had even built a small hotel called La Casa Nevada on a granite flat between Vernal and the higher Nevada Falls. Albert and Emily Snow had invited Lucy to visit and lecture about the legends and meanings behind the old Ahwahneeche names, Pai-wai'-ak and Yo-wi'-yee meaning "white" and "twisting" waters.

John Conway, the valley's most ambitious trail builder, had opened a zigzagging footpath four miles up to towering Glacier Summit to enjoy James McCauley's new hotel named the Mountain House. In addition to affording a spectacular view of the valley, McCauley's guests were treated to quite a surprise. To the initial consternation and then delight of the hotel's guests, McCauley would throw his pet hen over the side of the three-thousand-foot cliff. The chicken would shoot downward squawking like crazy but always landing softly. Lucy had heard that McCauley had someone waiting on the valley floor to retrieve the hen so that she would not be too exhausted for her next day's big flying performance.

The Cosmopolitan House had eclipsed the Hutchings House as the best hotel in the valley and, besides its lavish guest rooms, boasted an opulent saloon, a billiard hall, private bathrooms, and even a barbershop and reading room for its high-toned guests. James Hutchings and his family didn't even try to compete with that new establishment.

Besides fishing, billiards, hiking, and watching a flying chicken, visitors to Ahwahnee had many other interesting and enjoyable activities with which to occupy themselves. Lucy's daily summer nature walks below Cho'-lok and through the old village of Koom-i-ne as well as her lectures on the life and legends of the Ahwahneeche, drew large, attentive audiences. She seldom spoke on the same subject and her knowledge of her lost culture was all-encompassing. Lucy discovered that she could speak for hours on how to make the traditional meals, clothes, and cedar-bark huts. Thanks to Ouma and her mother, and sometimes the extensive botanical knowledge of John Muir, Lucy knew the names of all the valley's plants, trees, and flowers. She often delighted visitors by nibbling roots, bulbs, and greens and inviting the tourists to do so as well, right where they were found.

Lucy especially liked to demonstrate Ahwahneeche cooking. Visitors were amazed that her baskets were so tightly woven that they could hold boiling water and steaming acorn mush. Lucy's coiled and often intricately decorated baskets were now so cov-

eted by the visitors that recently one had sold for almost two
hundred dollars.

Rich and famous tourists also were flocking to Ahwahnee,
men like Horace Greeley and Ralph Waldo Emerson, both avid
readers of James Hutchings and John Muir's increasingly popular
articles extolling the beauty of this valley. Emerson had departed
from Yosemite swearing that he had never seen such natural
beauty and geological magnificence, promising to return at the
first opportunity.

It seemed that the Hutchings family, as well as the other pioneers relying heavily on tourism, should have been jubilant, but
Lucy knew they were not. Because of Ahwahnee's new park
status, the State of California finally had won its long legal battle
that had gone all the way to the United States Supreme Court.
As a result, Hutchings and the other private owners were being
forced to sell their property rights and vacate the valley. So, instead of joy, there was sadness. Lucy was especially worried
about ten-year-old "Floy" Hutchings, the first white child born
in this valley and a free spirit who had never seen an American
city but would have to leave with her family and relocate to San
Francisco. Floy was as wild as the surrounding mountains. Lucy
fretted about this child of whom she had grown very fond.

"Mr. Quaid finished stringing barbed-wire on his homestead
this morning," Dan said. "He's claiming the best part of the north
meadow. Says he's going to plow the whole section and plant it
in corn and beans next summer and to hell with the Supreme
Court's eviction decision."

Lucy's joy at receiving her brother's first letter evaporated at
this news. Mr. Quaid, like so many others, still defied the State
of California and continued to farm his land. Sooner or later,
either the state would have to enforce its rules against those who
were shamelessly exploiting the valley or, as John Muir and others were beginning to suspect, Ahwahnee was going to be made
a national park like Yellowstone.

"Floy saw your letter and asked if it was from Kanaka," Dan
said, dropping into a chair. "That girl has been dying to meet
him. She tells everyone that Kanaka is half-man, half-spirit."

"Floy has a very rich imagination," Lucy said, folding the

letter and placing it in her apron pocket. She then picked up her latest cooking basket.

Dan leaned back wearily and closed his eyes for a moment. He was working harder now than he had when he'd been employed by Mr. Hutchings. Lucy worried about him. After John Muir had finished building the sawmill, Dan operated it for several years, then had gone into business for himself as a blacksmith and wheelwright. He also made some extra money guiding tourists into the high country. But Mr. Hutchings did that and so did John Muir, whenever he was staying in the valley, and there were many others working as park guides. Competition was pretty stiff.

Lucy felt a quiet, inner pride that her income from making baskets was helping support her family. They ate well, Dan had several fine horses, and they could now afford as many glass windows as they wanted. They could take a long vacation. Lately, they had been talking about a winter trip to the California coast. Lucy remembered that her grandmother and Spanish grandfather had fled the black sickness from the coast. Maybe she could walk beside the ocean and summon the spirits of those two never-forgotten ancestors.

"What did you tell Floy about the letter?" Lucy asked, starting back to work on her basket.

"I told her that the letter was from an old friend."

Lucy looked up with amusement. "True. But did Floy accept that?"

"No," Dan said. "And unless I misjudge that little snippet, she's already regaled our William and Mary with new tales about Kanaka."

"I must speak to Floy about all this imagination."

"You're almost as much at fault as her mother," Dan complained. "Between your legends and Elvira's fairy tales and wild imaginings . . . Is it any wonder that Floy has no grasp of reality?"

Lucy, who knew of her husband's disdain for Elvira, did not want to discuss this again. "Did you see John Muir this morning?"

"Yes, but he was off to the high country for the day with a

famous landscape artist. Floy was disappointed that she wasn't invited to go along. You know how she adores John."

"Yes," Lucy said, "and how that irritates Mr. Hutchings. I just hope that John has time to join us for a nice long visit and a good supper one evening."

"Don't get your hopes up," Dan said. "You know how busy he's gotten."

Lucy did know. John was spending more and more time living in San Francisco and writing articles on his glacier theory, which was being hotly debated by academics and prominent geologists around the world. His Yosemite articles championing the preservation of the wilderness were becoming extremely popular. Lucy knew that their friend was becoming a celebrity and that Floy was disappointed because John seemed to have so little time anymore to hike or hunt for mountain treasures. Muir had great affection for Floy and called her "a tameless one." Floy went camping alone in the remote wilderness for days at a time and recklessly raced her horse bareback across the meadows, shrieking joyously at the top of her lungs.

"Do you think it would be possible for us to go visit Kanaka this winter?" Lucy asked.

"I don't think that would be a good idea," Dan said, as he headed back outside to work. "Besides, with the state taking over, I am a little worried about our own circumstances, given what is happening with this last Supreme Court decision. Lucy, we may actually be evicted ourselves."

"They may take this cabin and our land, but they will never make me leave Ahwahnee," she vowed.

"I know that," he said. "And I would never, never allow them even to try."

After her husband left, instead of going right back to work on her basket, Lucy reread the letter, savoring every word. Dan and Elvira had taught her to read and write during these past winters. Sitting before a warm, crackling fire at the Hutchings House, or in front of her own modest stone hearth, Lucy had discovered the special joy of books.

Later that afternoon, Floy appeared. Characteristically, she wasted no time with greetings or small talk. "I took the letters right off the stagecoach," she said in her most adult fashion. "I just jumped up there and asked the driver for our hotel's mailbag. Then, I sorted through the mail for everyone and found that brown letter from Kanaka."

"It *wasn't* from Kanaka," Lucy said.

Floy's eyebrows shot up. "Then who was it from?"

"It's really none of your business."

"Then it *was* from Kanaka!"

"It was from someone named Muaga."

Floy put her hands on her slender little hips, just as Elvira had a habit of doing when she wanted something from her brow-beaten husband. "May I read it?"

"Absolutely not."

"I've been thinking that I might ride up to Tuolumne and visit Kanaka."

"He is not there anymore," Lucy said. "The sheriff, his posse, and all those bloodhounds learned that the hard way after a two-week search, remember?"

"They didn't know anything about the mountains. They were just a bunch of flatlanders. Kanaka could easily have hidden away from them."

"Floy," Lucy said, "I'm telling you that Kanaka is no longer in Tuolumne."

"Cross your heart and swear to die?"

Lucy crossed her heart. "I swear to die if I am telling you a lie."

Floy's shoulders slumped. "All right. I believe you, Lucy. I just want to meet Kanaka."

"You will."

"But when!"

"I don't know. Perhaps next year."

"They say he looks a lot like you," Floy mused aloud. "Handsome and tall, with your color skin and the same eyes."

"Who says that?"

"John Muir."

Lucy shook her head and tried to appear serious. "Kanaka looks nothing like me. He is short, fat, and balding."

Floy's brown eyes widened, and then they both started to giggle at this ridiculous caricature of Kanaka.

"When," Lucy asked a short time later, "is your family leaving?"

Floy's smile died. "Next week. The state paid Father twenty-four thousand dollars for our land and hotel. My father says he's being swindled but we have no choice but to move. We're going to live in San Francisco at my grandmother's house, but Father promised that we'll be back every summer."

"Your father is a man of his word," Lucy said, eager to lift the child's spirits.

Floy gazed around the cabin where she had spent so many happy hours visiting and hearing about the old Indian times in Ahwahnee. "Will your family stay here?"

"We'll have to sell out, too, but the commissioners have granted us permission to continue to live and work here. They need my husband's blacksmithing skills to repair the stages and shoe the horses."

"They wouldn't dare kick you out because you're the last of the Ahwahneeche," Floy said, raising her chin and looking determined enough to fight.

"We'll see," Lucy replied.

"I'd better go now," Floy said. "I'm going to ride up Tenaya Canyon and meet John on his way back down with that stuffy artist."

"You do that," Lucy said. "Enjoy every precious moment and hold onto them all this next winter and then we'll collect new ones like spring flowers in the meadows. All right?"

"All right," Floy said, chin quivering. "Bye!"

"Bye," Lucy said, watching the child race off to the stables where her horse waited.

A week later, Floy and her family boarded the stage to complete the first leg of their long, sad journey to San Francisco. Almost everyone in the valley came to give them a warm send-off, but that couldn't change the fact that Floy looked absolutely devastated. It almost broke Lucy's heart when Floy said a last farewell to her beloved horse, which Dan had promised to care for until her return.

"In addition to my *California Magazine,* I'm going to be working on what I've already titled my *Yosemite Guide Book,*" Hutchings vowed to everyone just as they boarded the stage. "It will really put this valley on the map! And we'll never give up our fight to win back our hotel."

Everyone shouted encouragements and promises to write. Everyone but Floy, who was so heartbroken that she buried her tear-streaked face in her hands and sobbed uncontrollably.

"That poor child will never be the same," Lucy said that evening to Dan. "Her spirit will be broken in a big city."

"Floy is a fighter," Dan said. "If she can't adjust, she'll find a way to return . . . with . . . or without her family."

Lucy supposed that was true. And despite Floy's sometimes annoying impudence, she was a generous child, willing to give away her special Yosemite treasures, even to friendly strangers. Furthermore, she was always sweet and very protective to her own two younger siblings, as well as to William and Mary. Lucy knew that everyone would miss Floy more than her parents or Mrs. Sproat, whose inclination was to be bossy.

That winter was long and cold. Without the Hutchings and several other families who had been forced to sell out to the State of California, there was little social life in Ahwahnee. Muir's old friend and fellow mountaineer, Galen Clark, had been appointed resident superintendent of Yosemite, but he was not an overly sociable man and many resented the fact that James Hutchings had not been given that highly coveted new post.

In the spring, the Hutchings family did return, but without Elvira. Lucy overheard that James Hutchings's pretty but aloof wife had abandoned her family for a younger, handsomer man. James Hutchings had filed for divorce before leaving San Francisco and Mrs. Sproat had remained loyal to him and her three grandchildren. Her popularity among everyone in the valley soared and now, unfettered by the responsibilities of cooking, cleaning, and running a full-service hotel, Mrs. Sproat blossomed into a very charming and sociable lady.

That spring brought a second letter from Kanaka, now Muaga.

MAY 23, 1875

DEAR LUCY, DAN, WILLIAM AND MARY:
   I HOPE YOU GET THIS LETTER. I AM FINE. JOHN
WANTS ME TO SPEAK BEFORE A NATURALISTS'
SOCIETY ABOUT THE AHWAHNEECHE INDIANS
AND THE PLUNDER OF OUR VALLEY. HETCH
HETCHY IS ALMOST AS BEAUTIFUL AS AH-
WAHNEE. COME AND VISIT! I AM GETTING BET-
TER AT READING AND WRITING BUT CALEB
HELPED ME WITH THIS LETTER. HOPE YOU CAN
COME SOON.

                                    MUAGA

After reading this letter, Lucy was determined to go and see
her brother in the storied valley of Hetch Hetchy.
   "All right," Dan agreed. "We could both use a little time off.
Start packing."
   Lucy had never seen Hetch Hetchy, but she knew that Chief
Tenaya and many of her ancestors had often gone there to hunt. A
strong young Ahwahneeche could travel to that valley in a single
day. but Lucy thought it would take her family two days. William
and Mary would have a difficult time climbing the steep, switchback
trail flanking Cho'-lok. Once above the falls, they would skirt
Yosemite Creek over a high, rugged plateau and then make a sharp
and precarious descent into the Grand Canyon of the Tuolumne
before following it down into the valley of Hetch Hetchy.
   That evening, while they were preparing food for the trip, John
Muir returned from his day's outing in the high country. Muir
looked fresh despite the day's exertions and he was in good spirits, especially after learning about Kanaka's letter.
   "He's going to be a fine wilderness spokesman," Muir promised. "You won't believe the changes Kanaka has undergone
since leaving Tuolumne. Not only does he *look* different, but
he even *sounds* different. And wait until you see Hetch
Hetchy!"
   Muir then glowingly described the canyon where Kanaka and
Caleb were living. "Since my first visit in 1871, I have always

called Hetch Hetchy the Tuolumne Yosemite because it is almost
the exact counterpart of this valley, not only because of its sub-
lime rocks and waterfalls, but also because of its forests and
meadows."

"Is it big?" Lucy asked.

"Not as big as your Ahwahnee," Muir conceded, "but it is just
as magnificent and it has a striking granite monument called
Kolan, the very counterpart of Yosemite's Cathedral Rocks. It is
also blessed with the most beautiful, graceful waterfall I have
ever beheld."

"Even more beautiful than Cho'-lok?" Dan asked.

"At least its equal," Muir assured them. "This waterfall drops
perfectly free for a thousand feet, ethereal in its airy, dancing
beauty."

"Mostly," Lucy confessed, "I want to see my brother."

"Of course! Of course!" Muir exclaimed. "But when you witness Tueeulala Falls, floating as soft as thistledown, mighty Wa-
pama Falls roaring and pounding through a shadowy gorge, or
Rancheria Creek, with its pearly pools filled with trout, you will
see why Kanaka is so content."

"I'm sure that we will," Dan said expectantly.

"Yes," Lucy said, still thinking only of her brother. "Did you
know that Kanaka changed his name to Muaga?"

"I'm afraid that it was necessary . . . for his own protection."

"John," Lucy asked, unable to silence her fears, "if he speaks
before whites, is there a danger?"

"There is always a danger in truth," Muir said. "But there is
often a far greater danger in silence. And don't forget, your
brother was a hunted man in Tuolumne. He needed to leave there
for a while."

"Yes," Lucy agreed. "Now, he is safer in Hetch Hetchy."

John Muir could not stay long that evening, but he left in high
spirits and with a large wedge of Lucy's wild blue elderberry pie
in his stomach.

"You always look too thin," Lucy chided Muir as he left.

"Better so that I can slip through the forest without getting
stuck!" he chuckled, fading into the meadow moonlight.

* * *

The journey over the mountains to Hetch Hetchy was as difficult as expected, but William and Mary were good hikers and excited about finally meeting their infamous uncle. The weather was perfect and, two days later, they gazed into Muir's "Tuolumne Yosemite." Now Lucy could see why their celebrated friend was so impressed with Hetch Hetchy's spectacular cliffs, domes, and waterfalls. The Tuolumne River was a ribbon of silver and the entire valley was blessed with thick stands of Ponderosa pine, spruce, incense cedar, black oak, Douglas fir, and maple.

"Look!" Mary squealed. "Deer and flowers!"

It was true. They could see deer and even a few elk grazing contentedly in the sun and cloud-dappled meadows now brilliantly colored by wildflowers. Even at a distance, Lucy could identify all her favorites, including Western azaleas, Mariposa lilies, and California golden poppies.

Three hours of descent into the canyon brought them in sight of Caleb's log cabin, nestled up against the base of a granite cliff almost the equal of El Capitan. But, for Lucy, nothing compared to seeing her brother again. Kanaka had cut his hair short and he seemed taller in his white man's clothes and work boots. Even more apparent was the open, assured way he spoke.

"And you," he said, dropping to his knees before the wide-eyed children, "must be William, and Mary!"

The children flushed with excitement, especially William, who blurted, "Is it true that you changed your name to Muaga?"

"It is true."

"But why?"

Kanaka gently mussed William's hair. "You change your clothes when they get dirty, don't you?"

"Yes."

"Well, I changed my name so that it would be clean again."

"I didn't know you could change your name?" Mary said, eyes wide with wonder.

"Oh, sure you can," Kanaka told them. "From now on, I *am* Muaga."

He looked right into the children's eyes until they nodded and then he glanced up at Lucy and Dan.

"Muaga it is," Lucy said quietly.

"I want you to meet Caleb," Muaga said. "He's off fishing but will return by sundown. He's a fine, fine man."

"John wants you to start speaking out for the protection of Ahwahnee," Lucy said.

"I'll be leaving soon. I owe John Muir everything. Lucy, did you get my letters?"

"Two."

"That's how many I wrote," Muaga said. "How long can you stay with us in Hetch Hetchy?"

"A week or maybe two at the most," Dan said. "I've got work piling up every day that I'm gone and . . ."

"The work can wait," Muaga said. "Stay a month and I'll really show you the *second* most beautiful valley on earth."

"We'll stay," Lucy said before her husband could answer. "It's time that we got to know each other again, for we have both changed."

Muaga nodded and Lucy discovered that his eyes had lost the wariness of a hunted animal. This Muaga, she decided, was infused with an aura of confidence and determination. Lucy was happy but she harbored a silly, unbidden regret that her Kanaka was no more.

Twenty-six

Sacramento, California, 1880

The elegant dining hall was stuffy and, as far as Muaga was concerned, the genteel conversation over their fund-raising luncheon might just as well have been in Greek. John Muir was probably doing his best to talk about the preservation issue, but he was seated at a different table and those around Muaga were absorbed by the issues of politics and money. Muaga, unfortunately, had been seated between two gossipy women who seemed to care not a whit about wilderness preservation.

Even worse, Muaga felt queasy because the air was hazy blue with cigar smoke and he had liberally partaken of the luncheon's delicious clams, oysters, and rich sauces. Muaga's stomach, unaccustomed to such spicy fare, was fomenting a rebellion. Had Muir not specifically asked him to say a few words urging this group of Sierra naturalists to support the federal management and protection of the Yosemite Valley, Muaga would have bolted for the nearest exit.

As it was, all he could do was gaze wistfully out the window toward the mighty Sacramento River with its procession of steamships and pleasure boats. The immense seafaring ships were especially interesting to Muaga, for he had never imagined anything powerful enough to cross oceans and then propel mountains of cargo upriver against the broad Sacramento's current. A footpath traced along the grassy riverbank and Muaga watched families strolling about, some feeding ducks and others just enjoying clean air and sunshine. Muaga longed to go for an invigorating walk to clear his mind and pacify his stomach. His reflection in the window confirmed that he was pale and his forehead was glistening with the cold perspiration of nausea. There were threads of silver in his hair now and Muaga hardly recognized himself in an itchy woolen suit, stiff, starched collar, and choking tie.

His reflection mirrored the unwell face of a stranger trying to impress this affluent group which Muir hoped would donate funds for the legal battles necessary to preserve Yosemite. Still concerned about being recognized by someone from the past, Muaga had grown a full beard and mustache. When Muaga returned his attention to the room, he discovered that an attractive woman in a yellow dress was studying him with more than passing curiosity. In fact, her expression showed a good deal of concern and now her lips formed a simple sentence. Muaga thought she must have been speaking to someone at her own table, but when he did not respond, she actually came over to his side.

"Are you all right?" she whispered, leaning close and filling his nostrils with the perfume of wild Sierra roses.

"Yes, of course," he replied a little defensively.

"You really appear quite unwell."

"I am *fine*," he insisted, aware that people were beginning to stare.

"I don't think so," she declared, before returning to her table.

Muaga toyed nervously with his napkin. After a few moments, the swirl of conversation resumed and Muaga dared to raise his eyes and really look at the pretty woman who had demonstrated her concern. He judged her to be in her mid-thirties, a brunette with a heart-shaped face and wide-spaced, intelligent eyes. She was engaged in conversation with an older, distinguished gentleman whom Muaga did not believe to be her husband. Once, she seemed to feel his gaze and arched an eyebrow in question. Muaga ducked his head and refolded his napkin.

"Ladies and gentlemen!" John Muir announced, rising from his table and using the handle of his knife to tinkle his crystal water glass until he had the gathering's full attention. "Ladies and gentlemen, if I may interrupt, I first would like to thank you for your wonderful wedding present."

Muir lifted a beautiful tea server so that all could see the fine gift. "Mrs. Muir and I shall treasure this tea set and earnestly invite all of you to join us for tea as soon as we are settled into our domestic bliss."

"What bliss!" an older, red-faced man wearing muttonchop whiskers called.

"Now, now," Muir said, enjoying the ribbing and the laughter. "We all know that marriage is a fine institution. In fact, since dear Louie Wanda consented to marry me, I remain astounded that I waited forty-one years before entering into this happy state of union."

"John, the logic behind your delay will come to you soon enough," a short, balding man across from Muaga called around his smoking cigar.

There was more laughter, brought on, in no small part, by the large quantity of California red wine that had been consumed before and during the luncheon.

Muir tapped his glass several more times for silence and then said, "I assure you all that, when my dear Louie sees this beautiful gift, she will be just as touched by the generosity of the Sacramento Naturalists' Society as I am. *And,* I am sure that you will continue to support the vital work and legislation to preserve the magnificent Yosemite Valley."

Muir's smile slowly dissolved and his gaze gently passed over every individual in the entire dining hall. "Ladies and gentlemen, I have said it before and I will say it again that man does *not* live on bread alone. Everyone needs beauty as well as bread, a place they can pray in as well as play in and where, my dear friends, the beauty of nature may cheer and give strength to the body as well as to the eternal soul."

Muir paused and bowed his head to inhale the clean scent of the greenery that he had taken to wearing in his lapel several years earlier. Muaga wished he had adopted this habit, for the cigar smoke was so noxious and vile it clouded his senses.

"The *soul,* my dear friends," Muir continued, as he raised his eyes toward the chandeliers, "rejoices in the beauty of nature. And we must always remember that wilderness is not something that we as a people ought to preserve out of some dry sense of duty."

Muir paused and then thundered, "Rather, man *must* understand that he is not a separate entity endowed with some divine right to subdue and plunder all other creatures, as well as nature, for his own profit, but instead that he is an *integral* part of the harmonious whole that forms our infinitely beautiful and wondrous universe!"

The audience erupted with an ovation and Muir finally raised his hands for silence before adding, "I am sickened by what I have lately seen taking place in our mountain parlor of paradise. The Fresno and the Kaweah groves of giant sequoia are already being ravaged by loggers and the King's River stand, with trees every bit as magnificent as those in Wawona, is terribly threatened!"

Muir, shaken by the depths of his own passion, calmed himself for a moment before continuing. "My friends, Yosemite Valley and all its surrounding environments are also being plundered by the logger, the stockman, the farmer, and the miner. In a few more years . . . if Yosemite's precious stewardship is not wrested from the State of California and given strong federal protection, there will be nothing . . . absolutely nothing left of its God-given grace and beauty to pass on to the generations that follow."

A troubled silence followed and then Muir's eyes came to rest on Muaga. "Today I have the special privilege of introducing a very dear friend. Muaga is one of the very last of the Ahwahneeche. As anyone can see by his physical appearance, Muaga is a man of two races, someone whom the ignorant and less than charitable would term a 'half-breed' or 'half-blood' . . . though I assure you he has as much blood as any of us."

The audience chuckled and many eyes skipped to Muaga as Muir continued. "My Ahwahneeche friend will tell you a few things about his lost people. Muaga was raised in Yosemite and his father, a mountain man who came west with the Joseph Walker expedition in 1833, was a good friend of the legendary Chief Tenaya. Muaga survived the slaughter and subjugation of his Indian people, and I have asked him to speak about his life and sad experiences."

Muaga struggled out of his chair, legs feeling as stiff as wooden stumps and stomach flopping. He received warm applause and somehow managed to reach the podium, which he gripped with both hands, praying that his mind would not go blank and his body fail him completely.

A moment passed, then several more before Muaga cleared his throat and dared to look out at the well-to-do and politically influential audience. They were smiling, and that helped, but Muaga focused on John Muir, whose calm serenity slowed his racing heart. The lady in the yellow dress who smelled like wild roses also met his eyes and gave him courage. Muaga had memorized a speech, which Muir had warned would probably be forgotten. As usual, Muir was right, so Muaga just opened his mouth and was quite surprised that he could even speak.

"I . . . I could not dream that someday I would stand before you without hatred," Muaga haltingly confessed. "Many winters ago, my father tumbled from the cliffs into our valley of Ahwahnee. He was found and saved by my mother, a great tribal medicine woman named Anina. I remember my father well and never thought of him as anything but Ahwahneeche. Neither did my people. My father was much respected and became a tribal elder before he was killed by the whites during the Mariposa Indian War."

An edge of bitterness crept into his voice. "But it was *not* a war! It was a slaughter. The destruction of a people who only wanted to live as they had always lived before James Savage and others found our home. The People are almost all dead now, only their spirits fill the great valley of Ahwahnee."

Muaga used his coat sleeve to wipe his face dry. "Death awaits all living things. New people are born, grow old, and die. Peoples kill other peoples. But when the *land* is killed, it cannot be reborn. Trees and rivers and animals die in silence; no one hears their passing. Nature cries only to a God when the ax strikes, the plow buries the grassy meadows, or the bullet kills for nothing but sport."

Kanaka released the podium and swung his head about, speaking to everyone now. "This is wrong! Since the creation of Earth, the People lived in Ahwahnee and nothing ever changed except the seasons. The rocks, the meadows, the trees . . . they did not change. But now . . . in only a few years, everything has changed and this is wrong. My people are almost all gone and can do nothing for Ahwahnee . . . only you can help now."

Muaga swallowed and felt his stomach roll even as he thought how crude his words were in comparison with those of John Muir. A fresh rash of clammy sweat burst across his forehead and Muaga knew that he was going to be sick, so he whirled and dashed for the nearest door, barging into the kitchen.

"Outside!" he gagged, wild to escape.

A man in a tall, white, puffy hat pointed and Muaga lunged across the kitchen, through an exit, and into the sunlight. He ripped off his choking tie and sprinted toward the river, where he dived in headfirst to be embraced by the warm Sacramento. Muaga knew before surfacing that he had ruined his new suit, but since he did not intend ever to speak to such a group again, he did not care. Muaga allowed the water to carry him a few hundred feet downriver and then, feeling clearheaded and well again, he swam back to shore.

The woman in the yellow dress waited. Ignoring her, Muaga yanked off his suit coat and hurled it back into the water.

"No more suit or stuffy luncheons?" she said, looking amused, as he sloshed up to join her on the grassy riverbank.

"No, no more."

"Feeling better now?"

He ran his fingers through his hair, deciding that he would not cut it so short again and he would go back to using his father's Green River knife and resume shaving.

"Who are you?"

"My name is Elizabeth Eden." She stuck out her hand, ignoring the fact that Muaga's palm was muddy when they shook. "But you may call me Beth."

"Why did you leave the room to see me like this? Do you find me amusing?"

"Of course not! I came because I found your words inspiring and because you are very . . . different. My father owns the *Sacramento Gazette* as well as the *Mariposa Times* and the *Sonora Signal*. They are all weeklies, but our subscriptions are rising fast. Muaga, I would like to write a series of Yosemite articles for my father's papers that would not only be sympathetic to federal protection of Yosemite, but also to the Ahwahneeche. Of course, to do that, I need your help."

"I'm sorry, but no," he said, seeing John Muir emerge from the dining hall and begin to walk rapidly toward them.

Beth Eden spluttered in amazement. "But why in the world not! If you *really* want to reach the hearts and minds of the public and influence the politicians to save Ahwahnee, then what better way than to run a series of articles on the valley and its lost Indian people?"

Muaga shook his head, thinking about George and the vengeful Pierce brothers and of fleeing bloodhounds and bounty hunters. And about his father being escorted away in chains and shackles. These memories and images passed like a jagged bolt of lightning across the darkest reaches of his mind.

"Excuse me, Miss Eden," he said, turning to leave.

She caught his arm and angrily exclaimed, "I really don't understand! When you were speaking, I deeply sympathized with you, but now . . . now I see that you are a fraud. A fraud because I have just offered something that you and Yosemite desperately need . . . a widely read and very human slant in my editorials instead of more dry geological and botanical writings . . . but you refuse this opportunity for reasons I cannot begin to fathom."

"Muaga!" Muir called, hurrying to join them.

"Never mind," Beth said, turning and rushing away. "Congratulations, Muaga, you certainly had me fooled."

"What's the matter with Elizabeth?" Muir asked, head swiveling back and forth between Muaga and the departing young woman.

"Nothing." Muaga focused on his friend. "I am sorry for the words I spoke . . . and could not speak."

"Sorry?" Muir's bushy eyebrows shot up. "You were *wonderful!*"

"No."

"Yes!" Muir draped his arm across Muaga's dripping shoulder. "You spoke right from the heart and they understood that. The money is pouring in at this very moment."

"I forgot all my good words."

"You mean the *big* ones that you had intended to try and impress those folks with?"

"Yes."

"Muaga, my friend, never try to be what you are not. Nature is honest. It is infinitely complex, yet wondrously simple. It is *itself,* and you must be as well. You could not have spoken better and I cannot tell you how favorably your words were received by those fine men."

Muir clapped him on the shoulder. "You did well, my friend, and you will do even better as you become more practiced. Just speak simply and from your heart. That is the true, best way."

"You want me to speak again?"

"If you did not, I would be devastated. You should see how many diamond-studded hands reached into their pockets for funds after you spoke!" Muir looked around. "Where are your suit coat and tie?"

"I . . . I threw them in the river."

"Never mind them anyway. I should never have agreed to let you dress up to look like something you would not even want to be. The next time you face an audience—any audience—wear your buckskins and moccasins." Muir tugged at his beard. "You will speak again for Ahwahnee, won't you?"

"Yes," Muaga said, powerless to refuse his great friend.

"Excellent!" Muir took his arm and they began to walk quickly downriver, indifferent to the curious sight they presented. "Now," Muir said, "how long has it been since you have seen Ahwahnee? And by that, I mean *really* walked its cool, life-restoring meadows and felt the warmth from its rocks upon your back and tasted its delicious and healthful waters?"

"Many, many years," Muaga admitted.

"I think that you should go back to live there again," Muir said. "I think that it is time at last."

"What about . . ."

"The bounty hunter was an outlaw and killer himself. As for the Pierce brothers and their banker?" Muir wagged his head back and forth. "Banish them from your mind. After all these years, they are but illusions. Ahwahnee, however, is slipping away and *you* are needed. But remember, use words, never violence."

"What about you?"

Muir sighed. "Being newly married, I must attend first to my lovely bride. However, last year I began some important geological and glacial experiments in the Pacific Northwest and Alaska. That work *must* be finished. I'm afraid that, for a time, the welfare of Yosemite is in your hands and that of other good men like Galen Clark, Mr. Hutchings, and . . ."

Muir interrupted himself to turn and watch Elizabeth Eden stride across the grass to disappear inside the dining hall. "She did appear upset, don't you think so?"

"Maybe."

"I had better speak to her and find out what is wrong. I expect that she was moved to great emotion by your tragic account of the Ahwahneeche. As soon as the donations and pledges are collected inside, I'll find out what is bothering Miss Eden, don't worry."

Muaga nodded, but the thought occurred to him that he *would* worry . . . or at least wonder.

Muaga passed through Hetch Hetchy on the way back to Ahwahnee to say good-bye to his friend Caleb Witt. When he told the lean old hermit his plans, Caleb became upset.

"Now why do you want to go and do something that might put your neck in a noose!"

"Because I am a part of Ahwahnee and it is a part of me. I can no longer ignore what is happening there."

"And you think that you're going to change anything?"

"I can try."

"You'll get into a fight and then thrown in jail. Someone will figure out who you *really* are and you'll get your neck stretched."

Muaga knew this was still a possibility. But it didn't change the fact that he had not walked the meadows of Ahwahnee or visited Ouma's spirit in the pool of the Po'-loti witches below Cho'-lok in over twenty years.

"I know what is *really* bothering you," Caleb said accusingly. "You're gettin' older and you want to take a wife and have sons . . . maybe even daughters!"

"No, that . . ."

"A man can do that clear into his eighties and, that being the case, you'd be far better to go back over the mountains and live with the Mono Indians. Take a young one for your wife . . . take two if you think you can handle 'em both."

"That is not the reason," Muaga said, already thinking about how much he would enjoy helping Lucy and her children gather the autumn acorn harvest. Suddenly, he wanted to eat acorn mush until his belly was ready to burst. And he would build a cedar hut, an u'-ma-cha, just like the one where he had spent his happiest years as a boy. No more cabins. No more dark, cold caves.

"I think it *is* the reason," Caleb was saying. "But listen, Muaga, young women will kill you . . . if the law doesn't first.

I told you I been married three times—once in Kentucky and then out here twice to Indian girls, and every time it was awful, just hell. Women are all the same—they just want your money, especially the young and the pretty ones. They want to work you to death."

"My mother did not want to work my father to death and Lucy does not want Dan to work so hard either," Muaga said with exasperation.

"Well . . . well, they're one in a million! I'm telling you that it's better by far just to get a horse or a good dog. They don't ask for nothing but to be fed. And I taught you how to read. Beg, borrow, or steal books. All you can find. Read and read 'em again. You can learn more about the world than you can any other way."

"There would be no books among the Mono."

"Then stay here. We get along good. Muaga, if you leave Hetch Hetchy, someone's gonna recognize, arrest, and then have you hanged. The West is still an Indian-hatin' country."

Muaga knew that he needed to leave at once before he began to have second thoughts. "Goodbye, my friend," he said.

"Oh, dammit," Caleb Witt muttered. "Maybe I should go along, too, just to watch your backside and keep the evil ones away. You know that I can get feisty."

"Yes, I know. And if I get in big trouble, I'll come running back."

"I may not be here," Caleb said, thin shoulders slumped with disappointment. "I been thinking that there's been too many hunters and prospectors and just plain gawkers comin' into this valley the last few years. Maybe I'll be moving on to the north. After hearing all the good things that John had to say, I might even try Alaska. 'Course, there never was country . . . even desert . . . that he didn't think was a Garden of Eden."

"That's true."

"You takin' your old Sharps?"

Muaga had given this matter considerable thought. "No. It's yours for all you've done for me, Caleb."

"Too shiny a gift."

"Just take the rifle or it could be traced back to Phillip Pierce and get me hanged."

"Got to trade something back to you," Caleb said. "I got something you can use now."

"What . . ."

But Caleb was already hobbling into his cabin. Muaga figured he'd get a book, but Caleb surprised him by unwrapping a beautiful buckskin shirt decorated with beads and fringed sleeves.

"Here," Caleb said, handing him the shirt. "It ought to fit. Way too big for me anymore but it fitted when I was young and strong like you."

Muaga unfolded the shirt and held it in front of him. "It's the finest thing I'll ever wear," he said, meaning it.

"Won it a long time ago from a trapper up in the Colorado Rockies." Caleb winked. "Won the pretty Ute girl that made it, too!"

"Your second wife?"

"Yep." Caleb's smile withered. "She died bearin' my child. It died, too. I married a Shoshone gal three years later, but she weren't so good to me. Always jealous of that shirt 'cause she couldn't tan hides worth a damn nor do beadwork nor much of anything but complain."

Muaga stripped off his own shirt and tried the new one on. "It fits perfectly."

"You look mighty handsome. You'll find a wife if you're wearin' that shirt."

Caleb cackled and Muaga grinned and said his goodbye. At the edge of the clearing, he had a thought and stopped to turn around. "Caleb!"

"Yeah?"

"Alaska is too damned cold for your old, aching bones."

Caleb scratched at his board. Muaga thought he saw the man's head dip in agreement, but he couldn't be sure. "Got a piece of advice for you, too!"

"What is that?"

"Don't hire out no more to be a huntin' guide!"

They both laughed, the sound of it bouncing around in the great hall of stone that was Hetch Hetchy. Then, Muaga turned his face toward Ahwahnee, not exactly sure what he would find or even if he could adjust to the changes that John Muir had so often decried.

When Lucy first saw her brother standing at her door in his handsome new leather shirt, she dropped a frying pan, spilling beans across the cabin floor. "Kanaka!"

"Muaga," he said with a smile, as he stepped inside and scooped Lucy into his arms.

"I can't believe that you're really back!" Lucy cried, hugging him tightly. "But . . ."

"It's been too long since I walked this valley," he said, "and many, many years since my fight with those Eastern hunters."

"Almost sixteen," Lucy said, eyes misting.

"Where are Dan and the children?"

"Dan and William are working on a cabin up the valley. Mary is off playing with a friend."

"Will the acorn harvest be good this year?"

"Very good."

"Can I borrow a gathering basket?"

Lucy clapped her hands with delight. "Are you sure that you really want to gather acorns with us?"

"I am."

"You look tired and hungry," Lucy said, taking Muaga's arm and leading him over to a table. "Sit down and I'll pick supper off the floor and give you some of it to eat."

"Thanks."

Muaga was hungry and, after he finished eating, he and Lucy went for a walk that ended at the old village of Koom-i-ne where Muaga said to his sister. "You've kept our old bark hut in repair and the granary, too."

"Our mother and I made them, long ago," Lucy said. "I use them to show the summer tourists how The People once lived."

"But there is no more ceremonial or sweat house," Muaga said, eyes searching out the places where these structures once stood for his people. "If you like, I will build them."

"You can do this?"

"I am the last Ahwahneeche hunter," Muaga said. "That was what you called me on a day that we walked in Tuolumne. Yes, I can make a ceremonial and sweat house."

"For the tourists?"

"In memory of The People and so the tourists can better understand what was lost."

Lucy was very pleased with this and when, arm in arm, they started back to her cabin, they saw a young woman on a sorrel horse come galloping full speed across the meadow with her long, dark hair floating on the wind. She was riding bareback and without fear as Kanaka once had ridden on his golden stallion so many years ago.

"This is Floy," Lucy said. "Her father, Mr. James Hutchings, finally has been given the post of resident superintendent."

"I have heard you speak of this family many times," Muaga said. "Does this girl always ride so recklessly?"

Lucy laughed. "Almost always. And she has *always* wanted to meet you."

"Will you tell her who I really am?" Muaga asked with sudden concern.

"No, but she will guess," Lucy said, as the girl dragged her horse to a standstill. Floy Hutchings jumped off and let the puffing animal begin to graze, just as Kanaka had allowed the stallion to do without worry that it would ever run away.

The girl was dark and willowy with an open, guileless smile and a boyish, free-swinging stride. Muaga thought her beautiful.

"Hi, Lucy!" she called, her eyes never leaving Muaga's face.

"Floy," Lucy said, "this is Muaga."

She walked right up and extended her hand, eyes sharp and penetrating. "You're the mysterious letter writer. My full name is Florence Hutchings, but everyone in Yosemite just calls me Floy."

"The 'tameless one' that John Muir speaks so fondly of," Muaga said, shaking her hand.

"Just visiting?" she asked.

"No," he said. "I've come . . . to stay."

Without blinking an eyelash, Floy said, "You've come home at last, haven't you, Kanaka."

When he said nothing, Floy gazed off toward the new Sentinel Hotel, then said, "Kanaka, I'll bet that nothing is the same in this valley and whatever is new disappoints you. I'm talking about all the big hotels, dusty roads, and so many people."

"Floy," Lucy began, "I think . . ."

"Don't worry. I'd rather die than tell anyone who you *really* are. But everyone is probably going to guess anyway. You have exactly the same features."

Floy bowed slightly and started to turn back to her horse but then changed her mind. "Muaga?"

"Yes?"

"Have you visited Cho'-lok yet?"

"No."

"Would you like to now?"

Muaga was a little taken back by her directness. He started to say no, but Lucy squeezed his hand and said, "She's going to pester the daylights out of you for stories, so you might as well tell her about Ouma and the witches before suppertime."

"I am not a good storyteller. I haven't had much practice."

Floy smiled radiantly. "You don't have to say anything, Muaga. Just finally being with you is like walking with a famous *ghost.*"

He couldn't help but smile, and when Floy touched his buckskin sleeve, Muaga decided that he might as well tell the "tameless one" everything, because he had a feeling she was not going to leave him alone until all the ghosts were laid to rest and her curiosity was finally satisfied.

Twenty-seven

The permanent residents of Yosemite accepted Muaga as Ahwahneeche and treated him with respect. During the time that remained of summer, Muaga worked very hard to build a traditional granary and ceremonial house where he had grown up as a boy in the ancient village of Koom-i-ne. The old family u'-ma-cha, that Muaga now called his home, still warded off the occasional but sometimes heavy summer rains and continued to be an important tourist attraction.

Muaga worked on the new hang-e and listened to his sister give tourist talks about life back when they were children in this village. She did it so well that Muaga himself often was transported back to those happy days. And when a tourist asked about the new ceremonial house Muaga was constructing, he did his best to explain. It felt good to be back and Muaga did not mind when tourists came to visit and ask questions about the old Indian ways and the sad changes that were changing the face of Ahwahnee.

In the autumn, the family went to harvest acorns. Muaga and Lucy's children climbed high into the oaks and either plucked the acorns or shook them free for gathering in Lucy's winnowing baskets. It took a week before Lucy finally decided they had enough acorns to last through the winter. In the old days, the Ahwahneeche had kept at least a two-years' supply in case of a very bad harvest. But now . . . with livestock, regular supply wagons, and even truck gardens flourishing in the valley . . . there really was no need.

Lucy and Mary gave frequent demonstrations of how they handled the cracking stones to break and then shell the acorns before using the old bedrock mortars and stone pestles to pound them into a fine yellow meal. To eliminate the bitter taste of tannin, the acorn meal was steeped in Lucy's beautiful baskets and washed with hot water until the tannic acid was gone. Afterward, the meal could be prepared as mush, soup, or even the delicious acorn patties which they baked on hot, flat rocks. At age twelve, Mary already was a skilled basket weaver. She and her mother could not make nearly enough Ahwahneeche baskets to satisfy the heavy tourist demand.

Now that John Muir was usually away managing his father-in-law's fruit ranch and busily writing his articles on saving Yosemite and the wilderness, Floy became the valley's most

popular guide. She always called out to Muaga and waved as she
led parties of tourists off for a day's outing.

"Someday," Lucy said, as Floy led a group past Koom-in-e,
"Floy is going to realize that she is a pretty young woman of
sixteen."

Muaga smiled. "The boys have noticed."

"So have the men," Lucy said. "It will be interesting when
she falls in love with some handsome young man but doesn't
understand her own feelings."

"When that happens," Muaga said, "you must talk like a
mother to her."

Lucy blushed. "I know very little about love and courtship."

"You know enough," Muaga said, without looking at his sister.

Lucy snorted, but she was still smiling when she went back
to her family. Muaga continued his ambitious work on the large
hang-e, or ceremonial roundhouse, which was forty feet in diameter and was to be an exact replica of the one he'd known as
a boy.

"Why do you make this hang-e so big?" William asked, as he
helped one afternoon when the wind was cold and the trees were
filling the air with their rainbow leaves. "There are no more of
The People to fill it."

"That does not matter," Muaga told his nephew, already a
strapping lad of fourteen who could lift logs as easily as most
men. "When I was younger than you, the ceremonial house was
the most sacred and important place in our village. In the win-
tertime, when the snows fell and the winds cut at the bare trees,
all The People would gather inside around a big fire. We would
listen to the elders talk of many important things and then tell
and retell the old Ahwahneeche stories. The first one that I ever
heard was that of the Yel'lo-kin, the giant bird who grabbed disrespectful children by the hair of their heads. He would carry
them up through the hole in the middle of the sky, land on top
of the world, and eat those bad children."

William scoffed. "That is a child's story. One I've heard over
and over from my mother."

"Well . . . it could be true, so you had better be good to your
mother and father . . . and to your uncle!"

William smiled and helped put a ceiling pole in place, over which cedar bark and then dirt would be packed to form the dome of the ceremonial hang-e. The entire roof was supported by four big peeled logs, each as thick as Muaga's waist. These posts denoted the four winds and corners of the world. The Ahwahneeche also believed that there was balance and beauty in a perfectly formed square under a circle roof. In the old days during the ceremonies and special celebrations, there had always been a fire tender and a door tender. Now, they were both unnecessary.

"It's going to storm in the next few days and Mother says that I have schooling to do and firewood to cut," William said as the shadows grew long.

"You should always respect your mother's wishes," Muaga told him. "The heavy work is done. I can set the last of these ceiling poles and the cedar bark alone."

William slapped dust and bark from his pants as he straightened. "I enjoy helping you, Muaga."

"I know that. And you can come this winter to spend nights around a great fire that I will build for us in our new hang-e."

"Why?"

Muaga hid his disappointment well, realizing that there really wasn't much incentive for William to spend hours beside a fire with an uncle who sometimes talked too much about the old days in Ahwahnee. John Muir, Galen Clark, and a few others would be good company in a spiritual place like this, but it was expecting too much of a boy who had grown up in the white man's world. After all, William and Mary had far more white than Indian blood.

"There is no reason," Muaga said. "Run along."

"Are you sure?"

"Yes."

The storm held off for the next two days, but Muaga knew that, cradled high up in the mountains, his beloved Tuolumne was already being blanketed by heavy snow. There were times when Muaga gave serious thought to leaving the valley and returning to the quiet beauty of Tuolumne. Those solitary years had been good, especially after John Muir had entered his world and begun to train his mind and eye not only to see the beauty but also to study and appreciate the physical forces that formed and governed all of nature.

But, just when Muaga's heart carried him back to Tuolumne, he would always notice something of great beauty right in the valley. Perhaps it would be Cho'-lok with a strong wind weaving a ribbony rainbow in her hair, or the sun burnishing the profile of El Capitan, or the evening sky turning pearl, or a sunrise with an ocean of dewy diamonds, weighing heavily on the long meadow grass. At such times, Muaga would pause, his heart would swell, and he would know that he would never again leave Ahwahnee.

Floy galloped over to watch Muaga work on the hang-e's nearly completed roof. She folded her arms across her chest and announced, "I have just decided that I will never love a man. Yes, that much I have *definitely* decided."

"Why?" Muaga asked, as he carefully laid the final ceiling poles to form a tight web over the hang-e.

"Because men are so conceited and self-centered!" She winked. "All except you, Muaga. You're different."

He was amused. "Not so different."

"Oh, yes, you are. You enjoy being alone . . . like me. I think nothing of going off by myself for days, but my father expects me to be a tourist guide. Why, if it wasn't about to rain, that's what I'd be doing right now, and all for nothing but grubby money." Floy paused and her brow knitted in a frown. "You *never* worry about money."

"I have no need of it."

"Then you are truly free."

"But if I had a horse," Muaga mused aloud, "I might need money to have it grained and shod."

"Lucy told me that once you had a fine stallion and I bet you never had it shod or fed grain."

"But my stallion was tougher than your mare."

"Ha!" Floy cried. "Why, my mare could outrun and outlast your stallion any old day!"

Muaga knew he had walked into a trap because, next to talking, Floy loved to argue.

"What are you smiling about?" Floy asked.

"Grab some cedar bark," Muaga said. "If I have to listen to your chatter, I expect some help."

"Nope," Floy said, heading for her mare. "I'm going to watch the raindrops fall on Mirror Lake. Anyway, why are you building this thing so big?"

"Maybe I'll turn it into a native hotel."

Floy was still laughing when she galloped away. Muaga returned to work with the musical cadence of the mare's hooves accompanied by distant thunder. Muaga felt a few cold drops of rain. Glancing up at the threatening sky, he felt sure that Ahwahnee was in for a big storm. No matter, the old family u'-macha would keep him dry and there was a good store of firewood and a bearskin robe inside to keep him warm.

As the sun began to set, a lone figure came striding swiftly across the meadow from the Sentinel Hotel. Muaga felt annoyance because he would have to send the fool back before he was drenched.

"Hello!"

A square of cedar bark spilled from Muaga's hands because the visitor was Elizabeth Eden. Beth wore a heavy coat with a fur collar turned up around her pretty face. She seemed oblivious to the pelting raindrops and the lightning that forked like the tongue of Snake from the dark underbelly of clouds gathering to assault Ahwahnee.

When she halted, Beth simply said, "How are you, Kanaka?"

His first thought was to correct her about his name. But he found he could not. Instead, Muaga stammered, "So, you know."

"Everyone in this valley knows your real name. I learned about it several months ago from a stagecoach driver. He swore me to secrecy. But guess what?"

"What?"

"No one cares, not even the Pierce brothers. Phillip Pierce died almost ten years ago. And there is more." Beth dug into her pocket and handed him a square of newspaper. "You need to read this."

The rain began to fall harder, blurring Kanaka's vision, even as Beth's nearness caused its own storm of unexpected emotions. "Just tell me what it says."

"It's Allan Pierce's obituary. He died this spring and, since he and his brother had once owned a big hotel in Mariposa, my father's newspaper thought his death was worth mentioning. You really should take a moment and read his obituary. My father did a nice job writing it."

Kanaka unfolded the article as big drops darkened the paper. Even so, he read slowly. Allan Pierce lived only fifty-eight years. He was a millionaire and had divorced two wives and fathered three daughters, all married and living in the East.

"And so," Beth shouted over the gathering storm, "are you *finally* willing to bury your past and help John Muir and our Sierra Club to preserve Yosemite?"

Kanaka ground the soggy obituary in his fist, the rain driving down ever harder. "Yes!"

Beth shivered and reached out to touch his cheek as she pressed close. "I still want to write those articles on The People's traditional way of life. Maybe we could start them out by my description of a real Ahwahneeche bark hut."

"It is called an u'-ma-cha!" Kanaka hollered over the deepening growl of thunder in the high mountains.

"Is it warm and dry so that we can be comfortable while I take notes by firelight?"

Kanaka nodded because, even in a fierce downpour, Beth smelled like the wild roses of springtime.

Epilogue

Glacier Point, Yosemite May, 1903

President Theodore Roosevelt and John Muir had already stood poised on famed Overhanging Rock, thirty-two hundred dizzying feet above the Yosemite Valley floor. Now, the two men sat quietly together on top of Glacier Point with the magnificence of Yosemite and the High Sierras spread out before them like

God's great feast. There was snow and ice even this late in the spring, but neither man would have changed a thing, not the campfire nights nor even the raw, windy days they'd spent riding and discussing the plight of Yosemite. And most of all, from the president's point of view, not this delightful morning, when they'd awakened under five inches of snow.

"The waterfalls will be thundering this spring because of all the snow," Muir said, his eyes drinking in the entire valley. "Soon, the meadows will be filled with flowers and the air will be sweet."

"And I will be in Washington," Roosevelt sighed with resignation, "and you will be surrounded by this paradise."

Muir turned his head sharply. "But, as I have been saying, Yosemite Valley is a paradise lost. Tomorrow, you will see the many unsightly structures that litter the valley . . . the meadow flowers and grasses all trampled and devoured by livestock. Trash collects everywhere. You'll even smell a pigsty! Mr. President, the valley may appear beautiful from way up here, but it is an affront to nature. Trees chopped down, the river polluted by stock . . . everywhere, the abomination of barbed-wire."

"John," the president said, "you've all the tenacity and single-mindedness of a Scotchman and, for days, you've talked of little else but how Yosemite needs federal protection. Your newly founded Sierra Club grows more powerful and your wilderness preservation articles ever more urgent and popular. Now, I can finally see why we must hasten to give all of Yosemite the same protection we have given Yellowstone."

"Then we *do* have your support!"

"Yes. I will do everything in my power to rescind the state grant and create Yosemite National Park."

"If you do that," Muir said, shaking with emotion, "you will have done your greatest act as president."

"I'm going to do even more," Roosevelt vowed. "Before I leave office, I'm going to see that we also have a Grand Canyon National Park."

Muir did not fully trust himself to express his gratitude. After all the years of fighting; at last, a hard-won victory was within his grasp.

"Point out some of the landmarks, John. I want to burn them into my mind."

Muir raised a long forefinger. "Across the valley is mighty El Capitan, and off to the right . . . as you can guess . . . is Half Dome, and that next peak is called Clouds' Rest. See the two valleys forking around Half Dome?"

"Yes."

"To the left, in the more northern direction, runs Tenaya Creek and, if we had a few more days, we could ride up to Tenaya Lake and then to Tioga Pass."

"I've read about Chief Tenaya. Where does the bigger canyon lead and the Merced River form?"

"Past Vernal and then Nevada Falls and on up into the Cathedral Range near Mt. Florence."

"Florence?" The President frowned. "Is a mountain named after that young girl you wrote about so poignantly?"

"Yes," Muir said quietly. "Florence Hutchings. Our darling Floy. I called her my 'tameless one.' There was nothing she loved more than the wilderness."

"What happened?"

"Last September," Muir said, clasping his hands tightly together, "while guiding tourists up here to this very point, Floy dismounted in front of Sentinel Rock to gather ferns. A falling boulder struck her down. She lived just one more day and then was buried in the pioneer cemetery near Yosemite Falls. It broke everyone's heart."

The president touched his arm. "John, I can see that you were also quite affected."

"Floy was as pure and free as the west wind now caressing our faces."

President Roosevelt was silent a long time as he gazed down into Yosemite. Finally he said, "I will never forget this trip, John. Never. it has been one of the finest times of my life. And, when we reach the valley, I hope to visit Floy's grave and pay my respects."

"If time permits," Muir said, "I would also like you to meet a couple of Indian friends of mine, Lucy Marble and Kanaka. They will delight you with the lore and legends of Ahwahnee.

Brother and sister, they are the valley's most treasured historians and even knew Chief Tenaya and his only living descendant, Totuya."

"Yes, you told me about the tragedy of those native people. Does Totuya also live in Yosemite?"

"No," Muir said. "But we hope to see her return someday."

Roosevelt gazed out over the incredible panorama. "John, I wonder, did the Ahwahneeche Indians put up a *bully* good fight for their Yosemite?"

"Aye," Muir said, accenting his deep Scottish brogue, "a *bonny* good fight!"

Author's Note

The main characters in *Yosemite* are fictional, but a pair of fugitives like Jacinta and her husband, the brave and desperate Spanish captain, might have brought the "black sickness" into Ahwahnee. Tenaya himself spoke of this terrible epidemic and judged that it happened about 1800, forcing the remnants of his once-numerous people to flee their beloved Ahwahnee and live among the Mono Indians. Chief Tenaya was born near Mono Lake on the eastern slope of the Sierra Nevada Mountains. When he grew into manhood, he led The People back to Ahwahnee after a twenty-year exile.

Ezekial Grant is fictional but, the ordeal of Joseph Walker's party's near starvation during their attempt to cross the Sierras in 1833 is a dramatic page of American history. This group of explorers were the first white men to look down into Yosemite but were prevented from entering it by the valley's sheer cliffs.

The "Mariposa Indian War" was an infamous campaign during which the Ahwahneeche and their culture were almost destroyed. James Savage and the major events of that pathetic conflict are woven into the fabric of this novel, although Ezekial, Ouma, Lucy, and Kanaka's roles are entirely fictional. There was a Fresno River Reservation and Tenaya's favorite son was shot down while trying to escape his captors. It is said that young Muaga's death almost broke the spirit of the last true chief of the Ahwahneeche. Tenaya and several of the tribal elders were murdered during a game of "hand" by the Mono Indians and it seems reasonable that the last of The People scattered, some fleeing to hide in Yosemite and Tuolumne, others simply giving themselves over to the care and protection of the Americans or else intermarrying into other cultures.

James "Grizzly" Adams was a swashbuckling character and great fun to research and write about. And yes, he did capture "Gentle Ben" and the mighty "Samson" just about as I have described, and took them to San Francisco, where he opened the Mountaineer Museum and later toured with Barnum and Bailey. The death of "Gentle Ben," as well as Adams's own sudden death in 1861, received national attention.

John Muir was born in Dunbar, Scotland, in 1838 and grew up in Wisconsin with a passion for the wilderness. After walking a thousand miles to Florida and then arriving by ship in San Francisco, he hurried to Yosemite and fell in love. Muir never held public office, but his appreciation of nature and his unwavering advocacy of wilderness preservation marked him as someone far ahead of his time. Muir was also a gifted inventor and student of the natural sciences. His glacial theory was at first ridiculed and then wholeheartedly accepted by the academic community. His notes, observations, writings, and even his wilderness sketches are national treasures and are as relevant and brilliant in their clarity as they were a century ago.

Muir never considered himself adequate to the mission of saving *all wilderness.* He was a poet, yet found writing to be a laborious task, which he described as "rigid as granite and slow as glaciers." But everyone who met John Muir avowed that he was a spellbinding speaker, and it mattered not if Muir were seated around a Sierra campfire or standing before a huge and adoring audience.

As I researched *Yosemite,* I was touched by the tragic and premature death of Florence "Floy" Hutchings. In the excellent book, *Yosemite, Its Discovery, Its Wonders and Its Peoples* by Margaret Sanborn, there is a picture of Floy taken, I would judge by the sadness in her dark eyes, about the time that she had to leave her beloved Yosemite. She was a beautiful girl and her untimely death was mourned by everyone. If you visit Yosemite, be sure to stop by the old pioneer cemetery and pay your respects to Floy Hutchings, along with many of the other pioneers that you have met and become acquainted with in this novel.

Yosemite ends on a note of hope in 1903 as we see John Muir and president Theodore Roosevelt together at Glacier Point, each committed to saving a valley desperately in need of federal protection. There was every reason for them to be hopeful. On June 11, 1906, the valley of Ahwahnee finally joined with the surrounding wilderness to become Yosemite National Park. Thanks in large part to John Muir and President Roosevelt, Arizona's Petrified Forest and the Grand Canyon also soon became National Monuments.

Sadly, John Muir's last years were filled with disappointments as he and the Sierra Club fought to save the beautiful Hetch Hetchy Valley from being flooded as a water and power supply for San Francisco. Muir and the Sierra Club waged a long and courageous battle, but finally exhausted their appeals and Hetch Hetchy was flooded in 1913. Today, that once-beautiful valley's hanging waterfalls and spectacular granite formations overshadow an ugly, silt-filled reservoir, and one has to study old pictures of Hetch Hetchy to appreciate the lost beauty that earned it Muir's sobriquet of the "Tuolumne Yosemite."

Today, the environmental legacy of John Muir lives on throughout the world, and the United States is blessed with hundreds of national parks, monuments, and historic sites, all administered by the National Park Service. Each is unique in its own historical significance yet all share a common natural beauty which brings to mind the following words written by John Muir in 1890:

> "All the world is beautiful, and
> it matters but little where we go
> The spot where we chance to be,
> always seems the best."

And finally, in July, 1929, after an absence of seventy-seven years, Totuya came home.

Yosemite Chronology

1800 Black sickness and death of Jacinta. Anina born. Ouma leads surviving Ahwahneeche over mountains. Mono Lake exile of Ahwahneeche among Mono Indians. Chief Tenaya born.

1821 The People return to Ahwahnee.

1833 Joseph Walker party trapped in high Sierras. Ezekial tumbles into Ahwahnee and is saved by Anina.

1848 Gold discovered at Sutter's Mill on American River.

1850 *Summer* James Savage exploits valley Indians to bring him gold. Ahwahneeche raid for guns and horses. *December* Mariposa Indian War begins and Mariposa battalion formed to defeat Yosemites. Ezekial dies.

1851 James Savage invades Yosemite. Chief Tenaya first seen by whites, then captured. Son Muaga shot down while attempting escape. Yosemite Indians driven under guard to Fresno River Reservation but soon return to Ahwahnee.

1852 Eight prospectors killed by Yosemite Indians. Many Yosemite Indians recaptured and executed by firing squads or hanging. Others escape to live with Mono Indians, intermarry, never return to Ahwahnee.

1853 *Summer* Mono horse thieves and Yosemites raid into California. *Fall* Tenaya and other Yosemite elders stoned to death by Mono Indians while gambling.

1854 Grizzly Adams arrives with Lady Washington. Traps cubs Ben Franklin and General Jackson. Kanaka helps Adams to trap giant Samson.

1855 *June* James Hutchings arrives.

1856 Grizzly Adams's "Mountaineer Museum" fails in San Francisco. "Lower Hotel" first permanent structure.

1858 Gentle Ben dies. "Upper Hotel" opens in Yosemite.

1860 Grizzly Adams goes to work for P.T. Barnum Circus.

1861 Grizzly Adams dies.

1863 Anina and Wolf-dog die. Lucy left alone in the village of Koom-i-ne.

1864 Hutchings brings wife, Alvira, and mother-in-law to open "Hutchings House."

1864 "Floy" Hutchings born. First white child born in Yosemite. Yosemite Valley and Mariposa Big Trees granted to California as a public trust. Yosemite becoming artist's and photographer's mecca.

1868 John Muir walks from San Francisco to Yosemite.

1869 John Muir is Tuolumne shepherd. Appalled at destruction. Goes to work for Hutchings. Builds saw mill and cabin.

1870 John Muir explores the Grand Canyon of the Tuolumne.

1871 John Muir's "glacial theory" too progressive. Ralph Waldo Emerson visits to spend time with Muir.

1874 First stagecoach into Yosemite.

1880 Floy returns from San Francisco at age 16. Highly popular guide. John Muir marries at age 41.

1881 Floy Hutchings, the "tameless one," accidentally crushed by a falling rock.

1889 John Muir returns to Yosemite. Failing health and spirits restored.

1890 *October 1* Yosemite National Park created although valley itself remains under state control and inadequate environmental protection. Legal conflicts persist between California and federal governments over rights to protect Yosemite.

1892 Sierra Club formed to save Yosemite. John Muir elected president.

1895 Ahwahnee being plundered, overbuilt and commercialized. John Muir and Sierra Club vigorously campaign for the valley's national park status and protection.

1896 Last grizzly in Yosemite is shot.

1903 President Teddy Roosevelt arrives. Camps with John Muir.

1905 Victory! All of Yosemite finally under federal protection as a national park.

1906 John Muir persuades Roosevelt to make Arizona's Petrified Forest and Grand Canyon national monuments.

1908 Preservationists begin fight to save Hetch Hetchy.

1913 Courts approve Hetch Hetchy as a reservoir.

1914 John Muir dies.

1923 Hetch Hetchy is lost and flooded after long legal battle by Sierra Club and other environmentalists. Becomes San Francisco reservoir.

1929 Totuya returns at age 89, after 77 years.

1931 Totuya, last descendant of Chief Tenaya dies.